Vernella Fuller was born in
She moved to England to join
Vernella is currently a Head o
She lives in Sutton with her da
of *Going Back Home* (The Women's Press, 1992). *Unlike Normal
Women* is her second novel.

Also by Vernella Fuller from The Women's Press:

Going Back Home (1992)

VERNELLA FULLER

Unlike Normal Women

First published by The Women's Press Ltd, 1995
A member of the Namara Group
34 Great Sutton Street, London EC1V 0DX

British Library Cataloguing-in-Publication Data
A catalogue record for this book is available from the British
Library

ISBN 0 7043 4431 9

Phototypeset in 10/13pt Bembo by Intype, London
Printed and bound in Great Britain by
BPC Paperbacks Ltd, Aylesbury, Bucks

For my mother and my daughter, Alisha Nadine

Acknowledgements

I would like to thank my friends Mary Condé, Maggie King, Zaline Roy-Campbell, and Stella Mbubaegbu for reading and commenting on the script; Kathy Gale and Helen Windrath, at The Women's Press, and Lynn Taylor for all their work. My mother, my late father and grandmother, Aunt Bea, for everything. And Top Mountain for those formative years.

Chapter 1

Ashes seeped through the gaps of Aunt Vie's wattled kitchen settling momentarily on the nearest of four dirt tracks. The light breeze mingled dust and ashes, sprinkling them around the yard.

Aunt Vie was oblivious of this sudden dust cloud. Although her eyes were not what they had been, that was not the reason why today, despite her efforts, they constantly misted. Surreptitiously, from time to time, she wiped them with the back of her good hand, purposely not using her handkerchief so that she would not further alarm the people who were in her yard, in her kitchen and in both the rooms of her house. Each sigh from them, every concerned expression, the continuation of scenes from past nightmares. Her left hand, limp on her lap, refused to budge, her leg, even more stubborn, would not be cajoled into getting up to join the women in the bedroom, help them to get Babydear ready or even allow her to sit and gaze at her for what she was certain was the last time. Occasionally she bit on her twisted bottom lip to confirm consciousness, rubbed her lame leg on the red tiled floor of the verandah to accelerate its sluggish circulation.

First her daughter and husband had sent for Delores, the eldest grandchild, four years ago, then Wilbert two years after that. In her heart of hearts, as the last two years had gone with no mention by the parents of their plan to take her, Aunt Vie had thought that they would leave Babydear with her. A faint

1

smile slipped over Vie's lips. Everyone said that Babydear was the apple of her eye. It was true that Babydear was special to her, this youngest grandchild she knew, had been her hands and feet since the stroke a year ago.

'Aunt Vie a bring you some fever grass tea.' Ruthlyn Maxton, one of her neighbours, mounted the three steps of the verandah, a white enamel cup in hand, steam curling over the top.

'Ruthlyn a told you, I don't feel like anything yet.'

'What you mean by yet? You want to get bad stomach?' The woman was not prepared to let her have her way as the other women had been; one by one they had each returned cold cups of tea to the kitchen. Vie reluctantly took the enamel cup with no intention of drinking from it but the younger woman, equally adamant, had no intention of moving until she had.

'For heaven sake Ruthlyn give me some pace no!'

Ruthlyn reached out and rubbed her arm, 'I know it must be hard.' She sighed, 'God knows I don't know which of you to feel more sorry for.' Then as if speaking to herself she launched into a diatribe about how she had almost wept with Babydear at the Watch Night Service the previous evening when one by one mournful farewell songs and recitations were rendered for her.

'Between the old Cleary clan and England, this little District is being bled dry.' Catching herself, the distant look in Vie's eyes, Ruthlyn feared she had said too much, getting up hurriedly, forgetting her mission, she disappeared among the other women in the yard.

The taxis could be heard pulling up in front of her landlord's, Ezekiel Samuel's shop. Instinctively Vie peered through the cluster of trees, past the pig-sty at the end of the middle track to catch a glimpse of them, as if to check that her grandchild would be transported safely to the airport. Babydear's grip was passed out onto the verandah. Littleman who was hovering beside Aunt Vie, hoisted the pristine case on his shoulder and set off towards the waiting cars. As eyes followed him there began a debate in the yard as to whether it was worth sending clothes to England with Babydear. Ragu, unhindered by his lack of sight and utilising his carpenter's precision, spoke authoritatively, that having himself had first hand experience of Europe, most of it albeit in trenches, dodging German gunfire, he believed that wearing thin cotton and seersucker dresses in the cold climate of England, was tantamount to walking about without any clothes at all. Hadn't they heard about the winter, six years ago, 1962, when blizzard, snow and ice-cold rain had eaten off fingers and toes of those foolish enough to dig their way through pillars of ice surrounding their homes and venture the streets. Even inside, he added, paraffin heaters had all but frozen over.

That kind of talk, far-fetched though it seemed to her, served only to deepen Aunt Vie's depression so she made a concerted effort to move, to join Jane, Miss Dee and the other women in the room, they would not be so full of pointless chatter. But what answers would she give to the questioning, confused look in Babydear's eye? Vie sighed. Since it was all now inevitable she wished her gone, the farewells said and the taxi away, but most of her wished that she would wake up soon and find it was one of those vivid dreams of hers relating scenes about somebody else's life.

'You mustn't worry about Babydear you know. They'll take care of her in England. And the world is small.' Jane came out of the room, perspiration bathing her face. She sat down next to Aunt Vie. 'I know it's hard but you really mustn't worry so much.' Aunt Vie rubbed her bad hand but said nothing.

'Anyway,' Jane continued, 'She's ready now, you want me to send her out to you.'

Aunt Vie nodded heavily. 'Yes. Get Miss Dee to put a stool behind the house for me . . . away from everybody . . . I want to look at her alone.' Jane got up.

'Thanks,' Vie added after her.

Babydear stepped tentatively onto the verandah adorned in a red and white frilly cotton and lace dress, matching red shoes, ribbons, socks and bonnet. She hesitated at the door as Aunt Vie turned to look at her, the corners of her lopsided lips moving indecisively into a half smile. 'You look nice Babydear.' She said finally, trying hard not to focus on the little girl's puffy red perplexed eyes. 'Let's go behind the house.' Vie made to stand up, instinctively the little girl reached out and helped her grandmother up, threaded their arms together and supported her off the verandah and behind the house seemingly oblivious of the silence that had fallen in the yard.

'Aunt Vie I don't want to go.' Babydear broke down immediately they were behind the house. 'I don't want to leave you . . . I can't leave you . . .'

'Shee . . . Shee dearheart . . . Babydear.'

'There will be nobody to look after you. Who's going to fetch water from the pipe for you, go to the shop for you, help you to mount the donkey, thread the needle for you . . . Who . . . who . . . who . . . Who's going to read letters for you? See the scorpions when they come and shoo the lizards out of the room? Who's going to make sure you don't fall over when you walk . . .?'

'Shee my baby . . . Shee . . .' But she couldn't stop the child's tears nor could she find her tongue to reassure the child, so in need of reassurance and comfort was she herself. But eventually when she thought her near convulsion she had to do her best. 'I don't want you to keep crying like this my Babydear it's not good for you little heart.'

'But you're crying too and I don't like it when you cry . . .'

'I'm only crying Babydear because I miss you so much already.' She wanted to say too, and because I know you are in as much pain as I am and there is nothing I can do. Nothing I can do to make you better, and because I know I'll never see you again, but she felt the burden of those words would be too much to place on the already overburdened child not quite twelve. Instead she wrapped her up in her arms and reminded her of stories that used to make them laugh together and found herself drawing vivid made up pictures of a warm home in a far away and beautiful country where there would be a loving mother and father with a brother and sister she knew and missed and a new brother and sister to meet. She seemed to be succeeding for a while until their two dogs came, whining and yapping, sensing the situation, it seemed, rubbing their bodies against the child's legs. 'Rex! Buster! Sit down,' Aunt Vie ordered. But the dogs moaned and cried all the more around Babydear's feet, licking her hands before folding themselves on the ground beside her, started her crying again. She bent down and stroked them, promising with child-like confidence that she'd be back soon, that she knew she would not like England and would be asking her parents to send her back as soon as she landed. Aunt Vie sighed and held her tighter.

When she was quiet again Aunt Vie spoke to her gently, 'I know I must look really old to you with all my grey hairs, bad foot, lame arm and twisted mouth . . .' She found a smile for the child remembering that time years ago when a discussion about her toes had become one of their very own treasured memories. 'And my crooked toes,' she added.

'I love you toes,' Babydear said as always with child-like sincerity, clearly remembering too. Aunt Vie kissed her on the forehead keeping her mouth pouted to receive Babydear's own lips. Finding the resolve to lie to the child did not come easy to her, yet she reiterated, 'I know I must seem old to you, but when you growing up you don't really feel any older . . . unless you're sick . . .'

'But you are sick.'

'I'll get better. I'm only sixty eight and if God willing I've got a lot of years left . . .' Babydear watched her for a minute and when her grandmother didn't say anything else she lowered her head on her shoulder, her ear remaining alert for consolation and reassurance. But Aunt Vie couldn't go on because even then there were pains. Aches and pains that had been part of her life for as long as she could remember. Aches from bending over to hoe ground hardened from months of drought. From walking miles to get water and retracing with heavy steps, the precious liquid on her cricked head. From weekends haggling in Carnation Street or Spanish Town markets in the bid for precious coins followed by the weekdays futile hunt for Day's Work, defying the malicious heat of the sun when at last some big shot from the Clearys' class took pity on her and had her stand all day picking coffee, shelling, parching, beating, bagging or some such task, for little and nothing in payment, the landowner adding to his already considerable wealth through their labour.

She did feel old and sick and tired. She had always felt old. For as long as she could remember. There had never been a youth for her. There was just that time as a baby. Then a woman. And womanhood meant more unrelenting hard work without any of the respite of childhood. In one sense she was glad that Babydear was going. Away from the District with all its inevitabilities. Escaping history's nasty habit of repetition.

When it was time, Miss Dee peeped round the corner and cleared her throat. 'Babydear, Aunt Vie . . .'

The little girl stiffened. 'Come dear. I don't want you to miss your plane,' her grandmother persuaded. The grandchild started to cry again and the grandmother tried to be strong.

Chapter 2

The BOAC thundered overhead leaving a weighty silence in the hills of Top Mountain. Yet everyone still languished in Aunt Vie's yard well after the reluctant taxis had returned braving the stone road and sourly picked their way back out of the District again, the hefty fares small consolation for their newly acquired slow punctures and damaged axles. Only then did Vie manage to persuade most of them that there was no need to stay any later. Still her immediate neighbours, the Maxtons, Samuels, Ragu and with them, Littleman, Miss Dee, Aunt Jane and one or two other families dawdled, whispering inconspicuously their concern about her having only picked at food all day, sitting in that one spot on the verandah staring into space, about the very real possibility of her sending her blood pressure up with the worry and pining and having another stroke.

The well-meaning shaking of heads, clicking of tongues and continued talk about the snares of England did nothing to lift the burden of Vie's grief, only intensified it, moving as they did with authority from its ungodly weather, the practised wicked-ness of the people, to the madness that overcame Jamaicans soon after they disembarked and felt the cold, saw the houses they mistook for factories, signs linking them with dogs and people who only noticed they were there when they wanted to insult and abuse them.

'I for one would never live in a place like that, especially now

7

that we have our Independence in Jamaica. Now that our blessed Independence has come at last,' Amos said. There were appreciative and enthusiastic nods, affirmative words and smiles as the hope, promises, even the memory of the jubilant celebration of 1962, six years ago now, revived. 'Besides, I hear *say* how the place cold cold that when you talk the breath freeze as it come out of you mouth.' Amos continued reiterating the sentiments of Ragu's earlier point.

'More than that is how the place affect them mind. I was on this bus the other day coming from Town, one of them who must have been the first one to go over in the fifties, come back on holiday. You could tell him a mile off, in him wool three-piece suit and tie and sweating like a hog. The best joke is half way out of Spanish Town, him stop the bus. We did all think him getting off but him whisper something to the driver before him step down. And you never know what the man do?' Amos waited but meeting incurious silence he told them, '. . . I tell you, the man got off the bus, brazen as day, empty him bladder . . . take tissue paper out of him trousers pocket, excuse me ladies, wipe his teely with it and then put the self-same paper back in him pocket . . . You ever hear anything like this before . . . ? I tell you madness take them over in that place . . .' Half-hearted laughter resounded in the yard, his wife's, as usual when he spoke, the loudest, starting first and lasting longest. Yet it was she who first noticed that Aunt Vie wasn't sharing the joke and suggested, as he seemed ready to launch into another story, that they should go and see to their children.

When no one moved, Aunt Jane, unusually patient and quiet since her return from the airport, got straight to the point.

'Come on everybody have some consideration, Vie must want to lie down now, all of you have home to go to.' In the same way that they usually found plenty to irritate them about her, they found her tone annoying but no one said anything to that effect, one by one they offered Aunt Vie yet more condol-

8

ences, the false jollity of a moment ago wiped from their faces as soon as they were out of her sight. They left Miss Dee and Jane, who followed as soon as they had seen Vie washed and with everything she wanted for the night. 'Vie you sure you don't want Miss Dee to stay with you tonight?'

'I have my things,' Miss Dee encouraged.

Aunt Vie said she was certain but once they had left and she was faced with the impenetrable darkness of a moonless night in a cold bed too large for one, the latent fear of sickness with old age magnified and would not be dislodged from her mind. Despite youthful dreams, of husband, children and the security of grandchildren, she was to be an old woman alone, no close relative that she knew of within reach, sick and poor, dependant on fortnightly postal orders and the charity of the District. Living in a rented house, owning only an acre of land in another dying District, a patch that needed to be coaxed and tended to produce, promising everything but needing the labour she could not now possibly put in, those days having died a year ago when she had the stroke. And her other little ground behind the house, her donkey, Greystripe, to see to, how could she do it all when she could hardly walk? Perhaps it was best that Isadora and Leopold had taken their three children after all, she was in no fit state to mind them anymore.

She was still in bed, her senses numb to hunger and the stiffness in her bad leg when first Miss Dee passed to fix her breakfast and later Aunt Jane, insisting that she got up out of bed and walk down to Dora and Ezekiel's shop with her. 'Lying here grieving and feeling sorry for youself won't let them put her on the plane and sent her back.' Aunt Vie obeyed, not wishing to deprive Jane of this rare occasion when she was not on form, not the queen bee that everyone in the District thought she was. Jane insisted that they sat with Dora until the late afternoon, Vie only half hearing them make and laugh at stale unfunny jokes.

The only thing that slightly amused Vie was that the two most reputedly miserable and chronically sour women in the District were reducing themselves to laughter on her behalf.

In the evening, Aunt Vie's yard was full again with men assaulting her table with dominoes, their mirthless rum induced laughter competing with the women's attempt at serious conversation. Despite her objections, rotas were drawn for washing her clothes, preparing her meals and for keeping her company. Nobody considering it all unnecessary, conveniently forgetting that even when her grandchildren were around, hardly an evening passed when she did not have people in her yard. She was after all the mother of the District. Over the years she had been their unpaid midwife, their advocate in disputes with the despised Clearys, their counsellor and adviser on every conceivable matter. She was the only person they could depend on to find the extra shilling to help them out with school books or uniform, kerosene oil, corn meal or salt fish, to make up their rent or lease in a tight week. Although she had always been a woman without a man by her side, she was one of the few in the District uncowed by those the rest of them feared or revered, did not understand or hated; like Deacon, Azora or the Clearys.

Vie was alone later because it was church night and those who weren't saved or in need of righteous entertainment and diversion that night, ambled home, some to bewail the hold of Deacon and the church on the District over the years in scuttling their campaign to get a licence for the District to have its own rum bar, as an alternative to church. Others, to rest weary bones before their pre-sunrise start the following day.

As Vie laid in bed listening to the sound of tambourines competing with hand clapping, Ragu's banjo and Amos' mouth organ, it dawned on Vie that despite her position in the District, people would soon tire of her if she persisted as she had done that day, seemingly helpless, quiet, sorrowful. Besides it wasn't in her nature to give up, to bow out without fighting. But the thought of fighting wearied her. She had had enough of fighting. Yet, she had defeated harder times . . . much harder times, what with the life she'd had and a family like the Clearys to deal with over the years. The hate and disgust that she had always felt for the Cleary family, for the way they treated the District, the way they used its women, had not just been an obsession for her. She could not remember a time when she had not harboured the determination to challenge and destroy their power.

As if she was lord over her own life, she had vowed years before that she could not die before she had witnessed the demise of their power and influence over the District. Time she had thought initially would do the trick. Through young eyes, she could not see districts like hers remaining content to lease land from the Clearys when they could buy, pay rent when they could own, bow and scrape and say yes sir, no sir, when they could walk tall, just say plain yes or no, or not even answer if they so desired. Then when time did not herald a change, she had waited for some other miracle, events external to herself, like 1962, Independence Year. Somehow she had dreamt, like Amos and most others in the District still did, that with the unseating of the British, the power of their lackeys, among them the children they had bred with local women, the reluctant and the hopeful, would have waned too, leaving spaces for people like her, those who were too black to sit facing customers in banks, take seats in parliament, go to the best schools. But this historic year came, she bought the commemorative cups and glasses, waved the new flag and sang the new anthem, and went. Six years later, the Clearys remained living proof that little of the changes she had hoped to see had occurred. At least not in Top Mountain. Perhaps in town or in some other district but not in the districts she knew. So even now, there were still, in her view, shackles around the District's minds and around their small string purses. So how could she let herself die, give in, when their change had not come?

The fireflies were playing silent ring games around her house but the croaking lizards competed with the frenzied barking of the riotous crazy dogs charging through the District pursuing restless spirits on fearful mission, disturbing innocuous ones reclining under cotton wool trees. Vie tried to ignore the dogs, concentrating instead on the stars lighting up the sky, not tonight the counting of them, reaching 100 and dropping dead as country children believe. Strangely she realised it all made her sweetly melancholic. How time flies and how little time there must be left, she thought, no need for spirits sent to harm or for superstitions to bring her down. All she need do was bide what little time she had left. True there was no Babydear to listen to, to hear say prayers on her behalf, to read to her, to cream her toes, to rub stiffness from her hands and legs, to blow out the kerosene oil lamp. No little arms to wrap around her neck, no soft breath to caress her face as she tried again to find a comfortable position.

The church service now in full swing quieted restless spirits and dogs and imposed on her thoughts, taking her mind back inexplicably to a time when Babydear must have been about five. She had come home crying from the nursery school run by the church. Someone had called her maga and she didn't want to be thin but plump like all pretty girls should be. She could not be persuaded by her grandmother that fat or thin she would always be pretty. Later, in bed with her older brother and sister fast asleep in the adjoining room, Aunt Vie tried to show her how important it was to love herself. 'Do you love all yourself?' Babydear had questioned.

'Ummm. I do.'

'Everything? Every part?' Babydear insisted.

'Yes, I do.'

The little girl sat up. 'Your hair?' She stroked her grandmother's silver-streaked hair.

'Yes.'

'Your forehead?'

'Um um, my forehead too.'

'Your ears?' Her little fingers played with Aunt Vie's ears, and so she went on asking and stroking each part. Aunt Vie affirming and smiling.

'Your toes?' She cooed taking her grandmother's feet in her hands. Vie tried to pull them from her little playful fingers. 'Your toes?' She pressed.

Aunt Vie hesitated. 'Do you love your toes?' Babydear asked with urgency. Vie considered, her toes were among the most ravished parts of her body bearing the scars from accidents with machettes, painful contact with stony roads losing the tops of some, nails of others, broken bones suffered while picking coffee on hillsides and losing her footing, it being cheaper to bandage them herself and press on with the much needed Day's Work than go to a doctor. Then there were the corn and callouses, the punishment of ill-fitting, passed-on, borrowed, loaned, given, shoes. No. She could not love her toes. Seeing the hurt that her words engendered in the little girl, Aunt Vie wished she had lied. '*You don't love your toes?*' The little girl asked holding firm and studying them.

'No! I do not love my toes,' Vie found herself repeating quietly. Babydear looked at her with renewed confusion then bent to kiss her grandmother's toes. Aunt Vie pulled them away. 'Don't do that sweetie. They are so ugly.'

'I don't think they're ugly. I love your toes,' she said, brushing her lips over her grandmother's toes. 'I love your toes.'

Aunt Vie smiled, remembering. What would that little girl think if she hears that I have died a few weeks after she has left? She got up and stumbled down the steps of her verandah and into the kitchen at the side of the house and made herself tea. It's too easy to die, harder to live, she thought. On the way back to her room she remembered that Littleman had made and brought

13

a walking stick for her earlier. That boy is so thoughtful, he's the only one who seem to realise that now that I don't have Baby-dear to lean on, I need something else. She reached for the stick that was leaning in one of the corners of the verandah. She wondered where Littleman was tonight.

She sat on the verandah, drank her tea and dozed off, waking to the sound of familiar footsteps coming from behind the house. 'Littleman.'

'Night Aunt Vie,' he said as he climbed the two steps to the verandah. 'I just came to check that you all right.'

'You went down to the meeting?'

'I was outside the church. It just finished but they all still talking.' The verandah lamp wick had almost burnt down, he turned it up for Aunt Vie, suggested that he should see that the lamp in her room had sufficient oil, filled it from the oil pan in the kitchen when he noticed that it was almost empty. Vie thanked him, unable to stop a wave of pity for him. He was a changed man since his grandmother, Nana, had died eighteen months before.

The District was now almost totally quiet, that hush when mid-week services had just finished, as the brethren, sinners and backsliders sauntered home in contemplative moods. The brethren, to reprimand children who fitted their newly acquired interpretations of disobedience, and reproach slothful husbands who more often than not went only as far as the church windows when they needed a special favour from God. The sinners and backsliders, to pray for yet another chance while their emotions were still high.

Then the dogs would start their frenzied barking again, Ragu may strum a few tunes on his banjo or mouth organ possibly joined or even rivalled by Amos Maxton on his own mouth organ or flutina. One or two in this lower part of the District would even dare to play dominoes spurred on by those who had gone to Kitson Town to drink and returned with unconsecrated

14

jollity. Then there would be that quiet again for the few hours that they slept to rise just before the sun. This was the normal run of events four nights a week, including Sundays, and despite the periodic inebriated criticism, church meetings provided much filling of the spirit for the saved, and equal amounts of excitement and diversion for the unsaved who sometimes would sit at the back or be strung around the outside by the windows, sometimes joining in, at other times laughing and jeering. Only occasionally in awe.

When Littleman finished tending the lamps, he collected water from one of the drums by the side of the house and heated it up for Aunt Vie's wash. She smiled at how he busied himself, and at how when he came to see her, even when Babydear was there, even before his own grandmother had died, he would just find things to do, help out without being asked or without expecting gratitude. When he came and sat back beside her, she tapped his leg. 'You are a good boy . . .'

'You use the walking stick yet?' was his embarrassed reply. Aunt Vie rested her hand on his arm for a moment, 'Thank you, Littleman,' she said, 'it is a great help to me.'

Chapter 3

Littleman stirred, disturbing the bundle that was his pillow. It slid off the tomb onto the red dirt. His ears, unaccustomed to the coldness of his granite bed, quickly absorbed the chill, relaying it down his body. He folded himself more tightly into the foetal position, twisted and turned until his half consciousness realised that all was still not well. His eyes bulbous and red, shot open.

Groping around the edge of his grandmother's tomb he found the bundle, replaced it, shifted into position, closed his eyes. But the cock crowed. He jumped up, as if feeling for the first time the culmination of the mosquito bites that had been ravaging his half-naked body all night, slung the bundle over his shoulder and moved out from the family graveyard, his grandmother's the sole beggar among them, surrounded by the thunderous chorus of cocks, frogs, donkeys and seemingly demented crickets.

He pushed aside the last bramble that led out into Deacon's yard, brushed the dried bushes from his body, stood contemplating for a moment, one hand in what was left of his pocket, the other holding his bundle in place. He listened, as if for a sign. On hearing nothing unusual, he walked over to the kitchen erected someway from the main house, peered through the wattle, not quite sure exactly what he was looking for. Finding nothing unusual there either, he perched himself on one of the wooden benches outside to wait.

Eventually, he heard noises coming from one of the many windows that opened into that side of the yard. Before Deacon's and Sister Netta's children had moved, one by one, to England, Littleman had known who was in each room. Now he wasn't ever sure. There could be someone from the church staying or some out-of-District relative . . . More unusually, they could be by themselves. He stood up, hoping that it would be Sister Netta who came out first, allowing himself to wonder, not for the first time, what it would be like to have one room in a big house like that. Or in any house for that matter, without stringent and crippling conditions. It was at times like that when fragments of memory that he still had of his parents came back. Helped no doubt by the pictures they sent each Christmas. Perhaps it was the pictures most of all that created the memories. He was only two when they had left him with Nana, first for town and then for England. He had never seen in real life, the sisters and brothers that grew over the years beside them in the photographs.

Littleman was overcome momentarily with the desire to look at them again, especially his mother whose face could have been the grandmother whom he had been left with. He sighed heavily at the thought of her. One picture of her was in his bundle too. But before he could make up his mind, a door opened and Sister Netta came out into the yard, headed, with her face basin, flannel and some clothes slung across her arm, to another outbuilding at the other end of the yard.

'How long you been sitting out here?' she asked when she returned washed and changed. 'Good morning, Sister Netta,' he said standing up. She groaned knowingly and stepped past him into the kitchen. Littleman hesitated for a moment, turned to look back at the house then tapped gently on the side of the opened kitchen door. Sister Netta looked over her shoulder at

17

him, cut her eyes and turned to arrange the firewood on the stove. 'Why you no just come in and stop you foolishness.'

Inside, Littleman sat astride the bench in the kitchen gratefully sipping the bush tea and eating the buttered hardo bread that she gave him.

She was trying hard not to look at him, feeling as usual a nagging guilt at having given him the chipped enamel mug and plate. They were reserved only for him, hidden away afterwards. Her guilt was exacerbated by the sincerity of his thanks and the other ways he would undoubtedly find in succeeding days to express his gratitude to her – it was the same whenever she fed him – he would weed the flower beds around her house, sweep up her yard, go to one of the several fields she and Deacon owned, to weed, dig yam or climb trees to get dried coconuts and firewood for them. Even going on errands to Spanish Town, on foot. Sometimes it crossed her mind that he might die of overwork; there were so many people for him to work for. But she couldn't be expected to take it all on; there were other people in the District who should have consciences too, they had done their bit when Nana was alive, had even given her a burial plot. Yet, Sister Netta had to try hard to suppress the guilt, replacing it with thoughts that she was too old and too tired after raising ten children of her own. Now they were all abroad she was secretly glad for the release. How could she be expected to take on more at her age? What with the church work and all? Being Deacon's wife, having a big house and owning the second biggest acreage of land behind Cleary in the District, came with responsibilities the poorer ones of them could not imagine. Besides he wasn't fatherless or motherless.

Sister Netta sighed loudly, dismissing with it the burden of Littleman's lot, concentrating instead on her work in the corner of the kitchen where the three stones perched equidistant apart in a triangle formed her cooking stove. She needed to have her husband's cornmeal porridge ready when he woke up. Both of them had a busy day in front of them. Deacon had his visits to the sick and shut-ins to do, she, her stint at Aunt Vie's for the rest of the day. Poor Aunt Vie, yet another ageing grandmother deprived of her hands, feet and eyes. Littleman should count himself lucky that Nana had had him with her to the end. And Nana fortunate that his parents hadn't sent for him at eleven going twelve years old as most of the others had done. She herself was fast losing hope of ever seeing the grandchildren that letters and photographs reliably told her she had, despite her contrite prayers.

The thought of the lone old people adding to the already heavy load of the church, increased the weight that Littleman had ushered in. Still, she was glad that she didn't have to crouch down to the stove as she had done over the years. Today she was sure, she wouldn't be able to get up again. Littleman, noticing how arduous it had become for her, bending her back to fix firewood in place, fanning and blowing until the fire was kindled, had gone to town last Christmas, bought concrete and raised the base for her. She sighed. Why did that come back to her now? She glanced over her shoulder at him. 'You want some more tea?' He thanked her and took his cup over to her. As she poured the tea she reached out and took his hand with the cup, giving it a little squeeze before releasing.

The sun was just coming up when Littleman passed Deacon's and Sister Netta's water tank and turned right out of the yard. He walked purposely a few yards along until he came to Miss Dee's shop. He knew she had stayed there the previous night and he planned to stop there on his way to Aunt Vie's yard. He supposed she had a lot of organising to do having just recently opened it. Like everyone at that end of the District, he was excited about a grocery shop opening at the top end of the District, to rival the Samuel's shop lower down. But unlike most of them, his excitement was mainly unwarranted. The only time he had money to spend on items from a shop was at Christmas when he got his registered postal order from his parents in England and then it was certainly not on food that he lavished it.

He entered the yard behind the shop, found himself a spot and sat down by a breadfruit tree to wait. It wasn't long before he heard sounds he imagined to be Miss Dee getting ready, coming from the bedroom adjoining the shop. Although the doors were firmly locked, he averted his eyes and ears, trying to concentrate instead on the cacophony of stray hungry dogs roaming the streets, and the chickens in neighbouring yards cackling and scratching for worms, just before their main course of corn.

Wishing to further distract himself in case Miss Dee suddenly opened the door, he set his bundle down and undid the knot. He took out a can opener, a penknife, various bits of clothing, none more whole than the other, a Bible, a water can, lastly a pile of airletters and a few registered envelopes. He untied the string that held the letters together, found an envelope containing the photographs, sifted through until he found the picture of his grandmother. He relaxed against the tree remembering vividly the day when he and Nana had dressed up and gone to Spanish Town to take it. They had taken six in all that day, a couple of both of them together, two each of her and him alone. She was to send them all to England to her daughter, his mother, but he had begged her to keep that one back for him. He was especially glad now that she was gone. It was not fully two years yet but he was finding it increasingly difficult to summon up her real face; the multiplicity of expressions that had made her face so interesting, one of the reasons why, although he liked the picture, he found it so disappointing. Her face so static, sporting only the half smile that somehow on that day hadn't quite reached her eyes. He hurriedly replaced the pictures, tied the string around the letters and envelopes and repacked his bag, trying hard not to think of the multitude of things that may have caused those sad eyes.

In this the most populous part of the District, people were up before or with the sun; men sharpening cutlasses, packing crocus bags for the field, women rousing children to their early morning duties before school, and preparing tea . . .

Miss Dee, too, came out in the yard with a large enamel jug, headed for her drum over by the side of the kitchen. Littleman cleared his throat intending not to startle her, it had the opposite effect, she jumped, dropped the jug and rested her hand on her chest. 'What are you doing in my yard? I'm tired of telling you not to come here. How long have you been sitting there?' She fired the words at him in her own inimitable voice. He got up and went to pick up the jug. 'Just leave it and get out of the yard. Please. The man could have killed me,' she said, retrieving the jug herself.

'I just come to see if you need any work done today . . . some fixing or sweeping . . . or anything.'

'No. No. Littleman everything is all right. Just go . . . ,' she said dismissively, exaggerating the practised correctness of her speech, walking away. Then as if to increase the weight of her words she looked behind her briefly, adding, 'Anyway I'm expecting Aunt Jane any minute now so if I were you I *would* just go, you know what she'd say if she finds you here . . .'

He was equally insistent. 'You know I can work Miss Dee so if you need anything I'm able . . .' He wasn't sure she heard him but he didn't want to take any chances and be found loitering by Aunt Jane but he lingered just long enough to follow Miss Dee surreptitiously with his eyes before collecting his bundle and continuing down the District. Jacob Cleary's jeep sped past him as he had steadied himself down the first grade, throwing up a cloud of red dust and gravel in his face and covering his already soiled clothes, adding further insult to the injury Miss Dee had inflicted.

Walking about the District was the only pastime that presented no challenges, no slight or rejection, to Littleman. He smiled wistfully, though reeling still from Miss Dee's treatment, he couldn't get used to it but he erased it from his mind, holding instead the memory of their past friendship and the security he felt in the womb of his District, Top Mountain. He could not bring himself to feel otherwise despite the ill-luck that had befallen him in it, in the last months.

Top Mountain, high on one of the numerous hills of St Catherine, surrounded by numerous others, from any of which the lights of Kingston in the distance could be seen at nights, with its stubborn red dirt, the rich soil for the subsistence grounds or fields that wove their way throughout the District and beyond. The tangled undergrowth and vegetation too varied and numerous even for him to memorise. Though between the few hundred inhabitants, each name was logged in the mind, if not on paper, and passed on from generation to generation, and valued as a balm or curse, in bath or tea for good or evil. He had at some time or other, walked on each lane that led to an eight or six or four or two-roomed house made from affluent concrete with verandahs and painted in blue or with white-washed walls, a standpipe and water tank in the yard, down to the one-roomed wattle and daub ones with water drums by the sides, no standpipe in sight, but zinc sheets leading into them from zinc roofs patiently waiting to collect rain or the less predictable water from one of the three standpipes placed equidistant along the main road.

Littleman knew each gully, hillside, field or ground and not just in the daytime when the blazing sun produced glorious lights from dawn to dust but in the pitch blackness of unlit nights when one could imagine bats soaring the roofs of caves, hear owls mark out their patch and dogs communicating ominous messages. When familiar landmarks took on sinister and threatening shapes, making it all too easy to be convinced by tales of duppies, rolling calves and hence for peace of mind, the power of God and /or obeahmen, women and wise old people.

So there was the church, first built years before by one of the John Clearys, on land he loaned to the District, a pledge that successive generations had seen fit to continually honour, despite subsequent and frequent offers from members and others to buy it. The church stood just opposite his big white unin-habited house, which itself dwarfed even Deacon's and Sister Netta's enormous home. It was ostentatious, yet on only a frac-tion of the vast acreage that the Cleary family owned, mostly unworked and seemingly forgotten.

Littleman had spent all his twenty-one years in the District, making only brief trips to the surrounding districts of Paul Mountain, to the north, where he had attended all-age school years before, and occasionally went now to collect letters from the Postal Agency; Eggsbury further beyond that and districts in the other direction: Guanobovale to the west; Old Road, Kitson Town to the south and further on the capital of the Parish itself: Spanish Town. He had long given up hope of ever going further. There was that brief time when he was approaching twelve when his parents had sent for him, two years after they had left themselves, to join them in England and alluded to an invitation for Nana too. But his grandmother had been adamant, Jamaica was all she knew, she wasn't prepared to go and die in the snow and if her daughter took Littleman from her, she would just have to die alone. Littleman had cried for days on end, threatened to run away, and even if they found him, no one would be able to get him on the plane, he had vowed with eleven-year-old sincerity. He would never leave her, she was after all the only mother he knew since even before his parents had migrated, they had left him with Nana, his mother to live as a domestic in town, his father to go on endless six-monthly contracts to cotton fields in the southern states of America and once to Panama. Nana wrote back to her daughter about her son's distress. His twelfth birthday came and went and nothing more was said. The fortnightly postal orders came, the parcels at Christmas. Nana insisted especially because of his 'hardhead' that he continued at all-age school until he was fifteen, she lived in hope that he would eventually retain even a little of what the teachers tried to drum in. It had all seemed to him so secure and certain apart from those brief but poignant discussions of the certainty of her dying before him. 'But you don't have to worry they'll send for you then. They will have to . . . ,' she had insisted, 'After you don't have anybody here to see to you . . .'

She did die, he was nineteen then, shattering his world, leaving him alone, the only relatives he knew well out of reach in England. He struggled to manage. His mother sent money for the funeral, something extra for him but no mention was made again of sending for him. The fortnightly postal orders became monthly, then quarterly, then annually, with strong admonitions that he was a grown man now who could work and support himself. But where could he find work? It was the second half of the sixties, the same conditions at the end of the decade before had driven most of the fit young men and women abroad. But Littleman tried. He had to find the rent for the one room Nana had rented from the Clearys. In between working the half acre on which it stood, he frequented Spanish Town, walking there because he had no money for the bus fare, going round all the supermarkets, the factories. Nothing. He did Day's Work in Top Mountain and surrounding districts but everybody was in the same boat, little money to spare for payment. He had to be content with food on the job or provisions from the fields. He sold what he could from his own field, made the rent for a few months but not for long enough. Mr Cleary evicted him, Nana had only been dead six months. He was overcome with having let his grandmother down, not tried his best, although he could not see where else to try. So contrite, he refused the offers of shelter from Ragu, Azora and even the Maxtons with their six children. He had to find a way to help himself, show Nana from the grave that he was not as worthless as it seemed.

The Samuel's shop and property on which the Maxtons and Aunt Vie rented homes stood three-quarters of the way down the District, just past the Clearys' house, a distance put between them by a road, Aunt Vie's lane everyone called it.

People were now stirring at that end of the District too. Those who were going to the fields had left before the sun rose. Littleman had passed the few remaining stragglers along the way. He turned right just before the Samuel's shop onto Aunt Vie's lane. But he wasn't going to her yet, he had first to see the Dr Azora; confusingly labelled herbalist, savant, obeahwoman or a bit of each. Ragu called out greeting to him, Littleman shook his head as he did everytime that happened. He still couldn't understand how the blind man whose one-room house stood at the foot of the Clearys' and way back from the road, could recognise everyone's walk in the District and from such a distance.

Azora was not there when Littleman arrived so he had to wait, again. When she eventually came from behind the house she was laden with a crocus bag slung over her shoulder. 'Littleman,' she said in greeting. Littleman stood up, 'Morning . . . You are coming home from work when everybody just setting off.'

Azora mounted the steps of the verandah and set her bag down. 'Sit down man,' she ordered, 'I'll go and make some tea.'

Littleman gazed at her, wondering not for the first time, how she coped with the weight of controversy that had always characterised her work, continuing to live as a recluse but affecting every part of the District, though most would not admit it, with her baths, herbal medicines and mysterious pouches. She was, despite warnings from the pulpit and cynicism from Aunt Vie – arguably the most influential person in the District besides the Clearys and the church. Aunt Vie alone refused to hold to the commonly held view in the District that whatever could not be understood should be feared and respected.

Perhaps Dr Azora coped with it, Littleman thought, because no proof could ever be forwarded or no secrets told, to contradict her infrequent assertion that she simply used what God had naturally placed on the earth.

So, fuelled by Azora's own practised silence, her reluctance to defend her reputation and her character as a recluse, a trait not hitherto known in the District, many who sought her, on whatever account, came surreptitiously, some at nights, some in the early mornings, confident that they would not be exposed, at least not by her.

Littleman was the only one of her clients who did not care. His grandmother had unashamedly sworn by Azora's medicines and had believed to her dying day that but for her she would not have lasted until she did. It was Littleman who had related her ailments to 'the doctor' and returned with preparations for medicines and baths. He had got so used to the errands that when Nana had finally died he had not stopped visiting Azora. 'I want you to do a little thing for me as well,' Littleman said when she returned with their tea. She set them down and was returning to get the cassava bread she had offered Littleman.

She stopped. 'What is that now?'

'Something for Aunt Vie . . .'

'What you say?' Azora looked up, 'Aunt Vie sent you?' She lost her footing and slipped off the verandah, Littleman caught her just before she fell. Azora pulled herself up and repeated her question.

'No. She didn't send me.' What seemed like a very distant hope, died in Azora's eyes.

'I should know better,' she said, faintly, resting her back on the edge of the verandah.

'I just think now that Babydear gone and she's all by herself she need some little protection . . . She looked so old and lost the other day when the taxi drove off.'

'Littleman I'm tired of telling you that I have nothing that can protect people who don't believe . . . Besides . . . ,' she said pensively, '. . . Aunt Vie wouldn't thank you if she even know you call her name in my yard. She doesn't understand what happens here and she thinks the worse,' she sighed.

'Anyway, soon come.' When she returned with the bread she was smiling.

'You are one young man who love old people, eh?' she said, handing over Littleman's share. The young man smiled agreement.

Sensing that Littleman's mood had changed she cracked jokes about whether his period of self-flagellation had ended and whether he was feeling himself now deserving of a room with a bed and a roof instead of the skies and a tomb, albeit his grand-mother's. But she had misjudged Littleman's mood. 'You get cross when people don't understand you,' he said quietly. 'Try and see my position. I am a man. If a man don't work, he should not eat . . . or sleep in comfort for that matter.'

Azora sighed. 'You didn't understand your granny. She didn't mean that if is she you quoting.' Azora got up suddenly not waiting for him to reply and went into one of the two rooms leading off his verandah, returning with a bag of corn which she flung absentmindedly at the fowls scratching around the yard. They competed for single grains until it dawned on them that there was plenty to go round.

Azora sat down again. 'If a man or woman for that matter fall into a pit, he deserves to suffer and die in there if he refuses the hand trying to pull him out . . . Whoever the hand belongs to,' she said seriously.

Chapter 4

Miss Dee has never known her father and cannot remember her mother. She was raised by a Godmother in Guanobovale until she was seven and then 'adopted' by Aunt Jane. The period up to seven is a complete blur to her. It did not matter to her how common this giving away of children was and how many children she knew who were like her; being raised by someone other than their parents, someone to who they were not even related, she was angry in her heart and grew up with an over-whelming resentment for her mother and did her best when thoughts of her invaded her mind, to dismiss them rapidly. But not only was she resentful of her mother but her father too, apparently, a red skin big shot, from some vague memory of a distant conversation she had overheard or maybe dreamt, who had taken advantage of her young mother when she worked for him as a domestic in town, throwing her out with a bagful of threats and warnings before his deeds could be exposed, causing the hurt and confusion in her mother that led to Miss Dee being passed around and finally ending up with Aunt Jane.

Over the years, despite their see-sawing relationship, Miss Dee had eventually been left in no doubt by Aunt Jane's deeds, if not her words, that Miss Dee, flesh and blood or not, was dearer to her than her own life. But Miss Dee frequently had her doubts, she knew that although Aunt Jane passionately desired it and had done almost everything in her power to bring it about, she could not have children of her own. Miss Dee would find herself wondering many times whether it was she that Aunt Jane loved or the idea that she might have been her own child, the one that she could not have.

Miss Dee remembered that initially she was seen as a sullen and ungrateful child by her aunt who recited daily in the first few weeks that she did not know what she had taken on herself. That was, Miss Dee felt, until it was discovered in Sunday School that she could sing. In a district that was talent hungry and where activities centred around the church, which provided the main source of amusement and entertainment, she had in one Sunday carved out for her little self a highly respected niche. The attention she suddenly attracted miraculously transformed her young life, changing she felt her relationship with her aunt and for the first time in her short life, she viewed, with the optimistic eyes of a seven-year-old, the world as a bright and joyful place.

Though like her aunt Miss Dee was not saved, that was not held against her in church even though everyone was aware that participation by the unsaved in church services was a departure from practised doctrine. Soon after that first Sunday school rendition, Miss Dee graduated to singing in proper services in the District and fast upon that to representing the District at Parish and National church conventions.

Gloriously out-smarting the other children in attire and manners, as Aunt Jane would boast, Miss Dee did not miss a service, her head obligingly covered, occupying the front seat in the church and not one at the back or peering in at the window from the outside like the other unsaved and backsliders. Miss Dee was swept off her feet and became hopelessly besotted with her aunt, her new life, the church and Top Mountain. But it was not long before the praise and attention lavished on her by the District, and even more by Aunt Jane, generated another side that at seven she could never have predicted or contemplated.

29

Jane, not the most loved of people in the District, took to demanding in little ways gratitude from the District for having 'cultivated' Miss Dee's talents. When she was met with scepticism, she took to unnecessarily restricting Miss Dee's activities, even on occasions forcing the child to drop out of planned events on which her performance depended, making, it was angrily claimed, the District a laughing stock.

As criticism mounted, tearing the little girl's allegiance, Jane, during some weeks of seeming temporary insanity, dealt heavily with Miss Dee, blaming her. Because they lived past the Samuel's shop on the way out of the District on the border with Old Road, in the only house for at least a mile, Miss Dee often felt alone, her cries, when Aunt Jane took the strap to her for suddenly not measuring up, were drowned by the rustle of leaves whipped up by the wind and lost in the bark of the countless trees, shrubs, vines and suckers, the very ones which represented all that was fruitful and promising about Top Mountain District.

Miss Dee had been given her duties from the first day she was brought to the house and they had been no great burden, but after Aunt Jane fell out with the church, stopped going and forbade Miss Dee from doing so (despite entreaties from Aunt Vie, who she would normally have listened to), Miss Dee feared that the first two blissful years with Aunt Jane had been a delusion.

Now nine years old, it seemed to Miss Dee that Aunt Jane enjoyed finding fault. She was not now content to take Miss Dee's word that she had done her duties, that the girl had more often than not gone over them three or four times to be sure, and would have done anything to avoid the strapping that doubled if someone on the road had upset Aunt Jane, which often was the case.

Miss Dee must have been about ten when she first realised that the District thought something was seriously wrong with her aunt. At least once a week it seemed Jane would return from errands in the heart of the District furiously murmuring to herself. The only words that Miss Dee could ever manage to decipher were, 'Is not my fault, yet they keep calling me a mule, I'll give them mule one of these fine day.' Miss Dee did not understand but had finally decided that her aunt was being likened to a mule because of how hard she was known to work and because of her strength. She could not understand what the problem was.

Her aunt's unhappiness, Miss Dee's own confusion and both their estrangement from the District, made Miss Dee's days anxiety-ridden and her nights plagued with recurrent nightmares where she was left alone by her aunt on a moonless night on one of the lonely mountains of Top Mountain or sometimes in one of the precipices dug deep beneath them, for failing to measure up to some simple task. At first Miss Dee would awake with a vague unease that something untoward had transpired in the night in her dreams but later the dreams became so vivid that some days she would painfully relive each aspect of them.

Rigid with fear she would lie whimpering as the cold night air seeped through her thin cotton nightdress. Somehow in her dream she would make her way back to her yard but with no moon and with all the shutters from the house closed not even a faint light broke the darkness. The long lonely path leading from the front of the house to the road seemed closer than the house itself. Even in the day time, it haunted her imagination; the large tree trunks with barks for eyes, branches for hands reaching out to grab her, threatening her with unrecognisable sounds in the wind. And underneath them, the thickets, secretive; snares for mongooses, rats and lizards. And the robbermen, the blackheart men who ate children and made their spirits into souls that cried day and night, haunting other children and luring them to their deaths.

The habit of doing things more than once, of reading Aunt

Jane's face to see if there was any sign of new unhappiness became habitual, second nature, to Miss Dee. Relieved that she had not really been made to sleep outside on the tombs, she was always the first one to get up in the mornings and the last to go to bed at nights. This went on until she caught a bad cold and couldn't sing at a big annual concert in another District that Jane had adopted to get her own back at Top Mountain. It was only the first of a number of minor and serious illnesses that, one after the other, Miss Dee began to fall prey to. But she passed her common entrance exam and got into High school. Proud of her and worried by her frailties, Aunt Jane banned those early morning and late night sessions, forbidding her from doing anything but the mere minimum of duties, showering more kindness on her than she had done even in those first two blissful years. Miss Dee became herself again and her nightmares disappeared with her gloom.

The year of 1959 and the two years following it, Miss Dee still remembers as her best ever with her aunt. The year had not started well as far as Miss Dee's health was concerned. It had been a normal Saturday. Miss Dee had got up, had her tea and together with her aunt had done the usual Saturday chores, cleaning the house and yard, washing and hanging clothes out to dry for ironing later in the afternoon. Chores accomplished, Jane took to her sewing machine. Miss Dee sprawled out behind the house on one of the tombs that presented no threat to her now, just a coolness which emanated from its stones and from the branches overhanging them. She finished the composition that she had to do for homework, went on to her basic algebra and then trigonometry.

She would have loved instead to be playing out on the road or at Aunt Vie's house where she could at least hear the sounds of the District. She had to be content instead with the purring of her aunt's tireless machine. It was hot. She could almost see the leaves that formed a bed of carpet under the fruit trees around her, drying under the heat. Lizards moved even more purposely, seeking shade on yet another limb as the sun moved in on them. Their three dogs lapped constantly at the trough of water by the side of the house, retreating soon after to defiant shades.

Miss Dee looked up from her books as a shadow fell on them, expecting to see her aunt standing over her, not registering that the sewing machine was still purring. She frowned when she did not see her and went back to her book. Perhaps she had caught the shadow of a hovering skylark. But something rested on her head, soft, like an errant lizard but uncharacteristically still, not scurrying away as even the most brazen lizard would have done.

Aunt Jane heard her scream. Froze. Then using the back door was behind the house and by Miss Dee's side in no time. Seeing the lifeless form on the ground, feeling the unusual heat coming from the girl's body, Aunt Jane was in no doubt as to what had happened. In minutes they were on the back of her donkey headed for Azora and had it not been for the bath she immediately gave Miss Dee, followed by the protective pouch that she pinned to her underclothes, Jane was sure that Miss Dee would have died. She blamed someone in the District as having set obeah on her child, widening further the gap between herself and the community. And they, oblivious of Miss Dee's illness and her miraculous recovery, interpreted Jane's behaviour as yet another example of her irredeemable nature, haughty, bad-minded and undeserving of a place among them. This did not seem to affect Jane, she seemed content to hang on to the tenuous relationship she had with Aunt Vie and Dora Samuel. Miss Dee could not help but notice that once she had recovered fully, Jane seemed at her happiest. Apart from still insisting that she kept away from every family in the District except Aunt Vie's, where Miss Dee was petted and spoilt by Vie's daughter Isadora who would let her play with Delores, Wilbert and Babydear. Best of all the strappings ceased.

33

Her aunt's general manner too was miraculously transformed, gone was her former irascibility. Her cheeks got plump, she smiled a lot, said nice words to Miss Dee often, would stroke her face out of the blue and hug her without warning. Her aunt would have her sit in front of her on the floor as she took her time plaiting her hair in the sweetest styles, even when they were not going anywhere special. She took Miss Dee to town and had her choose fabrics for new clothes, ribbons, socks and shoes to match with no Christmas in sight and the two real Christmases that came and went with her in that mood surpassed the ones in between. Miss Dee was happy, with only a nagging wish that she could run about the District barefooted like other children, hop, skip, play ring games, hide and seek, mummies and daddies. But she was lucky, she could have everything they did not, so she did not dare be ungrateful.

Then suddenly one night, her aunt had started to scream. Uncontrollably. Miss Dee ran into her room to find her aunt's nightdress and bed clothes covered in blood. She had to run to Aunt Vie for help, and watched later, confused, as Jane was driven down the lane to hospital returning days later sadder, more irascible and unpredictable than Miss Dee could ever remember. Even at fourteen and clever by all accounts, Miss Dee could not work out what had happened to have changed Jane so in those two years and why it had all come so viciously crashing in. Seven years later she was no closer to finding out.

Later, as Jane further ostracised herself from the District and in return was included by them only on sufferance, she attempted it seemed to Miss Dee to draw closer to her just at the time when Miss Dee hungered most for friendship and closeness that was not sanctioned by her aunt. But her pity for her aunt, she did not then call what she felt for her aunt love, meant that she did not spurn her affection. Miss Dee reciprocated in full and at times found herself exaggerating her devotion, so mixed up as it was with the gratitude and debt she owed this complete stranger who had given her a home and raised her above most other children in Top Mountain District and its surrounds.

But underneath this ostentatious show of obedience, compliance and devotion, Miss Dee was stubbornly own way, her hand often on the annually renewed protective pouch Azora had made for her. She secretly defied her aunt in winning and keeping for a time the friendship of the barefooted, dunce and well-below-her Littleman and the force-ripe, woman-before-her-time Rose-marie. She knew Aunt Jane would have been appalled if she knew those she had picked out to befriend. Miss Dee often mused on which of the two her aunt would have objected to more, Littleman or Rose-marie, who lived in the humble house that she shared with her family in Kitson Town and did not pass her common entrance exam to go to High school, let alone do a business course as Miss Dee had done, but had worked unofficially as a domestic in town, to help her family out, when she should have been at school.

Together Miss Dee and Rose-marie were an incongruous pair. While Miss Dee was not fat, she could not be called thin, Rose-marie had to be called thin. As Miss Dee was 'tall for a woman', Rose-marie was said to be short, 'even for a woman'. Rose-marie did not have the thick, strong, long hair that Miss Dee had, only, 'picky-picky' stubs that resisted coaxing and would not grow. And though some could not see it, most thought, even grudgingly, that there was something nice about Miss Dee's looks. Not individual parts of her, but taken as a whole. That debate did not occur where her friend was concerned. But, had anyone the gall to let Miss Dee hear any of this comparison, she would have dismissed it as irrelevant and foolish, and her devotion to Rose-marie remained constant over the years.

Chapter 5

Miss Dee took her time walking to the shop, she was missing Babydear more than she had expected and was finding it difficult to be enthusiastic about anything. Despite the difference in their ages, Babydear had been mature and had been the only person in the District under fifty that she had any kind of relationship with. People, even Aunt Vie, said they resembled each other and they themselves sometimes joked about being cousins. As she walked up the final grade before her shop Miss Dee glanced to her right throwing a scathing look at the new sun, surely too hot for March. Once or twice she kicked a stone irritably, sensing the start of one of those days when she knew she would be aggravated by the world; the heat, the flies, the stray dogs, the constant stream of customers that would call for credit and by Littleman. She didn't know why but of all the people who annoyed and irritated her in the District, he had become the worst. There were so many things. His recently acquired pathetic ingratiating manner, the way he refused to get the message that she would no longer associate with him, but more than that his plight. Why did it make her so uneasy? Sometimes she wondered fleetingly whether it was because it made her reflect on how it may well have been herself in his shoes had Aunt Jane not taken pity on her when her Godmother had not wanted her anymore and her mother could not be found? But how could she compare herself with a man? She had been a child. She sighed, wishing that he would simply keep away from her, give her conscience rest.

When she had opened the shop three months ago, to see in the new year of 1968, she was fooled into thinking that everyone was pleased by the convenience of not having to walk all the way to the other end of the District to the Samuel's grocery shop. She had soon learnt; all they wanted she was convinced was another place to trust from. Although they did pay eventually their presumption irritated her, it was at their convenience rather than at hers that they chose to settle their debts. But she now had plans, ones she knew would exacerbate hers and her aunt's unpopularity, to limit credit for each family and be firm on the amount each would have to pay against it each week to continue getting further credit from her. She was past caring. At one time she was aware of actually being liked and pitied by everyone, or perhaps it was just pity; she was aware of the rumours that Aunt Jane wasn't treating her well; fuelling the District's dislike of her aunt. But eventually along the way Miss Dee felt she had been put in the same barrel with Aunt Jane. After all they said, Miss Dee herself had never seen fit to accept their friendship. Many, they said, would have fallen at her feet in the early days. 'She so nice and pretty, she can sing nice and she bright at school . . . you can tell she going to turn out to be something . . .' They would smile grudgingly. 'It won't be long before either Mr Cleary Junior or him one-son, Jacob, start seeking her out . . . You know how these big shot like their concubine . . . She really ripe for them . . .' A mixture of disgust and suppressed envy in their tones.

Initially it was as if Miss Dee's friendship was the more desirable because it was hard to obtain. But after a while when no one succeeded in winning it, everyone felt collectively stung and rejected, shared the resentment, shifting blame from Jane to Miss Dee herself. 'Jane grew her up to be selfish but she's woman now, why she no mix more? Pride goes before a fall, somebody should warn her . . . ,' the older women said.

'Is just because she got pretty clothes in all the colours of the rainbow and shoes and handbags to match that she so boasty . . . She think she better than us . . . She think she too nice for us. She carrying on as if she's one of the Clearys.' And everyone withdrew from her, to watch her from a distance, to wait for her fall. And when her shop was opened they patronised it, getting physically closer to her than they had done over the last few years, yet no closer to knowing or understanding her.

Feeling critical eyes from yards and verandahs, Miss Dee endeavoured to make her steps light, to move her hips in the way she had practised as a teenager when she had stolen time to be with Rose-marie, to laugh, talk and play vulgar. They were brazen then, in Miss Dee's pilfered, secret times, frolicking shamelessly on Rose-marie's mother's polished floors.

As she thought, Littleman was waiting for her, sitting on a boulder outside her shop. She did not disguise her irritation. She did not want him to remind her daily of all that was awful about life in the District, its ignorance, destitution, hopelessness and poverty. Not now. It was not that she did not feel guilty. She sighed. But for him in those early days, school would have been intolerable. But that was then. She scowled as she approached him, a do-not-say-a-word to me, look on her face.

He ignored or could not read it so she emphasised it by ignoring his greeting, cutting her eyes at him when he reiterated his offer to do jobs for her. She would be crazy, she thought, to have him scurrying about her yard leaving his trail of rancid smell behind.

Once in the bedroom adjoining the shop, she changed quickly into her work slacks and blouse, mindful that it was nearly opening time. She hurried through the sitting room, lingered in the shop for further minutes, dusting the counter, ensuring the glass display cabinet underneath had the usual pre-packed goods, like toothpaste, blue and soap. She checked the stocks in the barrels, they would be in demand especially it being a Saturday, flour, rice, sugar, cornmeal, saltfish, salt pork and mackerel. The glass cabinet on the counter was empty of bullah, cake and bread, there were just a few candies and coconut drops. She glanced at her watch. The bread van would be there soon. She gave the counter one last wipe, swept the floor front and back, popped back into the bedroom to have a quick glance in the mirror before unbolting the shop door.

'Littleman, why are you still here?' She began feigning patience but unable to sustain it. 'Why don't you just leave me in peace . . . ,' she said, with anything but confidence in her voice as the thought crossed her mind again of how true a friend he had been to her in the past, when she had needed him even more than he seemed to need her now. How despite having now to beg her, he had never reminded her with bitterness, or otherwise, of those years.

'Don't mean to worry you Miss Dee. Sorry.'

A little boy was coming towards the shop reciting a list. 'Two pounds a sugar, four ounces cocoa, tin a sardine, a loaf a bread . . . Two pounds a sugar . . .'

Miss Dee was about to repeat her dismissal before serving the little boy when she noticed that Littleman was clean, his clothes weren't torn and . . . she sniffed, she couldn't smell him.

'Miss Dee please to sell me . . . ,' the boy interjected.

She recited his list back to him, enjoying his obvious amazement, set about weighing and wrapping his order. She always served that family with enthusiasm because they took pride in never taking anything on trust.

'Thank you Miss Dee, you look beautiful today Miss Dee,' he said, taking his change and running off. 'Just mind you don't break the paper bag and let the goods fall out,' she shouted after him.

She turned back to Littleman, curiosity getting the better of her. 'Where did you get those clothes from?'

'Miss Dee, me clothes didn't die with Nana,' she thought she detected a tinge of bitterness then in his voice but she ignored it, wanting instead to demand, why then have you gone round the District since you lost the house looking like a vagabond, but she restrained herself.

'I just come to tell you that you don't have to worry about me bothering you anymore.' He stopped as if to emphasise a point that he felt she should understand.

She fingered her credit record book. 'Littleman I don't know why . . .'

'I will be living at Aunt Vie's now. And what I need now, I will buy. And . . . ,' he observed her closely, 'I will leave you alone but I just thought I should tell you . . . so that you won't feel the need to scorn me anymore . . .'

Miss Dee swallowed, 'Living at Aunt Vie? What are you gabbling on about?' She lifted up the counter flap without thinking and made to move to his side to challenge his lie. Littleman stretched out his hand as if to block her but without touching her, turned and left the shop.

Miss Dee looked after him long after he had disappeared out of sight. Convinced that if it was true, Aunt Vie must have allowed her sympathy to cloud her mind. How could she take on responsibility for a grown twenty-one-year-old man? It's funny, she mused, quashing any surfacing guilt and regret, as she set about weighing and packing the usual Saturday orders that would be collected later that morning, how things can change. The child-man, everyone had called Littleman as he grew up, though he had struggled with his school lessons from day one, making little progress throughout, he had been mature taking responsibilities beyond his years. To Miss Dee he had been her saviour. When she had first come to the District and others had spurned and mocked her, the new-out-of-District, awkward skinny child she was, shy and unsure though he was, he had found the courage to stand up for her, played with her at recess, walked with her after school until he had to turn off home. And when she had passed her common entrance and gone to High school in town and he had not, had stolen time between looking after his ailing grandmother, dodging Aunt Jane, to be with her, finding words to keep her sane.

She could not have helped noticing then how unlike the other boys he was. He did not get into fights when he was teased about washing his grandmother's underwear, ironing his own clothes and 'doing things that gal picknies should do . . .' Miss Dee had admired him for taking it in his stride, for being shameless in showing his devotion to his grandmother, had once even been heard to say at school recess, 'I love my grandmother . . .' And when she had taken ill, he had done everything for her, washing her, feeding her, leaving the house only when somebody else stayed with her for him. Nana's death had shattered his world and their friendship. How could they have remained the same when he had suddenly started wandering and sleeping on her tomb?

It wasn't my fault, she heard herself say, there was nothing I could have done. Aunt Jane was right, there was nothing he or any boy in the District could do for her, so it was best to shut him out as she had done and would continue to do the others.

Chapter 6

Aunt Vie awoke with a severe pain in her side. Its unfamiliarity rather than its intensity concerned her. It was not like the pain she felt that other time when she had had the stroke. That had started with a numbness to her left side, then her arm had dropped followed sharply by the side of her mouth, she had only known that saliva was escaping when she had raised her right hand to rub her mouth. At least Babydear had been around then, in the room with her, had run to call Ruthlyn Maxton.

Now the pain was getting worse, she could hardly move, there was little to do but resign herself to it. She tried to lie on her back, the natural dying position but she found that arduous too. Eventually with a great deal of effort she managed it and closed her eyes, her arms stretched out by her side.

As the dawn broke and no relief came Aunt Vie found herself looking forward to the prospect of her demise; after all death couldn't be all that bad. In her time, she had seen many people make their exit, the majority seeming to radiate an inexplicable glow. Of late, she had spent hours contemplating it, coming to the conclusion finally, despite her occasional church attendance, the regular visits from band leaders led by Sister Netta, that she was free from the image of it as the entrance to the trial of sheep and goats. But what to replace it with? She still struggled with that. At sixty-eight, with people in the District living well beyond the allocated three scores and ten, she had felt she had time. Now it didn't seem to matter. What was clear though, she would not be doing any wandering on this cursed earth again, as rolling calf or duppy, however powerful and persuasive the obeahman calling her. The thought, for some perverse reason, enlivened her and Azora came to mind. She would be the first to try and get her back, Vie thought, to give an account for having poured scorn on her carryings-on.

Dismissing her, Vie found in her mind a certain joy in the possibility of at last being freed from the weight of a life of responsibilities and regret.

First it had been her daughter unplanned and herself barely nineteen, the result of whispered promises, sweet words, few choices and little else to do that was thrilling.

When her stubborn period had refused to show as it had finally done for the first time only four months previously, she had sat behind her house for days, staring in space, moving only to eat and answer the call of nature, bringing down suspicions that somebody had set obeah on her mother's one child. Vie knew better and she was ashamed. For as long as she could remember she had been warned about and kept away from the omnipotent eyes and rapacious hands of the hated Clearys. Vie's mother had vowed that her daughter would not be one of those despoilt by them. But her mother had not foreseen the snares of an out-of-town government land surveyor, his sweet words and promises, camouflaging his commitments to a wife and children in town.

When it was evident that she had fallen and confided to her mother who had impregnated her, there was no choice but a conspiracy of silence between them. For the government official, the affair might have been a simple sting by a mosquito, erased from memory in a second. He frequented the District as before until his work was completed, boasting of the birth of his son, who through some inexplicable twist of fate had been born on the same day as his unacknowledged daughter. Before he left

Eggsbury, never to be seen again, upon a chance meeting with his country diversion and child he would look over their heads as if they were the wind he could not see.

Vie shook her head unconsciously. If only I knew then what I know now. Isadora's birth had been the start of her life of endless responsibilities, supporting her, protecting her from the other countless sweet-mouthed town men who chanced through the District but mostly from the Clearys, the ageing John Cleary Senior and his son John Cleary Junior who, though Isadora's age, could, with the weight of his three-quarter whiteness, his land, lineage and power, demand and take what he liked from a district indebted to him for the homes and part acres they rented from the family.

She was the hawk who guarded Isadora. They may be struggling home from ground together, her and Isadora, loads on their heads, or catching water from the standpipe, when father and son would stroll by, surveying the District they owned, Mr Cleary Senior, Sir, and Mr Cleary Junior, Sir, she would have had to say. Vie would watch the younger one, casting lustful eyes over her child. She would catch the eye of the father, the white of hers turning red and she would hope that he could read: warn your son or gallows for me and you know what that would mean for the two of you. Even when the son, John Cleary Junior, married and his wife had a son, Jacob, Vie did not let down her guard. Being married had never stopped his father seeking out country women.

Vie was glad that Isadora was reticent and proud and understood without much telling. Yet only when Leopold came along, one of their own kind not half or even quarter, not the proud progeny of slave-owners with only a hint of denied blackness – a poor country man with nothing much to use as bribery or to make grand promises with – and at nights no untoward vision disturbed Vie's sleep, did she relax a little and let her daughter find herself with him. The bonus for Vie was that

44

the marriage came albeit very late, Isadora was thirty, without any sign of a belly, but that was just the start of another anxiety for Vie, too many men hauled and pulled women around as soon as the wedding ring was in place. Vie took another vow, that would only happen to her one daughter over her dead body. But three children later, ranging in years from six to two, no gallows in sight, Isadora and Leopold, moved away to England leaving the three children with her. Separated by so many miles there was nothing Vie could do about anything where they were concerned, only take seriously the responsibility for the children that they had charged her with.

It only then dawned on Aunt Vie, pain now rocking her body that she was at last, with Babydear gone, sorry though she was, free of responsibility. Free to die in peace. To let down her guard. To rest. The District, although they held her as the centre of their lives, their counsellor, advisor, mediator, would on her demise find another to lean on, to succour them.

But there was Littleman sleeping in what was the children's old room. It had been empty since Wilbert left, Babydear having refused to sleep by herself, only going in there to play with her dollies when it rained heavily and made the verandah uninhabitable or when she was sent for something.

Vie allowed herself a certain satisfaction in what she had done. Her conscience had been bothering her since Nana had died and he had been turned out by the Cleary Junior, made to scratch and scrape and overwork to stay alive. But Littleman was a big man, didn't need looking after like a woman. She had done something by giving him a roof over his head, one that she would be paying for anyway, until anything happened to her. And hopefully before it did, she sighed heavily, she hoped she would have the time to arrange it so he could farm her acre in Eggsbury and help himself, putting a little aside to pay the government taxes. Isadora wouldn't be coming home for years, if ever, to claim her little inheritance. Vie was sure that even if she did, she wouldn't come back to the country and wouldn't mind leasing the land properly to Littleman then. She would see to that today, get Deacon also the JP to arrange everything. She would also speak to Ezekiel about allowing Littleman to keep at least one of the rooms if anything happened to her. There was also the little ground behind the house . . . if he's prepared to work hard . . . He could even build a little house at Eggsbury if Ezekiel wasn't willing. She could leave him all her furnishing. The poor thing had to sell Nana's old things to survive. And her donkey. Greystripe, he is strong and can work, Littleman could have that too. Vie's mind was a buzz with all the plans, her pain temporarily forgotten . . . She would get Littleman to write a letter to Isadora as soon as she got up . . . was her final thought before she dozed off.

Later in the morning a light knock on her door awoke her. She knew his knock and called out to Littleman to enter but couldn't fix her face in time before he came in and realised that she was unwell. 'Aunt Vie. Why you never call me? You sick!'

'Littleman, calm yourself. I'm all right . . . ,' but before she could finish he was at the side of the bed rubbing her arm and enquiring what he should do.

'Me going to call the Doctor Azora,' he said as he lifted Aunt Vie bodily and straightened her on the bed. Her whole body was numb now. Before she could protest, he had straightened the covers and was out of the door. She heard him running on the path behind the house, unable to stop him she thought that perhaps it didn't matter that Azora might be seen in her yard for the first time. She wouldn't be alive to hear the talk about it.

The Doctor arrived on her mule not long after, Littleman close behind. Littleman's rambled concerns and his hurry to get her to Aunt Vie's yard left Azora little time to confirm and reconfirm whether Littleman was sure that Aunt Vie really wanted her in her yard.

Azora had been in the District over thirty years and Vie's was the only household that had never consulted her on any matter. Yet Vie's presence over those years was all pervasive in Azora's yard as it was around the District. Each person who came seemed to bring her along; quoting sayings that Azora learnt to recognise as hers, the conventional among them expressing concern about rumours they had heard of her supposed other activities, even as they expected her to work miracles for them. Those who wanted deeper and greater things from her, wanted her to call on powers, and beings that were neither God or Satan, whispered concern about the possibility of Vie finding out.

At first Azora simply wondered at the power of a woman who wielded such influence, then she was irritated, then angry, and finally intrigued. But there was little opportunity to get to know Vie, just the brief greetings and stilted conversations as they crossed paths in the District and the row two years ago. Even then at the outset, Vie had seemed deceptively innocuous.

Azora dismounted with a tinge of triumph at Vie's imminent humbling but as she mounted the verandah trepidation took over and, recognising this, she was disappointed with herself.

Littleman left them alone to go to field in Eggsbury. Aunt Vie had only managed a smile of gratitude, too preoccupied with her pain and the figure hovering at the door, to say more.

Azora entered the room briskly, opened her mouth to greet Vie but Vie spoke first. 'Before you start anything I'm reminding you that I don't want you to bring any of your daft deeds into my house.'

'You know I wouldn't dream of coming in your house with anything like that,' Azora retorted, making light of Vie's serious words. Without ado and smiling she bent and took Vie's pulse, ran her hand over her arms, squeezing her joints, released and proceeded to rummage through her bag until she came out with various items: two small bottles of oil, one green, one pale

47

yellow and a neatly tied bundle of herbs. 'I think you just have cold in your joints.' It was on the tip of Vie's tongue to challenge her, to say she couldn't possibly know what she was talking about and shouldn't feign knowledge but the pains were so severe she would have taken anything for ease. 'I'll burn this.' She held up the green bottle. 'It will relax you. You see you drawing you body up and it making you condition worse . . . I'll boil these herbs up for you to drink and then . . . ,' she held the bottle with the pale green oil, '. . . when you finish it, I'll give you a herb bath and in no time you'll be yourself again.'

'You are going to do nothing of the kind,' Vie said getting up too quickly and feeling a stab of pain in her side reminding her of her condition. 'Jane is coming over later, so you can just burn the oil if you have to, take you pay, leave the rest and go about your business.' Vie caught a look in Azora's eyes she did not understand but it was gone before she could work it out.

'As you like.'

Azora's failure to persuade her incensed Vie. If Azora noticed this she showed no sign, she set about pouring the oil in the top of an earthenware contraption she pulled from her bag and setting light to a small wick underneath. Setting it on a table on the other side of the room she disappeared out of the room. Vie heard her rummaging in her kitchen, returning later with a mug of deep green piping hot tea. She set it down on the bedside table to cool and pulled up a chair and lowered her towering frame. 'I have always suspected that you are an odd woman.' Vie gazed at her, half-amused now at the unlikeness of the situation.

Azora laughed, 'A case of pot calling kettle . . . eh? Which one of the two of us you think more abnormal?' She laughed out loud again and then said in a voice more serious than her eyes, 'In case you are wondering, because you so suspicious of me, this drink is just a mixture of ginger, nettle, sage and peppermint.'

Vie grunted, 'Is just because I can't do any better this morning. Because Littleman left me no choice.'

Vie allowed Azora to help her up and took the tea she offered, its sharp sweet taste immediately warmed and comforted her whole body. Azora sat watching Vie as she drank as if there were years of familiarity between them. She waited until Vie had finished before collecting her belongings, 'I've left some more of the tea in the kitchen, you can get somebody to warm it for you until it finish and since you don't want me to bathe you, you can ask Jane or somebody to do that too. I've left the barks and bushes. It will help you . . .'

Vie indicated where her money was kept. Azora shook her head. 'This is a favour, after thirty years I can afford to give the formidable mother of the District something . . .'

Vie ignored the attempt at reprimand. 'I don't want to be indebted to you Azora, for you to have it to tell the whole District . . .'

Azora didn't let her finish. 'It's clear you don't know me. Besides, what is ever a secret in this District?' She picked up her bag. 'Goodmorning Vie . . . You can always send for me if you need anything else . . . Women should not be at war, especially women like you and me.' Vie frowned at the effrontery. 'Don't dare link us, we have nothing in common . . .' But Azora was gone. Vie listened to the sound of the mule's hooves as they receeded along the back lane, turned left onto the stone road and cantered away. She sighed, feeling guilty and ungrateful, she hadn't even thanked her, offered to send back her earthenware oil burner or pretended she was feeling a little better.

Vie has never made any secret of her disdain for what she always referred to as Azora's dark deeds. Like her hate for what the Cleary family stood for, and how with the help of the church they controlled the minds, pockets and bodies of the District, Vie despised what Azora was. Despite what the District said to the contrary, Azora, she believed was a common obeahwoman, no different from the chicken-slaughtering, gibberish-chanting varieties around the Island. The only difference between Azora and the church was that *she* disregarded God, tampered with the devil and the dead, claiming she could raise the latter and have them obey her command, binding those in the districts with warped hopes, fears, grudges and dreams, to her. To Vie they were all despicable, untruthful, sinister, working on the fear and superstitions of vulnerable minds, used over the years to being fooled and manipulated. If as she said, she was only a herbalist, she would have no quarrel with her, but she had heard enough whispers over the years not to believe or trust her.

Soon after her stroke when she had been taking a walk with Babydear out on the road, Vie had met Azora and she had suggested giving Vie something to speed her recovery. Vie had rejected her offer, especially so because Azora dared to bring that to her in front of the child. Incensed, Vie had said curtly, fully intending to put her in her place, that she did not deal with obeah, not having planned to use that word but finding it slipping from her lips without her having power to stop it. Azora had clearly been stung and had retorted equally angrily that all she ever used were nature's herbs and plants. 'The rest,' she had said in an even more caustic tone, 'is left to their minds or to their faiths.'

Vie had been adamant, unprepared for Azora to have the last word, 'You know all of them think you are an obeahwoman, dabbling in things best for God or the devil.'

'I challenge you to point out one person who tell you that I deal in any devil work.' She glared at Vie before jabbing her mule into a trot leaving Vie frustrated and angry with herself for having got involved so publicly.

As the morning wore on and the heat intensified, Aunt Vie twisted and turned trying to make herself more comfortable.

She wondered at her folly in not demanding that Littleman get the proper doctor from Kitson Town. It was all right to feel tired and wish for death but discomfort was altogether another matter. Yet surprisingly, towards mid-morning, she began to feel better, comforted that soon Jane would come and make her the cornmeal porridge she now had a desire for, she could then get up and sit on the verandah and talk. Perhaps even seek her opinion yet again on what exactly Azora was about. Littleman would eventually be around later to keep her company when other visitors had come and gone. Warmed by those thoughts she didn't notice when the numbness receded completely.

She got up and dressed, expecting the numbness to come back as she moved around but it didn't, so instead of waiting for Jane as she had planned to, she made herself the porridge, pottered around in her little vegetable garden behind her house, stopping to have sugar 'n water with Ruthlyn and later Sister Netta who read from the scriptures and prayed for Vie's complete healing of mind and body. Ragu came by after them and they sat on the verandah and talked, Ragu's wit enlivening Vie further before he felt his way back home to continue with his cabinet-making. She could tell they knew Azora had called, amused that none of them, not even Ruthlyn, more than partial to a little gossip and the dissemination of such, did not mention it. For her part Vie decided that her illness must have all been in her mind. Yet despite her scepticism, she could not deny even to herself that Azora puzzled her. Azora was certainly not unusual in the District in knowing the power of the multiplicity of herbs and barks that they grew or that sprung up despite them, but where she differed from the rest of them, it was asserted by everyone, was that it was never with her a case of hit and miss. From what Vie had heard, Azora was always precise, certain, correct. Vie grunted. That's why I know, she is more than she pretends to be.

In the thirty years that she had been in the District, Azora had

51

generally kept herself to herself. She went to nobody. They all went to her. Aunt Vie often heard them, sometimes at the dead of night, sometimes at the crack of dawn, creeping behind the lane to consult her just as the stray concubines of the Clearys did, though under different pretexts. It infuriated Vie. To see the District throwing away good money in payment for what they could get for free from any old man or woman next door to them. Herbs! They could pick and boil those themselves.

She had heard that Azora was learned. That she had stocks of books, that she was a thinker. Vie knew for a fact that she was totally self-sufficient. She kept a range of animals and lived totally from the land from cultivating what she ate, to making her own soap for bathing down to that for washing clothes.

Jane finally appeared in the afternoon. Despite feeling better, Vie took no chances, she asked Jane to rub her down with her own mixture of bayrum with pimento seeds, myrrh and various barks. She had carefully hidden Azora's oil burner and the other bottle she had left. Jane, though characteristically prickly, swept the house and yard, washed and cooked beef soup for their lunch, sat and chatted.

Towards evening just before Littleman was due back Vie told her that Littleman was now living at the house. 'He need a home,' she concluded, predicting Jane's response.

'I really think you take leave of you mind.'

'I don't see why. Nothing is wrong with him.'

'No? You must be the only one who blind in this whole District. Littleman is a worthless good-for-nothing.'

'You know something? This District is packed with hypocrites. The whole lot of them fill up the church on Sundays and afterwards close their eyes to the needs around you.'

'I don't claim to be no Christian.'

'Who said anything about Christian! Most Sunday everyone dress up and go to Church. Is not the same thing?'

Jane wasn't to be mollified. 'Littleman has been offered help but preferred to wander the District like a vagrant.'

'He was confused and in shock for a little period . . .'

'He saw you coming. The boy should make way by himself. I did. I had to . . . You mark my words, that hard back man going to wring you dry at a time when you should be taking time in your last few days . . .'

'Who tell you these are my last few days?' Vie said angrily. 'I have plenty days left. Plenty sixty-eight years old people living when some fifty-three-year-olds like yourself dropping dead,' she concluded pointedly, regretting it immediately knowing how superstitious Jane was.

Chapter 7

Mr Cleary Junior came to his big house on the hill with his food truck. As usual nobody had known beforehand that he would be coming. But helped by criers riding the back of the trucks, the news got around the District and by the time the free groceries were being divided up and shared out, it appeared that the District had been waiting all night for him.

Littleman was there too, with his calico bag, in the line that stretched from the annexe, all the way down the asphalt drive to the standpipe near the church, collecting, not for Vie, but for the lone old people who could not be there themselves ensuring, as at other times, that every household, apart from Jane's, Vie's, Azora's and the Samuel's, was represented, sometimes two or three in different parts of the queue waiting patiently despite the midday sun and the leisurely pace of the servers. They had learnt over the years that if there was any sign of disorder, the command was given to halt the distribution, pull in the back of the truck and wait, or even worse, return everything to Town.

Mr Cleary Junior and his only son Jacob were somewhere in the big house, asphalt running one hundred yards on either side of its large white iron gates. Checking, everyone supposed with silent grudge, that all their possessions, left locked up and unused in the house for months on end (except for the supposedly clandestine liaisons with one or other of the now two active men of the family and their country women), were intact and untouched. People in the queue were silently puffed up about that too, but were not in a position like Vie and the few others to boycott his charity. The present family like their Scottish forebears before them, who had along the way only slightly tainted their colour with choice slave women, the main testimony to that now being in the stubborn texture of their hair, owned most of the land in Top Mountain and Eggsbury, most of it left to waste, uncultivated. Only oblivious fruit trees, true to their nature, resting and bearing . . . unburdened only by daring children and hungry adults who ignored the signs threatening prosecution for trespassers.

The gadgets that were said to rest behind the closely barred doors, fired the dullest imagination; generator powered fridges, lights, washing machine, and other such unbelievable contraptions. And that was just the beginning, the District was fully aware of the family's position in Town, houses rented all over Spanish Town, large supermarkets here and there and their big house on one of the hills of Kingston and St Andrew. When members of the family travelled to America, it wasn't to do backbreaking seasonal farm work like their men had to, it was to shop, to holiday. They wondered how the Senior's wife could have allowed herself to die, eighty years old or not, and left it all. Heaven in the skies couldn't be sweeter than they imagined her life must have been. Despite how often Deacon and Sister preached and exhorted them against covetousness, the District could not help itself.

But despite the depths of their envy they were overcome with gratitude to Mr Cleary Junior for their share of weevil-ridden flour and corn meal, rice, milk powder, oil and, if they were lucky, a few ounces of salt fish. They were lucky, because as well as all that, there were tins of sardines for the taking too this time. But as they received it, their gratitude made them ashamed and confused and worse because nobody in the District knew or asked where Mr Cleary got the stock that he showered on the District from time to time.

The Samuels and now Miss Dee and Jane, were sure that Cleary came bearing gifts, out of malice, to wreck their own businesses, and to keep the District under control by keeping them grateful. 'Him not a fool, you all really think the food free that him giving up. You must be joking! Him put the cost of every single penny of it on you rents and leases. I would bet me life on it.' Ezekiel Samuel bewailed and once or twice when he used to be saved and a member of the church, he had used that as a topic for his exhortations. But in the church, built on Cleary family land, a situation uncertain from one year to the next, members only nodded tacit agreement, asking themselves: what can we do? each absolved and secretly warmed by the Holy Scriptures that assured them how hard it was for a rich man to get into heaven, forgetting even this unspoken solidarity the next time the truck rolled up.

Vie watched it all silently, no one understanding even when she had fallen upon hard times in the past, why she had never joined the queue. Why even when the Cleary Senior had been the beneficiary he had never seen her bow and scrap in his presence as was customary. Why she had never rented land or house from him? Why her attitude to their landed master had been so totally uncompromising over the years. Why she said, when asked about her stubborn overt hatred for the family, that even mangy dogs had their day.

When Ezekiel Samuel had bought his thirty acres from the Clearys on which he later built his shops and plots that now housed Aunt Vie and the Maxtons and later when Azora had come to the District and had amazingly been sold two hundred and fifty acres and even later Jane her ten, many old enough to see the change had been encouraged and had felt that was what Vie had meant, that it was after all possible to get the Clearys to sell. Many whose families had for generations leased land and rented houses from the family, had started to save. But after that the Clearys had pulled in their reins, had only grudgingly sold off single acres in Top Mountain, Eggsbury and in other districts they owned, much keener to lease or rent the houses on land they still firmly controlled. No one rivalled them, not even Deacon whose family lands though not as vast, were like theirs, scattered over the District and passed down to scions fallow and intact.

Miss Dee shut up shop furious but not without a tinge of excitement. If she was lucky she'd catch a glimpse of Jacob Cleary on her way home. The last time they had come with the truck, four months before, around Christmas, she had sent Babydear; unbeknown to her grandmother, to join the queue, for the sick and shut-in, Babydear nervously answered the questioning looks around her, glancing periodically at her grandmother's small figure tottering around in her yard in the distance below. Babydear's task had been to describe to Miss Dee everything about Jacob, what he wore, every single expression he sported, how he moved, what if anything he said. On her return with scathing criticisms of him and his high and mighty attitude, Miss Dee had shrugged. Nothing Babydear could tell her would alter her conviction that he was the most perfect person there was.

Miss Dee was certain now that being the Easter break he would be home from university, sitting on the side of the verandah, away from the throng, chewing on a bit of grass, his head thrown back, his face trying to look more than his twenty-one years. What must it be like, she mused jealously, to be rich, to have a father who can just throw food to the poor and destitute? To have more land than he knew what to do with? To have everyone respect you, so much so that they daren't look in your eyes when they spoke to you but said sir to you after nearly every word? What would it be like to be whisked away from her monotonous life, from her common country life to a big house in town, with servants and money to answer all her needs?

As she made her way down the road from her shop now, she tried to dismiss all the contradictory thoughts that flooded her head, whispered conversations that she had overheard since she was a child, about generations of Clearys especially Jacob's own father, John Cleary Junior, and grandfather, John Cleary Senior before him, taking country women against their wishes or with unfulfillable promises which basically came to the same thing, only to forget them when the speckled children arrived or even before, when signs of those stolen moments were evident. It was even said that when they could get away with it the Clearys made obeahmen expel newly formed foetuses. Those women are fools, Miss Dee thought, dismissing them, remembering instead how Babydear had described Jacob, exercising his dogs on the parched lawn newly cut by their gardener from town, and later standing, his legs wide apart, eyeing the crowd, '. . . his skin pale like a ghost . . . ,' she had said making Miss Dee laugh.

'I think he should sit out in the sun more,' Babydear had rambled.

Half way down the road Miss Dee was stricken with nerves and decided to turn back. Jacob would not be milling around with the throng and there was no way she could be like Baby-dear pretending to beg for the old and shut-ins. She would bide her time, take the opportunity to go for a quiet walk behind her shop. There would be no one around to see her so she changed back into her work slacks and flat shoes. She felt free and relaxed, no critical eyes, imaginary or real to watch her. Past the yard behind the shop, she followed the lane leading to where all the fruit trees were; mangoes, sweet and sour sop, naseberry and countless coconut and breadfruit trees. The leaves, in their differing shapes and contrasting hues, encouraged her to toss off her shoes and wander among them picking some up with her toes, caressing others in her palms.

Perhaps, she thought, lowering herself on the ground, I should get someone to introduce us properly, that's what he's used to. But who? She laughed out loud at the thought of someone in the District attempting to do it. Preoccupied in her dreams, she didn't see Leroy as he came up behind her. He coughed after watching her for a while. She jumped to her feet.

'You shouldn't do that you know.' She fumbled for her shoes.

'I must be the only man in this District who see the lovely Miss Dee without her high heel shoes,' he ventured looking down appreciatively at her feet. She cut her eyes at him, 'I should know that a woman can't have any peace in this District. Even if she finds a hole to bury herself in.'

'I hope you won't do that Miss Dee, you will leave a lot of us man frustrated,' he said laughing.

She started walking off not seeing or sharing his joke. Despite not having any time for the men around her age in the District, Leroy was the only one who unnerved her.

'Where you going man, stay and talk with me awhile no. Me notice you close up shop so there's nothing to go back to so fast.' He stepped in front of her.

'Listen, just get out of my way if you know what's good for you.' She looked him up and down threateningly, feeling anything but that under the circumstances, she side-stepped him and walked off with confident strides.

'You one lady who full of fart,' he shouted after her. 'Somebody going to pull that high and mighty throne from under you one of this day.'

She was fuming. How dare he approach her? talk to her like that. Hadn't he still got the message? She had perfected the insults she threw at him almost daily over the years. 'Just go and wash yourself,' she said without turning.

'One day when you dry up like you aunt you are going to be begging me for a piece of loving, dying for it. Wait and see. You going to regret that you think yourself so good. When you

59

dying for it there will be nobody to give it to you.' He screamed after her, his raucous laughter following her back to the shop.

Miss Dee didn't know if she was more furious or depressed as she eventually walked down the hill home. She felt the need to see Aunt Vie before going home but she was embarrassed. Babydear had been gone two months and she had not kept her promise to stay at least some nights with her. But how could she with Littleman there?

She had done as much as she could, gone there on one or two Saturdays, when she knew Littleman had gone to see Ragu to learn the cabinet-making she was told he had now set his mind on. That would be a joke, Miss Dee mused, the actual blind leading the mentally blind. Aunt Vie as usual had been understanding, accepting the excuses she gave, saying that since Littleman was staying with her there was no need for Miss Dee to put herself out. But those words Miss Dee felt held covert criticism of herself, perhaps a hint of mistrust, or was this her own conscience plaguing her. Whatever, it increased Miss Dee's guilt. She wanted Aunt Vie's regard above any other. Aunt Vie had always been good to her; made time for her even when she had her own grandchildren to look after, listened to her, advised her, helped her to make sense of the confusion that had sometimes over the years characterised her existence with Aunt Jane, been the grandmother that she had never had. Now when Aunt Vie needed her help, she had disappeared out of her life, leaving her to the caprices of Littleman who she felt must be a poor substitute.

Chapter 8

Miss Dee decided to go to Spanish Town to have her hair done leaving her aunt to run the shop for the day. It was Saturday so the truck came twice to Top Mountain to take the market sellers to Town, once very early in the morning, well before she was up and another later on, but Miss Dee categorically refused to go on the truck. Only cattle travelled like that, she said to herself as she walked instead to the asphalted road of Kitson Town to pick up a taxi, cursing the bad stone road of Top Mountain for the reluctance of the taxis to venture beyond Kitson unless on some especially lucrative errand, like an airport trip or the ambition of a taxi driver to get some other reward for taking a female passenger back. That was why Miss Dee usually had no problems getting a taxi back to the lane that led to her house and despite the abrupt end to her sweet inviting manner as soon as she neared the lane, they never learnt and continued to live in hope.

First, Miss Dee decided that she would go to the wholesalers and place her order and have it delivered to the shop in the week. Then she would go to the material shop to get fabrics for Aunt Jane who was sewing for an out-of-District wedding in a few months time. The rest of the day would be hers. Most of it would be spent in the beauty salon, having her hair pressed and styled, her nails painted and her eyebrows shaped. Who else apart from herself was there to show the other women in the District how a woman should look after herself? After the salon, she would spend the evening in Kitson Town, with Rose-marie. Miss Dee would not have to worry about her aunt spending the evening alone, she would be spending her evening with Aunt Vie. As Aunt Vie was unwell she would not be called away to pacify some angry wife or hysterical husband, reason with an errant child, embalm a recent dead or bring a new life to the District.

Miss Dee entertained a self-satisfied smile as she made her way. She enjoyed going to town. She could be dressed and not feel out of place, wear her high heels shoes without people laughing behind her back, as she knew they did in the District. But best of all was the anonymity. She inhaled deeply at the impending luxury as she walked through Old Road ignoring pointedly the unwelcome attention of the occasional man who hollered her name in moanful tones as she passed.

She arrived in Town frazzled and bad tempered after the cramped taxi ride, vowing that her next project would be to learn to drive and get a car, an Austin Morris or even a Morris Oxford. The thought of being the first and only woman in the District with her own car bolstered her spirit, she regained her composure, her slow purposeful stride, her swinging hips, just enough to make it seem natural, the straight back and the mouth showing only slight disdain for the world.

Miss Dee had just about exorcised Top Mountain from her mind when she thought she saw some way ahead of her, Little-man turn into a pharmacist, one she knew was owned by the Clearys. He's everywhere, she thought angrily.

Moments later, she saw a man leave the shop in a hurry, handing over, in a movement almost too quick for one to be sure, a brown paper bag to another waiting at the door. Yet the speed of their synchronised actions and the look of urgency on their faces held her attention. Each scuttled in different directions. She dismissed them without further thought but as she came level with the shop door, she almost collided with Littleman who was charging from the same shop, panic written over his sweat drenched face. Miss Dee stumbled out of the way but before she had time to wonder what was happening or to connect the scene she had just witnessed with the two men, she saw another group rushing from the shop screaming, 'Thief, thief . . . , one gone but catch that one . . .' Among those giving chase, Miss Dee caught sight of a furious Jacob Cleary. They were chasing Littleman. Miss Dee looked confusedly from that group to the faltering Littleman who was getting hopelessly caught up in pockets of bemused Saturday shoppers, her mouth opening and shutting, her right hand wavering between her shoulder and her mouth.

Experience, if not fitness and agility, was on the side of an oversized security-man-with-dog. The dog got to Littleman first sinking teeth in his ankle, the security man grabbing him around the neck and wrestling him to the ground, throwing blows and kicks for good measure. Saturday shoppers and sellers ran towards the foray echoing expectantly the cries of '. . . thief, the brute. This one not getting away. Them catch this one . . .' anxious to get a look at the accused, even, Miss Dee knew, ready to throw blows before the police came.

Miss Dee's eyes widened as eventually Littleman was wrenched from the crowd and frogmarched back towards the shop. Somehow he saw Miss Dee and for a moment their eyes held. She dropped her head and backed into the crowd away from his pleading bloodshot gaze.

In less than no time police cars with their armed protagonists were on the scene. Miss Dee hesitated for a moment longer, long enough for it to sink in that Littleman was being arrested for something he had nothing to do with, the real culprits having long disappeared. Littleman was a lot of things but not a criminal. Of any sort. But why was he running? The fool, she thought angrily. The fool, she repeated in her mind. The idiot, the idiot, she heard herself say aloud. She spun round and retraced her steps. Away from the frenzy, Miss Dee tried to compose herself but could not, her mind was a confusion of thoughts, doubts and fear for Littleman. She should go back and help him. But what could she do? Perhaps she should tell the police what she saw. But Jacob was there. How could she let him see her defending the simpleton Littleman? He would forever link her with him. And what if they did not believe her? Or think that she had been acting with him as they were from the same District? The mere thought was unbearable. She continued on her way hurriedly, taking the long way round to the salon, finally managing to compose herself, allowing herself once there to be pampered from head to toe, hoping that the police had realised that Littleman was not a thief. Hoping that even though he was such a fool, Littleman had managed to convince them.

On the way to Kitson Town, sitting wedged in the front seat between the taxi driver and a market woman, Miss Dee listened silently to the conflicting hearsay versions of the country boy who had with another collaborator robbed one of the Clearys' tills in broad daylight. He was, it was mainly asserted, a regular thief around town. Even been in and out of jail. This time, they said, he had gone into the pharmacist, dug his hand into the till, stuffed paper money into a bag and handed some to his friend who had hurried away. Miss Dee covered her mouth and bit her lips, hard. Poor Littleman, she thought.

When she got to Kitson Town, her mood plummeted further when she found that Rose-marie wasn't home, apparently she too was in Town and rightly not expecting Miss Dee until much later.

Miss Dee, not able to wait, left a message that she would see her the following weekend. She decided she had to go back to the District and see Aunt Vie, praying that by the time she got there Littleman would be safely home, his innocence established.

'I don't know what would be happening to me if Littleman

wasn't around,' Aunt Vie was saying as she tidied around her room, Miss Dee helping her by changing her sheets. 'The stick he made for me is really like a leg and him go to Eggsbury regularly and sorting things out round there for me. Somebody tell me that in the short time, him billing out space to cultivate more things . . . When we finish here we can go behind the house and you can see the yams, beans and other things him helping me to add to what me had there already. The little ground behind there is a lot better than when I was pottering about in it by myself . . . I can tell you that boy is really a God-send . . .'

Everything crowded Miss Dee's mind at once and she could hardly think.

'Eh Miss Dee . . . Miss Dee you all right?' Aunt Vie was saying.

'Sorry Aunt Vie I was just . . . My mind was . . . What did you say?'

'I said did you see Littleman in Town? I'm surprised he's not back yet. He only went to pick up some medicine from the pharmacist for me.' Miss Dee's heart stopped. 'Are you ill Aunt Vie?'

'No. Not specially. It's just me blood pressure tablet. I have the last few in the bottle. He been telling me to let him get them for the last few days but I didn't want him to tired out himself anymore so I did tell him to wait until today. But him should come back by now. So you didn't see him?'

Miss Dee looked over Aunt Vie's head. Her heart had not settled, 'No,' she said, her breathing getting shorter and heavier.

'You tired Miss Dee?' Aunt Vie asked, looking at her with concern.

'No,' she mumbled standing up. 'I'm sure he'll be back soon. Aunt Vie, I'm not going to stop long. I have to pop up to the shop to see if Aunt Jane wants me to do anything.' She lied without thinking, finished what she was doing, collected her bag and started for the path but stopped short.

'Aunt Vie do you want me to get you something before I go?'

Aunt Vie got her stick and walked down the side lane with her. 'I'm all right you know. Everyone keep treating me like an egg. But I can manage. This stick Littleman made me is even stronger than Babydear's little arms.' She smiled. 'I miss her so 'till,' she said almost to herself. 'I tell you that I getting letter from her every two weeks.' She sighed heavily. 'The last letter I get, she tell me she cry every day. That she start school now and that she hate it and everything else. You remember how she was bright and used to love school.'

Miss Dee nodded, tears welling up in her eyes. She turned so that Aunt Vie would not notice.

'I hope they send her back before she take ill over there. Her heart so young, she can die of unhappiness.'

Miss Dee turned suddenly and hugged Aunt Vie. When she pulled away, Vie noticed her tears. 'I know you miss her too. You and her was like sisters.' Vie shook her head. 'But what to do?'

Miss Dee needed to go, what with the weight of uncertainty about what was happening to Littleman, a rising guilt and now this. If anything happened to Littleman Aunt Vie would never forgive her, especially since she had never hidden her anger about the way she treated Littleman, her scorning him, was the way Aunt Vie put it . . . *in the same way the wretched Clearys treat the District. The way none of us in the District should ever treat each other.* 'So you don't need anything Aunt Vie?' Miss Dee asked, squashing her thoughts.

'No me dear, Littleman even cooked this morning before he left . . . run down he made . . . I'll stretch my legs over to Ragu, see if Littleman did mention that he had anything else in town . . . Him hardly go to town, perhaps him got lost or one of the half-dead bus might even break down with him.'

When they got to Ragu's, Miss Dee found a shaky smile for Aunt Vie, 'All right then. I hope Little . . . he comes back soon.'

'Later, Miss Dee,' Aunt Vie said after her.

'Yes Aunt Vie,' she said not able to look back, returning Ragu's shouted greeting as she walked away. She heard Aunt Vie's faltering step, Ragu's dogs leaping around her feet, she hurried on, her high heel shoes clashing with the stones on the road, glad for the hundred yards of asphalted respite either side of the Clearys' gates.

Chapter 9

Littleman ached all over. He couldn't speak because he couldn't trust himself to do so without crying. Perhaps he was born under the wrong star or somebody had worked obeah on him. What else could cause this succession of misfortunes? Despite his fatalism, he tried nevertheless to imagine what mistake he could have made with Miss Dee since his grandmother, Nana, died. Why had she not helped him when he had suddenly been pointed out in the shop, accused of being a thief and set upon for stealing what he did not know.

Handcuffed in the police van, unconcerned about his bruises, he was a jumble of confusion. He wondered whether before he was jailed he would be given the chance to apologise for whatever it was he had done to her, make things right so that when he was released they could be as they were when they were children. She had to know that he would sooner be lashed with the cat-o'-nine-tails than offend her.

At the police station, he was searched, his personal belongings confiscated before he was put in a cell where he sat on the sole piece of furniture in the room, a long wooden bench. Left alone for hours to wonder when his interrogation would come, he felt detached and amazingly calm, undisturbed by the commotion in the station; suspects being brought in and out of cells, sometimes violent, belligerent protests of innocence, sometimes resigned contrite pleas. But somehow the lull that came periodically when he heard the incongruous joking and laughing of the police officers, began to produce more dread than the voices of the supposed hardened criminals, and gradually his numbness went and he started to be afraid. He recalled the many stories he had heard of the police treatment of thieves and robbers, his fear becoming so intense that he lost control of his legs first and then his bladder.

When at last an officer came, notes in hand, Littleman's clothes had absorbed the urine, and the fierce heat had intensified the odour mingling it with that of the others who had languished before him in the cell. The policeman did not seem unduly surprised or offended by the rankness, seeming to speak with his mind on other things. So detached and disinterested was his manner, calm and even his voice, that he could be mistaken for a bank clerk dispensing cash. 'So you are a thief?' Not put as a question but as a statement of fact.

Littleman opened his mouth to speak but the words lodged in his throat. The policeman waited, looking directly at him. Littleman lowered his eyes, connecting with the pistol hanging casually in a holster by the policeman's side. Littleman shook visibly then.

The officer watched him for a moment, a faint smile on his face. 'You not from Spanish Town?' Having clearly not read the details Littleman had given to the officer on the other shift, 'I don't know you.'

'No,' Littleman managed to find.

The policeman nodded slowly. 'So what you do with the money you take out of the till? Why you do it in broad daylight? You fool?' Littleman shook his head.

'So who forced you hand?' The policeman observed him, 'So you come to town often to steal?'

Littleman shook his head violently, 'I hardly come to town and I've never stolen anything in my life . . . Ask anybody in Top Mountain.'

'You come from Top Mountain? One of the Clearys' District and you tried to rob them shop, knowing that one of them could be in the shop and recognise you? You more than a fool.'

'I didn't steal anything. All I know was that one minute I was going to pay for Aunt Vie's medicine, the next minute a man pushed past me and ran out of the shop. Somebody shouted thief and pointed at me . . .'

'So why you run?'

'I don't know.'

The policeman frowned. His patience seemingly wearied by Littleman. 'Ummm. Start from the beginning again for me . . . ,' he requested casually.

Littleman hesitated for a moment but, seeing impatience in the officer's eyes, proceeded abruptly. The policeman listened without speaking, only looking up now and again from the note pad he scribbled on, to observe Littleman's face. When Littleman had finished, he grunted, 'So you are the Top Mountain thief then?' Littleman shook his head violently, he had just about convinced himself that the officer was believing him. 'No sir, it wasn't me. They made a mistake. I would never steal from anybody.'

The officer looked expressionless at him for a considerable time before walking slowly out of the room.

Littleman was awash with perspiration, his face and body throbbed with the combination of the blows he had received and the fearful tension of his plight. His bladder was again full to bursting, and he began now to worry about Aunt Vie. Unable to hold his bladder anymore, he was on the verge of screaming out when another officer unlocked the cell and came in. Littleman plucked up the courage, 'I need to use the bathroom, sir.'

'Wait!' The new officer ordered impatiently, his voice sharper and more abrasive than the previous one. Littleman sank back on his bench, pressing his thighs together.

This time he had to give a description of the man he claimed pushed past him in the pharmacist's and reiterate his full story.

Eventually he was allowed to go to the toilet. When he had finished, he was escorted to a new cell. This time with another prisoner and a bed. Littleman had not thought beyond what was happening to him at the time and had not visualised that he would be spending the night locked away with criminals: the mere thought of the word filled him with a self-reproach he had never dreamt possible, not even on those nights when he had slept on his grandmother's tombs behind Deacon's yard hoping that she would understand and forgive him for letting her down. Never in his worse dreams had he ever imagined, when he had heard the word *criminal* spat out with venom, when known prisoners were caught hiding in one of the numerous hills around Top Mountain and were driven handcuffed through the District, or when he had read something in the paper about some heinous crime that had been committed in Town, that one day he would be a criminal too.

No convict lived in Top Mountain, the District having always prided itself in having upright and hardworking people, so his life there would have to end too with all the opportunities that living with Aunt Vie promised.

As he manoeuvered his body carefully onto the bed, blotting the taunts of his cellmate, 'crybaby battyman,' he allowed himself to cry. Yet the more he cried the more pictures of the new life that he had today succeeded in ruining flashed in front of him. There was the shame he would bring Aunt Vie, they would say I told you so, that he had bitten the hands that had so unselfishly fed him, as they had thought he would.

71

Chapter 10

When Littleman had not returned by dusk, Aunt Vie became increasingly restless. Jane couldn't understand what all the fuss was about. 'He's a big man, Vie. It seems to me you got rid of one child and take on a baby,' she said, glad of the opportunity to criticise Vie again for letting Littleman stay with her. Vie chose to ignore the dig, felt for her stick under the bench and raised herself. 'Where you think you going?' Jane said.

'I'm walking over to Mr Maxton to ask him to take a walk with a few of the men at least down to Kitson Town to see if they hear anything. It's truly not like Littleman.'

Jane sighed heavily. 'This is madness, the boy is a big man.' Aunt Vie laughed at her. 'You don't even know what you saying.' But inside she wondered whether she was indeed being foolish. But she said, 'I'm going to follow my mind. Something wrong with him. He wouldn't just stay out without saying especially since him have me pills . . . ,' she said, more to reassure herself than to convince Jane. Jane got up with her then, 'You never tell me that he went to get you tablets. But you can't do without them?' Jane asked, more worried than was evident in her voice.

Vie hadn't thought of using that before. She wasn't at all desperate for them, she could do without them until the following day.

'I'll go and call Mr Maxton myself,' Jane said, following her off the verandah but stopping after a few steps, 'On second thoughts, you go. I'll go home and tell Miss Dee what's happening, she went to town, she might have seen him.'

'I asked her that already and she hadn't,' Aunt Vie said over her shoulder. 'I'm really worried,' she said to herself as she felt her way in the darkness. She couldn't understand it, Miss Dee hadn't set eyes on him in town all day and neither had anyone else who had gone and come, nobody could tell her anything they had heard or seen from him.

Hours later, the men who had walked through Kitson and half way to St John's Road, returned with no light to shed on the whereabouts of Littleman. True they hadn't wanted to go right into Town, convinced that Littleman had passed safely, in one of the taxis that sped past them as they walked.

Now they were in Aunt Vie's yard, proven wrong, making contradictory plans about what they would do in the morning if he hadn't appeared by the time Jane had returned, which she did not long after they had exhausted all the options. Even in the dim light cast by the oil lamp on the verandah, Aunt Vie saw a look on Jane's face that she was sure meant bad news. After Jane's customary curt greetings to everyone, she motioned to Vie to follow her into the bedroom, where she made Vie sit down. Before Jane started her story, a million tragedies flashed through Vie's mind. But when Jane had related what she had got out of Miss Dee, it seemed in comparison to what she had imagined, a worse reality. 'Miss Dee said she saw what?' Vie shouted, visions of Littleman at the hands of an angry town mob, knowing full well what fate befell even suspected thieves when such mobs got hold of them. She didn't know what was worse – that, or his fate if he survived it and landed in the hands of the police. She scowled, failing to comprehend what had come over Miss Dee, causing her to keep the story to herself throughout this time of questions and worry. 'Why Miss Dee lie to me? she tell me she hadn't seen him? Why she never talk up for him when she see they accusing him wrongly or make sure she follow him to the police station. Or even run find somebody from the District in the market. And when she come back why she hold she tongue about the breed of wickedness. The gal mad or what? She just as bad as the mob.'

Jane wrung her hands, 'I can't tell you Vie. I can't tell you. Calm yourself Vie, you know about your condition . . .'

But Vie could not calm herself. For all she knew Littleman could be dead. 'He could be dead!' she exclaimed, articulating her thoughts '. . . And the child come to my yard bare face and brazen as morning star, with her lying wicked self . . .'

'Aunt Vie what we going to do?' Jane said, more panicked and confused than Vie had ever seen her.

'The gal wicked, the gal wicked, the gal wicked,' Vie moaned at the top of her voice.

'Aunt Vie please,' Jane pleaded with her in an attempt to get her to lower her voice. Vie, like her, registered the hush that had fallen over the verandah. 'She must have had good reason,' Jane defended feebly, visualising the polarisation that would occur in the District: her and Miss Dee on one side, the rest of them on the other. Aunt Vie became suddenly cross at her attempt to defend the indefensible, she raised her voice, 'Don't tell me no nonsense.' Aunt Vie rubbed her hands across her face, twisted and turned, clasping and unclasping her hands. 'I never hear anything like this in my whole life. What a breed of evilness.' She made to get up, Jane restrained her, worried about Vie relating in anger what she had just told her to the eager ears on the verandah. 'Vie, please. Don't make this worse than it is. Dee wasn't the one who accused him, or threw blows at him. Perhaps somebody work obeah on her and make her lose her mind for that moment.'

Aunt Vie jumped up then almost tumbling over. Jane got up to steady her, Vie pushed her hands away, grabbing instead on to one of the iron bed posts. 'Don't come with no foolishness to me Jane. Nothing like that happen. Nothing like that can happen. Don't look for any foolish excuse . . .'

Jane became suddenly belligerent. 'Don't bother to pretend that is Littleman you worried for. Is not Littleman, is yourself. You have nobody left but the one and two of us who take pity on you and giving you charity. Is not my fault any of this happening to you so don't come playing the kind hearted angel with concern about Littleman's wellbeing. You selfish through and through and all this is because you want to use Littleman and work him like you half-dead donkey. The boy lucky if they beat him to death in Town.'

She threw her final words at Vie uncaring now as to whether she had been heard on the verandah. That would give them something concrete to be vexed with her for now as well the other list of gripes they held against her. What did she care? She owed them nothing. They were the ones who had treated her badly in the years she had lived in the District, called her names, denigrated her because of how cruelly nature had dealt with her. So why should she care? If on top of all that they maliced her for their beloved Aunt Vie, the one for who they overlooked everything, the one, unlike her, who could do no wrong, who according to them, was the oracle among them, what would it matter?

She got up to go but was momentarily unnerved by Vie's silence and the hush that rivalled hers, coming from the verandah. She hesitated, allowing Vie time to recover. Vie did. In caustic tone, an ominous pause between each word, she warned Jane, 'If anything happen to that boy, Miss Dee will have more than duppy to fear. People in the District love Littleman.' She studied Jane. 'You know better than me how they feel about you and Miss Dee.'

'But Miss Dee did nothing Vie.'

'Exactly.' With that, Vie turned sharply, flung the door open and disappeared without a backward glance onto the verandah. Jane followed and without a glance at anyone, disappeared down the darkness of the middle lane.

Everybody on the verandah was speaking at once, among the discordant barrage of criticism was the general criticism that they were not surprised about either what Miss Dee had done, how clearly and fully she had finally shown her true colours and how Jane's condoning of her wrongs was a reflection of her own thorough wickedness. 'Jane always think that because the gal had good looks and could sing, she was above us, one of the Clearys. She raise her wrong. You can't have somebody living among ordinary people who don't think she's ordinary. She gal deserve a lashing.' That was Mr Maxton.

'If you ask me, Jane think Miss Dee is herself, young again and with another chance. She has always wanted Miss Dee to be what she wasn't . . .' Ezekiel said quietly, his voice with a hint of reflection.

Vie listened to them. She thought it important for them to speak. But when she asked them to stop, they listened to her. Her anger had subsided and she could isolate facts from emotion. 'Yes Miss Dee was wrong for not running to us with the news, going to the police about what she saw. I can't honestly say otherwise, you hear I just tell Jane that and when I see Miss Dee again I will tell her that in no uncertain terms. But after all is said and done, she's not the one who accused Littleman, threw blows at him or arrest him. We must be careful not to turn on ourselves as we are prone to do, and let the real evil doers go free. Let's leave Miss Dee out now. She done her wrong already and we have no choice but to rectify the wrong ourselves. Tomorrow some of us have to go and get Littleman out. Even if it means she has to go with us to the police and cry blood.' Everyone agreed especially the women who had one by one joined the men in the yard to see what their delay was about. Vie thanked everyone after Ezekiel Samuel had taken the responsibility to ask the Deacon, as their JP, to go with the nominated group to the police station the following day.

Jane mellowed overnight, having spent most of it turning over in her mind the fact that Aunt Vie was the only true friend she had in the District, or anywhere for that matter; the one who over twenty-eight years ago, when she had sought refuge there, had initiated her into their strange ways, stood by her, supported her, borne with her, understood her, defended her idiosyncrasies against the intolerant onslaught that had waded in on her steadily over the years. So she got herself ready early and waited at the end of her lane for the group she understood would be going to Town to bail out Littleman, fully aware that she could not be alone and friendless in the District and there was nowhere else to go from there, not anymore. That was the only reason why she told herself, she swallowed her pride and went with them to Spanish Town. It was certainly not to offer any explanation to Littleman or worse to apologise to the District on Miss Dee's behalf but rather to represent her, talk to the police as her legal guardian, take the letter that Miss Dee had written containing what she had witnessed and offering to testify likewise if and when the need arose.

As it turned out Miss Dee's note and the deputation were superfluous. Littleman's fingerprints had not been found anywhere near the tills and more conclusively, another man had been apprehended with the missing cash and had volunteered all the details about his collaborator's activities to the police. The police would, they said, call on Miss Dee at a later stage if necessary.

Littleman was brought back home, still bruised but more than a little confused. The news of his return sped through the District and as on the day when Babydear had left, Aunt Vie's yard was full to overflowing, some using it as an excuse not to go to church, others coming immediately after, everyone anxious to hear the full story from Littleman's own mouth, oblivious or uncaring of his wish to put it all to the back of his mind since there seemed little prospect of understanding himself how easily he had become so embroiled.

He sat on the verandah, his palms pressed firmly between his thighs, his head down. Silent. Reflective. It was Aunt Vie who related to them what she had managed to get out of him of his side of the story, carefully reiterating his and her plea that Miss Dee be forgiven.

In the days when he had been homeless, he had sometimes tracked her silently. Hiding behind trees along her deserted lane, to see if he could understand why she had so suddenly turned against him, stopped him from creeping behind her house to see if Jane was out and they could sit on the tomb together and talk or walk way behind the house where no houses were. Where they had studied absentmindedly, lizards, birds and wild flowers together, he trying to muster yet again the courage to touch her, ask for a kiss . . . She, he did not know. Now he wondered how she was feeling. He sighed repeatedly, generating renewed gushes of pity from those in the yard and expressions of the certainty of the imminent downfall and tragedy that would befall all those who had hurt Littleman.

He tried to dismiss the curses, wished he could ask them to stop throwing their words so generally about, knowing for certain that bad-mouthing was worse than the evil eye. He was planning already to go to the Doctor Azora to see what she could do to stay their mouths, just in case. More than that he called up a reverie of Miss Dee at that moment, her blanket spread under the Julie mango tree at the back of her house, lying on her stomach reading one book, another by her side, the wireless blaring out, mainly Motown but occasionally a ska tune. Occasionally, she would get up and make herself a drink or go into the house to sit with Aunt Jane for a while and talk with her as she sewed.

Littleman was secretly relieved that she would not be leaving her yard to go to evening service like most everyone would do. He couldn't bear the thought of her having to face the criticism on his account. He feared for her, what was she going to do now in the District when there was now an excuse for a more public, unapologetic and unashamed hatred of her.

Some of the women had brought food, ground provisions: sweet potatoes, yam and dasheen, rice and chicken to cook. The smell of frying chicken, rice seasoned with onions, thyme and coconut milk, wafted around the yard, reminding Littleman of his hunger. Those who had come without their children sent for them, glad that they didn't have to provide food for the evening, or to cook alone, that task seeming more pleasurable and less arduous done in a group and with the excitement, woefully scarce in the District, of the event that had brought them there. So they wallowed in the sad joy of it, some wondering secretly what further mileage could be made of it, others waiting to see what would be the outcome.

As more and more people arrived, so more food was sent for. Temporary fires were lit behind the house, pots and pans dug out of Vie's trunk, plates and cutlery sent for from other yards.

It was a long time since anyone in the District had been arrested and kept overnight in jail. Even longer since anyone had been beaten up in Town, falsely accused of being a thief even though someone from the self-same District had been able to contradict this but had held her tongue.

It was as if the Clearys had come with their food trucks, most every household represented. Ragu, banjo in one hand, flutina in another, mouth organ in breast pocket, ready to make up a mento about the story. No one it seemed having ever told him that he was over a decade late, that other musical forms had superseded the mento . . . Only that in Aunt Vie's yard where

79

there were now both saved and unsaved, he had to exclude some of his more lewd verses.

When the appropriate moment came, he strummed on his banjo first then flutina, as Mr Maxton played the mouth organ, creating impromptu, verse after verse, one version of the story and then another, Miss Dee the villain, Littleman the saint, Cleary and Town the devils, the lyrics a mixture of pathos and humour. Some of them even enlivening Littleman. Only Aunt Vie was more than a little reflective, her mind, now that he was safe, on the row she had had with Jane. Why had the talk with her degenerated so completely the night before? How had both of them managed to secretly harbour so much ill will against each other yet had feigned such a deep friendship. When the yard was eventually empty she went to bed that night troubled both with what had transpired and an overwhelming longing for Babydear.

Chapter 11

The following morning to Littleman's surprise, Vie suggested that they go to consult Azora. Littleman was not to know that Aunt Vie had grudgingly admitted to herself that whatever it was that Azora had given her when she had been summoned by him, had helped – whether by accident or by design Vie would never be able to tell but she decided on Littleman's account to give Azora the benefit of the doubt again. This time by choice. Vie saw going to her with Littleman as a way of showing Azora that she conceded just a little that perhaps there was something in what she was about, to allude to it in that way without making too much of it or saying it in so many words.

'She'll have some bushes and barks to boil up and give you a bath in. It will help you,' Vie said nonchalantly, hoping the strange excitement she felt at going in Azora's yard for the first time wouldn't be evident to Littleman.

'I asked Ezekiel last night to lend me one of his donkeys. He brought it up and tied it behind the house this morning, you can ride that one and I'll take Greystripe.'

'Thank you.' Littleman wanted to hug her for everything but the only person he had ever hugged in his life was Nana and he didn't quite know how to reach out to someone who wasn't his own grandmother.

If Azora was surprised to see them riding up her lane she did not show it, greeting them as if she had been half expecting them, she helped Littleman to tie the donkeys up, offered Vie a seat on the verandah and stood waiting to hear what had brought them. Her composure irritated Vie.

After enquiring how Vie was feeling, she listened without interrupting as Vie took over from Littleman who was precising the story to the point of making it nonsensical. The expression on Azora's face remaining unchanged throughout. When Vie had finished, she excused herself and disappeared behind the house. When she returned she prodded Littleman here and there, enquiring where he hurt. 'I've put on the pan with the bush. You'll need a good soak and then I'll rub you down with . . . ,' she hesitated as if she expected Vie to interject.

When Vie did not she half smiled, her eyes, for a brief moment, brilliant in the early morning sun.

'We don't need anything mysterious,' Vie said for want of anything better to say.

'Aunt Vie,' Azora said as if Vie's name formed a complete sentence. 'I only mix herbs and oils that nature provide . . . Things that I prove.' Vie only slightly raised an eyebrow and did not reply.

Azora made to move off behind the house but seemed to reconsider. 'Littleman go and get yourself ready. I soon come.'

She watched him disappear before turning to Aunt Vie, her voice quiet, even, 'It is good after all these years to have you in my humble abode.' Her smile broad and welcoming. Vie was not about to assume friendliness so easily, she adopted the business-like tone Azora had used previously, 'I'm only here on account of Littleman . . . I know he believes in you.' Vie said with a provocative grin.

'I suppose everyone apart from the wise old Vie has to have faith in someone apart from themselves.' She studied Vie's expression, as she waited for her reply yet seemingly at peace with the situation, unruffled by Vie's stubbornness. 'Anyway,'

Azora said finally when no retort came from Vie, 'This is a day *I've* long waited for.'

Vie rubbed her legs, she needed to stretch them out.

'Please, you can go and lie down on my bed if you want to rest your legs. It's going to take over two hours to finish off with Littleman and as you can see my verandah let on the full force of the sun as it comes up. I can get out a clean sheet.'

Vie would have laughed out loud or at least protested if there wasn't such a deadly earnest in Azora's eyes. In thirty years they had hardly ever spoken and yet in two short meetings she was treating Vie as if they were the type of bosom friends one easily had in a District like their own and Vie was feeling so at ease with her that if she allowed herself to relax it would feel as if they had gone back years. She *was* tired after all the coming and going of the previous day and not getting to bed until near dawn that morning. She decided that there was nothing to be gained from protesting, laughing or puzzlement.

'OK,' Vie said finally, 'Thank you but don't worry yourself changing sheets. I'll just put my feet up and rest my back on your bedhead.'

Vie remembered her stick lying at her feet and was about to bend down for it but Azora got there before she had thought of how to manoeuvre her body into that position without falling over. Vie shook her head. This woman is at least ten years older than me but it might as well be the other way round.

Aunt Vie sat on the bed feeling suddenly even much older than her sixty-eight years as she watched Azora busying herself on the other side of the room, returning afterwards to arrange the pillows behind Vie.

'Can I offer you something to drink?' she asked now at the door.

'No. No thank you.'

When she left, closing the door behind her, Aunt Vie laughed aloud at herself. Collecting herself she stopped abruptly, fearing Azora would return to see if she had completely lost her mind. She turned her attention instead to examining the room. It was neat and well-ordered, would have beaten the condition of her own room any day. It was one of two adjoining rooms with the standard verandah, not unlike her own. To her left she could just about see into the other one, the curtain that separated them was not completely closed and from what she could see, it was used as some kind of a stock room.

Vie was on a huge four-poster iron bed. One of the old time ones that needed a footstool to mount, one similar to her own also. Babydear used to enjoy playing under it especially when it rained and raindrops made music on the zinc roof.

But unlike hers, which was covered with one of her patch-work sheets, Azora's bed was covered with a sparking white ready-made sheet. There was a trunk at the foot of the bed with three suitcases stocked on top. On the other side of the room was a table, spread with a white calico cloth on which was placed an oil lamp. The walls were painted white too, the only splash of colour in the room coming from the red stained tiled floor. On the whole length of wall facing her were white shelves stacked with books, most of which looked extremely old and well used, in fact more books than Vie had ever seen in one place in her life.

Aunt Vie eyed everything carefully, surprised at how immaculate it all was, as if Azora had been expecting visitors or regularly entertained. The thought made Vie wonder suddenly, whether Azora had a man friend. She had never heard any rumours in the District. But one could never tell. The road outside Azora's house continued to two other districts, directly to Guanobovale or the round about way to Old Road and Kitson Town. Perhaps she rode one of her mules to see him. Or them, Vie thought with amusement, a vision of Azora's nocturnal activities enlivening her thoughts. After all, why not? Azora is a handsome woman, Vie mused. But she old. Yet she could be forty in her looks, she's fitter and stronger than many thirty-year-olds . . . But which man would want such a strange, abnormal woman? How could they cope with a woman content, as Azora seemed to be, to live by herself, do everything for herself, never hankering after husband and children? Or even regular company? No. Man can't deal with odd women like her. Vie groaned. And neither can women.

The room was not unlike Azora, Vie decided when her thoughts exhausted themselves and there was nothing else to feast her eyes on. Quiet and at ease, just like her, Vie thought, relaxing further onto the pillows and closing her eyes, wondering for some strange reason how it was that life had passed so quickly.

Chapter 12

Miss Dee was defiant, refusing to hide in her house as Aunt Jane implored. 'Give them a chance to forget that you didn't go to Littleman's help. Just leave the shop close for a week or so.' Miss Dee dismissed her concern. 'Besides I didn't do anything to Littleman . . .'

'Yes you did,' Jane shouted, then sighed. 'You know because it's you, they'll insist that you did. You know they been watching for years to find an excuse to bring me down.'

Miss Dee dropped her shoulders, frustrated, 'Aunt Jane, you weren't even there. You are just overreacting. What can the District do to me or you? Don't worry.' Miss Dee picked up her handbag. She didn't have to obey her aunt now. She was twenty-one. At last.

She walked off but turned and kissed her aunt lightly on her forehead. 'You worry too much.'

It continued to amaze Miss Dee how as she got older her relationship with her aunt had developed. Her aunt had never said, I love you. Yet, everything she did showed Miss Dee that she was devoted to her. Almost too much, Miss Dee feared. It left her with too much responsibility, too much power over her aunt. It made her falter at times in her determination to eventually leave the District, go to live in Town or even better, England. She envied Babydear. Why did she not have somebody to take her out of the District? Away from its non–eventfulness, its boredom, its backwardness.

Only very gradually had Miss Dee realised that behind all her aunt's rage against the District and sometimes against even herself, despite her aunt's independence, the obvious success she had made of her life, with no help from anyone, there was a profound fear of being alone, an entrenched desire to be like all the other women in the District; normal women, her aunt sometimes grudgingly allowed. Miss Dee would never have thought it of someone who made a hobby of putting herself above those same women in so many ways. But there was the trap, Miss Dee feared, with only one friend in the District, Aunt Jane couldn't afford to lose her or Aunt Vie.

Miss Dee tried to dismiss the worry from her mind. The forty minutes walk to the shop she hoped, would clear her head, she had come to use that time to mentally construct her story of her ultimate escape from the District, not to find her long lost mother as Jane dreaded. Miss Dee's greatest vision, even ahead of England, was to be whisked away to be wife to some eligible rich man somewhere and eventually be mother to his children. That was how it was meant to be. She would not end up like her aunt, a dried up spinster, ridiculed and pitied.

Miss Dee had not given up on Jacob Cleary, usually he was the one who was behind the wheel of the vehicle that sped her away. Despite the reputation the Clearys had around the Districts for their treatment of country women, Miss Dee knew it would be different with her. She was unlike the rest of them.

She had only just turned out of her lane, the dream not yet in full flow, when she came across a group of young women, Bellinda Jerr and Sibble Williams, from the upper end of the District, two of the faces she picked out. Miss Dee knew immediately by the way they stood, that they were way-laying her. She approached them, as she was bound to, careful not to trip or acknowledge their presence, came level with them and passed but without a word from them. She was just thinking that she had misread the situation when they started to speak, ostensibly whispering but loud enough for her to hear, Bellinda Jerr's voice the clearest of them leading a chorus of abuse for Miss Dee's treatment of Littleman in town, the worst of them, with a pretence at sympathy, wondering at how it could ever be possible for Miss Dee to be normal if even her mother had thrown her away . . .

At first, Miss Dee took her time walking as if they were not talking about her, as if she couldn't hear them . . . but this riled them more and they intensified their abuse. Miss Dee quickened her step, her high heels catching between the stones, making the group roll about with laughter.

Although the two homes she was passing were set well in from the road Miss Dee wondered still whether the inhabitants had heard, whether they had witnessed her humiliation. She stopped when she was round a bend and out of sight, glanced behind her to make sure the young women weren't following her, taking deep breaths, brushing her hands across her face, as if it too had been soiled by their words. She lingered further to adjust her hobble skirt, regretting now that she had not worn something less restrictive but on hearing footsteps ahead, she collected herself and started off again. Expecting the normal greetings she opened her mouth ready to respond but the couple passed without a word, their eyes over her head looking into the distance.

For the rest of the journey to the shop, Miss Dee was anxious. Her eyes flitted around trying to catch other critical eyes, her ear other abusive voices. But if there were any, she didn't see or hear them.

As the day wore on no one appeared at the shop, not the men on their way to field to pick up items for their lunch, children on their way to school or women to get provisions for the evening pot, only Sister Netta, who crept up from behind the house to inform her that she would be visiting her later that night to speak to her and pray with her. Miss Dee was outraged, it was the first time that Sister Netta had come herself to her shop since she had opened, content before with sending children from neighbouring homes or more usually her daily help. Now she hardly greeted her, spoke to Miss Dee as if she had a contagious disease and would have left in the same high-handed manner had Miss Dee not told her that she would be busy that night and would not be able to see her. Sister Netta shook her head and took her leave, deflated, the expression on her face more grave than when she came but not before letting loose a tirade of scriptures especially chosen for Miss Dee, vowing retribution on the wicked.

For the rest of the day, Miss Dee pretended to busy herself behind the counter as others passed one by one, making a show, she thought, of keeping their heads straight, as if neither she nor her shop existed.

Towards evening, when still no one had come, having been bored to distraction and too restless even to read or even to examine her features in the mirror, she decided that she would lock up and go home. She had tried all day to push the apprehension she felt about walking home alone to the back of her mind, wishing now she had taken Aunt Jane's advice. That she had at least even asked her to stay at the shop with her. Not for the first time she wished that Rose-marie lived in Top Mountain, was within reach or even that she had Littleman to turn to as she had been able to in the past.

But no one bothered her on the way home and for part of it Miss Dee almost wished they did, anything but the deathly silence that they adopted one by one as they met and passed her on the road. Not since the day when she had first been brought from the electric lit street and houses of Kitson Town to Top Mountain and seen mongooses leaping in and out of bushes, trees taking on ominous shapes in the darkness, had she felt so foreign and alone as she did then.

Back at home, Aunt Jane was anxious to know what had happened. Miss Dee lied. 'Nothing,' she said nonchalantly as she poured water in her basin to wash her face and hands before her evening meal. 'So there was no need for you to lock yourself in the yard all day,' she continued, convinced that everyone would be back to normal the following day.

But they were not, nor were they for a whole week. No one acknowledged her existence as she walked through the District or sat behind the counter in her shop, not even Sister Netta who Miss Dee prayed would come again to press her about a prayer meeting for her sins. Or Ragu who would usually hear her passing and call out to her. She dreaded meeting Aunt Vie and would almost hold her breath as she passed her lane. The rest of the District she cursed, dwelling on their hypocrisy, wondering why most of them called themselves saved and why all of them dressed like peacocks and went to church on Sundays. As for Littleman, when she was not wishing that they were friends as they had been in the past, she almost relished the thought of seeing him to challenge him for turning the District against her, for it must surely be him who had told lies. But she did not once set eyes on him in that week and underneath the bravado she was distraught, fearing for herself but also now for her aunt who had only left the yard in the week to go in the other direction to Town.

On Saturday, a week after the incident, she was sat in the bedroom adjoining the shop wondering as she had done over the last two days whether to open up or not. There would be no respite for her mind, at home or there in the shop. At home she feared she saw for the first time a level of pain and hurt in her aunt's eyes that she had never noticed before. Pain perhaps of other hurts that she had been subjected to over the years by the District that was now manifesting itself tenfold because of something not she but Miss Dee had done. In the past, regardless of what had gone on Aunt Jane had sewed for the District, gone to their christenings and the funerals, their weddings, sat in their yards on evenings when she had nothing else to do and, on rarer occasions when she felt the need for religion in her life, worshipped with them.

Miss Dee sighed repeatedly, vowing that regardless of the situation, she would get herself together. Perhaps this was the cue for her to leave, set about getting a position in Town and soon after that finding a way to go to England. She had lost much sleep over the last few nights, had not taken care with her hair or her make up, had even worn the same clothes two days in a row to the shop. That could not continue, she couldn't let herself go, give the District the satisfaction. She got up to examine herself in the mirror and what she saw, dark ridges under her eyes, pimples on her forehead, confirmed her fears.

She decided to lock up and go home. They would win that week, she would go home and sort herself out, get some sleep and think what to do the following week. If she was being maliced about something else, not the precious Littleman, she would have gone to seek solace at Aunt Vie's. At the thought of him, her blood boiled. Why was she being punished so viciously on his account when less than four months before the District worked him like a donkey and left him to sleep on tombs.

She heard a knock on the shop door. She leapt up, ran into the shop and peeped through the crevice of the door. Jacob. Miss Dee took a step back, gasped. Covered her mouth. She couldn't believe it. She tiptoed back to the bedroom to see if she could repair herself quickly to face him. No.

She ran back to the door, peeped again. His jeep was parked directly in front of the shop. She wondered how long he had been out there knocking. Why today? She wondered bitterly. She couldn't possibly face him in the state she was in. She watched him through the door as he looked impatiently at his watch. He disappeared for a minute and she heard his footsteps going behind the house where he knocked again loudly on the back door calling out her real name, Deseree, not Miss Dee as everyone had called her since she had started to sing in church. Finally he retraced his steps to the jeep and drove off. As the sound of it disappeared in the distance, she found herself crying. She hated Littleman then. But for him, for the District, she would have been serving and making conversation with Jacob Cleary. At last.

She didn't open the shop that day. She sat instead staring in space until she heard the jeep speeding by again a few hours later.

She locked up then and headed home. It seemed that Jane had been waiting for her and as soon as she stepped in the room to greet her, she demanded once more that Miss Dee made things right with Littleman. 'What for? I have not done anything to him,' Miss Dee stressed, 'So he got a few blows. But I didn't cause them. That would have happened if I had begged them to stop, if I had said immediately what I thought I saw. Plus I might have got hit too. He's the man.'

Jane said she agreed, that so far as she could see, what had happened with Littleman was only part of why they were being punished by the District.

'Yet still they want you to say sorry you didn't try to help one of them.'

'Aunt Jane, they can wait for ever.'

Jane pressed her lips with the tips of her fingers, did not speak for a long time. Miss Dee sat on her aunt's bed, as if totally at ease.

'Miss Dee I know you been lying to me all this week. Why?'

'I haven't told any lies.'

Jane shook her head sadly, as if regretting many things, then changed her tone suddenly. 'You don't live in this District by yourself, you know Dee. You need people more than they need you.'

Miss Dee was angry too. 'You are the one who brought me up to think I didn't need them. That they needed you and me more than . . .'

'Dee! What you think in your head and how you behave don't have to be the same thing,' Jane sighed heavily. 'I know that nobody's come to the shop all week and that no one of them going to ever talk to you until you make some recompense to Littleman.'

Dee jumped up, 'They can go to hell first. I don't care if they don't come to the shop.'

'Don't be so foolish!' Jane threw the dress she had been hemming down on the bed. 'So how you think we going to live?'

'You can sew,' Miss Dee snapped, leaving the room before Jane could reply.

She went to sit on one of the tombs behind the house, her hand on her cheek, unsure now of what she should do next.

She heard Aunt Jane busying herself in the kitchen cooking. Sorry for her earlier loss of temper, she went to join her in the kitchen. Miss Dee said nothing for a while. Instead she tidied things that were already tidy, got in Aunt Jane's way as she cooked. Eventually Aunt Jane stopped what she was doing and turned to her. 'I don't have many people to call my own.' She spoke very quietly. 'I only have you. But I have one friend who has stuck close by me since I moved in this District well before you were born or I even knew you. I know this is not what I've been saying all these years, but there is a lot of things that I haven't said that I should have said and a lot that I shouldn't have said.'

Miss Dee's heart was racing at a pace. She had never heard Aunt Jane speak in such a self-pitying tone before. 'When I had to leave my birth place, for reasons that is best not talked about, I made it up in my mind that I was the only somebody I had, the only friend. I made up my mind not to depend on anybody for anything, to just make my way through life. But when I came here they didn't know what I was thinking and when they see me doing well, the men eyes grew bright thinking that I was available as plaything. And the women, seeing what was in their men's eyes turned against me.

'I didn't do them anything but they started to abuse me, calling me names; mule, eunuch, dry-up-womb; just because I wasn't blessed, wasn't normal like them and could have me own children. So when they wouldn't take telling and stop troubling me, I turned against them too. I started to hate the whole lot of them, to work meself in the ground trying to show them that I could be better than them, husbandless and childless though I am . . .' She stopped and stared out into the dusk. '. . . Better than the whole lot of them. And I succeeded. I went to town and learnt to sew better than any of them. I got the style books and made things for myself so that they would grudge me for it. And they did and one by one, the same ones who used to shout names at me as I walked about my own business, had to come with their tails between their legs. I scorned them. I have to tell you the truth. I scorned and hated them but I sewed for them nevertheless, bit me tongue and sewed for them because I was benefiting too . . . When did any of them manage to get Cleary Senior to sell them land?' But even as she gloated Miss Dee noticed, not for the first time, that Aunt Jane's eyes narrowed and her mouth twisted in a mixture of bitterness and contempt as she mentioned John Cleary Senior. Jane hesitated and seemed to trip over her tongue. 'Get Cleary to sell them land without . . . before giving anything to him that wasn't money?' Miss Dee frowned not fully understanding her aunt.

'Most of this time . . .' Jane sighed, 'Vie stood by me. I know I'm not an easy person but she bore with me . . .' She turned sad eyes to Miss Dee. 'Now after all these years, despite the rights and wrong of the situation, I don't want anything to disturb the

94

fragile understanding that we come to. I don't want you to spoil that Miss Dee. I can't let you spoil that because when you go, who will I have left? . . .' Her voice was almost inaudible, 'I'm not blessed like other women. I will not have grandchildren to look forward to . . .'

In her room glad to escape from her aunt's self-pitying, she made the plans that she would present to Aunt Jane as a *fait accompli*. If another week passed and no one came to the shop, she would go and get a job in Town, perhaps in one of Mr Cleary's supermarkets in Spanish Town, but that would be the final option. Jacob wouldn't even glance at her when there would be so many others like her, working behind a cash till, packing shelves, cleaning. She knew she could do better. Perhaps a job in one of the banks, or a post office would be better, more in line with her qualifications. She would give the District a week then whatever it took after that she would get out of the District, even if it meant walking out the whole of Spanish Town and Kingston. Then they could tell her who needed who. She would have the excuses she needed to dress up, they wouldn't know anything about her, they would just see her go and come until one day they would miss her and would find out eventually that she would never be back.

Having resolved what she would do, Miss Dee went confidently back to the kitchen, said she was sorry for everything, knew everything would be back to normal soon, sat and ate with her aunt, trying desperately to ignore the uncertainty and worry on her face.

Chapter 13

Whatever Vie had been doing in the week following her visit to Azora, weeding her vegetable patch, tending her flower beds, sweeping her yard, cooking or washing, even sitting at Ragu's or the Maxton's house for company, she had found herself pre-occupied anew with thoughts of how Azora had managed to get the Clearys to sell her land, two hundred and fifty acres of it. Just over thirty years ago, Azora had come riding through the District on a mule and then disappeared again, months later she moved onto land that once belonged to the Clearys, the District buzzed with the news that this lone, serious faced, over-tall woman had bought the land. The first the District had known to have broken the Clearys' intransigence.

It had crossed Vie's mind then that perhaps Azora had only been granted favours as a special concubine. But experience reminded Vie that John Cleary Senior did not feel the need to give favours to his country women, not even to the stray children he produced with them. The women likewise, seemingly demanded little from him or soon learnt the hard way that nothing was due to them. Vie had spent many years counselling the young, even when she had been young like them. Trying to show them that the Clearys meant them no good. That, whatever their promises, they should spurn their advances and, more than that, broadcast to the District any attempts they made to spoil them. For that is what she considered they did.

Vie had moved with her daughter Isadora from Eggsbury to Top Mountain after the death of her mother, seventeen years before Azora arrived. Then twenty-one, Vie had started considering herself, like everyone else did on the onset of that age, a woman. She had awoken to the hold the Clearys had over the District, making it her vocation to be a thorn in their sides; she lead deputations to them when they abrogated their landlordly responsibilities, as they frequently did, when there was yet another plea to the family to sell land, and not least took it upon herself to warn young girls in Top Mountain, to appeal to them, not to be blinded by the big white house on the hill, the promise of money, other big houses, servants and shops in town. Most listened to Vie and to their own mothers. But there were always a few for whom words from a family so rich and powerful, were sweeter than reality.

Vie could never imagine, despite everything else that she opposed about her, that a young Azora let alone one who was then nearer fifty than forty, was of the Cleary concubine ilk. So she had dismissed that fleeting suspicion. Now thirty years later, having met her properly, a sneaking admiration of Azora was creeping up on Vie. She did not know whether to entertain it and go back on three decades of scepticism and opposition, or dismiss it and continue as they had been. Vie feared that she was already caught up in the net that Azora had successfully laid for the whole District over the years.

Littleman, one of those firmly caught, was no help to Vie on this account. He sang Azora's praises almost daily especially on the day he returned to work in Eggsbury with no bruises or pain only a week since his severe beating in Town. He had not even sat around and rested as he had been advised to by the District. He had done all kinds of things around the yard: mended the walls of the latrine that had been letting in water for months, billed the weeds and brambles from around the edge of the yard, got down on his hands and knees and reapplied red stain to the verandah and the two bedrooms. For the rest of the time he had gone across to Ragu's to continue learning his trade. Despite all that he had recovered.

Ragu visited Vie at the beginning of that week, threatening to strum out a tune about her change of heart over Azora.

'Thirty years of malice is a long pole of malice to climb down from,' he laughed.

Vie advised him to go back to his cabinet-making and leave her in peace. Later that night there was an attempt at a reggae tune from Ragu's banjo; a change from the usual ska and mento tunes, Vie mused, covert references in his lyrics, as he had threatened, to Vie and Azora. Amused by his mischief making and not impartial to his joviality, Vie limped across to his yard, taking her lamp with her, as everyone did, and watched him alternate work with music.

Before Ragu had gone to fight in Europe, he had the reputation of being the best cabinet-maker around, making furniture for surrounding Districts, shops in town and parishes as far afield as St Ann, Clerendon, St Mary and St Thomas. Since his return, sightless, his clients both old and new swore that somehow he seemed to have perfected his craft. Not that there was great surprise that he hadn't returned and sat around, griping. Like Ezekiel Samuel who had returned leaving one leg shattered between the trenches, Ragu had continued to work for his living. Vie saw in Littleman an admiration akin to hero worship of Ragu and she was glad to encourage it especially now that he seemed lost and confused again.

'Seriously, Vielina . . .' Ragu was saying. 'What make you change your mind so suddenly about the Doctor Azora?'

'Who say I change my mind?'

Ragu looked in her general direction. 'Well, if not change it, everybody can see that you changing it.' Vie said nothing and after a few moments Ragu went back to preparing the wood for a wardrobe he was making, Vie to playing with her fingers and considering.

In Azora's bed the morning she had taken Littleman to see her, Vie had dozed off several times. That was the last thing she had wanted to happen, to have Azora catch her sleeping when she would lose total control of her mouth, when it would fall open and saliva would drain from the corner, to have Azora see her as she really was and pity her. Vie felt let down by her body, compared herself unfavourably with Azora who was in total control in every way.

When she did eventually hear footsteps coming from the side of the house, Vie had arranged herself in as upright a position as was possible but before she finished, there had been a light knock on the door. Why is this woman knocking on her own bedroom door, Vie thought. She didn't answer. The knock came again. 'Come in,' she said finally, but it was Littleman not Azora. He pushed his head around the door.

'Don't tell me it's two hours already?' Vie asked.

'It's more than that Aunt Vie. The doctor came in before but you were fast asleep, so she said we should leave you.'

'Oh.'

'So whenever you are ready Aunt Vie we can go.'

'OK, dear, just give me a minute to straighten myself. By the way how you feel?'

'Good. Very good,' Littleman said nodding briskly. 'Doctor Azora is a wonderful doctor. She works miracles,' Littleman said as he limped from the room.

When Littleman shut the door, Vie got up, slipped on her shoes, fixed the sheets back in place and left the room.

Azora was sitting on the verandah, her head thrown back, looking to the skies. Vie watched her for a moment before clearing her throat.

'Had a good rest?' Azora asked, so unruffled and patronising Vie thought that she was irritated afresh by Azora. Vie controlled her tongue. 'Yes. Thank you.' She pulled out the pouch suspended from her neck.

'Let me settle up with you.'

'That is all right Aunt Vie.'

'No,' Vie insisted, pulling a bundle of pound notes out to get at the coins.

Azora shook her head ignoring Vie's outstretched hand. 'I'll get your donkey. Let me give you a hand up.'

Aunt Vie left one guinea on her chair anyway and followed her calling to Littleman who had disappeared behind the house.

'He will have to come back midweek and at the end of the week for another treatment before he's himself again,' Azora said as Vie directed Greystripe down the lane and out of her yard.

'Aunt Vie,' Azora had called out.

'Woah.' Vie pulled Greystripe up. Littleman stopped his donkey a little way ahead of them.

Azora strolled up beside her. 'My offer still stands. Give me a chance to coax your limbs back to better use.'

'I'm all right,' Vie said, tapped Greystripe on the side and started off again.

'Just think about it,' Azora said walking beside the donkey.

'Good day Azora.'

Azora stopped, 'Good day to you Aunt Vie. Now you see for yourself that there is nothing sinister in my yard, perhaps you can give friendship a chance.'

A week and a half later, sitting alone on her verandah, Vie reflected on what Ragu had said about the thirty-year pole of malice that she had to descend. If she was honest she would have to admit that she had erected that pole. Would her reputation in the District survive the descent? She decided impulsively to go for a walk. She needed to talk to Ezekiel. Like Ragu he would give her honest opinions. At least on matters that had nothing to do with he and her. Unlike Ragu he would not couch his words in humour. Leaving her bedroom door ajar she started down the middle lane in the direction of the shop.

It was a good thing Ezekiel could not read her mind, since whenever she was in her reflective and uncertain mood her body chose that as the time to play up, calling for her unquenchable desire to be satisfied. She knew Ezekiel was always ready to answer her need but the thinking part of her knew that she could not take that road again, not any more.

Dora took over the counter from her husband after she and Aunt Vie had exchanged polite greetings. It was one of the strange mysteries of the District that although Dora's husband and Aunt Vie were close, sat many evenings talking, Dora and Aunt Vie were anything but. For Vie and Ezekiel there was no secret.

Because the shop was joined to the front of the house the Samuel's verandah was in a peculiar place, behind the house and not in front as was normal. Vie sat there to wait for him as he finished off in the shop, kept especially busy because of the boycott of Miss Dee's, and went to make a large jug of syrup with ice for them. They sipped silently for a long time.

When Aunt Vie had her first stroke, and had recovered sufficiently for him to joke about it, Ezekiel had laughed that as well as understanding each other on just about every subject, they now both understood what each other felt to have a lame leg.

'I don't know which is worse,' Aunt Vie had said smiling. 'How I got mine or how you got yours. I'm no hero.'

'Who said I'm a hero?' he had said seriously. 'Nobody considers me a hero. Not then. And certainly not now.' She remembered he had looked bitter for a brief moment but had not dwelt on it.

'The leg giving you any trouble at the moment,' she asked gently, feeling a need to be tender now. Ezekiel seemed to pull himself together with effort. 'No man. I'm fine.' He smiled then, 'You still dragging and pulling yours I see.' They both laughed then, self-pity and the burden to remember the past was eased. But Dora came from inside the shop suddenly.

'Why you don't sit down and have a drink with us Dora. Nobody in the shop now,' Aunt Vie coaxed watching her. They were about the same age and although she looked much younger than Aunt Vie having never been ill, her look was sour and harboured a permanent expression of someone wronged, had done so for many years now. 'No. I just . . . I just going over to the kitchen to fetch something.'

Aunt Vie lost her train of thought and although good sense told her that she should continue with a conversation to assure Dora that she and her husband had not been sharing a secret joke or one at her expense, she could find nothing to say nor it seemed could Ezekiel until Dora passed back through the verandah and into the shop. Ezekiel sighed heavily as if expelling great burdens. 'So what brings you down here Vie? You haven't blessed us with your presence for weeks.'

'Time flies, eh?'

'I know,' he said looking directly at her with a sadness she had noticed in his eyes ten years before. 'You still don't regret that you didn't settle down and have a family,' he asked out of the blue, his mood seeming to reflect her own. Vie didn't answer immediately and when she did, her voice matched his graveness,

'I had a family. I have a family. My daughter and grandchildren were my family. And now I have Littleman. He's my family now. And . . . ,' she smiled, 'I have the District.'

'You know what I mean Vie, marry and have other children.'

She smiled, her lopsided mouth feeling conspicuous. 'You don't have to marry and have children to have someone to call your family,' she insisted, concentrating on the light red dust blowing around in the breeze. '. . . Otherwise a lot of us in this country, don't have families.' Ezekiel nodded. 'But sometimes I worry about you. Littleman not settled. He cut out to be a wanderer. He can go anytime. What will you do then?'

She stroked her bad hand. He was the only one who could pity her and not leave her feeling angry, the only one she told that her daughter was constantly suggesting that she joined them in England and about her insistence that she would never leave Jamaica.

He sighed with heaviness. 'So what bring you down here I say?' He insisted, knowing her. 'Is it about Miss Dee? Since the whole District turn against her and you and Jane fall out . . . Or Littleman . . . ?'

'No it's not about anybody . . .' She stared absentmindedly at the chickens wandering around the yard, pecking at invisible delights. 'I have a feeling that he has a soft spot for Miss Dee though.'

Ezekiel laughed, 'At least what she do to him will make him get sense. Miss Dee think she too good for the best boys in the District let alone poor Littleman.'

'Young people foolish these days, you hear. They think looks make the man or the woman for that matter.'

Ezekiel smiled, 'That has never been different.' That was her cue.

'What you think about Azora?' she said, lowering her voice even though she could now hear someone with Dora in the shop.

Ezekiel looked at her fully. 'Azora? Azora?!' He asked knitting his brow.

'Um mmm,' Vie sipped her syrup as if she had other things on her mind and her question was just by the way.

'Well. Like what?'

'Anything,' she said dispassionately.

'You know she keeps herself to herself.'

'I know that.'

'She know a lot about herbs. I suppose you know as well as I do that she's the most learned in the District.'

'Yes. Yes.'

'What more you want me to tell you?' Ezekiel seemed agitated. She wanted to laugh at his impatience, but waited. Serious.

'I said everything you know already and you know as much or as little about her as I do.' She watched him, still waiting for what she herself did not know.

'People say she's well off. Have a lot of money.' Ezekiel smirked. 'After all she should, she charge enough for her medicines . . .'

'How you know?'

'I hear,' he said defensively. 'Anyway you can't criticise anybody now since from what me hear you turn one of her regular clients.'

Aunt Vie ignored that, wiped her forehead with her handkerchief feeling suddenly very hot. 'You know if she have a man anywhere? Or ever had one?' Vie didn't know why she was asking that. Perhaps suspicion about Azora and the John Cleary Senior still logged in her mind. Or perhaps she was hoping that she could find something to vindicate her opposition over the thirty years, even now.

Ezekiel sat back sharply in his chair. 'Why you want to know that?'

'Zekiel. Is me asking you the questions? Why you have to confuse up the situation?'

'How I to know if she have man or not?' Then as if realising that Vie had asked an impossibly ridiculous question he exclaimed, 'But you can see a woman like that never having a manfriend? Of course she must have manfriend. No doubt she have plenty manfriend even children somewhere about the place.'

'Don't judge her like you men should rightfully judge your

104

one another. She's not a man. She's a woman and we can do without manfriend.' She was half joking but Ezekiel didn't seem to be amused. He got up. 'You want something more to drink?'

'No, but I'll go. A lot of people coming and going in the shop. You go help you wife.'

He sighed. 'All right. I must pop up and sit with you one evening this week.' He watched her pick her way down the steps, careful as usual not to jump to help her. 'What evenings Jane usually visit you?'

She had never known why that mattered but she told him.

'The stick really helping you, eh?'

'Yes. God bless Littleman. You should ask him to make one for you,' she said teasingly but he didn't laugh as she expected him to. She stopped and turned. He was still watching her. 'I'm planning to get some treatment for the walk from Azora.' She watched his astonishment but continued in a calm dispassionate voice. 'She said she can do some physio . . . something on the leg and give me some herbs to control the blood pressure.' Ezekiel stepped down from the verandah after her.

'Vie I thought you didn't like the woman. You always made that clear.'

'I never said that to you or to anybody. People like putting word in my mouth too much.'

'But everyone knows you disapprove of her and only let her come to your house that once because of Littleman and . . .'

'Is that why they all creep pass me house each nights to get treatment from her?'

Ezekiel cleared his throat.

'All I say is that if the woman only using herbs that nature grew and her hand that God give her then I have no quarrel with her. We should be grateful we have someone among us who is as knowledgeable like her.' Vie heard herself defending the woman she didn't know and certainly had never, and still did not fully trust.

She started walking towards the pig-sty at the end of the lane that led to her yard. Ezekiel followed her battling with curiosity. She refused to take up the subject again telling him instead that the sty needed cleaning out. 'It so stink I can smell it from my yard. Get one of you grandson to clean it out.'

'You nose too sensitive but I'll look after it. Anyway . . . ,' he stopped walking. Aunt Vie leant on her stick wondering why he had followed her. 'Thank you for the drink.'

'I'll pop up this week then,' he said.

She nodded and walked on feeling his eyes on her back as she limped away.

Chapter 14

Miss Dee agonised over why it was that in the two weeks her shop had been boycotted, she had felt so lonely. How could that be when all she had got from the District over the past few years, was opportunity to secretly ridicule the way they dressed, how they spoke; saying him when they meant her, mixing up tenses and the confusion that is their grammar, when they had just been killing time for her until she found somewhere better to be, better people to be with.

Not even Jacob had come again. No doubt, she thought, if his family had heard that the business was in trouble and that they would eventually have to turf yet another one off their land for failing to pay the lease, they would have been up in a shot. Miss Dee wondered why the District hadn't just gone the whole way, tell the Clearys to give her notice now since they clearly intended to wreck her life and her livelihood.

It perplexed her even more that she hadn't bumped into Littleman for the two weeks. It was true he didn't have to pass her shop to go to Eggsbury if he didn't want to, there were various short-cuts he could take which would be quicker and easier on himself and the donkey than the stony main road. She found herself wondering time and time again what he was doing as she suffered because of him.

With that thought she packed away the flask and cup that had contained her packed lunch wondering whether it would indeed be her last day at the shop. How could she have imagined that no one would have appeared or spoken to her for two whole weeks. In two minds about whether to see the whole day through, the last of the days she had given herself, she heard footsteps coming from the bushes behind the shop. None of her customers ever came that way. She sat still listening to the footsteps as they approached, finally certain that someone had decided that they couldn't be bothered to go all the way down to the Samuels' shop and was going to break the boycott. Too lazy. Or too much credit down there. She smiled smugly. She would refuse to hide, and serve anyone.

She got up, put her flask away, straightened her clothes and made to shut the back door when it crossed her mind that it might be Littleman. Her heart missed a beat. He might be coming at last to take his revenge. She was quickly to the door, was about to slam it shut when Leroy stepped into the room.

'What do you want?' she snapped. 'I was just closing.'

'I come because I know you could do with some company.'

'I don't need your company.'

'From the way I see things, you can't choose.'

'Just go away . . .'

He remained calm, looking steadily at her as if suddenly no longer in awe of her. She cut her eyes and turned back in the room and with a sudden turn that took him off guard, she pushed him, sending him stumbling out of the room. Before he had time to pick himself up, she pushed the door shut and locked it. He laughed out loud. 'You may have to imprison yourself in there. You a fool. You still don't learn.' She only half heard him as she flew through into the shop but before she could get under the counter to block the door he was inside it.

'Miss Dee you don't want to lock out the only friend you have now. Do you?' he said smiling, the gaps between his rotten teeth large and red. 'Leroy just get out of the shop and let me close the door,' she implored.

'What if me say no. You going to call thief . . . You think anybody going to believe you?' She sighed, going back under the counter and putting some distance between them.

'As I see it,' he said, coming up to the counter and resting his elbows casually on it, 'You badly need a friend. You don't have anybody. Except of course that dry-up mule who you call you aunt.'

'Go to hell,' she shouted. 'Even if I had nobody I wouldn't want you . . . Why don't you go and provide food and clothes for you girlfriend Bellinda Jerr!' He rubbed his fingers across his mouth amused by her vehemence. Miss Dee's eyes followed his fingers to his cracked lips. She was sure she could see cakes of dirt in between the cracks. She wanted him out but she knew the worse thing to do was antagonise him.

'Leroy, I want to close the door, please go.'

He covered his mouth in an exaggerated show of surprise.

'What a hearing things! Miss Dee saying *please*? Rain really going to fall and water going to run through the pipes like . . .' She grimaced.

'Well perhaps good always come out of bad, as me grand-mother say. This whole thing seem to teach you a lesson. Well let me continue the lesson.' He took little steps around the shop, his hands locked behind his back as if he was a Cleary. 'I have decided that I not ready to go yet, so you will have to wait.' He stopped suddenly, rested his hand on the counter and made to lift it up. Miss Dee slammed her hand on top. 'If you make one more step I'll scream this place down, and though they hate me they'll come running because you know as well as I do that they're inquisitive as hell.' He laughed, stroked the top of the counter, reached out suddenly across and grabbed her arm, pinching the flesh between his fingers, 'I will see you in the lane later then. Mark my words, you owe me something and you going to give it to me.' He squeezed harder, his eyes fixed on her breasts.

109

'Get out of my shop,' she screamed, rubbing the sting he had left on her arm. The volume of her voice startled him but he grinned indifferently and using the help of one arm scaled the counter, ran through the back rooms, unlocked the door and disappeared the way he had come.

When he was gone she shook more with anger for having not spat in his face or at least used something in the shop, a slice of the rotting corn pork or mackerel to smack him with. When her anger had finally abated, she locked all the doors and sat in the shop, the radio off, knowing that she had no choice but to call it all a day, give the keys back to Mr Cleary and get out of the District, find something else to do. It dawned on her that she could bear everything else but she couldn't bear to be afraid.

When she had finished locking up she paced for a considerable time, not knowing what to do. She had to get home but she didn't want to go alone, he had said he would meet her in the lane. But who could she go to? She thought of Sister Netta, she could go to her and ask her for the prayer meeting that night, offer to wait for her until she was ready to go, they could then walk together and she would make sure the meeting was finished before Aunt Jane got home from market. She definitely could not walk home alone, stay in the house by herself, back there, no matter how much she screamed, there would be no inquisitive neighbour to come to her rescue. When she eventually left the shop, her face had contorted into a knot having lost its practised disdain. She was unable to measure her step, consider the eyes surveying her from the verandahs or take in the one or two voices of ridicule or warning that emanated from them. She forgot herself, almost running all the way.

She refused categorically to go back to the shop the following week, ignoring Aunt Jane's pleadings. Later in the following week, with them barely speaking she went off in a huff to Spanish Town determined to find something else to do as she had planned.

Aunt Jane went to the shop herself, the first time she had been to that end of the District in four weeks, to put up a sign on the door that they would be closed until further notice, resolving that she would not be defeated. She greeted those she met as if nothing had happened, as if she had not been in self-imposed exile and was surprised how brightly they returned her greetings, some even stopping to exchange trivialities with her. She couldn't understand how Miss Dee had said they had not spoken to her. Whatever their game she determined that she would either find someone from out of the District to run the shop for her, reducing their profit but more importantly keeping it going, or she would do it herself, sandwich her sewing in the early mornings and evenings. Even if they stopped asking her to sew for them in the District, she had plenty of other clients elsewhere and she would not let them down. But she knew they would not take their work elsewhere, regardless of what they thought of her, she knew they recognised her as the best dress-maker they had and she did plenty more besides. Who else would tramp through town to get the best and cheapest fabrics for them? Sew for them and let them have the clothes months in months out before getting paid. Who else would use remnants to make little clothes for their children and refuse to take pay for them? Bitterly, she thought them the most undeserving and ungrateful set of people she had met. Despite the way they treated her, what they said about her behind her back, they wiped their mouths off and came crawling back straight as for things. With those thoughts on her mind she kept quickening her steps when she passed Vie's lane.

Back at home, the complications situation faced her again. She had fed and looked after. She the shop for Miss Dee, in years, to school her and wondered where sh

pain of the whole a lot of expense to get lot of expenses over the Yes she had made mistakes, had blamed her wrongly for things, but she had tried to make up, done her best. Perhaps she should have stayed by herself, come to terms with growing old, childless and alone, accepting the label that she was a strange and abnormal woman.

For her part, Miss Dee spent her day walking Spanish Town, her school and commercial college reports and certificates in hand, begging for a job. She went from bank to building society to post office, Records Office, large supermarket, small shops. When all of that proved futile, on her way to Rose-marie in Kitson, she even went to the post office there, the pharmacy, the iron mongers but finding nothing. Those who had the time or inclination suggested she tried again at the end of the month or after Christmas but that was over two months away. She knew she couldn't sit at home for that length of time. Yet she was relieved that there was nothing in Kitson Town, people from her District passed through there all the time. There was an all-age school there too, to which most of the children failing their common entrance exams progressed from Paul Mountain Primary, there would be nowhere there to hide. The thought that she was indeed trying to hide startled her, making her feel suddenly ashamed. She should be facing and challenging them. Why should she have to hide?

Rose-marie was of little help to her. 'It's true you didn't cause them to ... Littleman. But, Dee Dee, it was terrible of you just to ign... shouldn't h... and pretend that nothing had happened. You there for you... ated him like that especially since he used to be

'Rose-mar... done already. I ...n't need any more talking to about it. It's it would cause a... mething I planned. How was I to know the bed in the roo... ble?' They were lying side by side on 'You do need so... rie shared with one of her sisters. tell you that yet.' ... about it though. I bet nobody

'Tell me what?'

'That you were wrong.'

'How could they tell me when none of them has breathed a word to me in two weeks?'

'Have you said anything to them?'

'Of course not.'

'It's for you to do something, not them,' Rose-marie laughed. 'Anyway I never understand how they all 'fraid of you so when you is just all show.' Miss Dee rolled over on her side and pinched her hard. Rose-marie jumped up and straddled her, tickling and squeezing her until Miss Dee's laughter turned to tears but Rose-marie only took pity on her when her mother called out to them, telling them to behave like the young ladies they were supposed to be. They settled down again to dissect Miss Dee's predicament. As usual Rose-marie was brutally honest. 'You have to beg his pardon, apologise to him and to the whole District, there is no other way round it.'

'I'll never do that. Never. I did nothing.'

'Fine but just content yourself with being alone for the rest of you life, Dee Dee. And for whatever children you have for them to be alone. What mommy and papa always say, the sins of the fathers . . . mothers in you case fall on the children . . . Wherever you run to . . . Jamaica is small Dee Dee.' Miss Dee sucked her teeth.

'You know as well as I do Dee Dee, that regardless of the ups and downs that go on in Districts like Top Mountain, they all as close as real families and if you hurt one of them you hurt the whole lot. And whatever you do they won't let you forget it until you pay. And . . .' she continued as Miss Dee was about to cut in, 'And they don't usually ask a lot, just that you admit that you wrong when you wrong.'

'I'll have to die first. I can live without them.'

'Who will you have then?'

'Well I have Jane.' They smiled simultaneously because that

was one of their ways, their dare, to call their parents and guardian by their first name when they were alone, so it was always Jane and Elizabeth and Daniel.

'So you have Jane. She old . . .'

'She's only fifty-three . . .'

'Old. What you going to do when she die.'

'I'll be married with my kids by then and be right away from them . . .'

'I bet Jane thought that too,' Rose-marie warned. 'Anyway I think Jane understands the District, their ways, you think she's going to go on living outside the shelter of that community for ever because of your stubbornness. No Dee Dee, don't fool yourself. Watch and see, she'll disown you first.'

Miss Dee protested and made she didn't agree with her friend but she did see and that was why she loved Rose-marie. She was the only girl she had met at Primary school who was not overawed by her bravado and was not afraid to tell her the truth. When she had the opportunity in those days, they had spent many hours hiding behind bushes sharing secrets, talking about their hurts and pains, laughing at unfunny things. Rose-marie was the first person she had loved, touched, from whom she had learnt that a hug could be pleasurable and safe.

After they had eaten dinner, they sat in the moonlight and sang old school songs together. Later, Mr Rowe accompanied his daughter as she walked Miss Dee home, keeping up the rear wondering what young girls could find to talk about so much. But he didn't interfere, he took the opportunity to smoke his pipe in peace as they strolled ahead of him engrossed in incessant chatter and laughter.

They didn't leave her at the end of the lane as she had asked them to do on previous occasions, instead, to their surprise, she invited them in, sat them on the verandah and made them tea and water crackers with guava jelly, summoning Aunt Jane who had no choice but join them and it seemed to Miss Dee quite

114

enjoyed her talk with Mr Rowe because when she and Rose-marie resurfaced, they had to wait for some time before they had finished their conversation and he was ready to go.

The following day, Miss Dee told Aunt Jane the plans she and Rose-marie had come up with, carefully presenting it as her own. She had been wrong in what she had done to Littleman. She would go back to the shop but not to sell food permanently. She would do a food sale. Buy one get one free or something like that, a bit like when Mr Cleary came but not quite because nothing would be exactly free. When the stock they had was finished, they would open the first clothes shop in the District. Aunt Jane could sew at home as she did now or on the premises, and they could sell what she sewed. She would get other things from Town. Nice things. Laces and satins. Seersuckers. Nylons. She would get the latest style books. Everyone could order direct from them any of the styles that were being worn in Town and not have to go to Town to get them. She could eventually get someone to help . . .

As Miss Dee talked, ideas that she hadn't even discussed with Rose-marie flooded her head. A new excitement came into her voice. She smiled for the first time in weeks at her aunt. She could do it. Make it work. The District wouldn't be able to resist it, resist her. There would be no competition. She could buy materials too, thread, patterns. For those who wanted to sew their own clothes. But since most claimed they didn't have the time business would thrive. Besides most wanted the status of having had things ready-made or things made for them, that was the fashion. She was buzzing with thoughts, plans and ideas. Jane, relieved that her loss of control of the past two weeks had ended, was swept along with her.

The following day Miss Dee packed her bag and set off for the shop with paper and pens to do the signs advertising the sale. Aunt Jane had left for Town earlier. Miss Dee's plans were to do the signs that day and attach them to posts around the District, over the front of the shop and wait. She had just gone half way down her lane when she heard someone coming up behind her. She spun round and faced Leroy. 'Not you again,' she shouted, momentarily deflated.

Leroy wore a self-satisfied smile. 'Miss Dee. I been waiting for you to come all morning.' She cut her eyes and stepped past him. He seemed to have expected her to stand and talk to him so he was taken off guard when she strode off. It was a moment before he followed her. 'Dee no go on so man. I was rude the other day. I come to apologise. I'm sorry.' She continued walking.

'I like you Miss Dee. I have always like you. I deserve you. Especially now that you don't have anybody else.' He stood in front of her smiling. She glared at him determined to get him to leave her once and for all.

He seemed temporarily startled by her look. 'You have a girl friend and even if you don't, if you want to find one, you are looking in the wrong face . . .' He rubbed his dirt caked hands on his equally soiled clothes as if wishing to tidy himself for her. She stood her ground. 'I don't want you anywhere near me and if you ever come near me again or talk to me, I'll report you to the police.' He laughed loudly then. 'You a joke. No true? Which police a go have time for that?'

She snapped suddenly, swung her hand at his face. His hands went up like lightening and grabbed hers. Laughing, he pulled her close to him by her hand and as if in a dance, quickly released her hand and grabbed her around the waist.

For a moment Miss Dee was dazed. She didn't believe what was happening, that his hands were tightening around her waist, her body being pressed against his. Tightly. She struggled to get out of his grip but his face was coming towards hers. The next moment their lips were pressed together. His tongue forcing his way into her mouth, her tongue pressing against gaps in his teeth.

He weakened temporarily as desire got the better of him and she found her strength, lifted her knee, came up with full force into his groin. He was taken off guard, doubling up in pain. She bent in a flash, took off her shoes and came down with the heel in his head. He screeched but she came down again and again as he stumbled around. Blood ran down his face and neck but his shock and confusion soon disappeared and he grabbed after her.

But she was running up the path screaming for her aunt.

'Bring the cutlass. Bring the cutlass. Come and chop up Leroy.' The practised rules of High school grammar discarded.

Leroy suddenly stopped chasing her, doubting now that he had seen Aunt Jane leave. 'Jesus Christ me dead. She chop me, she kill me.' Turning, he disappeared through the bushes.

Miss Dee stood for a moment collecting herself then, she picked up her bag, went back to the house, washed out her mouth and brushed her teeth. When she had finished, she washed and changed her clothes, picked up her bag and with a new resolve started back down the lane and for her shop.

Chapter 15

Ezekiel visited Vie full of the news that had spread through the District, that Miss Dee was all but giving her food away, planning to start a new business.

'I can't say I wasn't pleased of the boycott but now the pendulum swing another way and she taking not just her own customers but mine too.'

'But you talk like you have no sense,' Vie was saying. 'Is not you just say that she going to pack up the grocer business and turn to selling clothes, so in a few months you'll have all the customers you want. Just bide your time . . .'

He defended himself feebly outlining the need to protect his livelihood but faltering half-way, left that subject and was involved in more trivial banter when he spied Jane coming up the middle lane.

'I thought you said Jane don't come today.'

'I said nothing of the kind. I don't think you know what day of the week it is.' Vie squinted to try and make out the shape, couldn't but took his word for it. 'I'm as surprised as you are. I wasn't expecting her, she hasn't come up here in nearly a month.'

Ezekiel drained his cup and got up to leave. 'Where you going?' She gave him a slanted look. 'What is it with you and Jane why you two both can't sit in the same place together.' He mumbled something she couldn't make out and left.

They crossed along the path but didn't stop to talk.

Jane greeted Vie and sat down on the low-wall of the veran-dah. Vie studied her impenitent expression, wondering how it was that she could have maintained a friendship with Jane over the years. Yet Vie found herself searching in her mind for some-thing innocuous to say to break the unease that Jane brought.

Perhaps one of the keys to their uneasy friendship, Vie reflected, was her understanding and toleration of Jane's touchi-ness and secretive nature. She could have asked her over the years about her background, about what exactly it was that had brought her out of the blue to their District? Who her family were? Where they were? But she had restrained herself. Think-ing at first that Jane would fill the gaps when she was ready but twenty-eight years later nobody in the District was any the wiser. And in a place like theirs where it was crucial for it to be known who one's family were, Jane had put herself at a positive disadvantage by her unwillingness to fill in the past.

Vie got up suggesting that Jane made herself comfortable on one of the chairs instead of the wall but Jane did not move immediately until Vie returned with drinks.

'You went away for three weeks Jane?' Vie asked provoca-tively. Jane's retort was a cut eyes and an intolerant shrug of the shoulders. When Vie refused to fill the silence that awaited her reply, Jane rearranged herself in the chair. 'You know full well that I never went anywhere.'

'I know that. But what I don't understand is why you feel now you should come out of hiding . . . nothing has changed.'

'Listen Vie I don't come here to have you run up your mouth on me . . .'

'So why you come? I don't forget. People don't forget . . . I agree that Miss Dee was not to blame for what happened to Littleman but she must learn that in this District we have to take care of our one another.'

Jane put her glass down. 'Why you always feel that you the

spokesman for the whole of this District. You are not God . . . holding it all in your hands.' She raised her voice with the shrillness Vie found coarse and irritating.

'You're not in market now Jane, lower your voice.' It was as if Vie had risen to an invisible bait. Jane jumped out of her seat and in a voice that made her previous interjection seem now mild and controlled, she accused Vie of orchestrating a plot with everyone in the District to bring down herself and Miss Dee. Of being judge and jury, twisting everyone around her little finger.

Vie sat and listened without response until she felt Jane had expended all her energy, more worried about Jane's voice carrying to the neighbour's yard than about what she was actually saying. When she stopped for breath Vie said evenly, 'Jane why don't you just sit down and calm yourself.' Jane obeyed more it seemed through sheer exhaustion than obedience. Vie was not to be cowed by her silence, she unleashed likewise though in a calmer and more measured way. She did not support the boycott of the shop, she told Jane. But she understood why it had to be done. 'The District frustrated. They feel they needed to do something.' Jane made to speak, Vie stopped her with raised palm. 'Miss Dee could stop all the bad feelings, if she would lower herself a little and see Littleman . . . say she sorry she didn't try to help him when she could well have done. As her parent Jane, you should be able to influence her, get her to make things right. No amount of free food will raise her reputation, Jane. You must let her realise that. So she thinks she can use the District as bat and ball until she find something better, but tell her for me that wrong doings have a way of finding people out.'

'I'm not going to be your messenger,' Jane said refusing to be mollified.

'Well tell her I want to see her. Somebody has to tell her,' Vie insisted firmly. 'She cannot continue in the District when she thinks everybody owe her something. This goes well beyond what she did to Littleman.'

'I thought it was my fault,' Jane said sulkily.

Vie frowned. 'Jane I do put some of the blame on you, you let her get away with too much . . .' Vie softened her tone. 'You mustn't take all the blame. Miss Dee must know that in the long run she's only going to punish herself. People in this District with all their customs and ways have been here long before her and will be here long after.'

For the rest of the evening their conversation was stilted and Vie was glad when Jane left though she was unsure whether she would ever come back again. But she did. In the following week, Jane visited several times to talk, even helping Vie with her garden. At the end of the week she even took Vie's clothes to wash for her, careful not to have any of Littleman's in the pile.

On one of the visits, without her having planned to do so, Vie found herself talking to Jane about Azora, a hitherto prohibited subject. Even if Vie had wanted to pretend that her wall of suspicion had not been shaken, Azora had not allowed it. Over the weeks, though keeping her own distance as before, Azora had regularly waylaid the Maxton children as they played at the back or wandered on her property catapulting birds and lizards, sending little parcels with them for Vie; herbs to boil, oil to burn and even ground provisions from her fields. Vie laughed to herself when the latter came, she had never, since Leopold and Isadora had left, been so well provided for with food from the soil, between Azora and Littleman she had more than she could use.

When she had finished speaking, Jane looked at her for a long time, finally turning her gaze in the distance towards Ezekiel's pig-sty. Out on the road in front of the shop they could just about hear the voices of children. Perhaps tossing marbles, or playing cricket. In the Maxtons' yard the usual sounds of reprimands mingling discordantly with laughter and tears drifted towards them. Ragu in the yard on the other side was strumming on his banjo. Occasionally a truck or a taxi bumped its way over the stone road bringing people back from Town, just another normal Saturday evening.

'You know you're a born hypocrite,' Jane said dryly.

'How you mean?'

'You take Littleman over to the obeahwoman house. That no good, murdering woman.'

Vie frowned. 'You being a bit drastic. What you mean, murdering woman? No you tell me one time that she saved Miss Dee life? When since you start calling her murderer? I said, what you mean . . . ?' Vie insisted when Jane did not reply. Vie watched Jane's contorted silent face, deciding that Jane was demonstrating her jealous streak, her fear that she would be pushed out of Vie's friendship by Azora. There had been many challenges to their friendship over the years as Vie had drawn close to other special friends in the District. Ignoring Jane's dramatics she found herself defending the Azora she certainly still did not know, hardly able to believe it was her own tongue that had once pilloried her. 'Anyway there is nothing wrong in admitting it when you are wrong . . . admitting mistakes . . .' Vie concluded.

Jane pouted, ignoring her excuse. 'I never think I would see the day when you defending Azora.' Jane shook her head, openmouthed. 'I suppose the whole District now feel that since you sanction her, they can all go out in the open now . . . You're real hypocrite for true,' she repeated. Vie, unable to understand why Jane was taking it so personally, tried to make light of her new mind about Azora. But her animated too-youthful voice still hung around them reminding her of younger days when she had found a new best friend. 'Why are you so worried about what people will say? I don't see anybody would be interested . . . ,' Vie said.

'You know full well that nobody would criticise you . . .

They will just make the Azora more powerful now. God help us all.'

In the face of Jane's onslaught, Vie was anxious now to change the subject but Jane didn't seem in the mood to think or talk about anything else because try as Vie did, she could not get much else out of her and certainly nothing positive.

Chapter 16

Vie sat in the shade absentmindedly watching the men digging in unison; raising their hoes together, sinking them in the ground as one. Their digging songs of old with only one or two new impromptu verses, reminded her of Day's Work way back when *she* was young.

Day's Work was one of the traditions that hadn't died out, perhaps because it was the only way to get a lot of work done, be it the digging, planting or weeding of a new piece of land, or the working of an old, in one day, without the necessity of hiring paid labour. All the person holding it had to do was set the date, provide food and drinks and organise its preparation.

The day was looked forward to with great anticipation. For one there was the certainty of at least two good belly fulls on that day. There was the singing too, old time songs mingling with new ones; ones extolling the virtues of this or that person from the past, Beward, Garvey, Bustamante. Ones ridiculing others. Songs directing the movements of the hoe, bringing them up-to-date with most recent happenings in the District, ones prophesying the future. No other event it was felt afforded the camaraderie that Day's Work did; not christenings, Sunday school outings, migrations abroad, weddings or funerals. Because on that day, old scores were forgiven and settled, new ones forgotten, the ending of the day bringing a new start for everyone.

Ragu with his banjo, mouth organ and flutina provided the music and conducting. The children, glad for a Saturday with organised activities for them, fetched and carried in between play but mainly got in the way while those of them nearer adulthood than childhood prided themselves on their active part.

Vie remembered with nostalgia the day when she would be among the line of women behind the men planting or among those behind them covering the newly planted seeds.

Somewhere about midday, since they would have started well before sun-up, they were summoned for lunch and found places under various shaded areas to eat.

The amount and quality of the food provided on Day's Work won or destroyed the reputation of the provider. Today Mr Maxton's and Ruthlyn's reputations were enhanced; it was suggested that the food might even spoil but not seriously, since some of the women had brought empty pans and calabashes, just in case.

Well-fed, they were lulled by the early afternoon sun into catnaps as Ragu strummed out esoterically lewd tunes of the antics of Littleman and Miss Dee, Vie and Azora, encouraged by appreciative ripples of soporific laughter. On the rendition of his song, Vie watched Littleman's consternation as he sulked off to sit with the children; recovering from their own overindulgent unease they were sprawled out, too, away from the critical gaze of the adults.

Even though Miss Dee had refurbished her shop, had reopened selling clothes and was being patronised both by the District and surrounding ones, it was clear that all had not been forgotten and forgiven.

Ragu was still in full flow when everyone suddenly became quiet, even the children stopped teasing each other, one or two shouting out Miss Dee's name, half-sleep wiped from eyes, looks turned in the direction of one of the tracks leading to the field.

Jane, her swallowed pride evident even as she had carried out the cooking task she had volunteered to do, stood up and went to meet Miss Dee as she pushed her way through the last cluster of brambles.

'What happen?' she whispered anxiously. A Day's Work had never been graced by Miss Dee's presence before.

Miss Dee shook her head calmly and stood momentarily surveying the labourers, passing overtly critical eyes over adversaries such as Bellinda, Sibble, pausing at Leroy who, previously more soundly asleep than others, had felt the silence last. He woke with a start, caught in the confused limbo between dreams and wakefulness and finding her eyes on him dipped visibly, his hand on the scar she had made on his head. She cut her eyes, moved them on until she picked out Littleman in the distance.

In the pause that followed, one or two of the men unconsciously smacked appreciative lips, unruly eyes running over her body, its shape hardly hidden in their minds by her bright red slacks and frilly white lace blouse.

Miss Dee was serious, and Jane, no less so, resumed her seat, no more the wiser. Vie smiled, relieved that Dee had heeded the advice she had given her after the shop opening party.

'I've come to say sorry to you Littleman,' she began, her voice loud and clear, her eyes fixed on him. 'You don't deserve what happened to you in Town. You're a good man. I should have helped or at least not pretended it hadn't happened when I came back home. I *am* sorry.' Hardly giving time for the wind to carry her voice or for what she had said to sink in, Miss Dee inhaled deeply, as if taking her first breath after birth and left as she had come.

There was a stunned silence before anyone spoke and then they all spoke together, expressing surprise. Perhaps, some said, her heart was not like stone after all. Only one or two dissenting voices feeling her apology a ploy, a means to her own selfish end.

'That girl can't be trusted,' Sister Netta said, ignoring Jane's

126

frown. 'She's got too much of a prideful heart. But the higher we climb the harder we'll fall . . .'

'The girl come to say she's sorry,' Jane said, clearly fighting to restrain her temper, 'And you of all people, the big Deacon wife should be ready to forgive . . . it just goes to show what hypocrites . . .'

'No wonder the child come out so . . .' Sister Netta flared. 'If she really sorry, why she no wait and see if Littleman accept?' Sister Netta persisted. 'She can't mean it. She no mean it. She needs to repent on bended knees,' she insisted, looking around the group for support.

'She no care you mean,' Mrs Jerr, Bellinda's mother agreed. 'I knew from time that that girl was worthless,' then turning to Jane, echoing Sister Netta's words she shouted accusingly, 'A you raise her so.'

Jane stood up furiously. 'People in glass houses shouldn't throw stones. At least Miss Dee no go round opening her legs, trying to bear for every Tom, Dick and Harry.'

Mrs Jerr mouth dropped open, found Bellinda with a questioning look, finding no reply, searched for sympathy but got only shrugs and lowered heads. Jane resumed her seat in a heavy silence. Everyone no doubt wondering whether it was wise to risk another criticism of Miss Dee in her presence.

At that point, Littleman, whom they had all seemingly forgotten, cleared his throat, stood up and made his way to the centre. He glanced at Jane who cut her eyes at him and looked away. 'I do forgive Miss Dee. I did on the very day . . . weeks ago. So please let it drop. Please. For my sake.' The majority nodded but a few, Mrs Jerr, leading that camp, tutted and shook their heads.

'I believe Littleman is right. Let it all rest now.' Vie, who had purposely kept out before, said finally when Littleman had walked back across the field and taken up his hoe ready to lead

127

the afternoon shift back to work. 'Nobody have a grievance against Miss Dee save Littleman and we hear what he said.'

Towards evening, to the renewed surprise of everyone, Miss Dee returned. On seeing her, Leroy and Bellinda slipped away but she gave no indication that she noticed that or any other disapproving eyes. She spoke quietly to Jane, kissed Vie and touched Ragu on the arm before pulling up one of the stools next to them.

Ragu, encouraged by her presence and memories of when she was younger, tuned up the banjo and encouraged her several times, gibed her loudly until she capitulated and agreed to sing.

They had not heard her sing for years, had not felt that she was part of them even before she had been forced to stop by her aunt, had forgotten how good it had felt to hear her voice. To watch her, eyes closed, singing as if songs had been created for her. As she finished one, she was implored to do another, one of hers, one of theirs, until the sun was setting and they were packing up their tools.

Littleman almost wept when he was alone that night, more than the fact that she had said sorry to him was the fact that she had done it publicly and even more than all that was the way she had held his eyes and called him a good man.

Littleman did not ever believe that life could be so sweet as he felt it to be that moment. He closed his eyes and conjured up her face. Her body. So perfect to him. Her voice. He ran his hands down his body, gasped as he imagined it to be hers. He turned over on his stomach, buried his face in the pillow. Afraid that Vie might hear him. He saw her hands on his body, searching, seeking him out. He gasped as she found him. His heavy organ pulsated in her grasp. He laughed, beyond caring now, completely lost in the ecstasy that the touch of his hands, that were her hands, gave.

128

When at last he was expended, Littleman rolled over on his back, in wonder. At twenty-one, he had never so much as gone close enough to a woman to touch her. He was too afraid, worried by his obvious ignorance. He had not, like the other young men in the District, proved his manhood with children here and there to boast of, girlfriends to order.

Moving away from the damp patch on the sheet, he hated himself all of a sudden. Why hadn't he learnt at his age the right way of getting a woman's attention? The right combination of disdain and flattery, cynicism and disinterest that so succeeded with other men? When would he learn?

Chapter 17

Forty-nine years ago Vie had determined that no man would ever get the chance to humiliate her again as Nehemiah, her daughter's father had done. She had ridden the waves of loneliness, frustration and yearning to be married, matched only by the more lengthy periods of grim contentment when she had gloated that she was not like other women without the resolve to be alone.

Yet she had to fight. There had been times, too numerous to admit even to herself, when she would pass a house, with a man sprawled out on his verandah, resting after a hard day's work, his eyes thankfully closed. She would stand and watch him, eyeing every contour of his body. She imagined herself, stretched over him, covering his body with hers, taking without protest from him, all that she wanted. She would catch herself, be ashamed, hurry home, fighting to recapture her resolve.

When her mother had died and Eggsbury entered its terminal state, with migrations to town and other more hopeful districts, she too took her leave to Top Mountain. The only house available to her that was not Cleary's, was on Ezekiel's family land. At the time she had wondered at her wisdom in choosing to live on the land of a man who though engaged to be married in months had captivated her interest. But for nearly four decades she managed to resist the temptation of Ezekiel until nine years ago when for two years her body made wonderfully new and startling discoveries. But her guilt in keeping a married man could not survive more than the two years, it had seemed then.

Now, without Babydear to distract her, Vie was finding her body more and more riddled with tension, making her curse her foolhardiness seven years ago. What had it profited her now to have been so rash, to have dismissed Ezekiel, the only other man, though woefully late, she had known. She should have kept him, as he had begged, so that at times like now, when her body cried out for comfort and warmth, she could call on him. Why had she been so bothered about his wife? Why had she not been grateful that when aged fifty-nine she had learnt that desire knew no age. Why indeed had she not been warned when she was young that old age did not herald a quenching of desire?

Vie decided to visit Azora. She did not stop to think why.

Azora's three dogs were the first to spot her, they ran down the lane to meet her and Greystripe, frisked around until they brought Azora from behind the house. She approached with her usual controlled, almost reticent gait. Vie thought she spotted a wry smile on her face but it may have been surprise. 'Aunt Vie,' she said, her name the complete sentence she made it.

'Afternoon,' Vie greeted her, allowing Azora to help her down from her donkey, as if I'm her grandmother Vie thought.

Vie picked her way onto the verandah as Azora went to tie the donkey behind the house. Vie was finding that she liked the seclusion of Azora's yard. The road outside, named after herself, led to Guanobovale. The lane which came off that, led only to Azora's house and hidden as it was by a multiplicity of mature fruit trees and herbage, could not be seen from the road. And since only part of Cleary's seemingly forgotten acres, with its weather-beaten sign warning trespassers, bordered Azora's land, only those coming to consult her, mischievous or adventurous children and errant lovers ventured there.

Azora returned with a mug of drink, 'Some sorrel.'

'So early?' Vie said, making reference to the seasonal red drink.

'Christmas not far now, you know.'

Vie sipped looking around the yard for something to distract her. Something to talk about. She sensed that, unlike her, Azora was relaxed and at ease, did not seem bound to make conversation but her quiet made Vie suddenly feel the need to explain why she had come. But for the life of her she could not find an acceptable one.

'So you decided to take up my offer?' Azora said finally when Vie's discomfort was getting the better of her, her voice detached and professional.

'Oh yes,' Vie heard herself saying, wondering instead whether an apology for thirty years was in order before that could begin. She started but the twisted side of her mouth seemed to take over from the good side, affecting the smoothness of her speech. She was sure she was dribbling. She raised her bad hand to wipe the side of her mouth. It *was* damp. She stretched to put down the glass on the floor. Thankfully, Azora didn't rush to help her. Vie managed it without spilling. Azora got up then, 'Sorry. Let me get you a little table to make it easier.' She disappeared inside her spare room returning with it and placed it within reach of Vie.

'We can talk about what you want and when you want us to start.'

The way she was feeling, Vie would have wanted her to start there and then and why not? she thought. For almost forty years she had listened to others, being balm to them, now I want someone to do for me. But they arranged that she would begin the massage in a few days and after that was done there seemed little reason for Vie to stay, she drained her glass and made to leave. 'I'm sure you don't have to rush back. I was just about to put on some lunch. Stay and have some with me. I could do with the company.'

Vie looked fully at her surprised and glad for the offer. She didn't hesitate. 'All right. But let me help you,' she offered, wondering how Azora could so easily forgive her years maligning.

'No.' Azora smiled. 'But you can come behind the house with me and talk. You have hardly ever spoken to me without telling me off. I would like to know how it sounds. How it feels.' She extended her hand to help her up, as Babydear used to do. Once up, Vie was about to bend for her stick but Azora crooked her arm for her to thread her hands through. 'I don't know what I've done to make you think I bite.' Vie thought they must look an incongruous pair; two old women linked as they were, Azora though older, tall and erect, strong as one of her oversized mules, towering over her own crooked, frail form.

Chapter 18

Jane was waiting on the verandah when Vie eventually returned to her yard, her face contorted in an anger Vie could not understand, hardly returning Vie's lively greeting. Vie's spirit recently battered by Jane's mood swings, now enlivened by the surprise friendship that was growing with Azora, was not to be dampened, she took her time manoeuvering Greystripe behind the house to the small platform Littleman had built, dismounted and stood for a while basking in her light, fresh mood before making her way back to the verandah to join her. Life seemed for the time when she was with Azora to have pulled up a pace, Azora did not rush when she talked but handled her words as priceless gems, as if, in her words were the very unfolding of life. It was refreshing for Vie, to have someone listen to her, one who did not expect words of balm, wisdom or counsel from her. Azora was unlike any other woman she knew. Though old, in her mid-seventies, she did not appear so, indeed was ageless, Vie thought, conforming to none of the rules that Vie had thought inviolable for old people or even women. On reflection, Vie did not see her as either man or woman. She said as much to Azora who had been amused. 'Sometimes I wonder myself,' she had said with reflective gaze.

'But you and me are not very different you know Vie. Neither of us is like a normal type of woman.'

'So where you been?' Jane said, confrontation strong in her voice.

Vie now composed, said without recognisable emotion, 'I went round to Azora.' Without comment, Jane jumped up and went to the kitchen. Vie was amused by her expression and the suddenness of her movement and, though she was puzzled, she wasn't about to push her. Jane's secretiveness, she decided, would backfire on her tonight. It was getting towards evening so Vie went into the bedrooms in the meantime to check that the lamps had sufficient kerosene oil in them, found a mosquito coil and placed it on the verandah floor ready to light later on. The crickets sounded their discordant chorus, cocks bade good evening in the distance and one or two unintelligible conversations drifted towards them from the neighbours' yard. Her own yard was quiet, Littleman having taken the dogs with him to Eggsbury and her own usually riotous chickens were being kept for the time being in their coop to protect them from a particularly daring mongoose that had been plaguing that part of the District. There was definitely a Christmas chill in the air and Vie decided that she could not delay unlocking one of her trunks later on to get out the blankets for herself, and if he needed it, one for Littleman too, and one of the cardigans Isadora had sent from England, to wear in the evenings.

'So why you go and see Azora?' Jane said impassively, returning with only one cup of tea.

'To talk.'

'Talk? Talk? When did you ever have anything to talk to that woman about?'

Vie paused, then retorted calmly, 'Jane when did I ever have to explain my actions to you?'

Jane seemed to turn the answer around in her head. 'You doing some strange things since Babydear left,' she accused finally.

Vie laughed. 'Like what so?'

'You know more than me.'

Vie waited for her to say more but she didn't, Jane fixed her mouth instead in a tight knot.

Vie left her and went to make her own tea thinking she would rather spend her evening alone or in the blind gaze of Ragu, the thunderous verandah of the Maxtons or even with Ezekiel surrounded by the knowing eyes of his wife than with a permanently bad-tempered person like Jane. When she returned Jane was ready for her, 'You can't live here so and not see men creeping past at night, leave them wife and . . .'

'How you know so much?' Vie said irritably, more in annoyance of Jane's unwillingness to stop her barrage of half-expressed criticisms, only partially comprehensible to Vie. 'Why is it bothering you so? The road out there, doesn't just lead to Azora's house you know. You live in the back of beyond and can see what going on up at this part of the District? That must be a miracle itself. Or did she work some obeah on you to give you extra vision?' Vie added provocatively.

Jane took a deep breath, her eyes bulging in her bony face. 'I hear things.'

They didn't speak for some time, Vie wanting her to go but not able to speak her mind then. Despite her irritation with Jane, as always there was a stronger residue of sympathy, of desire to erase what she could of her friend's entrenched inarticulated pains.

'Anyway,' Jane was saying, 'There is a lot you don't know about Azora . . . A lot you don't know about her and Cleary.'

Vie frowned. 'What you saying now?' She asked with fading patience.

'Azora is a hard, devious and cruel woman. She's not like other women.'

'Jane,' Vie said, her new found confidence in Azora wavering slightly, 'I wish you would stop talking in riddles.'

Without warning Jane lost her temper, 'I didn't think I'd have to tell you this because I thought you had sense, but take my advice keep away from that woman.' And she was up and away down the lane. Vie sighed heavily, Jane was getting more tiresome by the day. Why had she not thought of telling her to stop behaving like a spoilt selfish child.

Vie's feeling of well-being gone, she decided to have a lie down when she heard Ezekiel call to her from the back lane. He was the last person she wanted to see. The look in his eyes when he appeared told Vie that he came to beg again as he had done periodically over the past seven years. Her impatience extended to him too. In cutting tones she dismissed him and went into her room, only to feel guilty and a little sad as she heard him retrace secret steps. What with Jane, Ezekiel and the permanent longing for Babydear, Vie wondered when respite would come.

Perhaps, she thought, taking to her bed, if I took up with Ezekiel again I would at least have some comfort in my last few years. She called on the memory of their two secret years but found no joy.

Her relationship with him had began unexpectedly a year after her daughter Isadora had left for England. It was 1959, in her own fifty-ninth year, nearly forty years since she had found how easy it was for pleasure to turn to pain and promises to falsehood, forty years since she had first felt the hands of a man on her body. Each hand that did not belong to distant bodies reclining on verandahs, was to her the lying, cynical touch of Nehemiah which years of scrubbing had not erased from her body. But at the Maxtons' wedding and for months afterwards those thoughts hardly surfaced and played no part in her behaviour. As always at weddings, her emotions were at a peak, the march down the aisle to the sound of Ragu's banjo causing her almost to hyperventilate, the recitation of the vows bringing tears to her eyes, not because like others, she was touched by them but because it affirmed yet again that the years had slipped

137

by and she was still not like those normal women, and being unsure whether she wanted to be like them or not did not help.

It may have been that search to know for certain, but it was more out of a new type of anger, frustration with her lot, nostalgia or simple madness but somehow Vie forced herself to see Ezekiel Samuel in a new light that night. Gone was the irritation that had characterised her dealings with him, beginning when she had come to the District and found him engaged and soon after married when perhaps aware of her controlled interest in him, he had tried to steal away from his new wife, making promises instead to her. He was not to know that Vie had had her life-time of promises, or that she would go to his wife and tell her of the suggestions he had made to her. And how was Vie to know that Dora would not accept her innocence but hold her from that day as a threat to her marriage and her life? And none of them was to know so many decades later, Ezekiel would be doing what Vie had so viciously spurned and his wife had so feared.

There were lots of other men at the wedding, many available to Vie but she concerned herself only with Ezekiel, aware of his presence the moment he had walked in the coconut bough marquee balancing glasses of rum on a tray.

When he danced with his wife Dora her eyes were on him. And to her amazement, he found her eyes as he wound round the tables. Towards the end of the evening, across the dimly lit tent, between the gyrating bodies, they flirted shamelessly with each other.

Not that Vie did not remember Dora. She did. Dora was still lovely, much lovelier than she, her face having not yet consolidated the sour and aggrieved look that had since become her trademark. Or the anger that resulted from the slow realisation that her husband had not been totally her own over the years.

During the reception, Vie went outside a few times and returned some moments later making sure that Ezekiel saw her

138

leave, hoping that he would follow her eventually. He did, at first just brushing past her and whispering in her ears, words that she would normally have spurned were sweet to her and when eventually they jived together her decision was set in stone. At fifty-eight, she thought, it may well be her last time to find out if there was a difference between men. If they were all, as she had suspected, all those years, like Nehemiah.

In the week following the wedding, she went to his shop every day until she found Dora absent. She had gone not really knowing what to expect, yet in her heart of hearts she did not think anything could happen, what with the open shop and the constant coming and going of customers. She had sat on the verandah at the back of the house as Ezekiel alternated talking to her with serving. Then without warning, as if stricken by her madness, he had shut the shop, putting a sign on it saying that he would be back in an hour. When he told her what he had done she remembered her sudden burst of sweet, nervous laughter. What could they do that would take an hour she had said, her coyness belying her years. In the heat of it all, his panting, her suffocation, she had imagined all the time his wife or one of his children from town stumbling in on them, or customers not heeding the note but coming round to insist that they be served. In reality, lost as she was, she heard puzzled voices, queries, curses but had no choice but to ignore them, engrossed as they were in her belated second taste of passion.

After that for nearly two years, they found time for each other. She often boasted to herself that theirs was the only affair that had gone on in the District for that length of time unnoticed. But somehow she suspected that Dora knew. As their affair continued, Dora seemed to get more sour, more drawn and twisted. But she said nothing and did nothing and that so incensed Vie that she became more determined to go on. Losing respect for a woman who would put up with it.

Sometimes her conscience would play havoc with her but she

coaxed it into submission. The relationship was ideal for her. At her age, there could be no possibility of unwanted children. She could be with him when she wanted without any commitment, without having to wash and cook for him. Take orders from him. Without waking up to find him next to her when she had no further use for him, or her having to submerge her wishes under his as wives had to do. But then without warning he had turned foolish and tried to demand that she took unnecessary risks, allow him to stay the whole night, when his house was only a stone's throw from her own, when her grandchildren slept in the adjoining room, threatening to tell his wife about them, claiming that what they did was not unusual. For how could a man, he demanded, be expected to stay with just the one woman all his life? But worse, he began making seemingly innocuous comparisons between Dora and herself in the District, calling on Vie at times when they had not arranged, displaying habits in front of her that only wives should have to tolerate; breaking wind, picking his teeth and even his nose, had even once used one of her nail files to dig encrusted wax from his ears.

So she decided that he was disturbing her life but even when she had been breaking the news to him, that she was not happy with him anymore, that their relationship had to end, she had not worked out how she would stand it. What she would do without him now that she had found that there were differences between men, but she had gritted her teeth and insisted, even when he begged her with swollen tear-filled eyes, even promising to leave Dora, and more besides . . .

Chapter 19

Over the years, Jane had grown to hate Azora and only next to her Cleary Junior. It still astonished her how fresh and new her hate remained. As she walked home from Vie's, the fury of it rose uncontrollably, convulsing her. So, Azora was now trying to take her best friend away after what she had helped the Clearys to do to her.

Not long after she had moved to the District, Jane had started to hear rumours about both the Clearys and Azora, especially from Vie. At first Jane had taken Vie's words that Azora's activities were dishonourable. She saw for herself what the Clearys were like but she overrode that and managed not long after she had arrived to get them to sell her land. Jane knew that it was part of that family's ploy to undermine those who had always lived in the District, selling land to someone new when others there long before her had all but begged in blood to do the same. She could not complain whatever their reason, although she knew it did not recommend her to the District.

So far as Azora was concerned, Jane only changed the views she had been given of her when in desperation she had taken Miss Dee to her and Azora had so miraculously cured her. Jane had been grateful but more than that it had dawned on her that Azora was her last hope. Finding excuses afterwards to go to her for this or that complaint, it nevertheless took her some time to muster the courage to ask Azora for a cure for her barrenness.

Azora was able but where could Jane find the man? Even Azora could not enable her to produce a child alone.

Knowing that time was slipping away, only six years before she reached her half-century, Jane looked around the District earnestly. But no man returned her look and if they did their's was peppered with ridicule. Cruelly the women labelled her a eunuch and rumours multiplied that she was not a normal woman, capable of giving or receiving from a man. For if she were, where was the man and where were her children?

As Jane walked home in the descending darkness, she drew to her that empty and lost feeling that seemed to have characterised her life. The culminated pain, the consequence of the wounding words thrown at her over the years; even before she came to live in Top Mountain, she had been branded a failed woman, a shell masquerading as a woman; brought a new desperation and anger she had thought was abating. From that innocent throw-away word of a neighbour way back, that she was taking long to prove she was a woman, when her sister was having babies and she showed no sign, to being ridiculed and labelled now; mule, barren, dried-up womb. Tears suddenly sprang to her eyes and burnt their way down her cheeks as all the hurt of her life combined in memory of how nearly that might have changed. She kicked a stone in disgust just as someone suddenly came out of the darkness towards her. Leroy greeted her.

She strutted past him without a word. Each house she passed with its dimly lit lanterns, radiated cosy security, the light-hearted chatter, occasional burst of laughter, shrill voices of contented, happy children, accentuated her own dire plight. In the distance, from where she stood, it seemed the picture of idyll. She caught glimpses of men; pottering, getting ready to turn in with his partner. Another sprawled out on a verandah, one just returning home. She always found herself looking at men. More and more desperately as the years had gone by,

142

unsure as to whether it was from inside her that the hunger came or from something expected outside.

After Ricardo, the one who, though fumbling, had given her the first taste of love and the possibility of the prized children, there had been a long period of drought because after him, she could not believe that men were sane. Now as she neared home, the memory of him suddenly and surprisingly changed her mood, bringing a foreign smile to her face; the peacock, she had nicknamed him because of the way he had constantly preened himself, finding broken panes of glass, mirrors, to peer into. She had even once caught him looking at himself through the back of a spoon. Now from the distance of time she was amused how he had constantly compared his looks with hers, boasted of past conquests, of the women who were lining up to be with him, by his talk of his sexual prowess, never quite tallying with her own experiences of him.

The luxury of amusement she now afforded herself contrasting with the time with him when she had lost the will to smile. Even that time when they had crept underneath her house he, in character, having wasted no time in pulling her frock over her head, almost suffocating her, oblivious and uncaring of what she was feeling, unconcerned of the parts above her navel, had not amused her. Her dog, Daisy, hearing the commotion, had come to investigate, and finding a scent he did not recognise suffocating his mistress, had sunk his teeth into Ricardo's bottom. Luckily, they were the only ones in the yard and his cries had gone unheard. That was the last time he came to her.

Amos came after him, the one who for some glorious months was more vital to her existence than food and air. She was just over twenty, apart from the church girls, the only girl in her District who was not pregnant or had a child by that age. Previously some had suggested that she was too ugly to get a man, conveniently ignoring the rumours that Ricardo had spread about having been her first.

Now, she made sure that they saw her with Amos, that they knew they were a pair, ignoring the cries that she was not pretty enough for him, the best looking boy in the District. When it could not be denied that they were together, it was said that he only wanted her for what she had, that being the land and house her father had died and left for her sister, brother and herself. She had dismissed all that convinced of his true devotion. But it wasn't long before they were proved right. Subtly at first and then more overtly, he started to put pressure on her to sell her share to her siblings. One day when they were in town, he even picked out the bicycle, clothes and shoes he would buy with his share when she finally did. His share! She was devastated. Not once did he even mention marriage to legitimise his claim. She decided that what was needed was her pregnancy, he would want to see sign that she would not later cast doubt on his manhood. So she relented, took back the vow that she had made to herself that marriage had to come before the first child.

Her brother left for America, her sister by now with her own three children, married the father of two of them taking over all but one room in the house their father had left. She resented being pushed into the corner of the house that was supposed to be one-third hers so she asked Amos to move in. He needed no encouragement. Their relationship deteriorated as soon as he did, becoming even more of a cat and mouse game than before, with his unrelenting plea for her to sell, her unremitting hints for him to propose. She came perilously close several times to telling him what her conditions were for selling but she stopped herself, knowing that to be tantamount to proposing to him herself. Something unthinkable, that was bound to come out and haunt her in the future. So as much as she would have given her life for his offer of marriage, she bit her lip and waited for the growing belly that she suspected would be the sign he needed to do it himself. But the more she resisted him, the more obsessed he got with the idea and the more it dominated their relationship.

Whether out of frustration at her stubbornness or anger that she refused to breed, as he increasingly put it, he started being cruel to her; calling her names that strangely would be repeated in another time in another district from different mouths, flaunting his relationship with other women in front of her. One day he even threatened to hit her. She had somehow found the strength to make it clear to him that the day he did would be his last.

He didn't seem to believe her, and soon after that, during an outburst of recriminations, starting with his accusations that either she was purposely stopping herself from getting pregnant or that she was a mule, he raised his hand to hit her. That he did not manage to was irrelevant to her, she rushed out of the room and grabbed the machette kept in the kitchen. It was only the strength of her sister and her husband that saved him. He moved out sensing that she had been deadly serious. But her temper failed to cool and was further aggravated by his daily pilgrimage past her house, a different woman, it seemed, in tow each day. Then the rumours began that he had fathered a child some-where in the District when they had still been together, rivalled by others that he had not one but several children scattered around. It pained her and she tried to stop searching for news about him, stopped subtly delving for reasons to hate him more and increase her own pain. But he himself seemed to find her as she went about her business, delivering clothes she had sewn in the District, in town, shopping for materials, or purposely as he took detours past her house, ridiculing her in many ways, but mostly because she had no womb, he said, because she was not a normal woman.

Each night she willed him dead. When that failed to work she did what he had wanted, she made plans to sell her inheritance. Her sister paid her part first. The day the postal order came from her brother, she changed it, hid some in her room and went to an obeahman out of the District with the rest, having little doubt that the item of clothing she had missed when she had flung his clothes after him that day, would be enough. She returned from her mission, packed her straw bag and waited.

She did not have to wait long, less than a week later Amos got involved in a fight with a stranger to the District. In the struggle with a machette, Amos's arm was dismembered. Jane went like everybody else in the District and saw it for herself, the broad hand that was certainly his, lying caked in blood, half-covered in dirt, witnessed the trail of blood that followed him as he ran stunned with fright and disbelief around the District until he had finally collapsed, senseless. He didn't survive it, not ever having had a tetanus jab and with the delay in getting him to hospital in town, he died soon after. On hearing the news she had expected, she left, headed for Top Mountain, a name she had only heard in passing from market women in town. She had been only twenty-five then and for the next eighteen years she avoided men, frightened that she could not trust herself when, as was inevitable, they wronged her.

Somehow, that story, twisted and changed, had made its way to the District and she knew that they had whispered about it, used it as one of their reasons to mistrust and dislike her even though no one had bothered to ask her about it, about her side, not even Vie.

Jane arrived home and sat in her darkened room. When Azora had saved Miss Dee and she had found herself hopelessly drawn to her miraculous possibilities, she had agonised for weeks about giving in again to another man, assuming she would find him. But at that impossible age of forty-four, in 1959, a chance meeting with John Cleary Junior in town, gave her the opportunity she knew would be her last.

It had been easy to find an excuse to see him after that. She would make arrangements to meet him at his house in Eggsbury as she had done when she had negotiated the purchase of her first acres of land, under the auspices of buying more. Eventually he started to invite her to visit him there when he was alone. She knew she was not the type of which the family's concubines were made but her determination outweighed past history. Months later as familiarity grew and even though she sensed a relief in him, that she did not come to him in hope for a share in what he had or that she did not hate his family as the Districts he owned did, there was no sign that he would progress beyond that. She realised that if anything was going to happen, she would have to take the initiative. That she did. And she was not rejected, as she had sometimes feared she would be.

On the day she chose, knowing that his son Jacob would not be coming to Eggsbury with him, and knowing his habits, she waited for him on his verandah. He had been in one of the outhouses for what seemed ages, the needs of her body taking over completely in that time. She got up uncertain even then of what she intended to do, eventually fastening her eyes on one of the doors leading off the verandah. Not knowing what overcame her, she pushed it open. The splendour and quiet order of everything in it made her blink. She took a step back and would have closed the door if she had not heard his footsteps coming from behind the house. She went quickly into the room and shut the door behind her. Once she had done that, she didn't know what she was going to do. How was she going to explain what she was doing in his room? But rather than frame an excuse, she started to undress.

She heard him on the verandah when she had removed all but her brassiere and pants. She spun around the room then not quite sure whether to rush under the bed and hide, taking all her clothes with her or to pretend that she had suddenly gone stark raving mad. She could hear his questioning footsteps, going back down the steps of the verandah and behind the house. She

147

imagined he thought she had gone the other way to find him. She ran then to the door and flung it open, rushed back and jumped on his bed. It was only when she was lying there that she felt foolish but by then it was too late, all she could do was wait as she heard his returning footsteps.

When he entered the room and saw her, as she was, sprawled out in semi-nakedness on his bed, his face was as it always was. Slightly disdainful and unperturbed. For one second she wanted to laugh aloud. To be him, watching her. To laugh at her until she got up and ran from his room in shame.

Then for an awful moment she imagined that he was going to tell her to get up and get dressed. Leaving the room as she did so, afterwards casually asking her not to enter his property again, then watching her leave, the vacant expressionless look still on his face. But worse than that his spreading it among his chosen concubines, burying her further under the shame of her already tarnished reputation.

Suddenly, she didn't know what to do. She felt stripped, exposed. She saw herself, her dark, bony body, the stubborn red dirt of their District caked in crevices all over her, her tie-head slipping, only now partially covering her uncombed hair. She hated herself, and a self-revulsion she had hitherto never experienced welled up from the pit of her stomach.

'But Miss Jane,' he was saying, his voice not as authoritative and calm as was usual, 'What are you doing in my bed?' He held his ground, his eyes steady on her face. Her body burnt. She found herself shifting backwards on the bed unable to find her voice. His eyes drifted over her body. Too slowly, she thought. But when their eyes finally locked, she relaxed a little, until he spoke, 'All right Miss Jane,' he said, a puzzling smile fully in his eyes.

'I . . . I . . .' but before she could decide what she wanted to say, he was lying next to her, his lips pressing down on her face.

When she got home that night, a confusion of self-reproach

and elation engulfed her. She didn't know which to harbour, which to encourage.

Eventually with great difficulty, she erased her seduction from her mind, harbouring only thoughts of those moments enclosed between his affluent walls, the smell of perfumed, town soap on his body, determined that this novelty, her mission, would eradicate too the memory of his abrupt touch, the single-mindedness that had characterised the few minutes his body had pressed down onto hers and the silence that should have been gentle words breathed in her ears.

As months passed although he was a gentleman, John Cleary Junior showed no sign of becoming as intoxicated with her as she became with him but he did not refuse her. He worked out with her times when she could go to him without fear of being discovered and Jane basked as much in the surreptitiousness of their meeting as in its essence. But at the forefront of her mind there remained the panic that time was running out for her. Yet, despite his own steadfast aloofness and distance, she did not want to lose the sweetness that she found with him.

She sometimes watched him by the faint light of the full moon stealing into his room. She didn't know what a fifty-nine-year-old man was supposed to look like, but certainly not like him, she thought. Unlike some town men, his stomach was flat, his back, the part of him she liked best was firm and taut. His legs, solid, like someone who had played cricket for years and had spent a lot of time standing up fielding, his skin though pale and seemingly unfinished, was certainly the smoothest she'd seen or felt on a man. She wished him permanently hers so that she could have, at will, his large hands exploring her body and hers his. But though intoxicated, she was not a fool. She did not need to be told that she was a diversion forced on him, until he tired of it.

With mixed feelings and unbeknown to Cleary, she went to Azora for the tonic that Azora had claimed would cure Jane's barrenness. Azora would not tell her all that was in the liquid she prepared, only that among the things she had boiled together were wild yam, ginger, raspberry leaves and other ingredients she said would mean nothing to her. She was to take a cupful three times a day. 'Just before your fruitful time and until your next issue come,' she instructed, explaining in the meantime how a woman could work out when she was ovulating. 'She should make sure she goes to her partner then.' Jane was amazed at Azora's confidence and allowed her own doubts to be subdued, focusing instead on her new knowledge that such few days could bring such havoc or such immense joy. 'It's a pity you don't have anything that could stop it for the women who've had their share.'

'There is something for everything,' Azora assured her.

Away from Cleary, she sat about working out the dates as she had suggested and took the advice to go to her partner. As she fumbled with her calendar each month and sought Cleary out she felt dangerously wild. In the first month she went to him every night for a week, hiring taxis from Top Mountain to his bachelor house in Spanish Town. She even went to his family house in Kingston once or twice, leaving Miss Dee with Vie, claiming once there to be nurse to his ailing father, Cleary having ensured that Jacob who knew her was well out of the way. She knew why she basked so entirely in their relationship, why she took such risks. She did not know, or really care, why he did.

Six months after she had started taking the medication, when her greatest will to keep faith was flagging, and after Azora had increased the consistency threefold, she found herself pregnant. When the nurse in the clinic in Kitson Town told her what she had known but had dared not admit, she sat limp, unable to move. The nurse, assuming that she was another who already had her fair share of children at home and didn't know how she was going to go home and say that yet another was on the way,

150

tried to pacify. Jane came back to her senses, sprang up and kissed her, grabbed her by the waist and waltzed around the room with her. She finally left in a taxi she had got the receptionist to call, feeling suddenly delicate, panicked by the thought of doing something to dislodge her baby. The precious, fruitful womb that was not after all a mule's.

When she got home she stopped herself several times sending Miss Dee to summon Azora to hold and kiss her. She felt she owed her more than she did John Cleary Junior.

A week later, on their usual day, she set out to meet Cleary. He was at his house in Top Mountain and it was the first time she would risk seeing him here. Miss Dee was fast asleep. She took the long way round, left out of her lane, through Old Road, up behind Top Mountain and past Azora's property. She would be turning left just past one of the tracks leading to Vie's house and up beside Ragu's house. She could hardly stop her face smiling. They had been together just over eighteen months and what now kept going through her mind was all the time she had wasted. If only she had met Azora in her youth, as soon as she had come to Top Mountain. She might have had the four or five children she wanted.

She sat in the cool of Cleary's air-conditioned house that night, an uncontrollable mixture of nerves and elation. She felt she had to tell him, thank him then bid him goodbye. The following day she planned to pass by Azora and get medicine to strengthen her womb, careful as usual not to disclose who it was had fathered the child Azora had given her.

She ate with Cleary that night, a second dinner, as she sometimes did, one hand on his lap the other holding the spoon. He was uncharacteristically light-hearted and playful that night too. Occasionally she fed him food from her plate and nibbled his ears in between mouthfuls. He said he liked her in that mood and was glad she was happy.

Now pregnant, having tricked and used him, she did not

151

know what would come of their relationship. It suddenly dawned on her that he may be angry. But although she couldn't quite see it, his anger in the past had always been feeble and short-lived, she wanted to choose the right moment.

They finished eating and as she cleared away and washed up, he said out of the blue, 'The thing I really like about you Jane is that you don't ask me for anything.'

'But you don't give me a chance to, you always giving me things,' she said looking at him.

'That's because I want to. You don't force me to give you anything. You're not after anything, you don't come cap in hand, mouth open.'

He was surprisingly generous. He gave expensive, exquisite fabrics that she would transform into equally beautiful dresses. In the past her best designs had been for others, never for herself. With him she pampered herself, excelling and glowing as he praised her talent, suggested she took work from town where she could display them and not restrict herself to the sameness of Top Mountain. Occasionally he would even buy her a ready-made dress, often too young for her but he would have her wear it, keep them in a trunk at his house and she would dress up when she visited. She would dress for dinner in unfamiliar nylon stockings, satin and silk dresses, fine mesh hairnets.

Reflecting on all that she said, 'John, I love everything that we have had.' He kissed her on the mouth, a gesture that had come late in the affair, and somehow that night she could not bring herself to tell him that he had helped her to give her the best gift ever.

But as the weeks passed, even though the size she swore had altered little, people in the District kept commenting on how well she looked. It frightened her, she knew that it would only be a matter of time before her waistline grew beyond the secret. Cleary, too, commented on her looks. She credited the tonics she told him Azora had given her. He surprised her by saying that his family too were some of Azora's customers, as were many of their town friends. Jane told him how surprised she was. 'Azora is a business woman,' he said with what Jane thought was a little malice. 'She dispenses tonics and medicines for even wicked, hateful property owners like the Clearys.' He had never made reference to his relationship with the District before and his comments made Jane uneasy. But he smiled. 'I cannot go a day without her strength-giving tonics and my father I'm sure would not have lasted so long without her,' he said. Jane did not need it but his sanctioning of Azora raised the herbalist in her own inflated estimation.

Around her third month, Dora especially would constantly say, '. . . nobody can call you, *dry up womb* again, girl, you really looking well, what happening to you? If I didn't know any better I would say you expecting.' She laughed loudly and for a long time. 'In fact,' Dora continued, when she had collected herself, 'Sister Netta said the other day if the Bible did say there would be two Marys and two immaculate conceptions, you would be the second Mary . . .' Hardly able to finish her sentence as more raucous laughter impeded, '. . . So many people come to the shop and say something like that,' she said punctuating her laughter.

Jane was furious. She couldn't laugh with her friend who suddenly became upset that she had hurt her. 'Jane it's only a joke. You know as well as I do that you couldn't be pregnant. But look at yourself in the glass girl, you looking like any young girl. And it's not just now, a long time people saying so. You no notice that the women keeping a close eye on their men. They don't want you to catch their eyes.'

Jane left her that day and went to Vie. She didn't know what she wanted Vie to say, all she knew was that the unhappiness of having to hide the unhideable was getting to her. Vie, in her usual honest diplomatic way smiled. 'I didn't want to say anything, but Jane, if it wasn't you I would put my head on the gallows and say you pregnant for true.'

Days later she saw Cleary, she noticed immediately that he was not his usual self but serious, hardly responding to her hug. Her heart leapt. She could have sworn she felt the baby's first kick. 'Why have you lied to me Jane?' She caught her breath and lowered herself next to him on the verandah. It was on the tip of her tongue to feign ignorance but she saw a deep seriousness in his eyes that she feared she should not trifle with.

'How did you find out?' She said returning his stare.

'So it's true?'

She nodded. He got up and fingered his lips. 'Is it my baby?' She was furious at the inference but she said simply, 'Yes', her palms resting on the small mound of her womb. He turned and looked at her for a long time without speaking. When he did finally, she felt sorry for him. 'You shouldn't have done that Jane. It's not right. And I thought all this time you were different from those other common country women.' His turn of phrase annoyed her immensely but she kept her temper. 'Lots of them claim they have my children.' He grunted, 'As if I told them I wanted children from them. I really thought you were different.'

Jane felt no hurt, the love that had grown for him could easily be subsumed under the joy of her fertile womb. 'I'm sorry John but it's happened now and I'm going to have the baby.' She stood up, not wanting to get angry with him or see the changed look on his face. 'I won't tell anyone it's yours. I'll just stop coming.'

He sighed deeply, 'But what about me? I love you Jane. You are the first country woman I've loved.' Jane looked at him unconvinced. She wondered when he had last said those words and to which light-headed young girl. She could not tell him that if she had to choose between him and the child inside her, as much as there was no choice, she would chose her baby.

A few days later, he turned up at her house, seemingly with a change of heart, happy for her, with promises to ensure that

154

neither her or her child would want for anything. Already Jane had dismissed him from her heart and saw his offer as superfluous. But she did not dismiss him from the yard. She sent Miss Dee to her room, invited him to sit on the verandah, made him drinks and chatted with him. He was repentant for his initial disapproval of her pregnancy, indulged in jovial chatter about who the baby would look like and how the District would take her news. She thought he might be looking for assurances that she would not divulge his role so she repeated it, reassured him, thanked him, as a child would do an adult for a desired gift. He said she did not need to thank him, said he was delighted he had made her happy, knelt by her chair, played with her stomach, kissed it through her seersucker dress and held her hands more tenderly than he had done in the months that they had been lovers.

Before he left he told her that he had got one of his own favourite bottles of tonics from Azora that he wanted her to take. Jane was touched by his thoughtfulness but anxious to hear what exactly he had told Azora. She did not want even Azora to know that he was the father. 'Nothing about you. She thinks she has given me tonic for a pregnant friend in town. Take it. It will keep your strength up through the months.' She thanked him only then feeling a wave of sadness. He bent and kissed her, brushed his fingers across her cheeks. 'Bye,' he said but not, see you tomorrow or later in the week, as he would do before.

'Thank you,' she said, 'Sorry. But thank you. Thank you very much.'

It was a week before her own bottle of tonic finished and she started on the new one. Taking Azora's medicine was like a calendar to her. She decided that night to finish the bottle then break the news to Vie first and then Dora and watch it spread through the District. She couldn't wait.

A day after the first three doses, the diarrhoea began. She imagined it to be the mangoes she had started to crave and had been eating incessantly so she gave them up but a day after her stomach was still ripped apart with pain and she lived in the toilet. Miss Dee got worried and suggested that she went for Azora but just when she would have done, the pain and diarrhoea stopped altogether. There followed a day when she was weak and nauseous but she did not panic until she started vomiting and she saw spotting of blood on her underwear. She took to her bed. She couldn't keep anything down but stuck to her tonic to replace what she was losing.

When she finished the bottle at the end of the week, the bleeding increased. Only then did she start to panic. She sent for Azora but she was away, then for Vie who immediately sent to Kitson Town for the doctor. Before the doctor arrived, she told Vie that she was expecting but wouldn't tell her who for. The corners of Vie's mouth turned up knowingly before she reprimanded 'I don't know why you never say. You needed care, especially because you just opening you womb and you getting on in age. What you hide it for? What wrong with you?' Jane listened too weak to argue.

'Just don't say anything to anybody. They won't believe you until my baby born anyway.' Vie shook her head.

By the time the doctor came, Vie had had to change the sheets twice and Jane had sensed by then that it was too late. Vie could not comfort her.

When the doctor confirmed that she had lost the baby and put her in his taxi for the hospital in town, her screams drowned the noise of the engine as it thundered through the District passing the groups of people who had heard that Jane was bleeding to death and even the big doctor from town could not say why.

Chapter 20

Miss Dee sat in her shop alone, basking in the peace and calm before the school children charged into the District from Paul Mountain, littering the road with their games and quarrels, causing mischief to people's fruit trees and teasing their paper teeth dogs.

When she saw Leroy approaching the door, her heart somersaulted. She had not come face to face with him since the incident in her lane. She braced herself, regretting having sent Rose-marie to town earlier and telling her to go straight home afterwards. But Leroy's appearance tickled her and momentarily she lost her unease. His trousers knocked around his ankles, his shirt, half in and half out clearly tight for him. The colour and style well past their day.

She decided not to say anything but continue with her work. He came in and made a big show of looking around, appearing relaxed, but through the corner of her eye, Miss Dee surmised, distracted. Finally, eyes skittish, hands not knowing quite where to position themselves, he spoke as if to somebody he had not met before, 'I looking for a pants length.' It crossed Miss Dee's mind that perhaps if he did something with his time like the other men in the District he might be able to afford a pants length but she knew he could not. 'How much do you want to spend?' she said, desperate to hide the disdain in her voice. 'The price no matter so long as it's the best you have.'

'Show me your money,' she said suddenly, surprising herself. He sprung round. 'You don't ask other people to show you money first, why you no just treat me like any other customer?' She resisted the temptation to tell him. But all of a sudden he seemed to change his mind about the pants and strolled over to the stool on which she sat hemming a dress Jane had sewed. Now there was no counter to separate her from her customers she felt at his mercy, for a minute she regretted emulating this new idea; women's fabrics and samples of pants lengths folded neatly in glass cabinets on one side of the shop with dresses hanging on rails that Ragu had built for her as he had done the drawers that contained underwear, shirts, blouses and other accessories, and the stool she was sitting on.

Leroy eyed her sceptically without speaking. She wanted to move away, but unable to do so without touching him, she stayed. He seemed then to have second thoughts, backed off but as he did so spat his words at her, 'Girls like you are like never learn. You would think you of all people would have learn by now. You is nothing without a man.' He stared at her with a new found disdain in his eyes, 'Look at you dried-up Aunt. The old witch of the District. Look at her and learn,' he warned.

She gritted her teeth.

'I'll be alive to see you turn like her, forming that you pregnant and lose baby, so people can think you are a woman and not a eunuch.' Miss Dee jumped off the stool. He backed away suddenly, as if remembering only then the last time he had crossed her. 'You disgusting slime! Get out of my shop,' she screamed. Leroy looked round in panic as if hearing for the first time the sound of the school children breaking loose, gesticulated and strolled from the shop without a backward glance.

Miss Dee wandered round the shop trying to contain her fury, wondering what nonsense he spoke about her aunt and pregnancy. Eventually she calmed down and went back to work. Mid week was not usually her busiest time for customers, but they had taken measurements for, and were furiously working to complete Christmas orders so the quietness in the shop was deceptive. Her aunt was all-but working round the clock to make up the orders.

Miss Dee could hardly believe her own success with the gamble she had taken, starting with what she considered in her heart the humiliating climb down in the trip to the Day's Work and the public apology to Littleman. She was fully aware that the District thought they saw through her motives, felt it was a means to an end but she didn't care and they didn't seem to be holding it against her because now only weeks after that, she had all their custom plus that of people from all the surrounding districts. So as well as her aunt sewing for the shop she had, in recognition of the talent in the District and the desperation for work, recently and due especially to the pre-Christmas rush, even contracted sewing out to women in the District, enhancing her own reputation and winning more reluctant families to her side. She had even purposely gone in search of those whose grudge against her aunt had not wavered since she had come to the District with her fancy sewing and taken their clients.

Left with the anger brought on by Leroy, she could not get back to work.

Although Miss Dee had become preoccupied with her business she had found herself reflecting occasionally on Littleman, unable to shift a nagging guilt that had taken hold of her especially since a few weeks ago when he had passed her on the way to Aunt Vie's ground. She had been ahead of him but had recognised his walk behind her. She sensed that he had slowed his walk. She had strained to keep her head straight, anxious to get past the turning he took through Paul Mountain to Eggsbury. But she did not have the strength of will and he, she supposed, was uncomfortable with the unusually slow gait he had obviously adopted to avoid passing her. She turned and met his eyes, greeted him, stopped and allowed him to come level with her. He took the cue but on coming level did not pass quietly as she had imagined he would but had returned her greeting, asked after her business, commenting that he had heard she had some help in Rose-marie and had wished her good day in a calm relaxed manner, respectful but un-deferential. Since then she had not set eyes on him again.

She was so deep in thought about the transformation that had come over him in so little time that she did not register the sound of Jacob's jeep as it stopped in front of her shop. He was in the shop before she realised that he was there. She composed herself with difficulty. 'Good morning Miss Dee,' he said looking around the shop. It was the first time that he had stopped by since she had changed her business. She cursed Leroy for his disruption robbing her of the composure she had cultivated for the very event. But Jacob hardly looked at her, his eyes flitting around the shop, whether sceptically or with admiration she could not tell. Noticing that, her anger with Leroy turned on herself for the way she had suddenly jumped to her feet when he had come in, like a dog lapping around the feet of its master, tongue suspended, salivating. She could not believe her anger or the sudden hate that erupted in her heart not just for Jacob Cleary but for herself too.

For a moment she tried to deny the months, even years, of pining after his type. What did she think he could give her now that she realised how much she could do for herself? How much respect she could get for herself. But when he did turn to her and she remembered Leroy she could not help but admire him, difficult as it was to eradicate or even separate her admiration from the years of deference that was part and parcel of being brought up in a District that was owned by his family. And there was no comparison between him and Leroy. He was fresh and clean, having clearly been bred on the right amount of sleep, in a good bed, all his life. The right combination of the right type of food, just the right amount of loving from his family. And more

160

than that all the security of never having to worry about where the next meal would come from or where he would find the money for the lease or the rent. And as well as all that he could have the semblance of a clear conscience like his father, John Cleary Junior and grandfathers before him, with his frequent doses of free food that they lavished on the District, quelling potential discontent, about the high rents and leases, the vast areas of his dormant land in the midst of dire need.

'Miss Dee. You have done a good job on the shop. Papa told me about it.' He rubbed his chin, like a true big shot. 'Don't you think though that it is rather wasted here.' As soon as he said that with what she was sure was a look of ridicule on his face, her back went up. She had a right to criticise and ridicule the District but he had none. 'No. We wear clothes like you,' she said defensively, surprising herself. He was clearly taken aback by her tone. She stood her ground, refusing to twist her hands like she had seen other people in the District do when his father, ageing grandfather, John Cleary Senior, or even he himself were around.

Jacob looked at her briefly as if what she had said was an insignificant outburst, then walked over to one of the shelves with the pants lengths. He ran his hands over some of the fabrics. Miss Dee sat back on the stool, her palms resting on her lap, her back so straight, her chin so high it hurt, despising the thought that had briefly entered her mind that she should apologise for her tone, cursing herself even for thinking it. He was just a man not even older than her, no better and perhaps even worse. She surprised herself again, a few months before she would have given so many things to be so close to him. She had so wanted to be in the position to engineer a meeting with him. Now she was disinterested. She didn't know whether it was Leroy that had done that to her, confused and put her out.

Eventually he turned back to her. 'Thank you Miss Dee for letting me look round.' Then as an after thought, 'I do know

161

that people in the District wear clothes.' He looked her up and down. 'I can see that you do.' Miss Dee's face burnt. She was furious by the affrontery in his eyes. She turned away. Noticing, he laughed. 'I didn't know that country girls blushed so easily.' Her anger rekindled, how could he think her bashful when all she wanted was to do was slap his face.

'There is a lot you don't know about us country girls,' she said instead, fighting to control her anger. 'It just goes to show, doesn't it, that money and family name is nothing without sense.' He stared at her as if he didn't quite believe what he was hearing.

'Excuse me.' Then as if suddenly realising that he should not accept her offensive tone he said slowly, 'Do remember, that this shop is mine and that you should watch your manners.'

'You father's shop you mean,' she said, refusing to be cowed or to relent. 'And we are paying rent for it.' She got up, turned away and started tidying items on one of the already immaculate shelves. She felt his eyes on her, heard his laugh, but didn't turn. She heard him leave the shop, heard him drive off, a wretched feeling of regret descending on her.

Chapter 21

As Miss Dee laboured over the stones on her way to Aunt Vie's home, she despised herself. Her body that she had so prided herself in all her life seemed now a liability. From her carefully pressed hair, piled high on her head, her powdered face, her full rounded breasts, her tightly pulled in waist, right down to her rounded hips, overly accentuated now by her tight 'hobble' skirt. For when it came down to it, what drew men like Leroy to her and made Jacob treat her with the disdain he had, could only come from the way she had presented herself to them albeit, she felt, subconsciously.

For as long as she could remember she had silently pined for Jacob's attention, spent many hours scheming, willing the impossible; marriage, but retreating later into the second best of being his country mistress, bearing children for him, as other women did for his father and grandfathers before him. Now she was disgusted with herself, glad at least that she had not even confided this to Rose-marie.

She had not imagined that it could be possible to be so dirtied by his salacious eyes, left transparent and powerless by his stray words. Not even when Leroy had confronted her in the lane had he left her feeling so emptied of herself. Why had she not hated him from the start like everyone else in the District? Or even more, like Aunt Vie.

Aunt Vie was surprised to see her. She put down the dress she had been darning, 'Miss Dee, long time.'

She returned Aunt Vie's greeting but was preoccupied trying to catch signs of Littleman's presence, to her relief he didn't appear to be around. 'I'm sorry Aunt Vie, I feel bad. I should have come before.'

'Don't worry now. It's still good to see you.' She stood up. 'Let me give you something to drink, I made some sorrel yesterday.'

'I'll get it. You sit down.'

When she returned she sat next to Aunt Vie not knowing quite what to say or why she had come, only that she had been desperate to get some distance between Jacob's words, eyes, smugness, and herself. Aunt Vie's yard was naturally the best yard for that. When Babydear had been there she had spent some part of nearly every day at the house. Most of that listening to Babydear's incessant chatter broken only by light comfortable silences. Now the silence on the verandah was not comfortable, just restless and obvious. Miss Dee felt Aunt Vie's eyes on her and a new and startling guilt stirred in her, making it difficult for her to meet and hold the old woman's eyes. Not only for the wrong she had done Littleman, but even though Aunt Vie could never have been party to them, for the past ill thoughts that she had harboured against the District. 'Aunt Vie, I was wrong in what I did to Littleman,' she blurted, losing control of her practised reserve, wondering at the same time whether she could trust herself to be as she was. 'I didn't only say it at the Day's Work because you made me do it.'

Aunt Vie studied her, then in a quiet reflective voice said, 'Yes, you were. Very wrong. Littleman didn't deserve to be left to the mob.'

'I know . . .'

'But I respected you for saying sorry, for how you said it . . . That took a woman.' She stretched out her good hand. Miss Dee put her glass down, got up and took and rubbed the hand she offered. 'Sit next to me,' Aunt Vie said. Miss Dee released her hand and did as she said. Vie turned to her smiling. 'I know things are not easy for you. You are trapped between what you would like to be and what others feel you should be.' She smiled. 'There is nothing wrong with that. So long as you know that's what's happening and you don't blame those who are on your side.' She squeezed Miss Dee's leg. '. . . There is nothing to say you can't write you own rules. Write them of course but you'll have to be brave. I wish I had been brave when I was young.'

Miss Dee tried to smile, not quite sure that she had followed all Aunt Vie's differing trains of thought but realising that she had missed Aunt Vie and her little talks, her ability to know what to say, to explain what was inside you. Things that you couldn't put into words yourself.

'You are an ambitious young lady. I can see that you don't want to walk in the same worn-out footsteps that settled from other women in the District generations ago. And who can blame you . . . None of us is worthy to be followed blindly by the young . . .' She sighed leaving that thought. 'It's refreshing to see a young woman who want to make her own footsteps.' She rested her hands on Miss Dee's lap and tapped them, 'You want to do things when some of the young people here only want to breed. You want to be different. Good for you . . .'

She left Miss Dee hanging again, she was glad that Aunt Vie could not read what had been in her mind for almost as long as she could remember, because it was quite the opposite of what Vie was thinking and praising her for.

So when Aunt Vie stopped speaking, Miss Dee felt uneasy for a considerable time, focusing mainly on the lie she felt she was allowing Vie to believe of her. But later as she put on one of Aunt Vie's old dresses and they cooked together, making green gongo peas soup with pig tail, she began to feel contented, cleansed and relaxed and as the dusk descended and the mosquito coil was lit, she settled down to chat with Aunt Vie, full of the success of her business, not even minding if Littleman should come, in fact even hoping that he would and see something of the real her again. So engrossed was she in their conversation that she did not hear him when he did approach. It was just after Aunt Vie had wondered out aloud what had happened to him.

She thought she caught a glimpse of surprise on his face but she could not tell for certain since his expression hardly altered as he greeted her and led Greystripe behind the house. But she was conscious of him as he returned to the kitchen shortly afterwards with his bag of provisions, passed her on the verandah to go to his room and later again with his clothes to go behind the house for his wash.

When he was washed and changed, he got himself dinner and made to return in the dark behind the house to eat. 'Littleman you're not afraid of me are you?' she ventured in her most light-hearted voice, glad when Aunt Vie supported her. He hesitated but then sat on the low wall of the verandah as she had done when she had come and again there was that same strained silence. She turned to Aunt Vie to see if she was about to ease it but Vie had rested her head back on the chair, her eyes closed. Miss Dee couldn't tell whether she had fallen asleep or not. It crossed her mind to leave but the distance between getting up and finding her way off the verandah and out of sight seemed too great. She was fumbling for a way out when he spoke. 'I hear your business going well Miss Dee.' She nodded, glad that the dim light of the gas lamp left the greater part of her expression to his imagination. He wiped a thin line of soup from the corners of his mouth. 'I was surprised,' he continued, 'when I came and saw you here . . .' he paused, 'because I saw your shop door opened.'

'What?' Miss Dee jumped up. Aunt Vie's eyes opened. Little-man looked around confused.

'But I locked up.'

'I thought when I saw you that maybe Aunt Jane was there.'

'No. God. She's not there. She went to Town today. How could it be opened? I locked up.' Her mind racing ahead to the Clearys, his family were the only ones who had keys apart from herself and her Aunt, she had not got round to cutting one for Rose-marie yet. Miss Dee spun around.

'Littleman how you mean you see the door opened?' Aunt Vie said calmly.

He was looking at Miss Dee with concern, 'Yes, the front door was opened.'

'Jesus.' Miss Dee said, stepping down off the verandah, 'I have to go up there. I know I locked it.'

'Wait,' Aunt Vie said. 'Was there light?'

'Amm. No. I don't believe so. But it was just getting dark,' Littleman said, taking the rest of his dinner to the kitchen. When he returned he offered to go to the shop with her.

'Thank you but what about your dinner? You've been working all day.'

'Don't worry. Afterwards.'

Both the front and the back doors were open. Littleman insisted on going ahead of her into the shop, leaving her outside with one of the flashlights they had taken. He called her a few moments after he had gone in. Inside, she breathed a sigh of relief as complete order met her eyes. She must have just totally forgotten to lock up being in the state she was with the confusion of Leroy and Jacob in one day. Littleman lit the oil lamp, allowing her to see more clearly than the flashlights allowed.

She looked over the shelves more closely, pulling out drawers here and there. It was then that she noticed that everything was not all right. 'Oh God,' she screamed. Littleman who was in the process of bolting the door turned sharply. 'What is it Miss Dee?'

'My God,' she said pulling out a dress from one of the

drawers. It was cut in strips from the hem up to the waist. She picked up another and another. She charged across the room looking more closely at trousers, at children's clothes, at material. Each had been carefully mutilated, some with prominent holes, some hanging in shreds.

'No! No!' Miss Dee cried. 'Why? Who?' All of a sudden she stopped and stared in Littleman's direction. He looked behind him, then realised that she was staring at him. 'You? You?'

'What?' he said. 'Miss Dee, not again. Don't come with that again.'

She caught herself and shook her head apologetically, erasing the sight of him breaking into the shop and taking scissors to her clothes. At last paying her back for what she had done to him in Town.

'You don't know who could have done this to me do you?' she said, throwing off her guilt and giving way to anger. He shook his head. She stamped around the shop throwing things off the shelves, finding that everything had been touched. Littleman watched her without intervening until eventually, she stopped, exhausted, and slumped on her stool in tears.

She hardly focused on him collecting the bundles strewn across the floor and piling them in corners. When he was finished he stood leaning on the counter watching her, shaking his head occasionally, a pained look in his eyes.

When she had stopped crying, Littleman went back to locking up the front door, went into the bedroom and identified the lock that was broken.

'I have to go next door to Deacon's house for a screwdriver and fix the lock,' he said. She looked at him for a moment before she registered what he was saying. 'I have one.' She got up and led him to the tool box. She heard a radio somewhere blasting out Desmond Dekker and would have sat down and wept some more if she had been alone.

When he had repaired the lock, they went together to Deacon's yard to explain what had happened. Deacon and Sister Netta went with them to see for themselves, asking too many questions for Miss Dee's fragile mood. Eventually the holy pair went back home in disgust leaving Miss Dee and Littleman, who walked back in silence to Aunt Vie's house from which he rode Greystripe to get the constable from Kitson Town.

Chapter 22

Top Mountain, if anything, was renowned for the fact that little happened there that was unpredictable. Walking through the District at a time of day, one would know with almost complete certainty who would be passed on the road, who would be washing on Mondays and who would be ironing, whose husband was on the prowl and which young girl would be soon be pregnant. In the same way when there would be a special service or otherwise at the church, when Deacon, Sister Netta, band leaders and church counsellors would be doing visitations or administering to the needs of the lame and shut-ins, back-sliders and unrepentant souls.

It was not surprising therefore that the unprecedented events which had plagued the District since Babydear's departure, had given rise to the view that something was amiss in the District. The saved put it down to the wrath of God, those without God in their lives to the work of the devil or even the wicked deeds of an especially malicious obeahman. Many even wondered whether the Clearys had a hand in it somewhere.

Not long after Littleman had returned from Kitson Town with the constable to investigate the latest occurrence, a small group of people congregated in Miss Dee's shop yard and in the absence of a full moon, with lanterns and torches, wagging their heads, whispering speculations about the likely perpetrator, remaining there long after the evidence was collected and the constable had left.

Miss Dee and Aunt Jane themselves finally left the shop well past midnight, a silent resentment growing against the District inside Jane, a nagging anxiety in Miss Dee. Names did spring to mind but she avoided pointing a finger even at Bellinda Jerr and her crony Sibble who had made their presence prominent to her as she left the shop.

The following day to her surprise and inexplicable pleasure, Littleman passed by the shop on his way to ground. In the activity of the previous night she had forgotten to thank him and was glad to have the opportunity. More than that she accepted gladly his offer to return after work to see if she and Rose-marie needed any further help.

Later that day when he had left, the constable returned but could not prise from her the names of possible culprits. Several times the names lined up on her tongue, led by Leroy followed sharply by Bellinda and Sibble, almost forcing their way out but she refused to speculate. She couldn't afford to make a mistake and so she held her tongue. But it hurt her, with no insurance she had lost most of hers and her aunt's investment and the culprit's apprehension would make no difference.

She did not open the shop for a week, spending most of the time with Rose-marie behind its closed doors, building up again, even regretting though she tried to fight it, the lowering of her reserve towards the District, wondering all over again whether she could ever be a part of them or indeed wanted to be. Her resentment threatened to completely overwhelm her had it not been for Rose-marie's encouragement and the now daily visits by Littleman who in his own way began to personify another side of the District's character to her, a quietly support-ive side that she had not noticed before.

She talked about it to Rose-marie after she had come and met him there one morning. Her friend laughed at her, 'You're just feeling hurt and grasping for any little acts of kindness,' she said gently. 'Littleman is no different from anybody else in Top Mountain or even Kitson Town, too much kind-heartedness for their own good.' She looked knowingly at her friend. 'Sorry to say Dee Dee, you usually so high up that you don't see the good people lower down.'

'You can stop being brutal to me for a little while you know fat-face,' she said angrily. 'You don't have to tell me your truth all the time.'

'Not my truth, the truth.'

'If they are so good why they do this to me shop?' she snarled, throwing off her practised rules of high school grammar and town accent.

'Miss Dee man, they didn't do anything. There are less than two hundred people in the District, it only took one.' Miss Dee didn't answer, she continued her work, separating damaged parts of clothes from undamaged part, tops from bodices, saving parts she could. It had been Rose-marie's suggestion, that instead of burning the lot as Miss Dee had planned to do they should go through this process and give undamaged parts away to women with children so they could make clothes for them, and knowing the inventiveness of the women, even the shredded clothes would be used for patchwork sheets and the worst bits for furniture dusters. Although Miss Dee had continually protested about wasting her time, that it would have been easier and would have satisfied her anger more to have burnt the lot, she went along with Rose-marie, but to show that her anger was nowhere near subsiding, she sucked her teeth and sighed periodically, provoking pleas from Rose-marie to give her ears a break.

When they were done, Rose-marie moved the bags for her, determined to support her friend and get the shop back together as soon as possible, and eventually this rubbed off on Miss Dee.

'The best thing I think,' Rose-marie was saying, 'is not to let that person destroy what you work so hard to build up. The sooner we can get everything back to normal the better it will be all round.' She looked for the first time with seeming understanding at Miss Dee. 'Come on, don't give them the satisfaction of seeing you beaten.'

Miss Dee sighed, a fleeting thought of how undeserving she was of all the kindness and support she had got from the District in the week, almost causing tears again. She had expected kindness from Rose-marie, after all they went back a long way, but she had not expected the encouraging words that she had had, the offers of help to clear up, to go to Town with her to restock or even from some of the women to make initial items for her and waive the charge. She had been touched by that particular gesture but had graciously refused that and the others. She had not felt able, however, to reject Littleman's contributions. He had come one day without warning, tools, new locks and wood packed on Greystripe, had set to work fixing new locks, repairing the door and in the meantime revarnishing and painting shelves and cupboards for Miss Dee. 'To wipe off the old memory,' he had said seriously.

She stood now, with all the evidence of malice waiting outside on the steps to be distributed, a mixture of guilt and anger competing in her. She only succeeded in shifting the former by a scepticism of the motives for the District's kindness, by believing it to be their anxiety to feign innocence, to remove suspicion from their own family.

Chapter 23

Aunt Vie had had weeks to think about Jane's warning about Azora. What was it that Azora, in league with Cleary, had done to Jane? When had it all happened? With increasing uncertainty and deepening worry as to whether she had let her guard about Azora down too soon or whether she should have done at all and flaunted this in the District, Vie still found her way to Azora's house, engaged her in conversation, wishing for some light to be thrown. Jane she supposed was not unaware of these visits, jeopardising further, Vie was certain, their friendship.

In the past two weeks, Jane had only visited after the troubles in Miss Dee's shop to talk about it and to find out whether Vie had heard anything about who it could be. Vie had wondered whether she had been making insinuations about Littleman and so the few minutes she had spent had been unusually strained.

But despite her own curiosity about Azora, Vie tried not to go to see her too often, once weekly she determined initially was adequate even though with Jane punishing her, she could have done with Azora's company more. If Vie was home alone in the evenings she would be inadvertently putting pressure on Littleman to stay with her instead of discovering the joys of his own new friends in and out of the District. Vie did take the opportunity to get about with the stick. When she didn't feel like watching Ragu work, darkness no bar to him, she would go to the Maxtons, but watching six children romping and fighting incessantly and Ruthlyn rushing here and there after them and her husband, made Vie appreciate the quiet of her home.

Sometimes, with all the opportunity of companionship around her, she was unbearably lonely, making it seem to her that she was viewing life from the outside and not a part of it. On those occasions she would wonder where the years had gone, those best times, when she had been fit and whole. She wallowed sometimes in the injustice of it all, the waste that her life seemed to be. Why had she never fully exorcised the mistake of Nehemiah, moved on, pranced around when she had good legs, walked, noticed birds, wondered at their habits, enjoyed the change from one season to the next, explored the low-lying hills in the District, reflected more on life, reached out more to the District. Found love. Loved? Forgiven herself and loved? For now when she felt the need to do all that, life was slipping away and sapping her energy with it.

When Babydear had been around, Vie had had someone to preoccupy her. She had thought initially that Littleman would have been the same, there at her side, predictable like the child who had been absent only during school times. But Littleman was a man who, like most of the others in the District, worked constantly, but even more than the others he had the added burden of disproving the rumblings of the more stubborn in the District that he sought to exploit Aunt Vie, that deep down his character was like the leopard's spots, unchangeable. The same ones who remained sceptical of Littleman's intentions, borrowed from Vie often, kerosene oil, sugar, flour, even money, and somehow conveniently forgot to return them but did not see their action as exploitative in the same way that Littleman was said to be. Vie watched him with anxiety sometimes as she did other young people like Miss Dee, wondering whether they could see life slipping by at the pace it was, frightened to tell them in case they would think like Jane that her senility was to blame rather than good sense for her panic.

Vie worried even more for Littleman than she did for the other young people in the District because her pity for him had been replaced by the more heart-rending emotion of love. Somehow, with the others, despite how hard it was to find work when they had finished school, ingenuity always triumphed, she had seen it time and time again. They would find something to turn their hand to, like generations from the District had done before, even though sometimes it meant going away, abroad or to town. The ones who stayed to work the land often needed great strength of character to resist the temptation of what might be elsewhere. But it was not on account of work that she worried for him. Even in the event of her death, she would ensure that he had a piece of land, and the way he was working, she knew it was only a matter of time, barring the Clearys, before he saw to that himself. It was on whether he would end up alone as she was. The young women in the District were, as she had been, blind to important traits in men, looking only to the transitory, preferring the improbable to the possible.

In her loneliness, watching time pass as if now it was in a perpetual state of winding down, she didn't know how to make it work for her because, though it amused her, the trips to Azora and the other friends around her, did not seem enough. She wanted to grasp more, take the time and enclose it for herself until she had wrung the substance from it. It was more than not wanting to be alone, it was desiring to utilise this time with absoluteness so that, even in moments alone, the last sweetness of life would be sucked from it.

She had often found herself wondering, as Ezekiel constantly put to her, whether she would have been better off married, like a normal woman who would now be growing old gracefully with a husband to ease the endless drag of time. But knowing so much about the lives of those normal women, so dissimilar to hers, seeing the reality of the lives she often envied, observing their roving husbands and the desperate stray children they fathered, viewing their wives' pretence of happiness covering their pain and hurt, most of the time Vie would think that perhaps she had made the right choice to be alone after all. When she had shared Ezekiel secretly with his wife, she had relished that she did not *have* to hear him snore all night, wash his dirty socks and underclothes, watch him dislodge wax from his ears, hear him clear mucus from his throat or wake up to him at her side. She had the choice. But more than all that, she would not have to wash or cook or clean for him, take orders from him or sit sinking in frustrated bitterness, biting her tongue, for the sake of peace, as he went in pursuit of yet other women, to affirm his manhood. For the first time she had got a true glimpse of what it must be like to be born a man and she strove to replace a lifetime of hate but found only envy. That was why she decided she was so gripped and fascinated by Azora. From what Vie could see, Azora had never needed to hate what men were or even envy their position, since she had made a life for herself more perfect than theirs.

Vie was deep in thought when she heard a knock on her bedroom door. She listened. It wasn't Littleman. He had gone to Town. It was only just after noon, he wouldn't be back yet. The knock came again. 'Who is it?' she called warily.

'Are you ill Vie?' came a no-nonsense voice. She would have jumped out of bed if she could when she recognised it to be Azora's. She looked around her room as if caught red-handed in somebody's ground. 'I'm coming,' she said, getting off the bed and straightening her clothes. She was glad she had decided to have a wash and change out of her night clothes despite how low she was feeling.

'I don't want to get you up if you're not well. I'm just passing,' she called through the door. Vie smiled to herself, she wasn't just passing, there wasn't the sound of her mule outside, she would not have missed that as she could easily do her soundless walk.

177

Azora was sitting comfortably on the verandah when Vie got herself together and went out on the verandah. She glanced in the direction of the front and middle lines.

Azora caught her, 'Do you want me to hide behind the house?' She laughed. Vie smiled and sat on the low wall of the verandah.

'I just thought it was about time I returned your visits . . .' Azora said by way of an explanation.

Vie left her and went to get drinks. Once there she remembered her stick, manoeuvering the tray up the steps of the verandah with her bad arm and leg wasn't going to be easy, perhaps, she thought, if there hadn't been all the ups and downs with Miss Dee she would have started the massage treatment as planned. She wondered whether Azora came to talk about that. Now with the gap since they had discussed it, Vie wasn't sure. She was still contemplating that and how she'd get back safely with the drinks, hating her frailty when Azora years older than her was the epitome of health, when Azora coughed at the kitchen door.

'I've come to help you.' She said it in such a matter-of-fact way that Vie wasn't offended or embarrassed, just grateful.

They sipped in silence before she spoke, 'I've managed to make the appointment at the opticians in Kitson Town for you.'

Vie was surprised. On her last visit, Azora had said that Vie did not have to put up with half a sight when glasses or perhaps a small operation would help her. Vie had half-expected it to have been idle promise.

'Oh . . . Thank you.'

Azora looked amused but Vie didn't ask her why. She didn't have to wait long for an explanation. 'The next thing is your body rub. You see that I haven't pressured you since we discussed it.'

'I thought you changed you mind and didn't think it would do me no good, seeing how far gone I am.'

'Far where?' Azora said. 'There is nothing the right herbs and oils can't do.'

'Perhaps I should change my own mind anyway,' Vie said remembering Jane's words.

'Umm. For what reason?' Azora asked calmly.

'I don't really think I can be any better,' she continued, 'This old and twisted body of mine is going to stay like this until I blow the last breath.'

Azora studied her face. 'That doesn't sound like you . . .'

'You don't know anything about me and my sounds.'

'I know enough to say that you don't strike me as someone who would let a common ailment defeat her.'

'What so common about my ailment?' Vie insisted.

'You know lots of people have strokes.'

Vie sighed, not quite sure if Azora was trying to tell her that she knew she was feeling sorry for herself. Vie was and at the moment she didn't care who knew it. But she decided on second thoughts to deflect attention from herself. 'I was talking to Jane about going to you.'

'She must encourage you to take the full treatment.' Azora said unperturbed. Vie watched her expression carefully but there was no sign of anything that would suggest discord with Jane. But she had never heard her discuss any of her clients or make the slightest insinuations about them so she did not know if anything could be read from Azora's expression.

'No. Jane thinks if I take more treatment from you, people in the District will say I'm a hypocrite. You know I've made no secret of . . .'

'That was in the days when you didn't understand . . . now you know better,' Azora said in a matter of fact tone.

'. . . Besides Jane class you with satan.'

Azora downed her glass and looked in the distance towards Ezekiel's pig-sty. When she spoke again her voice was reflective if not somewhat sad. 'I suppose I should say that Jane wouldn't have anything good to say about me, I think you should know that and not let that stop you from seeing about your health.' Vie was taken aback.

'What you mean?' Vie turned to her. 'How you and Jane know so much about each other?'

Azora didn't reply immediately but Vie waited.

Eventually Azora asked, 'Has Jane discussed me with you?'

'No. No. Not in so many words . . .'

'It's a long story.'

Vie waited.

'A few years ago I got involved, unwittingly, in her affairs . . . I was tricked into . . .'

Vie's mouth dropped open. 'You knew her before she came to the District?'

'No.'

Vie eyed her impatiently.

'It just goes to show that even you don't know everything that go on in the District,' Azora joked, a faint smile on her lips.

Vie demanded that Azora stop her games with words and say what she had to. She did, telling Vie that some seven years before, a man whom she refused to name had come to her asking for some medicines to bring about a miscarriage. 'It is a man whose family's actions and behaviour I have always abhorred, even though I must say that they are long-time customers of mine,' Azora interjected. Continuing, she said she had been assured by the man in question that the person who needed the medicine was a young girl not yet out of High school whose life would be spoilt by her pregnancy. 'This was not new, it is well known that the men of this family have made a habit of spoiling young girls' lives and then discarding them. In the past, and this might come as a shock to you, I have encouraged and helped many young girls to expel the wretched seeds of that family from their wombs and not just girls from this District.' Vie raised her eyebrows but did not interrupt. 'It goes

180

without saying therefore that when the man came to me, surprised though I was that he was instigating this, that he had even stopped long enough to hear from the woman that he was responsible, I was glad, overjoyed in fact, to destroy another of their seed, that I could have a hand in stopping their seed from spreading. So I gladly prepared and gave him the medicine. I even concocted an extra strong dose, I did not want to fail, convinced that I was stopping the destruction of another young life by that family . . . Only later, when it was too late, did I realise that it was Jane's baby that this cussed man destroyed with my drugs.'

Vie's mouth dropped open and she could not for some moments find words.

'I believe I can trust you. I would not have said anything if I didn't believe that you are discreet.'

'The Cleary,' Vie said knowingly, 'Jane was pregnant for the Cleary. The Cleary Junior? And him kill her baby? Peace divine. Why? Why? When none of that wretched clan have cared before who breed for them? And Jane why she bend down so low? I know she was desperate . . . and how she manage to now after all the years she wanted to?'

Azora told Vie how, without knowing who was Jane's lover, she had been treating her condition.

Azora got up 'You see why Jane hates me. She thinks I was in league with Cleary . . . Anyway, I only told you so that you'll understand Jane.'

'Why have you never explained?' Vie said, still reeling from the shock of Azora's revelation.

'I have tried so many times.'

Chapter 24

When Jane fell out with Vie, she would go to Dora in the evenings instead for company. It seemed of late that even Miss Dee could not be depended on for companionship. When they were together, Jane would try her best to make conversation but if it had nothing to do with the business, Miss Dee, too preoccupied in her own thoughts, answered in monosyllables, if at all. And even though Jane was often desperately lonely, she was reluctant to put the pressure of her aloneness and isolation on Miss Dee so she let her be. And since Top Mountain was not like town, with electricity, Jane could not stay at home and watch television, go to the cinema or even stand by the roadside gazing aimlessly at passers-by. Even the radio, after a time, though mostly a greatly appreciated link with the outside world, became an irritant.

Distractions were woefully few in the mountains, when people walked or rode their donkeys, mules, or went out in their drays in Top Mountain, they did so purposefully; going to ground or another equally important errand. Those with families, middle aged, old or settled, who were not regular goers to almost nightly church services, stayed at home in the evenings, visited neighbours or friends, playing dominoes, telling duppy stories, listening to the radio and talked of by-gone days adding spice to stories of life when, they vowed, it was more eventful and exciting. The young, those supposedly well brought up and disciplined, stayed on the periphery of adult company, waiting their turn to be admitted into that preserve of assumed comfort, knowledge and wisdom. The others crept around surreptitiously in the shadow of twilight and darkness, seeking others like themselves to bring excitement to their otherwise mundane existences. Only a few ventured into town to taste the sweetness of that other life.

To an outsider, the church goers – to the Pilgrim Holiness Church in Paul Mountain, Pocomania and Anglican in Old Road, the Pentecostal in Top Mountain, and a diverse band in Kitson Town and surrounding areas – had more eventful evening pursuits. At least there was always something going on for them; either services at the churches, house to house prayer meetings or visitations to the elderly and shut-ins or even trips out of the District to other districts and parishes, to gospel concerts, building programmes, parish conventions, revival meetings and various crusades all culminating in the biggest event of the year, the annual national convention in town, when there was a mass exodus out of the District to spend a week basking in the Spirit, in Kingston.

But Jane wasn't a church goer so as well as suffering from the double disadvantage of not having a big family, she was only included in District activities on sufferance, and did not have a choice of homes to frequent on those long empty evenings.

At first when she had stopped going to Vie, she had felt relieved of the burden of that habit but, as the weeks had passed, she feared that her irrational and senseless jealousy was only hurting herself. Vie was loved by the District, wasn't short of people to call on, wasn't so consumed with pride that she would not seek help and companionship if she needed it. Even that angered and riled Jane.

When she was young Jane had heard women she considered to be well past their prime, talk about past loves. She had laughed at them, imagining then that events of even the previous year were too old to remember with any clarity let alone harp on. She was convinced that once relationships had ended feelings too would be erased from memory. Little did she know that one can never forget.

She remembered still the minutest detail about John Cleary Junior, details that though pleasing at times, simply made her bid to procreate with him all the more enjoyable; his scent, the feel of his body, the multiplicity of his expressions, the things he liked, how it felt to be with him, the little things he had said to her, what had made him laugh or even cry. And cruellest of all, the end was indelibly stamped on her mind, still painfully fresh in her thoughts and heart.

Very occasionally she was glad of the early memory which belied Vie's and the District's perception of Cleary, would purposely call on it; the circles he made with his breath on her face, his light leisurely touch, the strength of his body as it made one with hers . . . then the memory of her child that he had killed would flood back, erasing the pleasure, knotting her stomach with bitterness and hatred.

In nine years, despite the smallness of the District and his infrequent visits, she had set eyes on him only a few times. She cursed herself even now that instead of facing and challenging him, as she had dreamt of doing every day, she had scurried past him, head bowed, as if she was the one who should be ashamed. When he was out of sight, she had contemplated several times spreading his deeds through the District. But who would believe her? She was not the Cleary concubine type, but a dried-up, almost old woman. Besides, deep inside her she had feared him, was afraid of the power he had. If he had destroyed her child so callously and in so cold and calculated a manner, he could find a means to destroy her too.

At Dora's Jane was embarrassed at not having timed her visit well. She had expected Dora and Ezekiel to have finished eating well before she got there and for Ezekiel to have gone about his business and left Dora alone as he normally did, but instead had arrived in the middle of what was by any account a tense conjugal meal. She refused Dora's offer to join them knowing that her husband would have choked on his meal if she had accepted.

She still did not know how to feel about why Ezekiel had come to hate and mistrust her so. It was during the most intense period of her relationship with Cleary. They had planned to meet but she had fallen asleep and woken up in the early morning in a panic that he would think she had let him down. Certain that no one would be stirring in the District and so see her, she took the route past Ezekiel's shop, turning left on to Vie's Lane hoping to creep past Ragu's then Vie's house, to the side entrance of the big white house. The full moon bounced off the path for her marking her path. Passing Vie's house, she glanced absentmindedly in the direction of her yard and saw to her amazement Ezekiel descending the steps of the verandah. He did not take the middle lane leading directly from her yard to his but turned left and headed towards her. Before Jane's brain had time to recover from the shock and to think what to do, he saw her. She was rooted to the spot and could not move as he approached, in which direction would she go? They stood facing each other for moments before he spat out, 'Why you sneaking around spying on us? You nothing but a common lowdown woman, if you can be called a woman,' before strutting past her, leaving her still fixed to the lane. Nothing else was ever said to her either by him or Vie about it so she did not think he told Vie and, embroiled as she was with Cleary, she too kept her mouth. Yet Ezekiel had not forgiven her for knowing.

Jane sat on his verandah now waiting for them to finish eating. She found herself straining her ears, peering around the trees to try and catch a glimpse of Vie's yard knowing full well that she could not make anything out apart from the faint gas light on her verandah.

'So Jane what going on now?' Dora said wearily as she joined her on the verandah. Jane waited for Ezekiel's steps to recede as he headed, without a glance in her direction, towards the Maxton's, to play dominoes, she supposed. Ragu was strumming out a Shinto tune on his banjo in the next yard and the dogs, as usual, howled messages to each other in distant yards. Jane felt suddenly a longing to live in that part of the District where there was at least sign of life, she no longer wanted to be alone where she was.

'Nothing much. Just passing to see how you doing.'

'Umm . . .' Dora seemed anything but interested in having company. Jane watched her, feeling her more deserving of pity than she was herself. At least if one is truly alone with no husband, she thought, then one was at least spared the bitterness of having one who was never at home. One could not tell for sure where he was or what he was doing. Although Jane had little doubt that Dora knew. For how could she not know when her husband crept into the bed beside her in the early hours, the scent of another woman fresh on his body? Jane's pity for Dora was perhaps why she liked to see her when she herself was feeling low, it always left her appreciative of her own sorry lot. So even though they could not be called friends, they could sit and talk and would do each other little favours but Jane was always the one who initiated this, Dora only reciprocating.

Minutes into her visit, Dora sullen and uncommunicative, Jane wondered why she had bothered but she persevered. She wouldn't want Ezekiel to return unexpectedly and find her gone and be fooled into thinking that his years of giving her the cold shoulder had finally had an effect. So she initiated topic after topic. Only the shameful events at Miss Dee's shop succeeding in enlivening Dora.

'Everybody admiring her. She is one young woman who has real backbone,' Dora was saying.

'I'm glad because I was thinking after the thing with Littleman that she would have to leave the District for sure.'

Dora finding a topic that engaged her, wanted to relax fully, she excused herself and returned sharply from inside the house, settling with a pillowslip, lit another lamp on the table by her side and started to embroider the edges.

Jane studied her dexterity. 'Is that for the shop? Dee tell me you agree to do some work for her.'

'Yes. God knows how I let her talk me into it. She's got me crocheting, embroidering and all sorts. She something else you know.' Dora laughed. 'For true though I enjoying it. It gives me something to do when I shut the shop and 'Zekie gone . . . ,' she whispered and lowered her eyes.

Jane waited until her discomfort had settled before going back to the safe territory of Miss Dee. It was not that it did not cross her mind to offer some support to Dora for the anguish she knew she felt but what could she do? She was not herself seen by any of the women in the District as a part of them; too many strange ways, an unknown past, not like themselves, with their husbands, children and grandchildren, fully known in the District like their parents and grandparents were. Besides if Dora wanted to continue playing games until her dying day it was up to her. Her brother, the Deacon had convinced her so successfully that prayer and dutifulness would solve it all in the end. Perhaps he's right, Jane mused. Perhaps the end he means is her death.

'Sometimes I feel so resentful,' Jane heard her saying without warning. It took Jane aback.

'Why?' she asked softly. Dora didn't answer, just shook her head and looked over her shoulder towards the noise that was coming from Mr Maxton's house. There seemed to be a lot of them playing tonight. They could hear the smashing down of dominoes, challenging shouts from the men and hysterical bursts of laughter from the women. Jane repeated her question, wanting to bring Dora back from the exclusion that mirrored in her eyes. 'Why you feel bitter and upset sometimes?'

Dora sighed for a long time. 'You didn't know me when I was very young. You weren't in the District then.'

Jane shook her head.

'I was lovely. Pretty as a picture they used to say. Everyone thought so and said so. I was hearing that from the time I was knee high.' She shook her head. 'I know you wouldn't believe it seeing me now.' She stared blankly at the embroidery she had rested in her lap. 'So out of shape and sour.'

Jane shook her head not knowing what to say to her.

'I know. You don't have to try and disagree. It all just crept up on me. I do blame Ezekiel but I know I shouldn't blame anyone but myself.'

Jane wondered how she could blame herself for him, for the children he was rumoured to have scattered in surrounding districts and in Town, for his lack of respect to her, but she kept her mouth firmly shut, her thoughts fully locked inside.

'I should blame myself,' Dora re-emphasised. 'No woman should give a man power to destroy her. Because we have to give them the power, they can't take it from us you know.' She stopped and played with her hands for a long time. Jane had been hanging onto her words. For so long she had envied women like Dora with their husbands and quiver of children, had treasured this envy despite the glaring evidence that perhaps she had pulled the longest straw.

'I used to think that my beauty was everything, that it would answer every question for me. I loved having so many men wanting me. And getting the pick of the bunch in the District. But the very day I got married I found it was all a foolish dream. Marriage just made me into a respectable servant . . . And whore . . . ,' she added in a whisper. 'And the funny thing is, I don't know why but I never never even liked it,' she lowered her voice as if there were children or men present. 'I never liked the bed part. Up to this day I don't know what all the fuss is about.' She made a face to demonstrate her distaste. 'But I did it because I had to have his children. I know that men have more need for it than women and even though I tried my best to please him, give him what due to him, I know I never quite managed it, never quite satisfied him. That's why I have to take the blame myself for how it all turn out for me, and him, why I turned a blind eye to all his running around.' Jane's eyebrows went up. Dora caught her, 'Of course I know about all of them. I don't know their names, not all of them anyway. Don't really know who most of them are, but I can always tell when he is with someone new,' she sighed, 'his eyes and walk are always different . . . His eyes especially, full of a kind of sweet guilty pleasure.'

Jane rested back in her chair, gaping.

'Now I see deep lines on my face that nights of sleep, Azora's best bush teas or balm can't begin to soften. And look at him! See his own smooth unlined face.' She sighed with deep resentment. She stopped suddenly and Jane waited, thinking that she would say more but she showed no sign of wanting to add more.

Jane wanted to touch her but couldn't, it had never been her way. She was thinking instead of how *she* had spent nearly all her life worrying about not being like Dora, Ruthlyn Maxton, Sister Netta . . . feeling abnormal, too preoccupied with it to create a space around herself in which she could be happy, alone. She had wanted so much to be like them that she had taken Miss Dee, struggled with her, had not even relished the most important relationship in her life that she had because of her obsession, when all the time women like Dora were feeling trapped and sought to escape to the life she resented.

Eventually as night deepened, they made milk-powdered Ovaltine and sat silently sipping, lost in their own thoughts. Later Jane contemplated leaving, rescinding on her secret plan to have Ezekiel find her on his verandah on his return. As she

189

wavered indecisively, she heard faltering steps punctuated by the drag of stick on the sun hardened ground, coming towards them. Dora strained her eyes against the darkness, but Jane recognised it immediately as Vie, regretting that she had not followed her mind and left earlier. 'Dora, it's me, Vie,' came the call through the darkness.

Dora got up to meet her, informing her before she remounted the verandah with her that Ezekiel was not at home.

'As if I can't hear his big mouth from Maxton's yard,' Vie said, if put out by the insinuation that she only visited to see Ezekiel, not showing it.

Vie, surprised to see Jane, tripped over her stick. Without thinking, Jane jumped up to help her, getting in Dora's way who was confidently steadying Vie herself. 'I was just thinking it's not like you to visit so late unless you needed to see 'Zekie.'

'No. I don't need him, just felt like taking a walk, thought you might be lonely.' Dora bit her lip and left to make the Horlicks that Vie said she would like.

'So how you do Jane?' Vie said, making little attempt to add cheer or friendliness to her tone.

'Life goes on,' Jane said but Vie was not prepared to coax her and sat scowling waiting for Dora to return, but she could hear her going further down the yard to the latrine. She could not tolerate the silence, 'So Jane what I do to vex you?'

Vie's directness never failed to surprise Jane. 'This is not the right place to talk,' Jane said, attempting to silence her.

'Why not?' Vie retorted, if anything raising her voice. Jane shushed her.

'I don't see why you don't want to talk, since you can't have much to say. I haven't done you anything and you behaving like a spoilt child, keeping malice.'

'I said I don't want us to talk about it now.'

'Why, you shame?'

'Vie you don't understand.'

'What's there to understand?' Vie had decided before in her quiet moments at home on the strategy she was employing if and when they met, as if unaware of anything that should make her do otherwise. 'All I said to you was how I find Azora . . .'

'Vie, Dora is going to come,' Jane said with panic.

'Why you always so worried? Just relax yourself because even if you can't be sensible, I will be. I'm warning you, I'm getting too old to let adult tantrums affect what I do.'

Jane's lips tightened as Dora returned, apologising for taking so long. She handed Vie her drink and left again, saying over her shoulder that she had to make porridge for her husband. 'He normally like a bit of cornmeal porridge after rum. He say it settle his stomach.' Jane sucked her teeth. Vie said under her breath, 'Him still turning her fool after all these years and that man so easy to control.'

'After you don't live with him,' Jane said, glad for a chance to vent her anger. 'See me and live with me, is two different things.' They at least agreed on that and it lightened the atmosphere between them.

Vie relaxed into her chair, already determined though tempted, that there was nothing to be gained from hearing Jane's side of the story Azora had told her. Like her own affair with Ezekiel still locked between them in history, her friendship with Azora and her new knowledge about Jane and Cleary had to be relegated likewise.

'One thing I have to say though Vie,' Jane started to say but caught Vie's frown, 'And you don't have to look like that. We still friends and I too can speak my mind, and I would not be a true friend if I don't repeat my warning . . .'

'So long as you don't go off in a huff and hide for weeks if I disagree with you.'

Jane frowned. 'You must *watch* Azora,' she emphasised. 'Go to her for your treatment by all means. She is good. She can do anything for you health.' Vie tried to maintain a blank expression, 'But more than anything she wants respectability in the District. She wants people to stop seeing her as a common obeahwoman. To see her as a herbal doctor. One with no hidden or evil ways. She wants to come out in the open. You are her passport to that. People in this place take their cue from you, she knows that Vie. Befriending you mean that all the hiding and crawling about to see her would stop.'

Vie watched her closely, unable to imagine Azora caring. She had done without her acceptance for thirty years, befriending the District, practised her craft. She had made no difference and so far as Azora was concerned she did not give her the impression that she wanted to come out of her isolation. That was part of her lifestyle that appealed to Vie. Someone who reflected her mood for the most part, not the part of her that was desperate to have company and not be alone, but the greater part of her that joyed in her separateness, independence and oneness with herself. But Vie said none of that either because in a small district, being part of the game that sought company and sociability was as natural as the rolling hills that surrounded them. And Vie would not deny that there was the most immense joy in being in company but she could not deny either that that same joy could be easily surpassed by the bliss of moments totally alone. In finding Azora, it occurred to Vie that she had found a kindred spirit at last. She did not think Jane would understand her so she said only, 'Jane I'm too old to take telling.'

'Have it your own way then . . . ,' Jane retorted.

When Dora came back with more Horlicks and Ovaltine, they talked trivialities, enlivened temporarily, no doubt, by the novelty of the three of them sitting and talking as they had done briefly together years ago, before the discomfort that Vie had found in living a lie to Dora and indeed to herself, had come between them. But even tonight, they were only together in body. Lost in their own separate thoughts, Top Mountain, despite the crickets, the dominoed voices of the men, manic howling of dogs and the strumming of Ragu's banjo, was very lonely for each of them that night.

Chapter 25

People in Top Mountain fell into two broad categories where church was concerned. They were either regular or not so regular church goers, since there was nobody in the District who did not go to church sometime, if not to the biannual Sunday school fair, Easter or Christmas services then to christenings, weddings, funerals or send-off services.

Sunday school fairs especially, were looked forward to with great anticipation since unlike the other events, they were not accompanied by any of the anxiety that often characterised them.

Deacon, who moderated and looked after the affairs of the church in the absence of the Pastor who lived in Town and had four other churches to minister, insisted on changing the Sunday school superintendent after each annual national convention of the church. He was not so ready to change other church department leaders, like the young people's, women's auxiliary and publicity leaders, often leaving them in their positions for two, or even four and five years. Deacon considered it vital to have new blood to stimulate the children in the District since to his mind they were most vulnerable to the wiles of the devil and had to be rescued and sheltered in the arms of the church as soon as possible.

The superintendent's role was more than that of selecting teachers, raising funds for literature from the church's main office in town and organising the District into groups according to age for classes on Sundays. He or she also had to run the District nursery school. Top Mountain had no primary or all-age school, all the children went to Paul Mountain or Kitson Town, or those at eleven lucky enough to pass their common entrance exam, to high schools in Spanish Town or Kingston. This was the ultimate ambition of every family in the District, so as soon as a child could talk and was out of diapers (and because of the incessant chatter of other siblings around, the constant wandering of neighbour's children in and out of each other's yard and the general expectation that to talk was as natural as the ability to recognise trees, herbage and birds around the District, this was without exception well before a second birthday), it was sent to nursery school.

The curriculum did not change radically from year to year, the only need being to respond to the wish of parents that learning nursery rhymes, to read, add up and say the times tables up to twelve, know singular and plurals, opposites, past, present and future tenses, the parishes of Jamaica, her national bird, dish and anthem, the capitals of countries, the names of the highest mountain, the longest river, the great oceans, proverbs, parts of speech, to sing and say recitations, all were to be mastered before primary school at seven. But of equal importance, young hands were to be trained in the skills that kept the District alive, cultivating grounds.

The termly fee of one guinea for each child with a reduction if there was more than one child in a family, though hard to find for some families, somehow materialised from most, but twice a year on a Saturday, a big fair was held in the church grounds to raise funds for those who, despite all efforts, could not afford it, as well as to provide additional equipment for the school, like slates, chalk, exercise books, pencils, crayons, occasionally desks and chairs, to pay the principal who was also the Sunday school superintendent and her assistant teacher and to help towards the annual nursery school outing which was distinct from the annual Sunday school outing.

Fortunately, it was no great sacrifice to support the biannual fairs, and people from outside the District came even though they did not often have the pleasure of seeing the uniformed toddlers from nine o'clock to three o'clock Monday to Thursdays and Friday mornings, reciting their lessons in between frenzied play in the mornings, and after their midday naps, cultivating their gardens way behind the church, planting, watering, feeding and exercising the donkey and petting the pigs and chickens.

Today everybody was in the church yard for the second of the two annual fairs. A fun fair had been hired from Town, with slides, swings, dippers and roundabouts. It was possible to test your wits against strong men, join in singing with the children, listen to singing and recitation competitions, even be one of the judges and of course to buy pre-cooked food such as patties, fried dumplings, cocoa bread, drops, roast yam and corn, rice and peas and curry goat, fried fish and chicken and so on.

Miss Dee had collected Aunt Vie on her way, ensuring that as in the past when Babydear was around, she would not need her stick. Miss Dee had quite liked the fact that Littleman was at home and she had had the chance to talk to him. It surprised her how much at ease she was in his company, and how when he had left before them to put the finishing touches to the marquee that had been constructed from coconut bough the previous day as shelter for the least adventurous, she wished he had stayed, how she had missed him.

Yet she contrived that she would be late. She could not resist the pleasure of having heads turn to look at her, having girls her own age, especially the hateful Bellinda, cut their eyes at her and suck their teeth, in sheer exasperation at how she managed always to look the best, ignoring the fact that her dress was

Chapter 26

Vie didn't ride Greystripe, deciding to walk, but regretted it as soon as she had turned off her path and on to the road that led to Azora's house.

For someone able-bodied, the walk would have taken no more than twenty minutes but she was still walking an hour after she had left home, dragging her resistant right leg behind her. Reproaching herself, wondering what she had been trying to prove did not help, but she did it nevertheless. More than once she thought of turning back but good sense told her that it was just as well to continue. She had sat on the tree trunks along the way but on the last occasion before she turned right on to Azora's lane, it had taken her ages to raise herself again. Her hope that someone would pass on a donkey or even better that Azora herself would come riding by on one of her especially big horses or mule was not realised, and Vie knew it was hoping against hope because only rarely did anyone take that road to the District or out of it, preferring to go the other way to Guano-bovale, which though longer was more eventful and less arduous on bare feet, precious shoes or even hooves of donkeys and mules.

When at last Vie stood by the path which led to her house, the thought of how she would get back home crossed her mind. Azora might be good at concocting herbal cures but there was no way she was a miracle worker. She did not, like the Deacon and his flock, claim the power of the laying on of hands.

As she got closer to the house and realised that it was locked up, the last remnant of her energy drained and she would have collapsed in her disappointment but for her strength of will and the good fortune that verandahs in the District were open and not hemmed in by grilles as they were in town. Mustering all the energy she could she mounted the steps and all but threw herself on one of the seats. Using her good hand she massaged the top of her legs, wishing at that moment more than ever that Babydear was around to rub her feet for her.

Luckily, she had set out when it was getting towards evening and it was not too hot. The early December breeze was lifting up the red dust and spiralling it around the yard. She slid her bottom down until the back of her head rested on the chair back, within minutes she had dozed off.

When she awoke Azora was sitting opposite staring at her. Vie rubbed her face in that moment of half-sleep half-wake confusion, wondering how long she had been there. Seemingly eager to ease her embarrassment, Azora looked away for a moment.

'Had a good rest?' Azora asked as if her sleeping on her verandah was the most natural thing.

'How long you been sitting there?' Vie asked, her tone suggesting that Azora had no business on her own verandah.

'Long enough,' Azora smiled.

One of her dogs jumped on the verandah and she bent to stroke it, distracting them both.

'Listen,' Vie said as soon as she had chased the dog away, 'I've come to start the treatment.'

'Good,' Azora said strongly, without obvious surprise. Vie waited for her to say more but she didn't, just excused herself, got up and went behind the house.

When Azora came back Vie listened attentively as she explained the course of treatment she would administer, the herbs she would concoct for her, the oils she would use for the rubs and what she hoped would be achieved. Vie struggled to be inspired by her confidence and failed but she did not let on. Instead she asked questions, whether Azora used only herbs she grew, had she successfully treated anyone else like her, only half-jokingly asked whether she had poisoned anyone. Answering her questions and fears authoritatively she itemised each herb, listing the parishes where those she did not grow came from, suggesting that she would be happy to have anything she used retested in labs in town if Vie was unsure.

'You are not the only one who at first fear that I will poison them. It's natural, even college trained doctors kill people sometimes.'

'I hope you've never though.'

She shook her head, characteristically not overdefending herself.

Then, 'So how it all seems to you?' she asked finally. 'I'm not saying anything will happen overnight. It would have been better if you had started getting treatment just after the stroke, but never mind, I think there will be improvement. You'll see the difference.'

Vie nodded, 'So when can we start?'

'Well, give me a couple of days to get the herbs together. I've got the oils already . . . Ummm . . . Say one week. Yes to be sure that everything will be ready give it a week. Or would you prefer to wait until after Christmas?'

'Whenever you ready.' That having been resolved, Vie informed her that Littleman would be picking up her glasses that were now ready in Kitson Town. Vie thought she should leave then but her legs were like lead and she had no delusions that she could move them let alone have them carry her home. Azora seemed to read her mind. 'You really try to fully destroy the leg by struggling here without the stick, eh? You really mean to test me to see if I can work miracles, no true?' She laughed heartily.

'Yes, I was foolish,' Vie said calmly when Azora had satisfied her glee.

'I'll take you back. But why don't you spend the evening here. Two old women should be able to eat dinner together now and again.'

'I have my dinner cook at home already.'

'What Littleman leave, have tomorrow, overnight food sweet you know. You won't even have to do anything, go and lie down and rest the leg until I finish.' The thought of the calm, quiet order of her room with its spotless white sheets suddenly appealed to Vie. But she hesitated. She did not enjoy playing the feeble old woman role.

'You not worried about Littleman?'

'No, I told him I would be coming round here. It's not that, I don't want to fall asleep again, if I do I will never sleep tonight.'

'That's fine. We can sit up and talk all night . . . Many night I see the night through round here by myself.'

'Doing what for peace sake?'

'Contemplating and plotting.' And she did not smile so Vie did not know what to make of that last remark.

Chapter 27

Littleman took to watching Leroy after what had happened at the Sunday school fair. Despite his bravado then, he still feared him, the way he had done when they were at primary school together, and wondered with trepidation what he would do if Leroy were ever to discover his surveillance and confront him on some dark lane alone.

At primary school, Leroy had plagued him. Unlike other thugs that dominated the playground and the walk to and from school, Leroy was neither crude nor obvious in his wickedness. But his iniquities were so permanent that children who had been subjected to them would never forget. So if it was perceived that Leroy was having a bad day on account of being beaten at home or at school or had to do duties at home that he objected to, children would go to great lengths to avoid him, even preferring to get a short sharp thump or kick from one of the other school bullies.

Littleman still bore the scars of the day after Leroy had been strapped in front of the whole school for cheating at sums in a test. He had crept into the classroom during the recess to check the questions that had been put up on the blackboard ready for the session afterwards. He was caught.

As was the practice, he was paraded in front of the whole school, made to stand during the afternoon blessings so the school could gaze on him with scorn as they sang hymns, listening to the reading from the Holy Scriptures and heard the notices.

The headmaster had turned to him, the long ruler, reserved for corporal punishment, lightly massaging the side of his legs. He had eyed Leroy for a while before turning to inform the school about his shameful act. More than causing the teacher extra work, since she had had to design another test and spend more time rewriting it on the board, Leroy had brought shame on himself. Only dunces and loggerheads, he informed the school, had cause to cheat and such characters could not be tolerated in his school. The school had resonated with the echoes of the ten lashes.

Littleman's mistake was to catch and hold Leroy's eyes as he had been marched down the centre aisle, classes in neat open-planned rows either side, to complete his punishment, the copying of lines about the proper ways to behave. Instead of pretending like the rest of the school, that they had not witnessed Mr Leroy's humiliation.

Littleman didn't fight, didn't believe in getting into arguments, preferring to admit defeat or that he was wrong. So after school, sensing that Leroy was not pleased with him, he had stayed behind to help the teacher clear up. He must have been about nine at the time, Leroy two years older. But even the most devoted of teachers had to go home and the school locked up for the night. As Littleman left the school building with the teacher he realised that perhaps he had made a mistake and that it would have been better for him to have gone home in the relative safety of other children.

Walking stealthily past the line of weeping willows that ended the school playground, past the teacher's turning, the standpipe in the centre of Paul Mountain and the last row of roadside houses, he knew that whatever happened between there and Top Mountain would go totally unheard since the remaining scattering of houses were well hidden from the road.

It was quiet. He looked around furtively, aware that the boys, normally on the road, changed out of their khaki uniforms and into their yard clothes, playing marbles or pushing cartwheels, were absent and so were the girls playing with stick and coconut rush dolls.

The walk from Paul Mountain School to his home at the top of Top Mountain was about half an hour. Littleman estimated that he had nearly done that and was reproaching himself for his wasted fear, contemplating rather the telling off he would get from Nana for being late, when he heard the whistling he knew to be Leroy's approaching him out of the twilight.

Littleman hesitated, then he started to run but not faster than the stones that whistled past his head. One caught the back of the neck. He felt the blood immediately, heard Leroy's laughter, but didn't stop to be hit again.

At home Dettol and gauze were carefully applied by Nana followed by a beating for getting into fights at school and being late home without telling her he would be.

Now thirteen years later Littleman was ashamed that he was still afraid of Leroy.

Yet realising that Leroy was spending a lot of his time at the back of Miss Dee's shop doing nothing in particular, gave Littleman the courage to delve more. He found that Leroy who always had his penknife with him, a machette by his side, would invariably be using the penknife to carve away at the tree trunk on which he sat. As Littleman crouched watching him, once or twice, Leroy's ears would prick up as Littleman's feet crushed dried leaves around him or broke a twig.

Littleman feared that Leroy had cause to be alert and it dawned on him that if anyone in the District was to be blamed for ransacking Miss Dee's shop, it had to be him. But what to do about him occupied Littleman many a night after he had turned in or when he sat with Ragu learning his trade or on those long days as he worked his ground in Eggsbury or when he helped

Miss Dee around the shop, as she had at last agreed he could. But at least Leroy would see him around the shop and have second thoughts if he had any other mischief planned. Despite having more than enough with which to fill his days, Littleman found time to clean up around the shop, made extra shelves when he worked with Ragu or just pottered around behind the house at a flower garden he was planting for Miss Dee. That part was particularly satisfying, it being less ingratiating and obvious than cutting flowers for her.

It pleased him that she trusted him and for some reason it seemed to him that having her friend Rose-marie with her, softened Miss Dee, made her more relaxed and playful than he had ever seen her. Even in those days when they had dodged Aunt Jane and stolen away to talk, he had never caught a glimpse of her as she was now. Now she did not wear a frown, did not speak in short dismissive sentences to him as she had done after he had fallen upon hard times and once again she was becoming more and more relaxed in his company. He was aware that his own response had changed too, he was not as frightened of showing himself up in her presence, was able to speak to her without stammering, to hold her eyes, although sometimes only momentarily. And better than all of that he did not see himself as an irredeemable fool unworthy of her presence. To him the way he was and his transformation was akin to the difference between the way the District bowed to the Clearys, and the way Aunt Vie did not. It was almost too subtle to be perceptible but palpable if you paid attention.

Now, she would talk to him freely, even asked his opinion on matters pertaining to her business, consult him on personal matters like colours she had chosen to wear out to a dinner party with Rose-marie, even laugh with him about her aunt's objections to her recent waywardness. She even insisted that he be one of her employees and be paid an hourly rate for things he did for her. He had refused at first but at the end of that week, she had grossly overestimated the hours he worked and so overpaid him, saying how hurt and offended she would be if he didn't accept. So the following week, he had kept a check himself, told her at the end, and had accepted her payment graciously.

He was happy. One evening, he mustered up the courage to talk to Aunt Vie about Miss Dee. He had been turning the words around in his head for days but each time he opened his mouth, the distance between Miss Dee and himself loomed larger than his feelings and he had kept quiet but that evening he was unable to stop himself.

'Aunt Vie,' he had said to draw her attention away from the patch of ground she had been weeding behind the house.

'You all right Littleman?'

'Yes,' he swallowed.

'You not in trouble Littleman are you?'

'Oh no.'

She studied his face. 'Let's pull up the bench and sit for a minute.'

He fetched water from the drum in a basin for her to wash her hands, did the same for himself, poured sugar and water from a jug he had made and brought to her earlier and sat down beside her.

'I think I put too much lime in this,' he said as he took the first sip.

'No man. I like the lime. Azora reckon it is the best source of some vitamin or other, I can't remember the exact letter she said.' Vie paused. 'So what this on your mind dearheart?'

'Miss Dee,' he said simply. He waited for some reaction from her but Vie only brushed a sand fly from her chin and waited.

'I . . . I . . .'

'You like her?' She helped him.

He nodded, feeling suddenly awkward and foolish as if he was saying that he loved and wanted a Cleary daughter. He was just about to apologise to her when she rested her hand on his knee.

She was smiling when he turned to look at her. The side of her mouth that was always out of control seemed softer and less obvious than before. He wondered whether it was because he had come to love her so that her flaws were less obvious to him, or whether Azora's medicines were helping her.

'One of the things that I feel, is it a great pity about the way us women are brought up. The way, for some reason that I have never been able to fathom, we think we should look for and like only the surface things in men.' She looked sad all of a sudden. 'So many of us could have lived better lives, if we didn't. If we didn't read a lot of fairy-tales and listen to a lot of foolishness about what is important and what is not. Don't get me wrong, men read the same fairy stories and listen to the same nonsense, so all of us trapped and few of us are happy.' He watched her, trying hard to follow her drift.

She smiled at him, patted his knee and took her hand away. 'I hardly know what to tell you. You know Miss Dee and you know Jane and you know this District.' She sighed heavily. 'There is nothing wrong with the way you feel. It's natural. Miss Dee is a handsome woman. A very handsome woman. And you?' She ran her hands over his head and down his neck. 'You are a good man. One of the best. I pray to God that some woman will look hard enough to see. I even wish I was young again.' She laughed and kissed him. The first time she had ever done so and the first time he had ever been kissed by anyone other than Nana.

Littleman smiled remembering her. 'The only woman I want to look hard enough to see is Miss Dee. I would do anything for her. Even give my life. Since I was at school I've felt that.' He had said a lot more than he had intended, more than he had ever said aloud even to himself.

'Littleman, Littleman. Sweetheart . . .' Vie said as she pulled his head on to her shoulder. But the way she repeated his name though she did not say it, spelt out for him the hopelessness of his dreams.

Chapter 28

Azora had her lying on a clean white sheet, her whole body covered with another equally spotless calico, only her left leg that she was to work on, was exposed.

Vie had been taking her medicines but this was to be her first body rub. As on the day when Azora had taken her to Kitson Town to the opticians, she had collected her from her house just as Littleman had been getting Greystripe ready for her. Azora's excuse was that she didn't want to waste the preparation she had made for Vie. 'So you don't trust me,' Vie had said, touched by her friendly and unpredictable gesture.

Prostrate, half-naked on Azora's bed, Vie mustered the courage to examine the herbalist's expression. In her heart of hearts, bearing in mind the past, Vie had expected a victorious expression or even ridicule, for this must surely be the most humbling position yet. But to Vie's surprise, Azora was masked by a totally new face. Gone was the contemplative, ready to break into a mischievous smile face, replaced by a purposeful concentrated demeanour. The prepared jar of oil rested on the bedside table and without further ado, not even a word to her, Azora poured some on her hands, rubbed them together and proceeded with her craft.

Vie felt she should have been self-conscious about loose areas of flesh that now characterised her hitherto taut and well-defined body, about the islands of scars that dug up her body, about her crooked toes that Babydear had loved. But she found that she was able to totally relax and allow her body to experience the firm, healing sensation of Azora's firm soft hands moving from her toes, her legs, her thighs and back.

By the time Azora had finished, Vie was almost asleep. 'Sleep if you like. It would be a compliment to me if you felt inclined to.' She pulled the sheet over her shoulders, went out and closed the door behind her.

Much later when Vie woke up and left the room Azora was sitting on the verandah, a mouth organ on the seat by her side. 'I didn't know you played?' she said still a little light-headed.

'I do sometime, when I'm in the mood. When I feel that the healing power walked through the hands,' she said with a broad grin. Vie had never heard her make light of her craft before and didn't quite know how to respond.

Azora didn't seem unduly put out. 'After a few months, when we see how you are getting on, I can give you a full body rub that will work even greater wonders,' she said.

Vie nodded, 'So, when you going to play?'

'You really want to hear me? I don't usually play in company.'

Vie wanted to ask why she had brought out the mouth organ but said instead, 'Pretend I'm not here,' thinking with admiration about the self-sufficiency of Azora. As if she is an island, needing only occasionally to interact, defining herself independently of what is common or normal. Despite her sixty-eight going sixty-nine years, Vie had never known a woman like her, never known that such women existed. She found herself both admiring and resenting her together. Admiring her skills, her self-assurance, her independence but resenting her aloofness from the District. Her arrogance.

'All right. After you tell me how you feel,' Azora said, still not having blown a note.

Vie tried to describe a sensation, the depth of relaxation which she said was a cross between how she imagined flying to feel combined with the luxury of half-sleep half-wake. What she could not bring herself to describe, even at her age, when she felt there should no longer be any inhibitions left especially in front of another woman, but was discovering new ones by the second, was the pleasure of having someone do something to her body when she did not have to reciprocate or feign any one emotion. She found herself instead asking with a grin if she gave the same treatment to men.

'But of course. Why not? I'm working . . .' She smiled as if there was more to be said but said nothing.

Vie changed the subject again exploring uncharted territory.

'So what you do for pleasure, all by yourself round the back here, that is, when I don't take pity on you and visit you? For the life of me I still don't understand why you never come round and join in what's going on. Get to know people. You not lonely?' she said all in one breath.

'I like my own company most of the time,' Azora smirked. 'You still don't think I know the District do you . . . ?' She observed Vie closely. 'Take it from me I know every single one of them.'

Vie looked at her for a minute. 'I suppose you do, in your own way.' Vie was tempted to be openly critical of her aloofness, of Azora's obvious attitude that she need not make the effort or put herself out to get involved in the District, since the District needed her more than she clearly needed it but Vie held her tongue on that and asked instead, 'How you do it though? Fit everyone in? Granted it can't be said that I frequent your yard, but still how come I never see anyone here when I'm here?' Azora thought so long that Vie did not think she could find an answer, then she said, 'A few years ago, I got people to make a kind of appointment. Roughly anyway . . .'

'I know that, but for emergency, nobody ever seem to come . . .' Vie hesitated.

'In daylight you mean,' Azora finished for her, looking at her, accusingly, Vie thought. 'Don't come and blame me. I had my view but I did not influence anybody.' Vie defended herself feebly.

'Aunt Vie you know that even if you blink, people in the District take your word as gospel,' Azora grunted. 'I even hear that Deacon himself once say that in the District, there are four forces that battling for the souls of the District; you, me, Satan and the Church.'

Vie had to laugh. 'The man can be so foolish at times. Why him leave out the wretched Clearys? Why him not preach them? Who else trap up everybody's mind, lives, pockets but them?'

'He can't criticise Cleary you know that . . .'

'Why not? That's what that cussed family depend on. Why you think they letting them borrow the piece of land the church on and give out free food?' The tiredness and tension that Azora had eased, came back with a vengeance. Vie didn't know how she had got on to the Clearys, the name she could not hear mention without accompanying headache and gnawing anger. She felt Azora's eyes. 'Don't worry about me blood pressure,' Vie said, even though willing back the feeling she had described. Azora's eyes were steady on her and, as if she knew what Vie was feeling, she rested a firm hand on her arm but it could not remove the bitterness of Cleary in Vie's mouth and heart. More and more as the days passed she was fearing that she would die and not have done enough to loosen the Cleary's grip on the District. To convince the District that they had to act, do something, instead of passively accepting their lot as they had done for generations.

Azora changed the subject. 'I don't believe that people should come to me just when they're ill. I think if more of us try we could prevent ourselves getting ill.'

'Sickness is a part of life Azora,' Vie said irritably, feeling her words a criticism of her own illness and frailty.

'Some sickness. Some caused by the way we live and eat.'

'That's true but something have to take us. None of us here to live forever.' Then 'I wouldn't want to live forever.'

'Sometimes I wish I could live forever,' Azora said looking in the distance. 'Vie,' she said drawing her attention again, 'You ever wonder why the older you get the more you wish that you could just have a little more time?'

'The things I want to see happen, what I want to do, need more time than I can ever have left.'

'What is that then?'

'You may well ask,' Vie said, not in the mood to resurrect the fading dreams she had had of unseating the Clearys, of bringing true independence to the District. How could she tell Azora that she could hardly resign herself to the fact that she would soon die, leaving things no better, even worse than when she was young and dreamt of changes. That she had accomplished nothing in her life. Influenced no one. That her existence had been a sham. Even the youth who could inherit her dreams had been taken away or dreamt not of seeing change in the District but of going elsewhere, town, England. She feared that Top Mountain like Eggsbury would die in fact or be so complacent that death would be the most fitting description of it.

Instead of saying any of that Vie asked, 'So when you going to play?'

'Now,' Azora said picking up the mouth organ and putting it to her lips.

As she began, one of her dogs started to howl, mounted the verandah and would not be silenced until Azora had set all the other dogs off in the vicinity. Vie wagered she could even pick out her own, Buster and Rex from the melee. Azora was not to be distracted, she drove the dog off the verandah, apologised and continued, with tunes she said she had composed the night before.

When she had played a few, she lowered the mouth organ and smiled at her.

'That was good,' she said sincerely. 'You are a talented woman. A total woman.'

'I wouldn't go so far. Just something to pass the long evenings with.'

'That is your choice.'

'What?'

'To be alone. As I said you could come and mix with people.'

'As I said, I like my own company. And besides, I get company in one form or another nearly every night.'

'You know something?' Vie said as if she had solved a long-standing puzzle. 'I think you purposely let good decent people in this District think you doing something dark and secret round here to drum up trade. You exploiting the superstition that entrench in this place.'

Azora didn't answer immediately, as if turning the words around in her mind. 'I'm all thing to all people Vie. That is the service.'

'And what you suppose to mean by that?'

Azora eyed her without answering and it crossed Vie's mind that obeah or not there was something about Azora that was not all it seemed.

'I said what you mean by that? You not Jesus Christ.'

'Some think I am and if . . .'

'That get them to go come to you and give you the money then that's all you need.' Vie suddenly remembered that when Azora had told her about Jane's baby she had mentioned in passing that she sold medicines to the Clearys, the shock of Azora's revelation about Jane had almost erased that from her head. Vie's tongue-in-cheek banter turned immediately into anger. 'And it's an insult to the people of this District for you to have any kind of friendship with the Clearys when you pretend to have our wellbeing at heart.' Azora looked confused and Vie felt a pang of ingratitude but did not relent. 'You're right there is no answer to that,' Vie said, but Azora's composure under her

217

onslaught took the steam out of her sudden anger. If I was still young and impressionable, Vie thought, that composure would be worth emulating but she did not allow her continued sneaking admiration of Azora to take root. She demanded a response.

'You too hard on me,' was all that Azora offered then. She picked up the mouth organ again and massaged her lips with it then said seriously, 'I see you chose to forget though what I said about helping plenty young people to throw away the Clearys children and why I been doing this over the years. It's not because I love the family.' Her caustic tone now was not lost on Vie. 'Anyway don't pretend you sad about me having bought land from Cleary . . . From what I hear, if there's a family who should fear your hate, it's that one and who can blame you. I, too, like yourself have been saying for the longest time that this District should loosen itself from their grip. Organise themselves, push the Clearys away from the District.'

Vie looked at Azora long and hard, surprised. Yes Azora had said she'd been destroying little unwanted Clearys. Yes that was a tremendous, brave and risky thing to have been doing, something if she had the opportunity she would have done. Vie broke into a smile. To have found a kindred in such an unlikely place in so unlikely a person. One she had so misjudged. Vie cursed herself for having taken so long. Now it was almost too late.

Chapter 29

There was the usual excitement that came with Christmas in Top Mountain. Nobody pretended as they did in the old days that it was just for children, Christmas providing the perfect excuse to end the year long deprivation that generally character-ised their lives. For once they didn't have to think about excesses when they unwrapped the money put aside in tins under beds, or the more daring, from banks, to make preparation for elabor-ate meals, new clothes, curtains, bed linen, shoes and treats for the children, like fire-crackers, bangers, candies, flutes, mouth-organs.

But one thing was different about the Christmas of 1968. Whereas in the past, the District had made pilgrimage to town to *buy up*, now, Miss Dee's shop provided everything they needed for the celebrations and more. And, if previously she had had cause to complain about business, the weeks preceding Christmas would have silenced her.

Miss Dee realised that, for one, she needed to have in stock a wide selection of fabrics from which every soul in the District could choose, the three separate items of clothing needed for the Christmas period. There was the one and most elaborate for Christmas Day itself, arguably the most important and well attended church service of the year where one had to arrive before the crack of dawn to secure a seat or bring one's own chair from home and sit in the yard outside and be content with the muffled sounds of the loud speakers positioned on trees around the church yard. Then there was another item of new clothing needed for New Year's Eve watch night service which heralded in the new year and of course one for later on New Year's Day itself. Watch night service, in line with the inherently superstitious nature of the District, was the most significant service of the year. The saying went that if you were found on your knees when the clock struck midnight and ushering in the new year, you were guaranteed God's richest blessings and so peace of mind for the entire year. The expected bounties some- how also came to be linked with the newness of attire worn on that night. New clothes, new year, new life, hopefully with the hitherto elusive wealth, prosperity in land. Some, despite the warning of the Deacon that this threatened to be idolatrous, regarded their new clothes as an even more important harbinger than being on one's knees in prayer when the clock struck twelve. The Deacon's warnings thereafter went unheeded to the extent that if he dared to open his own eyes on the striking of midnight, he would no doubt have caught many wandering eyes scanning the congregation in secret evaluation of who was the best dressed that night. So traditions and superstition, more embedded and deeply held than Christian doctrine, triumphed.

Now a couple of weeks before the first big event, Miss Dee and Rose-marie were rushed off their feet as was everyone else in the District.

In the midst of frenzied preparations, Azora persuaded Vie to go with her to Spanish Town to watch the jankuno show, saying she could have a chance to properly test out her glasses. Vie couldn't refuse. In the last few months, since knowing Azora, gaining confidence in her medicines, her life had taken on a semblance of carefreeness hitherto foreign to her. The longing for death was even slowly being pushed from her mind and Vie even found herself sometimes entertaining hopes of seeing her grandchildren, especially Babydear, again.

As a child, she remembered the parade, the grotesque masked figures prancing about with charity collection tins, herself nearby, half-buried in her mother's dress tail, tottering between the pandemonium of supreme happiness and crippling fear. Did those in the show really have faces like that or were they just masks as her parents had always insisted?

She did not of course tell Azora this, after all she was a big woman now and besides she was more preoccupied with how quickly it had travelled round the District that she and Azora were now bosom friends. No one apart from Ezekiel and earlier Jane had approached her with their views directly but Vie had been graced by many otherwise aimless visits from virtually all the women in the District dropping hints as questions, only to have them leave no wiser than they had come.

So as the car Azora had hired braved its way over the stones, only slightly less taxing than previously because of the seasonal work that came the way of the District to weed the grass verges and replace some of the larger stones along the way with others only marginally better, Vie was conscious of double takes from eyes on verandahs, yards and passers-by.

Aunt Vie only admitted to herself the excitement she felt as the taxi bumped its way over the last stones of Top Mountain, passed through Old Road and turned left onto the paved road of Kitson and the last stretch through St John's Road and into Spanish Town. When she had had her stroke she had thought that the only time she would leave the District would be in a casket. She had not bemoaned that, having vowed years before that she had had enough of the hauling and pulling. The days had passed when she had no option but to sit in the boiling sun haggling with market shoppers, bidding to shift the ground provisions, mindful of the pounds, shillings and pence for paying the rent, buying essentials like kerosene oil, cornmeal, flour, rice and salt fish. Now, as their taxi joined the throng of other cars, trucks and buses, the melee of hagglers and shoppers, weaving between them, it seemed to her more than ever that the paved streets attracted and trapped the heat, putrefying the smells, magnifying them and throwing them back with a vengeance at country folks. Vie could never be persuaded that humans were exercising sense when they chop down trees to make houses as close together as they did in town, leaving so little space for the wind to whip up good fresh air.

Feeling rejuvenated, Vie had made a special effort with her dress, having asked Miss Dee to make something suitable for her. She was fully aware that it was not Miss Dee but Jane who would eventually sew it but she did not allow it to concern her unduly, she had just told Miss Dee from the start not to let on it was for her. Eventually Miss Dee brought a dress which took a little getting used to and Vie found herself debating for days whether she could indeed wear it. Miss Dee and Littleman had joined forces against her and she let herself be convinced that the blue and white seersucker, pulled in at the waist with a belt and finished off with a buckle, was not too young for her. On showing Miss Dee the straw hat she planned to wear she had come the next day with a band from the same material to go round the brim. Only the shoes could not be in line, she was unable to find one from the two good pairs she owned that did not need to be slit to ease her bunion.

As the taxi picked its way to the area of town Azora wanted, Vie shared with her the memory of the days when she was not unlike some of the women they passed along the way, walking to Town with loads on their heads, no money to take a taxi or even a truck, hoping that they would return with a knot tied in their handkerchief, able to afford a cramped seat in a vehicle and settle overdue bills back at home. Or perhaps one of those riding a stubborn donkey, hamper laden with similar ground provisions or cassava bread, coffee, chocolate, pimento, even pulses. Or even later in her life, on a dray with a stubborn mule. She related a particular incident to Azora of going across the level crossing in the dray in question, and how she had nearly lost her life '. . . when the cursed mule had just barely stopped short of an oncoming train'. She had even been thrown when she was pregnant with her child and, God knows how, she said, she had not lost the precious child.

She leant on Azora's arm as they strolled now through the market, marvelling constantly at how clear the world seemed through her glasses and how novel it was for her to walk through the market for leisure. Vie could not help but wonder what sight they presented, two old women, walking aimlessly arm-in-arm, as if they were best-friends-school-girls. Seeing the respect that Azora accorded the women who Vie was once like herself, as they shouted to them to choose their tomatoes or yam, scallion, dasheen, sweet potatoes, coconuts and countless other provisions freshly harvested from diverse parishes, endeared Azora, who by all intents and purposes was a big landowner and a woman at that, afresh to Vie. That the women, baked dry by an unrelenting sun, were sprawled out on the market floor, ostensibly without dignity or the talents and skills that Azora herself possessed, and so undeserving of respect, seemed only to give her cause to revere them.

When they had their fill of walking, of the entreaties of the market sellers to choose from them, or even their curses when they handled their goods without buying, they took what was a vantage position in a bar to await the jankuno parade, Azora with a glass of rum, Vie with carrot juice, viewing the expectant crowd.

It was Azora's turn to reminisce, hers to listen. But Vie was not like her, she interrupted Azora constantly with her laugh, questions, points of her own. And for the first time Azora answered the question that Vie had not yet got round to asking her, about where she sprung from, what had brought her out of the blue to Top Mountain.

It was from St Thomas, the most eastern Parish on the Island.

223

She had made a name for herself as the best cyclist in her District. 'I was the best,' she said without any pretence of modesty. 'The best,' she repeated. 'They used to call me Put-A-Woman.'

Vie looked questioningly at her.

'. . . Because when I used to ride through the District, beating the hell out of all of them, my friends used to shout, Put it pan dem . . . Put it pan dem . . . I used to go everywhere on me bike, find any competition in the Island. Even went to Trinidad once . . .' Vie smiled because her voice had risen as the fit young men's did when supporting their cricket teams.

'So what made you stop cycling? I only see you ride horses and mules . . . as if you are a big shot,' Vie added, a provocative look in her eyes.

'It stopped me. I didn't want to stop. I didn't think I would ever stop. In those days, I saw myself riding until the day they nail up the coffin.'

'How it stopped you?'

Azora thought for a long time, as if she wasn't sure how to phrase her answer. When she eventually answered Vie, she had shifted her eyes and was looking out onto the streets, talking as if to herself. 'I was a woman. When I was young, they used to say, *She just a tom-boy. She won't want to be spreading her legs open over handlebars, horses and mules for long. Give her a chance, she'll grow out of her manly ways.*' She smiled an almost imperceptible smile. 'But I didn't grow out of any of it . . . any of my abnormal ways. They just got worse, they said, more entrenched. In the end nobody could tolerate me. My family was ashamed of me, ashamed of everything about me . . . For instance, look at the size of me. How many women you see who is so far over six foot?' She sighed and for the first time Vie spied sadness in her eyes.

'. . . And I had no hunger for men, at least not in the ways women normally hunger for them. I liked them, had them as

224

my friends, even now. But I didn't feel the need for any more intimacy. Never did. Never will . . . So as I grew and the name-calling and worrying about me got too much . . . Everything I did concerned everybody. If I walked they thought it was odd, if I ran, they laughed. When I studied the herbs and use them they accused me of practising obeah. So I moved from place to place, practising what I knew best, saved and worked, and looked for a place that would let me be . . . And I found Top Mountain.'

Chapter 30

Vie gave Azora a few days then she went to see her. 'I've just come to check you,' she said when Azora came from behind her house to greet her. Since they had been to Town for the Christmas parade, Vie had been left with a strange nagging worry about Azora's past. Vie was puzzled by her feelings. She had felt a lot of things about Azora over the years but never pity. But the way Azora had spoken about her past, the knowledge that Azora was not after all some special human being unaffected by the shackles of traditions and expectations, affected Vie. After hours of thinking about it, Vie concluded that it was not exactly pity she felt but anger. Anger against the people whom she did not know personally but whom she could know because they were everywhere in every town and district. People who would not let women be.

'Good of you to come Vie but I couldn't be better.'

Vie observed her closely and it seemed she was telling the truth, Azora wore the same look as she always did. Vie was relieved, she had imagined that the memory of the past would have engulfed Azora as it had threatened to do Vie herself. Relieved, Vie invited her to spend Christmas in the District but Azora did not feel the need to, instead she invited Vie to spend Boxing Day with her at her house.

Two days before Christmas Vie hung new curtains at the windows, took out her Christmas spread from her trunk and dressed her bed. The annual Christmas parcel had arrived the day before from her daughter, Isadora, with, among clothing and household wares for herself and Isadora's old friends in the District, little trinkets and Christmas decorations from Baby-dear. Vie took special care in putting these up and packing the new sheets, spread and dinner service away, for using, she did not know when. She was trying to get out of the habit of automatically putting things up, for a rainy day. At her age, she often thought, there would not be many more rainy days, just that last and final deluge. But old habits die hard.

The Maxton's eldest, Blue Boy, came over to help her. When he had made several trips for her, to fetch water from the stand-pipe in front of Ezekiel's shop, fetched and carried messages for her, the last one to Jane telling her that Vie had to see her that night, she gave him lunch, sixpence and sent him home with his mother's parcel that had come wrapped up from Isadora, know-ing there would be goodies in there for him too, he ran home, a broad Christmas smile on his face.

Vie had planned to have more people in her yard this Christ-mas than she would normally have entertained. But as usual the responsibility would not be hers alone. Ezekiel and Dora would be providing the goat, for the curry. The Maxtons the pig for corned and jerk pork and Deacon the chickens for the roast, other items for salad and vegetables would be provided from her ground in Eggsbury and from others around the District, as would drinks which would come from fruits and vegetables, sour sop, tamarind, pineapples, carrots. And rum. That certainly would not be scarce. So although most everyone from the Dis-trict would be in her yard sometime or other on Christmas Day, Vie would not be over-burdened. Her job was to buy whatever it had been worked out that she would contribute, get the house and yard ready in time for the setting up of the marquee on Christmas Eve.

Jane arrived when Vie had finally slumped, exhausted on the verandah rubbing her feet, wondering why she had not felt so beaten until she had sat down, hoping that she had not overdone it and would have to spend the next few days in bed. Jane carried items for storing in the kitchen, confirming to Vie without having to say so, that she would be suspending her malice at least for the day. Vie watched her as she returned, still wondering why she had to make life such a fight for herself.

Vie could not resist commenting on how tired she looked. When Jane said she had not been sleeping well Vie did not ask her why but heard something worse slipping out of her mouth, she could have pinched herself, 'You should check Azora, she's bound to have something to help you.' Jane stared at her with obvious bitterness, as if Vie's words were calculated to wound her. It flashed through Vie's mind to apologise but quickly decided to leave it, saying instead that she herself had overdone the cleaning. Jane was not to be sidetracked or manipulated.

'You send for me, what you want me to do for you?' Vie shook her head feeling suddenly sorry for Jane but more than that irritated by what she saw as her childish intransigence. She snapped, 'Jane why don't you grow up! I have done nothing to you to make you behave like this.'

Jane stood up. 'I have no time to waste getting lectured by you. I come all this way because I thought you needed something.'

'Jane sit down and stop you foolishness.'

'I tell you already, I've had me fill of taking orders from you. You forget that I find me feet now. I'm not the new girl in the District now needing your directions.' Vie passed her hand over her face showing her exasperation. There was then an uncertain pause, Vie not knowing what it was safe to say. Jane on the brink of leaving but seemingly not averse to taking an outstretched olive branch if offered.

'I miss you Jane. That's what I send for you to say.' Jane raised her head slowly and looked at her, opened her mouth, didn't utter a word to that but did not retake her seat either.

'Listen Vie, you always play big and mighty in this District. Everyone treat you like you some goddess. Don't mix me up with them.'

'If only I was really a goddess I would have been able to tell what really eating you out. Then I would end this carry on and get it out of you system for you.'

'You mean with herbs and rub downs,' Jane snapped.

'The way you carrying on not even Azora's best would cure you,' Vie retorted, matching her abrasiveness.

'It take away your shame though . . . the two of you parading in full view of the District. After all your condemnation. What I would like to know is what she do to change you so?'

'For God sake Jane,' Vie said now more amused than angry, watching Jane shift from one leg to the next, irritated that she would not sit down. 'Why don't you give yourself some peace girl? What past is past. I was wrong, so wrong.'

They were silent for a long time.

'Jane why you no sit down?' Vie repeated out of habit now, not expecting her to mount the verandah and comply but she did. No other words broke another weighty silence. Vie prayed that Littleman would not return and so drive Jane away. She hoped Jane would find the words to tell her what Vie already knew. Vie longed to have the chance to give Azora's side, to tell her that Azora did not knowingly help Cleary to kill her child but Jane had to raise it first. But after a while it was clear that Jane did not seem ready to say anything else or to change the sour, wronged expression on her face.

Littleman came and Jane mumbled greeting to him, but he was his normal affable self, he set about sorting out the goods he had brought from town, ate with them, helped to tidy up and disappeared. Vie watched Jane's expression carefully as he had busied himself, wondering if she knew Littleman's intentions towards Miss Dee, apprehensive about the uproar she was certain it would cause.

Chapter 31

On Christmas Eve as the men were setting up the coconut bough marquee in Vie's yard, women positioned stones in triangles by the side of the kitchen to hold the extra large pots and pans that were needed.

The tradition had come about years before as a way of ensuring that everyone in the District had something special to eat on Christmas Day, a sizeable number of them put together what they had, making a veritable feast. Old people who lived alone were relayed by the taxi Miss Dee had organised and paid for from Kitson Town, grandchildren from town who were spending the holiday with their grandparents, like Ezekiel and Dora, would make up the number.

Vie mustered up all the enthusiasm she could on the day itself, taking advantage of her increasing mobility and ability to use both her arms though still not equally well, if a little tired of the constant reference to her miraculous improvement.

First there was the feasting followed by the obligatory nativity play put on by the children, the dress rehearsal for the Christmas service at the church on the Sunday and the now standard rendition by Miss Dee and Ragu. Both contrasted with the uncontrolled riotous fun afterwards, as rum punch took effect, rivalled only by the frenzied romping of the children, setting off fire crackers and bangers, shouting Happy Christmas for the millionth time as they pranced around the yard showing off the single Christmas presents they had received from their families.

Ostensibly, Vie was enjoying herself too but throughout the day, her mind was taken with what Azora would be doing. All alone on Christmas Day. Solitary. Contrary to the dictate of normality and tradition. It was not without some anxiety for Azora that Vie wished her guests gone and the day ended so that she could have a good night's sleep. Only Jane, feeling she had done her duty and shown her face, obliged. The conversation of the rest shifting from one subject to the next with consummate ease; the flight of Leroy from the District under mounting suspicion that he was to be blamed for wrecking Miss Dee's shop and the shame he had brought to his grandparents. 'The District is better off without a boy like that,' Mr Maxton remarked. 'Top Mountain is a District of hardworking people. He was a lazy good-for-nothing criminal.'

'Nobody will miss him and his grandparents will be better off without his weight,' Ruthlyn Maxton offered.

Moving on to Bellinda Jerr, that she was hiding away at home because she had fallen and was carrying somebody's baby, some said Leroy's, others that they weren't so sure. The fatigued punctuated their contributions with cat-naps, shamelessly sprawled out on the floor of the verandah or even the hard red dirt. Eventually the children were driven home under orders to bathe and put themselves to bed, protests silenced with threats of Christmas spankings.

It was well after three in the morning when the inebriated taxi driver, among the last to leave, having earlier taken the old people home, vowing now that he was stone sober as he said goodbye, collapsed by the pig sty on his way to his car. Littleman gave him his bed for the night glad for the excuse if any was needed to walk Miss Dee part way home.

Vie made her way to Azora on Greystripe the following day as

232

arranged. A table was set and spread with white lace table cloth and matching napkins, on the verandah. Whatever Vie had expected, this was not it. She had expected to come and help her prepare and perhaps to eat later, fortunately she had only had tea in the morning and was rather hungry. Azora didn't allow her to lift a finger. Rather she sat and was waited on as she served one course after another, clearing away in no time, without fuss.

When they had finished and the table was returned to its rightful place in the spare room, they sat side by side on the verandah, night still somewhere in the distance.

'Azora I feel I must say how very regretful I am for the thirty years . . .'

'You don't have to . . .'

Vie sighed, 'I do and I would like you to accept it.'

Azora nodded faintly.

'And what I want to know besides is how comes you stayed in Top Mountain when people like me drove you from other districts.'

'No. Not people like you,' she smiled a beaming smile. 'You and me are more alike than you know. That's why it is so good, makes me so happy, to have won your confidence at last . . . After so many years I was beginning to doubt that I would.'

Vie felt ashamed. She was linked with those who had not let Azora be. Those who had turned her into a recluse, had driven her into solitude.

'It was perhaps a fortunate thing for me though,' Azora was saying without any perceptible hint of self-pity, regret or bitterness. 'This life, my solitude, frees me from the fetters of other women . . . Women like your Jane, Dora . . .'

Vie wanted to know what she called fetters. When Azora had listed almost everything that characterised the lives of women in the District, Vie said, 'Shackles can be broken.'

'Leaving scars,' Azora insisted.

There followed a heated discussion between them. Vie defending the women of the District whom she said Azora could never understand. Azora refusing, she said, to be patronised, showing Vie instead in minutest detail how many of the women she defended, fashioned their own chains, put them in place and threw away the keys.

Eventually, Vie decided that there must be some compromise argument somewhere. Something other than men or women who were to be blamed for the fetters. Neither of them could think who or what that might be.

Having reached an impasse there, Vie asked the question that had been plaguing her. How Azora had got the Clearys to sell her land.

'I suppose since I was out of the District, they didn't feel the need to keep me in my place ... Still the senior was more willing than the younger one ... ,' Azora said it had been a war of attrition lasting more than five years. Finally, she wore them down. 'They knew I wasn't going to give up. I suppose five years is nothing compared to how long people in the District have been waiting ... There has to be determination, willingness to not take no. Even independence come and gone. What else is there to come to give them the excuse or to give the District the will to make them?'

Vie watched her for a long time allowing her words to sink in. It still amazed her that Azora, a relative stranger to Top Mountain, with nothing to gain personally from changes in the District, was thinking her thoughts. 'I couldn't agree with you more Azora, if only you know. But what I still don't see is why a stranger to the District like yourself should want to see change, should care about people here. The Clearys not downtrodding you.' Azora replied jokingly that she did not consider herself a stranger still, after thirty years. 'But,' she continued, 'Stranger or not to this little District, I'm no stranger to the Island. There are

Clearys in every corner of this country, keeping the likes of you and me, yes you and me because we are no different, in the places they mark out for us, somewhere below them, separated from them, whether in the amount of land they own more than us, the amount of education, wealth, power, opportunities or their different colour shades. So every little victory that's won, that you and I win, in every little corner, is one less battle for others to fight.'

Vie nodded, she could not honestly say she was concerned about the whole Island, Top Mountain was her preoccupation. And time was running out. Yes, her health was improving under Azora's care but even Azora could not give her eternal life. She had to act now, especially now that she had found someone of the same mind, who needed nothing from the Clearys and would not be cowed into silence and inactivity. Vie resolved that a start had to be made to loosen once and for all the Clearys' hold on the District and more importantly imbue the youth of the District with the same determination so that when she went the fight would continue.

But she had made resolutions before and she could not help harbouring a tremendous sense of personal responsibility and failure. She had influenced the District on so many other things and yet not that, the most vital thing, getting the Clearys to part with land. She said feebly articulating half her thoughts, 'It's not for want of trying over the years to get them to sell land. They just refuse to sell. For the life of me I can't understand what good the hundreds of wasted acres are to them when in the District so many young have nothing to do. There could be more Miss Dees, more Ragus. They know so much they could pass on. Even Jane and women like them, but there is nowhere to build workshops and the like, to do more cultivation.

'Yes, that's why we have to let our good young people go, the Babydears . . .' Azora said in a lowered voice.

Vie studied Azora carefully. In all these years, there Azora

235

was living just behind her, thinking her thoughts, having her unspoken plans and she did not know. If there was anything she regretted, that was it. Vie spoke half her thoughts. 'I hope we haven't left it too late?' Azora didn't immediately follow her line of thought. Vie explained, how she agreed that if the District put its mind to it, with both of them at the helm, they could change the Clearys' mind, start a separation from the family, free the District from them, 'Get our *independence*. Before we die.' Azora nodded.

'And I'm sure after that, young ones like Miss Dee . . . Littleman, Babydear, if she comes back as she keeps threatening in her tear sodden letters, will lead the fight with the young . . .'

That evening was the kind Vie loved, breezy, almost cold, one of the nights when she would normally have dug out one of the candlewick spreads from her trunk, snuggled under and relished its comfort and warmth. Tonight she was more than happy to delay that, basking now in the greater comfort and warmth of friendship and hope.

Chapter 32

The start of 1969 was not unlike the start of 1968, 1967, 1966 . . . There was a quiet expectancy in the air, the hope for newer and better things, happier and better times. But behind all that there was the nagging silent knowledge that, as in previous years, the same insecurities, fears, uncertainties and struggles would continue unabated, the same stories told. Few things would be different.

The shops in the District re-opened and even the most recalcitrant farmers had returned to their grounds.

Miss Dee, having more cause for optimism than most, was nevertheless restless as she had been for sometime. Despite the impression she gave, she was not blind to Littleman's infatuation. It concerned and preoccupied her and she found herself petrified that he would say something to her about it. She talked to Rose-marie about it. Her friend did not allay her worry, just exacerbated it. So instead of basking in the new status that she had won for herself in the District, in the inspiration that she gave others; that they did not have to depend solely on the Clearys of the world, this or that brassiere factory in town; in her success in destroying their resentment against her, she found her mind in turmoil.

What was complicating matters Miss Dee reminded her friend, as Rose-marie sat practising on the new sewing machine that had been bought for her to learn to sew on, was that Jacob,

237

all of a sudden, had taken to calling on her more regularly now. Rose-marie had even heard around the District and as far as Kitson Town, and had passed on to Miss Dee, that Jacob was making it clear that he had private business with her. That he was on the verge of taking over the running of his father's business in the District too. And that meant, it seemed, Rose-marie had said, more than just his land and buildings.

At first, despite Rose-marie's cynicism, Miss Dee had been secretly flattered and could not help dreaming of what his friendship could mean to her, how there could be no comparison between him and Littleman, dear though he was. Yet, Miss Dee couldn't understand what she had done to suddenly attract Jacob's attention, when weeks before she was just a country girl who might or might not wear clothes. She examined herself in the mirror. Had she changed overnight? Suddenly got prettier, more shapely, more intelligent?

His one weekly visits became twice weekly then thrice and she found herself slowly being sucked in by the words he whispered to her when Rose-marie was out of earshot; the compliments about her looks, her business, her way of speaking, so different from others in the District, he said, making her he said, out of place and deserving of better.

More than that Rose-marie told her that it was being said in the District that she was to be his woman in the country, as this and that woman had been his father's and grandfather's before him. That was what they had expected of him. Of her they wondered whether like other eager, hopeful young women, she was ripe for empty promises and the kind of life he would lead her, hiding her away from his friends and family, stealing to see her when he felt the need for her, dispensing with her when he had had his fill, to marry a brown-skin girl from his class in town. 'Don't you see that she look so high up she can't see the mulatto children him father breed and leave in one district one after the other, as if he did not lie naked next to their

238

mothers . . .' And collectively they held their breath waiting for the signs that consummation of their relationship had occurred and she would have his baby and so signal the end to his games as they said had happened to the latest woman, Bellinda.

Bellinda it was being said now, had been caught once or twice in the dead of night, stealing over the fence of the big white house on the hill, when Jacob's jeep had been there and the generator drumming the electric lights on. They now wondered aloud whether it was indeed Leroy's and not Jacob's child that she carried. From what Miss Dee heard, Bellinda would not say.

'It'll be obvious when the baby comes,' Miss Dee said angrily to Rose-marie. 'Why doesn't everyone just wait . . . Anyway can you see Jacob wanting *her*?'

'You obviously don't know men like him,' Rose-marie said scornfully.

But strangely, despite her disbelief that Jacob could go to Bellinda when all the time he praised Miss Dee for being so different from girls like Bellinda, now that the rumours were being repeated too often to ignore and Bellinda's silence was too telling, it all jolted Miss Dee to her senses, her pride. But she did not know how she would extricate herself from the knot she had got herself in with him. She had not promised him anything but she had all but, as she had allowed him to take her hands, rub his lips over hers and breathe his tickling breath over her neck, knowing full well that when he was out of her sight, there was no hunger for him, only for what he was, for his life-style. What he looked like was immaterial, as was how he walked, how he smiled, what his hands, his teeth were like, only what he had was important.

But he was not easy to resist, for contrary to what the District said about him hiding women away, as his father did *his* concubines, one Friday Jacob invited her to a movie in town. She could choose any Saturday she wanted. 'See,' Miss Dee gloated to Rose-marie, only a hint of doubt, more in confusion. 'He's not hiding me away. I haven't given away anything to him . . . not yet anyway . . .' Rose-marie did not laugh with her. 'And he's taking me to town. He even said we can meet some of his friends afterwards and go back to his house on the hill in St Andrew, to listen to music . . .' She got no encouragement from Rose-marie, only disappointed looks, and since she could not tell Littleman about it, she blurted it out to her aunt that evening. Miss Dee was taken aback and confused by her aunt's response.

'That boy dare to bring his rudeness to you.' She was furious. 'You haven't . . . ?' Jane's eyes widened.

'No aunt, I haven't.'

'Don't let yourself down I'm warning you. I didn't raise you to be no concubine for that heartless murdering family.' Miss Dee raised an eyebrow, she had never heard her aunt express any strong feelings either way towards the Clearys. Miss Dee's confusion increased. Despite her doubts about Jacob's real intentions, his family's reputation in the District, she wished she was free to think for herself, make up her own mind. Jacob's attention was something she had only dared dream about in the past and now her dreams, amazingly had become real. Why was she now having to *think about it*, why did she need to listen to anyone?

'When *any* young man want your attention, he will have to treat you like a lady. It will be over my dead body before anyone, Cleary or no Cleary, rich or poor, dodge and hide you, you're not a whore!' Miss Dee covered her mouth in surprise at her aunt's language.

'He's invited me to town, to a movie and to meet his friends at his house.'

'He what?'

'He'll pick me up and return me home.' Jane's surprise silenced her momentarily, she gaped at Miss Dee. Miss Dee smiled and nodded.

'That still doesn't mean that boy has any claim . . .' Then as if hit by another thought her aunt said, 'I knew you wouldn't have to make do with any of these good-for-nothings in this place . . .'

'Aunt Jane? You just said . . .'

'I suppose it's possible that the boy can be different from his father.'

Miss Dee frowned, 'Why, because he invites me to town? Aunt Jane you're not making sense.'

'I'll make you something new to wear . . .' Aunt Jane said nonchalantly, lost in her own inexplicable and sudden change of heart. 'You deserve it Miss Dee . . .' Her expression belying her words.

'But I don't know whether I should go or not,' Miss Dee said, eyeing her aunt suspiciously, 'I have to feel something and I don't.'

Jane sat down. 'Feelings is nothing,' she said drily.

'And you've heard about Bellinda.'

'I think now that must be lie, you and Bellinda have nothing in common. She's a yard gal . . .'

'Anyway, I still *don't* feel anything for him . . .'

'Feelings soon go. Don't worry about feelings.' Her aunt sounded so wary, so unconvinced, that Miss Dee didn't quite understand her position.

'I have to,' Miss Dee said quietly. 'Besides even if it's not true about Bellinda I hear he has many girlfriends in town.'

'That's not for you to worry about. Think of yourself.'

'I am thinking of myself, that's why I won't go anywhere with him. I don't know what he wants from me,' she found herself saying. She had not meant to say that, hadn't made up her mind, despite Rose-marie, when she had started telling her aunt. Now she was certain. Her aunt, Miss Dee decided, didn't really want her to go, was only trying, most ineffectively, to persuade her because she thought it what she wanted. Her aunt could not be so different from others in the District who thought the Clearys should be avoided at any cost by anyone calling herself decent and with self-respect.

'Anyway I hate the way he comes to the shop, struts around as if he own it . . .'

'He does . . .'

'His father does.'

'Same difference. He's the only son . . .'

'That's not what I've heard . . .'

Jane turned away.

'Well he's the only one for the wife. The first born, the one that will inherit everything from him . . . The others are stray children.' Her voice dropped so quietly that Miss Dee could hardly hear her. 'They say stray children are like stray dogs, nothing due to them . . . Some feel they don't even deserve to be born.' With that she kissed Miss Dee goodnight and disappeared into her room.

The next evening Miss Dee went to Aunt Vie and told her what had been happening with Jacob. Vie stared at her long and hard with a look that Miss Dee had never seen before. For a moment she wondered if Vie was suddenly taken ill, about to have a second stroke. Miss Dee got up quickly and sat next to her, rubbing her hands. Vie turned to face her and spoke as emphatically as she could. 'That family is a dangerous family,' she said slowly and with an emphasis Miss Dee had not heard in her voice before.

'. . . They worse than the devil that the church says is like a roaring lion seeking who to devour. How can the worthless brute impregnate Bellinda and now bring words to you. Run the boy Miss Dee! Run him! You too good to be soiled by the likes of the Clearys. Too precious to us, to harbour his seed.'

Chapter 33

Jane had totally given in to her feelings over the past few months. Since she had known for a fact that there was no stopping the friendship between Vie and Azora, the threads that had been her life had finally disintegrated. She could not sleep at nights and her eyes that had, at the best of times, been cream where others were white, took on a yellow hue giving the effect of unceasing weeping. She lost the little body fat that she had been tenuously hanging on to over the years, making her look and feel the walking wounded that she was.

Now to add more burden to that already stacked on her, was the business with Miss Dee and Jacob. The shock of the knowledge had set her rambling, no real help to Miss Dee. Having now had time to think about it, Jane realised that some of what she had said absentmindedly and by impulse, was meant, though they had poured from inside her with little help from her brain. The public friendship of Miss Dee and Jacob would be the greatest retribution against John Cleary Junior, Jacob's father. Whatever happened, Jane vowed to see to it, that Jacob would not have her Miss Dee going the long way round through Old Road to his house; as his father had had her do, ducking and diving like a common thief and whore.

She would make sure, with the help of a good obeahman, like one who had fixed Amos for her, that Miss Dee knew how to behave so that Jacob would fall totally in love with her. And as one of the Clearys would be left with no choice but to marry a country girl. The high and mighty family would be powerless to prevent it. When it was all done, she would make John Cleary Junior know that it was she who had humbled his family.

But this new involvement with the Clearys, pained her more than she would let herself believe, twisting her heart. At nights when sheer exhaustion defeated her troubled mind and she would have slept, memories of her baby that never was resurfaced. And each time it came to her, the pain of her loss was fresh, engulfing her, bringing back the midnight weeping into her pillow.

Afterwards, Jane conjured vivid pictures of John Cleary's, following sharply by Azora's death. His painful death. Sometimes she imagined herself the perpetrator and would caress ominously the item of clothing she had taken when she had left him that night, when she had been overwhelmed with gratitude to him and Azora for working miracles in her body, a list of out-of-District obeahman lined up in her mind. At other times, his death was at the hand of some demented madman wielding a two edged cutlass but whoever, it was always painful. Torturous. A final and total revenge for the pain he had put her through. The pain that she had never even had time to share with him or even to hear him make incredible explanations for what he had done. She had not asked much, just that she be allowed to prove that she was a real woman like the rest, not a eunuch with a dried-up womb.

But in more sober moments, she feared her thoughts, cursed her thoughts. Feared the friendship she thought he had with the powerful Azora, because like everyone else, apart from Vie it seemed now, she was convinced that Azora was embued with supernatural power and mysteries that even the most fearsome out-of-District obeahman could but revere. Such was the extent of Jane's own superstition and her belief in Azora's powers that soon after she had killed them in her mind, she would have them resurrected with the incompatible combination of prayers, psalms and bits and pieces of incantations that had lodged in her mind from various suspect sources over the years.

So unable to reach them, she turned all manifestations of her anger to Vie and would now only visit her when she was driven to see if she would catch Azora there. But when she did on the night Vie had returned from town with her, Jane could not trust herself to be face-to-face with Azora and she had crept back down the lane hopefully undetected.

Vie called round now and again on Greystripe, determined at first it had seemed to ignore Jane's behaviour and continue as before. But their conversation was always stilted and strained. Now it seemed to Jane, Vie only came when she was sure Miss Dee was there and between them a constant chatter would be kept up until Vie mounted her donkey and left.

Tonight Jane was alone, Miss Dee was staying at the shop, as she had done since their disagreement about Jacob a week before. It was one of the nights which Jane dreaded. She had been on her own long enough to recognise the warning signs as soon as they appeared. She had had her bath in the usual way, powdered her body and put on her night clothes. The pitch blackness around her house was unbroken, as it usually was by pennie whallies. For some reason the fireflies that normally formed a row in front of her house were absent, and since there was no moonshine and being so far in the back of the District, she couldn't catch even a glimpse of glimmering lanterns from cosy homes. The reasons why she had chosen to live apart were the reasons she now hated having done so.

She put on her house coat and came out on the verandah, trying to ignore the senses that had for no apparent reason awoken in her body. She sat and stared in the darkness trying to distract herself, ignore the plea of her body for some kind of satisfaction, some easing of her tension, of the sudden aching in the lower part of her body, the sudden flush of dampness. An overwhelming desire to feel a hand, any hand over her body. Down her body. She got up, irritated and annoyed with nature, cursing it in her heart for not taking away the desire with the opportunity. She went to the kitchen but by the time she got there she didn't feel she had the energy to make the tea she thought would ease her hunger.

She went back to the verandah but unable to sit still, got up and went into her room. She lowered herself on the bed, her mind's eyes on him, Cleary Junior, she imagined an agreed pact to make a child, creating the scene as she recalled it; his strong aroma of expensive town soap, freshly laundered clothes, his hand exploring her body. Slow and deliberate. Down. Down. His hand. Her hand that was his hand, gasping as he met the waiting dampness. She rolled over onto waiting fingers, her breathing loud and uncontrolled, her body reaching its peak quicker than she had hoped, disappointingly quicker. She had hoped to linger awhile with him, with herself. She lay still in wonder at how easily her thirst had been quenched and yet how dissatisfied she was still. It was a long time before she realised that she was weeping.

It crossed her mind as she went about her daily duties the following day that in order to free herself and despite her fear, she had to bring her whole experience with Cleary and Azora out into the open. That would be the only way to free herself from the shame of her barrenness and expose the true Azora; the District would know that she was not abnormal after all, that she *had* conceived a child. They would replace their scorn with sympathy. She would show that Azora had been in league with the Clearys all these years, had been conspiring with them against the District, despite appearances. Perhaps murdering many children with the Clearys. After her night of tossing and turning, Jane's sense of urgency was all-consuming, she was convinced that she had to tell all now. Vie was allowing herself

246

to be completely seduced by Azora. If only Vie knew the truth, she would drop Azora like a hot coal and take up their friendship. Help her to drive her desperate loneliness away.

She just had to tell somebody. But who else was there apart from Vie? Deacon and Sister Netta? What could they do? The church's half-hearted condemnation of Azora had gone mostly unheeded over the years. Now everybody, despite what they whispered, was in her grasp, feared her. Throughout the day, she would stop what she was doing: resting on the broom handle as she swept the yard perhaps, gazing into the hazy morning sun as she fed the chickens and her dogs, standing by the water drum as she collected water for her tea, sitting in the bath pan, her eyes vacant, an antithesis of her mind that was a turmoil of unresolved thoughts and counter thoughts.

At her sewing machine, finishing off one of the many dresses ordered through the shop, she decided that she would have to do something about her unbearable loneliness, though as yet she did not know what. What was clear to her was that she did not want to be alone forever. Miss Dee would soon be gone . . . She still occasionally spoke of moving to town eventually, even to England. Marriage was more probable, Jane thought, even though I have not given her any example of how normal women are supposed to be. If only someone Miss Dee loved, like herself or Vie, Jane thought with sadness, had been a good example to her, found a man and settled with him and shown Miss Dee what was right. For what was enough money in the bank, land, as much food and clothes as she wanted when she had lived a fruitless life, would never have grandchildren like normal women? When she had to spend each night alone suffocated between ancient trees and oppressive uncaring desires.

When finally she went out to sit with Dora in the evening, her mind was calmer, though her face showed as did her companion's, the indelible scars of bitterness, anger, frustration and unhappiness.

247

Sitting with Dora, their silence broken by the occasional clash of Dora's crochet needle with the wedding band partly embedded in her flesh, Jane blamed the District afresh in her heart for the pain that she had seen creeping on her face over the years. Blamed them for their insensitivity to her plight. For the cruel names that they had made up for her useless, barren womb. For not having the faith to believe what the most perceptive of them had spotted from the start when she had carried Cleary's child. If only they had believed, trusted their eyes, the hints about it that she had dropped subsequently around the District, she would at least had been freed from that cursed label, even though it would not bring the child back.

Chapter 34

Miss Dee hadn't quite finished her meal when Jane, who had been eyeing her since she had come back from taking her bath, said, 'What are you going to wear to go out with Jacob?' That was the only way she had decided she could raise the subject again in an attempt to force Miss Dee. Jane was aware that more and more she was getting herself and Miss Dee confused in her head. But she could not help herself. Cleary had to be brought down, humbled by his own son's true love for Miss Dee. After him Azora would be next.

Jane had heard that Jacob had been stung by the coldness that had come over Miss Dee and had even taken to bringing presents from town for her to try and change her mind. What more evidence, she asked Miss Dee, did she want to prove she was special to him, as no other country girl had been to his family.

'Excuse me?' Miss Dee asked, fully aware of what she had said but not really wanting to talk. She was fast losing patience with her aunt who, despite entreaties, refused to discuss what had happened between her and Aunt Vie and what else was making her so unhappy. Miss Dee was now convinced that though she loved her aunt dearly, there was a limit to the morbidity and sullenness she could take.

Jane was not about to be silent, fuelled by her own bitterness and obsession, she paced her words, trying to disguise the impatience in her voice, 'I said what you going to wear to go out with the young gentleman?' Miss Dee sighed quietly, resting the tray with the remains of her supper on the floor of the verandah. 'I've told you Aunt Jane I have made up my mind. I have no intention of going anywhere with him.'

'Honey.' Miss Dee turned to her sharply. Her aunt had not addressed her with endearments since it had first been discovered that she could sing. 'Honey, I have thought about this a lot. It is true, the Clearys do not deserve you for true but you must see this as an opportunity to further *yourself*.'

'I can further myself without them, Aunt Jane. Definitely. I don't need them. I've made up my mind,' Miss Dee emphasised, though she was still uncertain within herself, were she to be honest, of what she should really do but resenting the pushy tone of her aunt, clear to her despite her aunt's attempt to disguise it.

Jane sucked her teeth loudly, losing her hitherto tight grip on patience.

'Don't talk foolishness. There is nothing to make up your mind about. You have to go.'

'Why?' Miss Dee shouted.

'Miss Dee,' Jane used an imploring tone. 'This *is* a good chance for you. Don't be a fool.' Jane bit her lips, the last words had slipped out unintentionally. All day, she had been turning the words around in her mind as she had sat over her sewing machine, catching up with orders that had been suspended for the Christmas rush. She had resolved not to lose her temper but to reason with Miss Dee, let her understand how important Jacob's invitation was. How many girls in the humble District would after all get the opportunity she was getting? And without scheming and plotting as she had done or Bellinda must have done. If Miss Dee was sensible she would not have to work as hard as she was doing in the shop, she could have anything she wanted, be envied, truly now, by all. Jane had carefully thought out how she would exclude herself from the spoils, showing

Miss Dee how this would be the answer to all her dreams. But the own way stubborn, ungrateful girl was letting her lose her temper. She inhaled deeply, trying desperately not to be further riled by Miss Dee's calm uncaring demeanour.

'You should count yourself lucky,' Jane tried again. Miss Dee got up. 'Where you going? I'm talking to you. Sit down.'

Miss Dee turned and looked at her aunt. It was a long time since her aunt had lost her temper with her. 'Aunt Jane excuse me. I want to go to the bathroom, I'm not feeling well.' Her aunt tensed noticeably but Miss Dee did not capitulate, she stepped down off the verandah leaving her tray and went behind the house. Once there she leant with her back against the wall trying to get her breathing under control. The meal that had been hard to swallow anyway churned over in her stomach. She had just about collected herself when she heard her aunt's steps coming. She didn't have the energy to move. Face to face Jane looked her over with an unhappy mixture of entreaty and impatience. 'You may have come of age and have money in the bank but you still live in my house. The shop you making all this great money in, is leased in my name, so don't go getting ideas above your station. You still under my control. I warned you about bad company.' Miss Dee tried to calm her aunt with a touch, to beg her to stop before her anger got out of control, before either of them was forced to say things they did not mean and would regret. Jane brushed her hand way, 'I think that's why you think you can stay in my house and carry on like you big. There can only be one woman in this house . . .' With that she wheeled off.

Later, Miss Dee lay sprawled out on her bed contemplating her choices. She saw herself as having just four; to live alone at the shop, the lease had three years to run, to go to Town or write to Isadora and beg her to get her to England. If that wasn't possible she could surely find work as a seamstress somewhere, but

251

Jacob's family owned practically everything worthwhile there or were friends with those who did and he was anything but happy with her for trying to humiliate him, as he said. Or lastly, she could battle on with Jane, go with Jacob, dismiss the plans she had for her life. Doing what Jane and Jacob wanted from her would bring peace. Perhaps Jane was right, being Jacob's country woman, having his children, Jane's grandchildren, would be an honour for a parentless waif such as she was. For who would have thought it when her mother gave her away, that she would eventually be noticed by a rich man's son, a man who stood to inherit more land and houses than he would have need of in one thousand lives. She could see him when he was ready, accept what he gave her gratefully until he found another girl somewhere to marry. She would not be treated like those other women. Unlike her, they had not been offered trips to town, invited to his big family house where she could meet his family, he had not seen them in broad daylight, brought them gifts, made public his affection for them.

But the thought of it all, of his family's history, Aunt Vie's words about them, filled her with such horror and disgust that she could not wait to see him again to drive him out of the bits of her life that he had invaded.

Miss Dee had just decided to take a walk to Kitson Town to see Rose-marie when she heard Jane's footsteps coming through the sitting room that separated their bedroom. Miss Dee sat up on the bed. Jane knocked and entered. 'Something else I wanted to say to you,' Jane said immediately, her face taking on more lines, her eyes sadder than Miss Dee had noticed earlier. 'I don't think we need Littleman creeping around the shop anymore, creating work to do when there is none. It's a waste of money paying him to do nothing . . .'

'I need him there,' Miss Dee said more emphatically than she wanted, almost hysterically.

'Need? Need? You change your tune all of a sudden. Is not

the same boy you allow a mob to beat to a pulp in town?' Miss Dee lowered her eyes.

'Besides, I'm sure he putting off the town customers with his dirty self.' Miss Dee resisted asking what she knew about it since she so rarely visited the shop, preferring to hide at home playing the wounded wronged soul in the District. She said instead,

'Aunt Jane he's only dirty because he sometimes comes straight from his ground . . .'

'His ground? What ground him own?' Miss Dee sighed inaudibly. Her aunt sat down on the side of the bed. Miss Dee stood up. 'Aunt Jane I'm going to see Rose-marie . . .'

'That's another thing, I never did give my permission to take that short, dry-head gal on either . . . Why didn't you ask my permission or at least discuss it with me?'

'I did Aunt, you agreed. And anyway that was months ago.' Miss Dee shook her head incredulously, adding, 'She's a good worker.' Then with an explosion of the anger she had so far managed to control, 'What are you trying to do Aunt Jane? Everything that I do is wrong for you. Every friend I have is not right for me. What are you trying to do to me? Why are you turning against me now?'

Jane's voice contrasted with Miss Dee's. 'Calm yourself. I'm only trying to let you see sense. Show you what is best for you.' Miss Dee stared at her.

'I have always thought you a sensible girl, able to take advice. Well I'm giving you the last one and leave it with you. Know a person by her friends. Learn from other people's mistakes, you won't live long enough to make them all. You have the world staring at you in the face, plenty opportunities and you choosing to reject it. You don't know how lucky you are . . . Nothing need change in your life just grasp the opportunities that you're being given.' She took a deep breath. 'Have Jacob's kids.' Miss Dee's face knotted in disbelief.

'All you need to is go through with the pregnancy . . . I can take the children . . . bring them up as my own . . . How many girls can . . .'

Miss Dee screamed objections and outrage. Jane stood calmly watching her for a long time, saying nothing else. Eventually she left her silence with Miss Dee and went to her own room. Once there, she folded herself in a tight ball and wept.

Chapter 35

Jane broke her self-imposed silence and her exile from Vie's home and went to complain about Miss Dee. Vie listened, outraged by Jane's lack of shame, in so brazenly admitting what she had been pushing Miss Dee into. Vie could not trust herself to say what she really felt, especially now that she and Azora had come so close to putting their plans into practice and needed everyone's help to pull the power from under the Clearys' feet. She kept control, and instead of driving Jane out of her yard as she wanted to, she said calmly, 'You and Miss Dee are not one. You are two separate people. You have to allow her to make her own mistakes. To find experience for herself and from what I can see, she doesn't want any experience from the Cleary boy.' The name almost sticking in her throat.

Jane was not to be convinced, she went over the same points as she had done with Miss Dee and finding even more sceptical and belligerent opposition, lost her temper, accused Vie of being an embittered old woman who did not like to see a young girl get what she had not been able to at her age. 'You cannot tell me that when you were young if the Cleary Senior had even cast an eye in your direction that you would have turned away. Of course you wouldn't have. A simple country girl like you, would have turned away from what he could offer you? You must think I'm a fool! I wouldn't have and neither would you. You were too poor . . .' She scorned.

Vie watched her, waiting to steady her emotions rather than to consider her words. 'Dee doesn't need anyone to do anything for her. You should know, you brought her up seeing you making life for yourself. Dee can do what she wants for herself, so give her credit and pat yourself on the back . . .'

Jane frowned, 'Pat myself on the back . . . I didn't bring her up to be disobedient and disrespectful.'

'That's not what I see. The girl treat you with plenty respect,' she hesitated, 'And you're trying Jane, take it from me. Your temperament is trying. The girl deal with you better than most people could . . .'

'That's all I ever get from you and this whole District. Criticism . . . Criticism . . . Where were all of you when I picked her up off the streets after she was thrown away by a mother who didn't want her after she'd been bred by a father who's never owned her.'

'You didn't pick her up off any street! You got her from somebody's yard so don't talk about her as if she's a mangy dog. And I'm not criticising you Jane. What I'm saying to you is that Miss Dee doesn't need anyone to make her, especially not a Cleary. She made herself already. She can decide for herself what else she need. And Jane, take care you don't get too involved and spoil the girl's life.'

'What you saying, I can't give her advice. Tell her what I think is right. She can take advice from you but not from me? That's it, is it? I see now who she's been talking to. I warn you to keep out of my business. You done cause enough harm already.' When Vie did not reply she said, 'When I was young as long as you in you parents' house, you were subject to them. She's still in my house.'

'And more than paying her keep,' Vie could not resist saying. Jane seemed momentarily lost for words and despite everything, Vie's heart went out to her. She pushed to the back of her mind her own impatience and anger, got up and perched by the side of the verandah where Jane sat and rested her hand on her friend's knees. 'You have too much inside you Jane. Too much pain that you won't let go of. What's the point of clinging to the past if it means clinging to unhappiness, if it remove you from people and make you lonely and miserable.'

Jane stared in space as if she had not heard her. Without warning, she lifted Vie's hand off her lap and got up. 'I will not be coming back to this yard and I will thank you not to come to mine.' With that she left without so much as a backward glance.

Chapter 36

Rose-marie did not think much of any of Miss Dee's four choices. 'You leave and work in some factory or as some low-paid domestic? And as for that boasty Jacob, if your aunt thinks he's so good, why doesn't she have him herself?' That made Miss Dee smile.

'She must want some spice in her old age . . .'

'Shee . . .'

'What you worried for, Elizabeth and Daniel are way out in the yard somewhere.' Rose-marie was sitting on the bed astride her friend who was at the foot. She was combing her hair for her. Miss Dee insisted as soon as she had arrived that Rose-marie removed the pins that had held the bunch piled high on her head, and comb it through, as she often asked her to do when she was particularly tense.

Despite her anger with her aunt, she could not help but feel sorry for her too and she could not hate her as much as she wanted to, and knew she would not leave her alone in the District or even be on bad terms with her. For who else would she have? Nobody else, not even Vie it had seemed of late, was able to understand and put up with her.

'So what can I do?' She pleaded with Rose-marie. 'I cannot do without either you or Littleman. You are the only friends I have.' She pursed her lips. 'Even though I do know he has other hopes about me,' she added quietly.

'That's something else,' Rose-marie contributed, 'I don't know how you going to deal with that without destroying him. He's really taken set on you.' Miss Dee frowned. 'I'm going to have to talk to him.'

Rose-marie, particularly peeved by the little Miss Dee had said about her aunt's view about her and Littleman, was anxious to get back to that subject. Trying hard to be objective she said,

'Listen Dee Dee . . . Just carry on as normal. She'll cool down. It's your life . . . She can't force you to do anything you don't want. Just try not to get into a row with her about anything. She knows she's only got you . . . She's not foolish . . . I just think the weight of other things come down on her and she has nobody else to take it out on but you.'

Miss Dee sat alone in her shop a week later after closing time and after Rose-marie had left, waiting for Littleman to come as she had asked him to do after work. She had taken Rose-marie's advice, adopted a sweet, childlike attitude with her aunt, avoided a row even when her aunt had shown her the fabric she had bought to make into a dress for her to wear out with Jacob, when she had set the date herself when she thought Miss Dee should go out with him. Taking Miss Dee's silence as obedience she had buzzed round her each evening pampering and petting her.

She knew Littleman would have taken the short cut from Eggsbury, by-passed her shop and gone home to wash and change before coming to her. She had carefully hidden the package that Jacob had brought for her that day and sent Rose-marie home early.

Earlier Jacob had skipped into the shop, a broad smile plastered on his face, a contrast to his normal impatient scowl. Miss Dee had only understood his jollity when he told her that Aunt Jane had waylaid him by her lane to give him the good news that her niece had set their date for the following weekend. He had been unable to hide his pleasure, had kissed her face continually, sucked her tongue into his mouth, had even seen fit to press a few crumpled notes in her palm before he skipped out of the shop to his waiting jeep. 'He's thinks he's buying me,' she had blurted out to Rose-marie, hardly able to hold back the tears.

'He thinks that because I'm a country gal, I'm cheap and easy and that he was right when he said I cannot possibly say no, not when he brings all these pretty little gifts, says sweet unbelievable words to me . . . And why is he giving me money?' She screamed, remembering her aunt's earlier words that had so stuck in her head, 'I'm not his whore.'

Miss Dee strained every time she heard footsteps going past the shop, relaxing only when she did not recognise them as Littleman's. Her earlier fury had been replaced by nerves. She left the sitting room that now doubled as a stock and work room and went into the shop. Once there she absent-mindedly ran her hands over shelves he had made for her at his class with Ragu, she stopped to caress a slender glass cabinet, his latest creation, that stood in one of the corners. Even looking into the mirror gave her more pleasure than it had done before because it was not plain as it had always been but framed with cedar wood that he had made and polished himself. She smiled at how unceremoniously he presented these items to her, as if he was doing the most natural thing in the world, how reluctantly he had taken the payment she insisted on giving him for them.

Lost in thought she did not hear his footsteps or his first knock and when she did it took her minutes to unbolt the locks. Even though no one had seen or heard from Leroy she did not take any chances when she was alone.

'Miss Dee, you not hot all lock up so?' he said, glad of finding something to say. All day at work, he had rehearsed words, phrases, sentences, hoping that when at last he saw her at the end of the day, he would not appear mindless and foolish. Despite the fact that he wanted more than anything to be alone with her, he had even hoped that Rose-marie might be around to ease his self-consciousness, to detract somehow from the overwhelming difficulty he found in being so close to Miss Dee, with no way of expressing how he felt, of letting her know how much he wanted her.

'The windows are open,' she said, catching a look in his eyes, one she'd been noticing more and more over the last few months especially when he came across Jacob at the shop. She wondered what he thought, whether he was like the rest, thinking that she was without virtue, mere property ready to melt under the weight of a Cleary's flattery and expensive gifts. But regardless of what Littleman and the District thought, Miss Dee felt ashamed and soiled by everything, by herself; her lips that she had allowed Jacob to squeeze with his, his hands that she had permitted on her body, though at those times always covered by her clothes and her pride, the touch itself had unclothed her. And ashamed too of the gifts she had accepted, of her aunt's scheming. She bit her lips, she would not be a cry baby with Littleman, he was not Rose-marie with whom she could be herself totally. Hot and uneasy she rummaged for two fans. She offered him one but he refused, 'I don't need one, is you I worried about, you sweating. You not ill are you?' He creased his forehead. She smiled and shook her head, noticing not for the first time how at peace he always seemed now with himself. She wondered if he still felt the need to sleep on his grandmother's tomb. How it helped? He sat down as she poured from the bottle of ginger beer Aunt Vie had made and sent for her. 'Sorry I don't have any ice.'

'It's fine. Thanks.'

'Have you eaten?' she sat next to him.

'I had a bite of bread and some tea at home. Aunt Vie cooking run down tonight so I don't want to spoil me appetite.'

'I love that too you know. It's my favourite food,' she said.

'What will the both of us do if all the coconut trees in Jamaica die and we can't have run down anymore?' he said laughing.

261

'I suppose then we'll have to move.'

'No man, you remember we used to say when we were little that we could never leave Jamaica.' It was the first time he had made reference to those times and it made her even more wretched and sad for him.

He sipped his drink seemingly relaxed but so aware was she of him next to her that she fidgeted constantly, stood up, opened a cupboard, sat down again, all the time conscious that he watched her steadily as he did always. She watched him now out of the corner of her eyes as he averted his to survey the room.

'So you have something for me to do?' She must have looked confused.

'You said you wanted to have a word. I thought you wanted to ask me to do something.'

'Oh,' she hadn't yet formed the words in her mind. 'No. No. I just wanted to talk to you . . .'

'Oh. You not worried about anything are you?' He leant towards her, made it seemed to reach out to her, but withdrew his hands. In the last few months as they had become friends she had noticed that same action. Yet, he had never touched her, apart from those accidental times when he gave her something and their hands brushed or when they squeezed past each other in some tight corner of the shop, or when she insisted on working with him to put a shelf up or pottered with him in the flower garden he planted for her, or when she wanted to draw his attention to something. She saw even then not pleasure in his eyes, as would be expected but an uncertainty and tension that broke her heart.

'Leroy come back? Is that why you lock up?'

'No.' She remained open-mouthed, touched by his outrage, his concern. 'Not at all,' she insisted. His face softened but was not totally eased of worry. She cleared her throat. He was still looking intently at her, waiting for her to speak. But even though the words lined up on her tongue, she could not bring

herself to say what she knew she had to sooner or later. 'Littleman,' she said finally, 'Littleman I just want to thank you for
being such a good friend to me. I will always treasure your
friendship and hope it will continue regardless . . .' He looked at
her, smiled eventually. She noticed his embarrassment but could
find no other words to ease his awkwardness or hers.

Chapter 37

'So what happening with you and Miss Dee?' Vie asked as Littleman sat down on the verandah with his dinner.

He tried to smile. 'Ahmm . . . well . . . nothing.' What could he say? Miss Dee had asked to see him alone. Despite reason and good sense, he had entertained a glimmer of hope. Then she had thanked him for his friendship. Told him she would always treasure it.

He had died several times in the silence before she had got up to lock up the shop and they had walked down the District together. He knew he should be grateful. The lovely Miss Dee treasuring *his* friendship, he so awkward, ugly, a known dunce. He should be happy but he could not be more wretched.

Vie, perceptive as usual, sensed that something was amiss. She squeezed his knee and changed the subject. Still he was anything but garrulous so she knew he needed time alone. She left him and went to spend her evening with Ragu.

That night he hardly slept, reflecting on how since Nana's death only in the last year had he had some peace. Less and less had he felt the need to sleep on her tomb. Even though he went there almost every day still, he did not feel the yearning to reach her as before, to excuse to her the mess he had made of his life. For now, he imagined her to be proud of him, of the way he had taken control of his life and work; like who his friends would be, where he would spend his time, what he would plant and, in line with natural cycle, when he would plant them. When he would diversify, what to send with the market women to sell in town and what to give away. Even at Miss Dee's shop and at Ragu's there were areas where he took control. He had proved himself in these areas, had imagined, foolishly he now knew, that his personal life would be under his control too. He cursed himself now. Why had he been so foolish? How could he ever have imagined that a lady like Miss Dee could love him as he loved and wanted her.

Miss Dee was with some out-of-District customers when he finally arrived the following afternoon from Eggsbury. Her look and smile, he felt, told him that she had indeed relegated him to the role of friend. Not that his elevation before was of her making. She had never misled him. He had deluded himself. She had just realised what was happening and in her kind sweet way had put him right.

He left the shop and went through the back where Rose-marie was sewing. She greeted him, he felt, with a knowing smile, he flushed under her cheeky gaze but she took no pity on him but exacerbated his embarrassment by commenting on how hot and bothered he looked. Remembering what Aunt Vie had once said in passing about young men in the District being undeserving of a woman like Miss Dee because none was as much a man as Miss Dee was a woman did not help. He took a seat behind Rose-marie and out of her amused sight but as if she knew how uneasy he was, she turned and studied him. He rubbed his hands across his mouth, 'What happen to you Rose-marie? I said something funny to you?' She raised and dropped her shoulders nonchalantly before returning to her work.

Miss Dee suddenly appeared, she wore a big smile and made straight for him. He stood up. She touched his arm. They exchanged views on the unimportant events of the day before she went back to the shop and he to finding things he could do for her.

In the week that followed a great deal of wheeling and dealing occurred around Top Mountain. Vie's friendship with Azora solidified and was much discussed. They spent many hours talking about how they would organise against the Clearys who more and more were monopolising Vie's thoughts. But despite their determination to challenge the family, they had to face the fact that there would be repercussions for the District. Eventually there would be a lot to gain but immediately there would be plenty to lose; Vie was well aware that the Clearys would not take any show of defiance from the District without a fight. Each defiant act, Vie was sure, would be met with some form of retaliation.

When Vie told Azora about Littleman and Miss Dee, and gloated about how, even though the Cleary boy had tried his tricks on her, she had fearlessly rejected him, Azora stopped her flow with what Vie considered pointless questions. Had Miss Dee *allowed* herself with him? Vie though a little irritated that Azora did not obviously share her celebratory glee at one of the Clearys' humbling, was nevertheless amused by her turn of phrase.

'Of course Miss Dee hasn't *allowed* herself with him. She's a decent girl.' Vie watched her but Azora did not add anything further. There was a long reflective pause.

'So aren't you going to tell me why you want to know that in particular?'

'How many Cleary babies do you want me to have to kill?' Azora said slowly and quietly, a serious determined look in her eyes.

'You *are* serious about this whole thing,' Vie said. Azora nodded, 'I couldn't be more serious.'

Azora's fears reconfirmed for Vie the urgency of the whole situation with the Cleary family. She knew for herself the mixture of confusion, uncertainty, wonder and excitement a baby growing inside, even an unplanned, unwanted one, could bring.

Azora was right, they could not afford to have Miss Dee become pregnant for a Cleary, especially now. Not Miss Dee who without knowing it had revitalised the years of antipathy towards the Clearys that had gnawed at her unavenged over the years. Now at a time when she would have given in, circumstances were bringing things to a head and what was more, she had found an ally in Azora. For her own reasons, some of which she was unclear about, she seemed as excited about how they would finally confront and challenge Cleary's preeminence as she did. It was three months since they had first discovered their allegiance but yet no plan had resulted. As one plan after the other came to them, so they had discarded them, seeing this one as too extreme, the other as too insignificant. Besides, would they get the support of the District? Would the plans work or would the District be left in a worse position than before?

As far as Miss Dee was concerned, two days before it was ordained by her aunt that she would see Jacob, she sent word to him in town that she had taken ill and would be indisposed for at least a week. She hoped that he would then keep away from the District and he would not stumble across her at the shop, fit and well. On cue at home, she confined herself to bed with a mysterious illness but was strong enough to reassure her disappointed and concerned aunt that, on feeling unwell that day, she had sent word to Jacob and suggested another day. Taking her heart in her hands she improved on the Saturday, recovered fully on the Monday and returned to her shop, fingers crossed, that he would not drive through in his jeep. She was to be lucky.

Rose-marie was on leave that week. So Miss Dee pressed Littleman to go to the shop after work each evening just in case Jacob appeared. After closing, she asked him to go for walks with her. Littleman took her to secluded areas of the District, parts he had long forgotten, areas that she had never known existed. They would disappear together, scrambling over hills, creating new tracks, until Miss Dee was sure they were away from the puzzled eyes and ears and ready mouths of the District. But she need not have gone to all that trouble to be secretive because, once alone, their talk was innocent and innocuous. And as far as the District was concerned, as it was when Jane was pregnant and the District chose not to see, though they had suspected something was not as it should be, so it was with Littleman and Miss Dee. As their closeness had grown, sheltered by the attention that Jacob turned on her, mouths that would have opened to whisper doubted themselves and closed again, silent. And Jane remained blissfully ignorant since Azora's now occasional presence about Vie's yard, had conspired to keep her more and more out of it and out of the District.

But Miss Dee herself began to worry. Although the time she spent with Littleman was of great solace to her, she began to fear that Littleman still wanted more from their relationship than mere friendship. It was not that it had not crossed her mind once or twice that he was a possibility as a lover, a husband even. Sometimes, when she was alone after a day or afternoon with him, she would spend hours thinking about it. Perhaps forming a relationship with him and making it public would solve some of her problems, get rid at least once and for all of the temptation of Jacob. Littleman would be devoted to her, would be there to help her, to support her. But she had proven she could stand on her own feet. She didn't *need* him in that way. Besides, a relationship with him would be unworkable. He would never see himself as her equal and she would never be able to accept him fully as such or treat him as such.

Hard as she found it, she determined that she would have to raise the subject with him again. Once she had decided, she did not delay. On her way home from work Rose-marie was asked to leave a message at Aunt Vie's for him to see Miss Dee at her shop urgently that night. He came washed and changed, looking relaxed and at ease. Miss Dee almost lost courage but she knew she could not put it off.

Miss Dee's main concern as they exchanged small chatter and drank tea was that she would not lose him as a friend. 'Littleman,' she said suddenly when she found a pause in their conversation. But the unrehearsed words that appeared on her tongue seemed in that split second too harsh and cruel. She reached out and took his hands, something she had not done before, her eyes sad, pleading understanding.

'Littleman, I felt I had to say now because I may have been giving the . . . I don't want to give the wrong impression.' She read confusion and a look akin to rising panic in his eyes but she continued, her voice soft but decisive. 'I like you so much. No. More than like, I love you, as I would do a brother. Even more. But I cannot find anything else, any other kind of feeling in my heart . . . I'm so sorry. I know you will think I'm not normal . . . I don't have, never had a boyfriend.' She sighed. 'I hope you can find it in your heart to forgive me.' She leant across and kissed his cheek. He looked at her momentarily then looked away. She did not know what else to say. She felt like saying sorry again but held her tongue.

Littleman did not move, nor did he remove his hands from hers. They remained in that position for minutes, only their breathing unsynchronised, disturbing the silence. Eventually, as if just aware that she still held his hands, he withdrew them and stood up. 'It's all right Miss Dee. Don't worry. Thank you for . . . for saying,' turned and left the room.

Chapter 38

Only a few things *can* remain hidden from the District forever. An aborted pregnancy, perhaps, a discreet and short-lived relationship maybe, but not a growing friendship between the two most unlikely people in the District. Nor the fact that Jacob had wised to the fact that Miss Dee had been playing little games with him, daring to make a laughing stock of him in the District and his friends in town. So the rumours started, extending too to include the new closeness between Miss Dee and Littleman and it was not long, in spite of her self-imposed seclusion, before Jane herself became aware of them. Unluckily for her, she did not hear what most of the District knew, that although Littleman had designs on Miss Dee, to her he was just and could only ever be a friend. Some pitied him in their hearts but none was surprised. Sweet as he was, hardworking as he was, Littleman could never be good enough for Miss Dee, they said.

So far as Jane was concerned, it was by accident that she overheard an idle speculation between Bellinda and Sibble outside the grocery shop. Whether by design or by accident, as she left the shop, she distinctly heard one of the young women say something in connection with Miss Dee and Littleman taking long walks alone together. Jane stopped, put down her bag purposefully, stooped to look into it as if she had forgotten something, cocking her ears at the same time. The woman paused, giggled, and Bellinda, now shamelessly flaunting her bloated womb, said maliciously, 'Who would have thought she'd dirty herself with somebody from the District . . . and with Littleman that even the least of us wouldn't touch? Who said we're the ones without ambition?' She laughed as if party to some great secret, mischief full in her eyes.

Jane's eyes widened and the bag she hastily retrieved slipped out of her hands. It was moments before she could collect it and herself properly and scurry away, conscious of the scheming eyes of the two women. At home, she denied what she had heard, aware that the women in question had never been on good terms with Miss Dee or herself. Yet she could not relax. The thought crossed her mind to go immediately to the shop to see Miss Dee but how could she bring that ludicrous conversation to her when she would soon be going to town with a gentleman. Despite Miss Dee's foolhardiness she was not that unambitious, could not be so shameless. Yet recollections of how Miss Dee's behaviour had altered over the past two weeks came back to her. Hardly ever at home after work in the evenings, she had even taken to closing the shop half day on Wednesdays. At home, Jane had never seen her as she had been, lighthearted one moment, contemplative and reflective the next. The previous evening was a case in point. Miss Dee had come home uncommunicative and sullen as if her mind was laden with unsurmountable difficulties.

Before that, it occurred to Jane, Miss Dee had been dismissive of her, but now she was attentive and patient. Foolishly, Jane had thought that maybe Jacob was having an effect on her, that he was taking her off to genteel places in the far reaches of his property, away from the gaze of the District, and that Miss Dee's pride hindered her admitting it. Now she waited impatiently for Miss Dee to return home to confirm which was the true story, hardly able to cook or do her other duties.

When well into the night, she heard footsteps coming up the lane, Jane dived into her room. She planned to come out casually and sit with Miss Dee for a while when she was settled, watch her to see if there was anything in her that was indicative of what the women were saying. But she heard voices and stopped when she had reached just inside her room and listened. There was a woman with her, Jane turned straight back and walked into the verandah just as Miss Dee mounted with Rose-marie. Jane frowned, looked to Miss Dee for an explanation, ignoring her friend's greeting. 'You know Rosy, Aunt Jane, she's come to spend the night, sorry I forget to tell you.' Rose-marie wore a self-conscious smile but was ushered past Jane into Miss Dee's room. Jane stood for a moment on the verandah unable to believe it. Jane tried to calm herself and called out to Miss Dee who seemed to take ages to hear her among the racket they were creating in her room, talking and laughing.

Miss Dee returned to the verandah, her friend in tow, smiling. Jane stared at them in disbelief. She did not trust herself to speak so she spun back into her room. Miss Dee followed her, enquiring if she was ill, if she had eaten, oblivious of or ignoring her fury. 'Why you bring that girl in my house?' Miss Dee looked questioningly at her.

'You hear what I said?'

Miss Dee watched her, her expression unchanged. 'Is there a problem?' she said coolly. Jane jumped up from the side of the bed and would have slapped her then if Miss Dee had not stepped back. 'You out of order . . .' She screamed losing control of her tone and volume.

'Aunt Jane what's the matter? What have I done? Rose-marie has come here before.' All of a sudden it seemed to dawn on Jane that what the girls had said must be true. She did not know why.

'Get out of my room,' Jane screeched hoarsely. 'I'll talk to you when you've sent that girl out of my house. And I will get the truth from you then.'

Miss Dee frowned, 'Aunt Jane have I done something wrong?' Miss Dee pleaded then, a questioning lilt in her voice.

'I said out of my room.'

But Miss Dee did not send her friend away and Jane laid in her bed listening to them chatting and laughing, wondering if she had made a mistake. Why had she turned so quickly from dismissing the malicious women to doubting Miss Dee?

Later Jane heard them on the verandah, then in the kitchen obviously eating the rest of the food she had cooked, then in the yard behind the house on the tomb. Finally Miss Dee called out goodnight to her as they turned in, as if she had no care in the world. Jane's blood boiled. Once in her room, whatever the friends had to talk about, was still unsaid, Jane heard their voices late into the night, preventing her already elusive sleep, allowing her no time to cool.

When Miss Dee and her friend were quiet and still she could not sleep, tears burned their way down Jane's face and the more it dawned on her that Miss Dee was reducing her to tears, the more she found herself unable to stop. In the dead of night, convinced that Vie and Azora must be behind it all, scheming with Miss Dee to humiliate her, hatred knotted her stomach, sending her scuttling to a shoe box under her bed where the items of clothing were stored; the underpants she had taken from Cleary the night she left with the intention then of remembering him; one of Vie's handkerchiefs, left behind when Jane had washed for her. She regretted not having anything of Azora's that could be used. There must be, she vowed, an obeah-man who was more powerful than Azora. Amos' death would be sweet in comparison to the death she would give them. She did not know when she fell asleep and the underpants and handkerchief slipped from her grasp onto the floor.

She did not see Miss Dee the following morning, the young women were up and out before she had stirred from her belated sleep. But in the evening, Jane was ready for her. She sought first to find out whether what she had heard in the streets about her and Littleman was true. Miss Dee she thought, feigned ignor-

273

ance. Jane's blood boiled. With controlled anger she spelled out for Miss Dee what was being rumoured around the District.

'That you creeping off in bushes with the simpleton . . . That you . . . that you . . . give yourself to him.'

Miss Dee remained calm, 'Nobody could have said that.'

'Said what?' Jane screamed.

'That I *give myself to him*,' she said, with clear disdain for the term.

'So what going on then? Do you or do you not go off in bushes with him?'

'We go for walks together.'

'What kind of walks? What for? What purpose for? she shouted. 'You mad and crazy? What will Jacob think?'

Miss Dee sighed. 'I don't care what Jacob thinks. He's nothing to me. Littleman is my friend.'

As the words left Miss Dee's lips, Jane became inflamed with rage. Was Miss Dee a fool? Did she not know she was playing with fire? Littleman would see her behaviour as invitation to take liberties with her. If she wasn't lying and had allowed him to already.

Miss Dee tried to walk away but Jane had not finished with her, blocking her way, she gave vent to her anger, to pains and frustrations old and new. Even Jane in the mood she was in knew it was a nasty and unpleasant scene, was aware that Miss Dee was the wrongful recipient of her venom. But who else was there to release it on? Fortunately it was witnessed by no one save their dogs that howled frantically as the row raged.

It was a long time before Jane's fury was spent and she stormed to her room and locked the door, as if she could not trust herself to come out again. Miss Dee did not resurface again either that night, not to wash and brush her teeth or to get her dinner. In the morning, up from a sleepless night, Jane watched her, her swollen eyes the only indication of what had occurred the previous night, as she moved around the yard getting ready for work.

A little later, sharply dressed, with thickly applied powder, high heels and bag as if nothing had happened, Miss Dee was half way across the yard when she shouted at her. 'You are an unfeeling street throw-away. I don't know what Jacob sees in you.' Miss Dee did not turn but continued walking. Jane threw herself off the verandah after her, running until she was in front of her, 'You will leave this house. I give you a week to pack and find somewhere to go, I don't want you here. You wring me dry already.'

Miss Dee, if she was shocked did not show it, only shook her head and said with the utmost calm, 'Aunt Jane, why are you destroying yourself? There is no need.' With that she stepped round her and continued down the lane.

Chapter 39

Aunt Vie sat impassively and listened to Miss Dee's almost incoherent account of the previous night's events, Littleman's pained expression and interjections, as he hung on to her every word, adding further drama to her descriptions.

As Vie expected, Miss Dee asked her to be intercessor.

Whatever Vie had imagined her reception would be at Jane's did not prepare her for the one she got. If she did not know better, she would have imagined that the row with Miss Dee had only just then taken place. Jane's temper had not cooled and Vie wondered, if that was the case a day later, what it must have been like the night before. Jane would not listen to her, would hear nothing of conciliation, of reasonableness or understanding, of having been young herself once wanting to make her own decisions, choose her own friends. And yes, Littleman and Miss Dee were just that. But Jane was adamant that Miss Dee had gone too far in flaunting her friendship with him around the District without discussing it with her first, of lowering herself, giving the wrong impression and worse, rejecting the attention of a young man from a respectable family for, and she searched around until she found a word that was all but what she wanted to say, a one time layabout. Adding that since a leopard cannot change its spots, Littleman could not have changed.

Vie was not foolish, she could see that Jane would not be reasoned with but she tried her best, the weight of Miss Dee's expectations heavy on her mind but every angle she tried was contradicted and rejected by Jane, who ended by dismissing Vie from her home, getting up and leaving her on the verandah when Vie did not budge immediately. Minutes later, when Vie was about to mount Greystripe, Jane returned, as if she had forgotten to say something, 'I'm giving her one week to pack and get out of this house and clear the part of the stock in the shop that is hers out.'

Vie was aghast. 'You what!'

'You hear me. Pack and go.'

'You do not mean that Jane.'

Jane surveyed her, wooden-faced, 'You don't think so. Let her try me. If she and the rest of you think I'm your play thing, your bat and ball, we will see. Is not the first time I'll take on the high and mighty and win . . .' Vie did not know what she meant but tried to pacify. Apologising for whatever Miss Dee was supposed to have done, for herself, the District. When Jane was not moved she said, 'Everything you fighting to achieve over these years you destroying in one swoop. Have sense woman and think. If you do this and lose Miss Dee who, with all her faults, will stick with you and provide you love and company, who else you going to have?'

Jane snorted, turning her most critical look on Vie. 'I only now realise that you and Miss Dee are one. Both of you would do anything, compromise your best principles, so long as in the long run you benefit and you the centre of everything. I only just now realise that. How selfish the two of you is.' She stood up. 'I wouldn't be surprised if you put Dee up to this. Plan it all from the time you contrive to get Littleman in your yard. Scheme it all so you don't lose out and die by yourself in your little two room rented house.' She nodded bitterly. 'You are a thief. Even your daughter know that but she wouldn't let you thief her children. So you plan to thief Miss Dee.' She hesitated, 'and God knows whose else's husbands and children you thief over the years.' Vie mounted Greystripe. Whatever had she unearthed?

'Jane I will come and see you again when you calm down and seeing sense.'

Jane's anger flared afresh. 'Don't talk to me like no child. I'm not one of the people in the District that you have in the palm of your hands . . . Just give Dee me message and none of you will have to come back here when she clear out . . .' With that she disappeared behind the house.

Vie was exhausted when she got back home and even more so when she had to relate to the two anxious faces that things were as bad as they could possibly be. Miss Dee broke into a weeping, the level of which Vie had not thought her capable of, genteel and proper as she was. Vie went to make tea, conscious that it would be only a matter of time before Ruthlyn called under the auspices of borrowing something or other but really to see what the loud crying was about and then it would only be hours before the whole District was party to all the intricate detail, most of it her own.

It seemed to Vie that she was dealing with the two most stubborn people in the District in Jane and Miss Dee because after cooling her fever grass tea with her tears Miss Dee announced that she would not be going home that night as Vie suggested she did anyway, and would only go back to collect her belongings.

'Jane is bound to calm down. Give her time. There is no way she's going to throw you out with nowhere to go. In fact I do really think you should swallow your pride and go home tonight,' Vie implored. But Miss Dee was adamant she would stay at the shop.

Later that night Ruthlyn and her husband sauntered into Vie's yard, followed later still by Ragu. Vie had foreseen that eventuality and had suggested before they came that the young people left everything as it was without shedding further light on what had been going on, letting it all continue as rumours, but Miss Dee would have none of that. 'I'm tired of rumours,' she had said. So, resolute and in a falsely animated voice she told her story to Ragu, Mr Maxton and Ruthlyn, reputedly the most reliable of all District criers ever known in Top Mountain. She told them that there was and never would be anything between her and Jacob. That she and Littleman were friends, best friends, as were her and Rose-marie. Nothing more, nothing less. And no one would stop her spending time with her friends, going where she liked and doing what she liked.

Vie's heart went out to Littleman as Miss Dee extemporised. For caught up as she was in setting the record straight, Miss Dee was oblivious of Littleman's pained expression.

Vie was not surprised that the weight of support from the Maxtons and Ragu rested with Miss Dee. She foresaw that as how the dice would fall in the District as a whole too. Over the years Jane had been more tolerated than loved, excluded rather than included. Some of the reasons for that Vie could not understand, it did not seem to her in the true nature of the District to treat people as Jane had been consistently treated. True, no one escaped some form of ridicule. It had to be expected in a district with so little diversion, so little excitement to break the monotony and drabness, that was an accepted part of life. But Jane chose not to understand it, to take it too much to heart and to hold it against the whole District, guilty and innocent, making what had started out as innocent sport a true vendetta against her, permeating the very consciousness of even the most holy and church going in the District.

That night Miss Dee did not feel able to sleep alone at the shop. As Vie squashed up against the wall beside her, she felt a rising anger with what Jane had brought on herself and the position she had put her in. She could only hope that before the week was out or the notice she had given Miss Dee expired, she would have cooled and seen sense.

But Jane did not change her mind nor it appeared did her anger quell. Miss Dee went with Littleman the following day to collect changes of clothes and from what Vie was told, Jane had ranted so much that Miss Dee had had to ask Littleman to wait for her at the end of the lane. Once he had left, Jane would not speak to Miss Dee apart from reiterating that all Miss Dee's belongings had to be out of the house before the week was up and from the shop two weeks after that.

The first Vie and Miss Dee knew that Jane had gone to town to rescind the lease on the shop was at the end of that week when a letter was delivered by hand to Miss Dee, stating that in fourteen days the shop would be repossessed. Much as they blamed Jane, they saw more the hand of the Clearys at work. So Jane had asked them to terminate the lease. It was *their* shop and land, not hers, the rent and lease were being paid. The Clearys had no ground to act so promptly or at all. When had they ever bowed so decisively to anyone's demand in the District? Besides, they knew that Miss Dee ran the shop almost independently of her aunt. Why did they not consult her? Suspend serving such immediate and final termination until they had.

There was no doubt, Vie thought bitterly and with mounting anger, that it was a vindictive act for Miss Dee's unprecedented rejection of Jacob. If Vie had had any doubt that this was the time to act, she dismissed it when she saw the look of disbelief and destitution on Miss Dee's face and heard Littleman when Miss Dee was out of earshot and he thought Vie otherwise occupied, venting his anger with expletives and curses she was not aware he knew.

By now the whole District was having their very public say about the events. Only a few talked about the higher the climb, the harder the fall for Miss Dee. On the whole even the most reluctant admirers of Miss Dee were outraged about what Jane and the Clearys were doing, full of admiration for Miss Dee, for giving Jacob Cleary his marching orders. A young girl, knowing the wealth and power of the Clearys, knowing the status, if only temporary and illusory that friendship with a Cleary gave, still having the confidence to reject him, was, they said, worthy of admiration, support and any sacrifice necessary. They repeated this again and again, in the grocery shop, in the fields, as they collected water from the standpipe, as they passed the time in yards, on verandahs or sauntered home after church. Miss Dee had chosen the District above the Clearys they gloated with disbelief and pride. Choosing us above his sweet words, big house and lands, they reiterated. Miss Dee is really something, they cooed. How many women would have acted like her? She is certainly not like the normal flighty girls with easily turned heads, they echoed. And they hoisted her in their heads and hearts on a rung not far from Vie and Azora.

Azora visited Vie in the middle of this furore. They talked of capitalising on the interest that pervaded the District, of channelling it away from gossip to action. 'People have always known how wicked and badminded the Clearys are, but they fear them. They *have* a lot to fear, most of us depend on them totally for our livelihood. But despite this they are realising, if still slowly, that the Clearys are *not* Gods. If one young girl can say no to them, how much more can all of us together do,' Vie said.

The following day, her resolve strengthened, Vie made concrete plans with Azora. For a start they encouraged Miss Dee to make plans to go to town and see the Clearys for herself. In the meantime they spent two days going from house to house, Vie on Greystripe, Azora on one of her over-sized mules, the younger people walking, talking to everyone in the District, directing their thoughts to the vindictiveness, as they put it, of the Clearys, discussing with them examples of their heavy handedness over the years, engaging them in discussion of the possibility of change, the advantages of change, for themselves, for their children and succeeding generations. Passions buried, grievances ignored and tolerated were resurrected and refuelled. As dusk fell on the second day every house, save Jane's, in the District had been visited and Vie, Azora, Miss Dee, Littleman and Rose-marie returned to Vie's yard, well-pleased at the hornet's nest that they had disturbed.

Imbued with the confidence at the stirring of agitation against the Clearys in Top Mountain, Miss Dee and Rose-marie left for town the following day, apprehensive but hopeful, to persuade the Clearys to ignore Jane's demand. When they returned and it was confirmed that the family were not prepared to make any concession, Miss Dee would have to vacate the shop, Vie was not surprised and was almost relieved. It would have been too easy, she thought and the greater battle would remain unfought.

Miss Dee told Vie afterwards that Jacob had been present too and so had his grandfather, Mr Cleary Senior. Jacob, she said, sporting a smugness and an expression she would not define as that of a wronged and unrequited lover. Vie remained calm, they had found the catalyst they needed and the next plan on their list would be effected. Later she left Miss Dee, Rose-marie and Littleman and went to Azora's home to draw up final plans, all inevitably involving some form of confrontation with the Clearys, Jane now completely out of the picture.

Chapter 40

Miss Dee struggled through her imposed final week at the shop in a state of suspended disbelief. She had seen for herself the papers with her aunt's signature terminating the lease, heard with her own ears that there would be no change of heart from either side but she still looked for a way out. She had removed the rest of her belongings from the house, storing them in various houses around the District, there being insufficient room at Aunt Vie's. She was surprised at the directions from which offers of help had come. She was however too distraught to enjoy the obvious show of affection. She had tried everything to correct whatever wrong she had done her aunt, writing to her, sending her small packages of gifts she and Rose-marie had purchased in town, cooked dinner and taken it for her. All to no avail.

A few days before the lease was due to expire, in desperation she sent a message to town asking Jacob to visit her at the shop. His journey through the District up to her shop did not go unnoticed and Miss Dee's last remaining doubters felt that they may not after all have to wait long to see her reconciled to her aunt and back home and Jacob Cleary have the country concubine he desired.

The District was not to know that the night before a great deal of intricate plans were discussed at Azora's house, away from the ears of chance passers-by and that this meeting with Jacob formed only part of them. Vie who wanted to involve the whole District immediately was outvoted and she had to be satisfied with going through the various stages that the others felt were necessary first, before, failing those, resorting to collective action.

Dee and Rose-marie were in the shop when Jacob arrived. The two women exchanged knowing glances as Miss Dee left her in charge of a full and intrigued shop and she escorted Jacob to the back room. Ironically the uncertainty about the future of the shop had drummed up trade, the shop could not be left unattended for even short periods. The line that was being given to her customers was that they would cease trading on those particular premises but would re-open somewhere else in the District soon after. Their guesses were as good as Miss Dee's and Rose-marie as to where that would be. For where else in the District would she find spare land that was on the main road, and with a shop? And who else would own that land but the said Clearys, their antagonists?

To Miss Dee's immediate annoyance, Jacob wore the same grin that she had noticed when she had visited his family the previous week. She wondered irritably whether it had been stuck since then. She knew her lines but she had had to rehearse them over and over again with Rose-marie before. Neither of them trusting her temper, nor her worry and irritation that Jacob might see the meeting as a sign of her submission.

Resolutely, she mentally revised the message she had to relay. She was able to take over the lease from her aunt, had enough stock and capital to run the business alone. Alternatively she could go into partnership with Rose-marie. She could speak to him with confidence, she would inform him because of the financial support offered from Rose-marie's parents, Vie, Azora, Ragu and amazingly even the Maxtons with their many mouths to feed.

She offered him drinks and sat on the other side of the room from him trying desperately to take control but losing what semblance of it she had when she saw his lascivious eyes on her. She tensed. Luckily before she could open her mouth he spoke,

'I knew it would only be a matter of time before you realise like this whole District, you cannot live without our family. You need us.' Miss Dee swallowed and would have got up and asked him to leave if she had not remembered her promises to Vie, Azora and Rose-marie, and more than that if she did not see vivid pictures of herself with endless days stretching before her and nothing to fill them, or trudging through town from office to office, factory to factory, house to house looking for work. Ignoring what he said, she outlined her points to him, imploring him to try and persuade his father to reconsider and allow her to take over the lease from her aunt. He seemed to be listening to her, she was surprised and encouraged by this, adding more than she had rehearsed with the group, animatedly relating her plans, her ambitions, her hunger to succeed, to expand so that more young people in the District and even surrounding ones, could get work. She was not even looking at him, so lost was she in the excitement of her dreams. Then something made her stop and shift her eyes to him.

His legs were crossed in the habitual manner of big shots, his face expressionless, his mouth set, making him appear older and wiser than his age. 'From what I can see Miss Dee you are in a predicament.' She cut her eyes at him in her heart but remained visibly expressionless, waiting. He crossed the room and sat next to her. 'I think the problem between us in the past . . .' he rested his hand lightly on hers, '. . . Is that we don't always quite understand each other.'

She withdrew her hand and wove them together away from him.

'It's my fault for not recognising this and spelling things out.'

He smiled and seemed to wait for her to respond. But she said nothing.

'Yes. Country women *are* different from town people, more well . . . need more persuasion. I do find this interesting, challenging, perhaps even quaint, like your little names, Miss Dee, Babydear, Blue Boy . . . Littleman.' He paused on that then repeated Littleman's name observing her closely. Her expression remained stoical. She extended herself in her chair, her back straight, her neck stretched, her chin up. When he still had not encouraged a response, he stood up and walked around the room.

'Yes quaint, so quaint that I find your little ways endearing. But most of all I find you endearing Miss Dee.' He looked at her steadily for so long she had to shift her own gaze. 'I haven't made any secret of it. I haven't hidden my feelings. My friends can't imagine why when I have more . . . well girls from my . . . many girls to choose from in town . . .' He paused but she stubbornly refused to assist him in his ramblings. Or worse, she thought to appear flattered. 'What I'm saying Miss Dee is that everything is in your hand. My father will do anything I ask but why should I give you something for nothing.'

Miss Dee swallowed hard, 'I will pay your father more than he got before, if that's what he wants.'

He looked her over. 'You are refusing to get my meaning Miss Dee and I know that you are not one of the country simpletons,' frustration and impatience now slipping from his tone.

'Jacob. I have made it clear to you that I am not . . . I don't feel we have anything in common.'

He laughed, 'I must admit I credited you with more ambition . . .'

'What the hell are you talking about? It seems like you are the simpleton. Ambition is precisely why I asked you here. Not to discuss what you want.' She interjected with quiet control, poised to call Rose-marie.

'OK. Choose your own country-man,' Jacob continued as if he had not heard her. 'That won't change what I want, how I feel about you.' She stood up her anger palpable. But he did not relent. 'Miss Dee, Deseree, I really want you. Love you.' He laughed nervously.

She stood her ground. 'Well I don't love *you* or want you,' she said quietly. 'Sorry.'

'I can't believe you're rejecting me. You! Rejecting me?'

'Why not?' She glared at him.

'How you mean why not?' He asked with incredulity.

'You mean how can I say no to a Cleary, one whose fore-fathers have made it their right to take and break country women, one who's so rich and powerful, no normal woman in her right mind could possibly reject.'

Jacob sighed, 'Miss Dee, Deseree,' he grabbed her hands and held them tightly. 'I cannot be blamed for what my forefathers have done. I thought you'd realise by now that I'm not like them. Have I ever tried to force . . .'

'Jacob.' She stopped him in mid-sentence. 'I know your vir-tues are many but I asked you here to talk about business.' He released her hand and paced the room, turned and lifted her bodily off her seat and held her to him. She made to call out to Rose-marie but he had predicted that, he clapped one hand to her mouth, grabbed her right hand with his other hand and pushed her back against the wall. Miss Dee's eyes widened in disbelief and shock.

'You are nothing. Just a country nothing. My family allow you to lease our land and rent our shop and you get ideas above your station. I tell you, you will *not* say no to me. How dare you say no to me,' he insisted on the verge of hysteria. Miss Dee recovering from the initial shock, tried to push him away. Fail-ing, she grabbed his ear lobe with her left hand and wrenched with all her might. He winced but did not release her, forcing her more firmly with his body against the wall. 'You will learn that I get my way especially in this God-forsaken hole of a District.' Empowered with fury Miss Dee tore at his ears, released and dug her nails the whole length of his cheeks, drawing blood. Jacob screeched, released her and backed away, his fingers covered the damage. 'Rose-marie. Help,' Miss Dee called out loudly, a thinly disguised panic in her voice. The chatter in the shop ceased and her friend was with her in a second. The two women stood together facing him. He looked from one to the other in confusion.

Miss Dee strung her hand through her friend's and said at the top of her voice, conscious of the cocked ears of the silent customers in the shop, 'I was just congratulating Jacob because Bellinda must be about ready to give birth to his baby anytime now.' She had not rehearsed that. Jacob's mouth dropped opened, he looked to the opened door leading to the shop, looked back at the women and without another word stepped off towards the back door. 'So I suppose all that is left for me to say is it was good doing business with your family,' Miss Dee spat out bitterly, unable to stop herself.

He turned, his voice matching hers in volume, 'Take the woman from the bush but not the bush out of the woman . . . Your education and pretty clothes . . . what a waste. I know what my grandfather means now when he says that you country women are strange, abnormal, not like our normal women . . .' With that he strutted from the room.

Chapter 41

It was Miss Dee's last day at the shop. She had done the final packing in the morning, divided goods for distribution around the District for storage. Littleman, with some of his friends, were left to remove the last fixtures and fittings and were to take them to Ragu's. Miss Dee and Rose-marie sat now on Vie's verandah, the former staring wretchedly into space, the latter trying her best to take her friend's mind off her troubles by attempting animated chatter.

Vie ran her hands over both their shoulders and left for Azora's having exhausted all her words of reassurance. She decided to walk. Her leg still dragged somewhat, lagging a little way behind the other one, but the improvement was such that with her stick, she could make the walk relatively easily and did not always have to resort to Greystripe or stop to rest.

She lounged around in the quiet of Azora's yard as her friend finished with a client and completed duties behind the house; feeding her unusually quiet dogs, throwing handfuls of corn to the chickens and sweeping behind the house. Vie watched absentmindedly as she moved about now in front of the verandah, sprinkling water on the ground to keep down the red dust before taking her home-made broom to the leaves and debris.

'You know Vie I'm glad we became friends after all these

years,' she said as she finally sat down next to her. Vie looked to her for a particular reason.

'A woman can get so used to being alone and think that it's the only way to be.'

'But I thought you liked your precious solitude.'

'I do. I do. But even when you are here, especially when you are here I don't feel disturbed. I don't think we disturb each other.' Vie wasn't sure what she meant and she said so. 'You must know that some people agitate you when you are with them, disturb your peace, even if they're not speaking to you . . .' Azora smiled at her, Vie nodded now, indicating that she understood.

A little later when Azora had fixed her something to eat, they returned to the subject that had occupied most of their conversation in recent months. Not now what Jane had done, but how the Clearys were seeking to destroy Miss Dee and the District, '. . . lifting their heavy hand to remind them, as if they needed to, who they were,' said Vie. The last time they spoke it had been to express little surprise at the attitude of Jacob when Miss Dee had met him alone, to gloat at how Miss Dee had fearlessly handled him. 'He'll have those scars to remind him not to tamper with her again. Or any of us for that matter,' Vie said.

'It will take more than that to convince the Clearys.'

'I know but it is something. It all help to keep feelings high in the District. From the day we went around from house to house talking to everyone, some people asking what more they can do. Some still frightened of course . . .'

'If we all stand together then there will be no need for anyone to feel afraid . . . But we have to convince people of that.' Vie agreed with that and added, 'In spite of Jane you know I think if Miss Dee had lifted up her skirt for him, she would still be in her shop now.' Yet, she was not devastatingly disappointed that it had all come to a head. Everything amounted to the opportunity she had wanted all these years. For one, there was of course the

District that was being made to see that though the Clearys were rich and powerful, they could challenge them. But more than that, and she could just about admit it to Azora, she relished the next stage in the plans they had drawn, of her coming face to face with John Cleary Senior after all these years. He, like his son was now doing, had left the running of the District to the Junior years before and had not come to the District himself for a long time and would no doubt never come again. She and Azora would have to go to him. 'One thing I think is a pity in all this though,' Vie was saying.

'What is that?'

'Jane.'

'If only she could realise what kind of woman she is. How many women are there like her in the District who with no help from any man can make such a life for herself.'

'For true,' Azora agreed.

'That's why with all the ups and downs she and I have, I love her and respect her. When a lot of us sit in this District making the Clearys fat with big rents, she work for herself, sit at her sewing machine for hours, raise her money and get him to sell her land, set Miss Dee an example so she turn out the way she has . . . It's a pity for true that she thinks we're not on her side.'

Vie looked at Azora, 'I wonder sometimes if she had had the babies she made rule her life, if she would have been different.'

'She wouldn't have had Miss Dee if she had. Perhaps she wouldn't have even come to the District.'

'I meant especially the baby she lost,' Vie looked sad.

'I wished I had not been so blinded with my bid to stop the spreading of the Clearys' seed,' Azora sighed heavily.

'You weren't to know.'

'I should have asked more questions.'

'It's not your fault, the brute deliberately lied to you. He's the only one to blame . . . Despite that though, I don't know why

Jane should have gone to him. Of all the men. Why him? He just finally wreck her fragile life.'

Azora shook her head. 'It's ironical though, with one hand I was helping her and with the other, unbeknown to me, I destroyed her.'

'You should go and see her. Yes. Why don't you go. Explain to her. See if she can bring herself to understand. See what you can do to ease the pain the brute left her with.'

Chapter 42

Sometimes Littleman felt so grateful for what Aunt Vie had helped him to accomplish over the past eighteen months that he was often overcome with the need to run around the acre he cultivated, to kiss the trees, root vegetables, peas, corn and whatever else he grew. But conscious of workers in other neighbouring grounds he restrained himself.

He wandered around his fully cultivated land now making things to do, finding little enthusiasm for the work he normally loved; a bit of weeding, a bit of hoeing, collecting mangoes that had fallen from trees here, uprooting yams or cassava there. Since the time when Nana had died and he had slept on her tomb in confusion, he had not known the level of depression and frustration that he knew now. That morning he had woken up alone as he had always done, a situation he could never imagine changing, not even in his wildest dreams. As it was when Nana had died and circumstances had changed around him and he had been powerless, so was he now. Why could he not think of something? How could he not persuade the Clearys to let Miss Dee continue with the lease? And more, why was Miss Dee unable to find anything for him other than the feelings of friendship? It was not that he did not treasure her friendship, even that was dear to him. But it was not enough. Would never be enough. If only he could show her that if she gave him a chance, she would never have to worry. He would look after her. Devote his life to her, to supporting her, to making her happy. But she had gently told him to cease dreaming. He was trying but failing abysmally.

The previous night she had stayed at Aunt Vie's, he had listened to her weeping, unable to do anything but disappear behind the house in the dark to shed his own silent tears, as Aunt Vie had hugged her and Rose-marie had repeated encouraging words. He had no faith in the Clearys to believe, as did Azora and even Aunt Vie, that they would make them change their minds when they saw him in town at the end of the week. Littleman did not see how that could be, when it was rumoured that Jacob himself wanted to restock the shop and continue the same line of business as Miss Dee had done, that he was looking for someone in the District to manage and run it for him. That had been the final blow for them. What Aunt Vie had said, that Jacob was being malicious, attempting to punish Miss Dee, seemed plausible. Yet Littleman could not understand. Why did he want to do that when his family had enough businesses in town, enough fallow land in countless districts to last through eternity?

Littleman was sitting to have his bun and cheese lunch when he heard the unmistakable steps of Greystripe picking his way through the bush towards him. His immediate thought was that something was amiss and Aunt Vie who rarely came out to Eggsbury needed him. He jumped up and pushed his way through the herbage and came face to face with Miss Dee, a broad smile on her face. He rushed to help her off. 'What are you doing here?' he said, returning her friendly hug.

'I was bored out of my mind so I thought I'd come and give you a hand.'

He laughed.

'Are you saying I can't work ground?'

'Of course you can work ground, it's in your blood,' he said, too quickly to dispel disbelief from his voice.

'Well then.' Her mood seemed transformed from the previous night and hesitantly, he commented on this, asking her why. Had they had news from the Clearys? 'No, better than that,' she said, smiling broadly and all but dancing around him. 'Aunt Vie got a letter from England this morning. Babydear is coming home.'

'True?' Littleman asked.

'True. True. True. Her fare has been booked and everything.'

'Is she coming back for good?'

'The letter didn't say but Aunt Vie thinks it's possible. She's not settle at all as you know, is not thriving. Her parents are worried.'

'That is good news, good, good news,' Littleman said.

They talked about it for ages, what it would mean to Aunt Vie and the District. 'Not everyone choosing England above Jamaica then,' Littleman said. Miss Dee agreed but said she feared that it was not the best time for Babydear to return with all the upheaval and conflict in the District.

That news exhausted and celebrated, he walked her around the fields showing his work with pride and satisfaction.

Suddenly she said, 'I've had enough of hopeless tears. It's my shop and I can't continue moping around. Those are Aunt Vie's words by the way,' she said half-smiling. 'I have to show that I believe what we are doing will work. And more than that, do things. For a start I plan to write letters, tons of them,' she said. 'To the national paper, to our local MP, to the prime minister, the Governor General. The Queen's representative himself,' she informed Littleman. 'To the radio stations, to every notary I've heard of in and around St Catherine and Kingston.' She said she would carefully detail the case of the District, their need to buy land from the Clearys, to get the family to change their attitude to the District. 'Reasonable demands by any standards. And what reasons could the Clearys have to reject our offer?' she asked. The District did not ask for charity, for concessions, she said. They would not be able to justify to the whole Island the acres left fallow and unused, year after year. What after all had Independence been for? Who did it benefit? If the status quo, the old structure remained intact. Ragu, Azora and Vie, she told Littleman, had agreed to pay the postage for her deluge of letters, which she said, would continue: she would send one to each person daily, until the District had achieved its aims.

'How can we lose with everything we've planned?' She asked. Then more soberly, 'I know it will be hard, a long struggle but we have to believe that it will be worth it. Don't you see?'

Littleman was hearing both Aunt Vie's voice and Miss Dee's together. He did not want to dampen her attempts at optimism by expressing his own fears, that there was little even all these Districts put together could do to stop the Clearys doing what they wanted especially fuelled as they were by Jacob's anger. 'I know what you are thinking,' she said, throwing herself on the ground next to where he had been sitting, pulling up a blade of grass to chew. 'Most of the people in all these Districts, especially in ours, live on their land, Cleary land, and it's easy for them to punish them. Us,' she corrected. 'You're right. That frightens me too. Especially that I might be the cause of it. But don't you see, that is it, what can he do to punish everyone without hurting himself too.' Littleman remained serious.

'Lighten up man,' she encouraged. He smiled at the relaxation of her language. She sighed. 'I do understand your fears,' she said speaking for him. 'I too hope we won't be wasting our time, making things worse.'

Chapter 43

The day before Vie and Azora were due to see the Clearys, the food truck trundled through the District laden with stacks of free food for the District. As usual, the boys riding on flour sacks, drums of oil, boxes of sardines, bags of cornmeal, with packets of oats and cane sugar around them, intoxicated with this occasional opportunity to earn a living both in kind and coins, had been bellowing the news as soon as their carrier had left Old Road and turned the corner into Top Mountain.

Usually by the time the truck passed Ezekiel's vexed shop, turned left into the lavish asphalted drive of the big white house on the hill, overlooking the greater part of the District, the long line, grateful hearts and empty bags, would have stretched down to the standpipe sandwiched in between the church and the grocery shop.

Today there was no one. Not even from the most desperate and destitute house. Vie, Azora and Ragu had seen to that, their success they thought finally clinched by Azora's promise of a similar handout, funded by herself, the week after Mr Cleary came, whenever that would be, if every single person in the whole District supported the planned boycott. That had been deemed unnecessary by the District. They were prepared, they said in unison, to make the sacrifice now and in the future to do without the Clearys' free food. For had they not survived in the months since he last came? Did he take them for vagrants and beggars?

Mr Cleary who as usual had driven up earlier with his son, to survey his house and grounds, to test his generator and to see that his water tanks had not been disturbed, was more perplexed than anything. He checked again and again from his new batch of seasonal workers that they had announced their arrival through the District though fully aware that this, though customary, was never really necessary.

Well into the afternoon, when they would have been finishing and when he had craned his neck from the upper floor verandah for more times than he had sat still, he was finally convinced that no one would come. His workers, in the dark about what had transpired over the past few weeks, were confused, even venturing on the road once or twice to way-lay passers-by, who in ostentatious show of ignoring then, sang or hummed aloud when they were told of the bags of free food on offer.

As the trucks trundled back out of the District at dusk followed sharply by Mr Cleary's big car, many though amazed and gratified at how they had stood together, shook their heads in silent fear of what the effect of their action would be, especially since more was to follow if on the following day when Azora and Vie went to see them, Miss Dee was not returned to her shop. And since the demands had even widened as Miss Dee was outlining in her string of letters, not just to getting the shop back as was the earlier bid but to force the Clearys to sell the ten acres of land on which the shop stood, the church land for the building of a nursery and primary school, plus other acreage that were earmarked for workshops, playground, farming. Many although they were going along with Vie and Azora wondered whether the two of them had taken leave of their senses, whether it was after all a good thing that Azora and Vie had become friends. Even though Vie, Miss Dee and Azora, who were at the helm in organising the District to action, had carefully catalogued and reminded the District of the Clearys' other heavy handedness over the years, their property that had gone unrepaired, the burdensome rent increases, their reluctance to sell even half-acres of their land, the waste that characterised their vast holdings, left fallow year after year, the white house on the hill, ostentatious and under-utilised when many households burst at the seams, many still doubted and worried even when, spurred on by the prospect of ownership of the church, even Deacon and Sister Netta sounded agreement from the church pulpit.

The four of them, Vie, Azora, Miss Dee and Rose-marie, went together in the taxi to Kingston. The young people too anxious to wait all the way in Top Mountain until they returned, preferred to wait in a restaurant in town so they could get the news fresh after the meeting.

Vie had refused to see Cleary Junior and after much to-ing and fro-ing of messages the previous days it had been agreed that she could see the ageing Cleary Senior as she wanted. Many conflicting emotions passed through her head as the taxi made its way with them to the Clearys' office in town.

At the office, they saw no immediate sign of life, shutters were drawn and a closed sign marked the door. Vie put on her glasses, looked in confusion as the taxi sped away. Azora checked and rechecked the address, the time the letter had confirmed. They were at the correct venue at the correct time. The two women stood silent, waiting, looking at the barred door, expecting it to fly open at their bidding. The minutes ticked into an hour, the unsympathetic unrelenting sun exacerbating their discomfort and fury, emphasising the degree of the insult and disrespect. Vie could not believe that the Clearys would have brought them all the way to town for nothing.

'They have to come,' she insisted to Azora who, after one

hour, felt they should leave. 'They would not dare do this to us, to the District,' she insisted, hardly able to speak those few words coherently. Azora sighed and shared the gourd of water they had brought with them as they rested on the low wall outside the office complex. When another hour had passed and none of the Clearys had arrived, the two women, outraged and disbelieving, took their leave, with bellicose, vitriolic expressions on their faces.

Back at Azora's yard, away from the wrath of the young people, Vie's own fury was such that Azora had to concoct a herbal infusion to calm her temper.

Before they went back to face the young people the two women determined together that, from now on, there should be no holding back where confronting and challenging the Clearys were concerned. 'They will live to regret their treatment of the District today. Mark my word,' Vie warned. 'Mark my word,' she repeated, the cloud that had descended over her face in town, deepening by the moment.

That night people gathered in Vie's yard to hear the outcome of their meeting with the Clearys. They had not expected a miracle but they had not expected what they heard. 'We cannot allow them to treat us this way,' Ragu inflamed, tapping the mouth organ buried inside his breast pocket. 'This is preposterous, out of order and rude.' Similar sentiments were echoed around the yard.

Vie was right, it was as if the District, angered and frustrated before, had suspended their anger and frustration as they waited for reason and a change of heart from the Clearys. Now that anger was grasped again and with it, determination and confidence.

Vie suggested the need for unity in the District, the benefits that support from surrounding Districts would give and plans were made to get both. From the following day Rose-marie, Littleman, Miss Dee, Vie and Azora were to split Old Road,

300

Kitson Town, Guanobovale, Eggsbury and Paul Mountain between them, going from house to house to solicit support. Ragu, the Maxtons and Ezekiel Samuel were to take Top Mountain itself. Azora suggested a public meeting at the end of the week to gauge the extent of the support received and gain suggestions for actions against the Clearys.

That night Vie lay in bed burdened and fearful. The District was determined to take the Clearys on as she had wished they would all these years, as she had incited. But instead of glorying in it she was overcome with the fear of failure, engrossed by the consequence of failure. She knew however that whatever her private thoughts, they could never be allowed to mar her public face.

She spent most of the night twisting and turning, unable to grasp much needed sleep. She had never imagined that she would spend the first week after hearing that her beloved Babydear was returning, so agitated and angry, hardly able to find a moment for the news to sink in. To turn it over and over in her thoughts, to celebrate it in her heart. She decided one thing though in the quiet of the morning, she would write to her daughter and ask her postpone the return of Babydear for a few months. She did not want Babydear to return in the middle of confusion and uproar.

Chapter 44

It was a sober public meeting at the end of the week. Vie, Azora and Miss Dee addressed the large crowd with its representatives from all the districts they had visited, outlining the case of the District, soliciting suggestions of how to proceed now that the Clearys had challenged them to battle, were Vie's words.

The solidarity was tremendous, matched only by the list of suggestions of how to proceed. This included an eventual protest march to town and various petitions. Miss Dee's letter writing campaign was endorsed as was Vie's suggestion that they embark on a rent strike if all else failed.

The following evening Littleman was alone on the verandah with Miss Dee. Vie had gone to meet with Azora to discuss the meeting of the night before. Littleman too had been carried along by the strength of feelings at the meeting and was ready to do anything but he was worried about the suggested rent strike.

'That is one thing I don't agree with. It will be blackmail. They can take people to court.'

'A lot of people to take to court,' Miss Dee said impatiently.

Littleman sighed.

'Littleman, don't you see we've tried reason, we've even offered more money than the shop is worth and they, Jacob especially, have been bloody minded. Look at the way they treated Aunt Vie and Azora. It's unforgivable. Now it's clearly not between us and Aunt Jane anymore. It's between the whole District and the Clearys. How can they win?'

'They can make us suffer. They have so many powerful friends,' he said bitterly remembering his own experience with the intransigent family, thrown out of the house that was to be locked up empty and still remained so. 'He can make us all suffer,' he repeated.

She was irritated with him, 'Well, it's outside our control now. I think people, not because of me or the shop, feel that it's about time they assert themselves for once and get together in the District to make some demands, instead of having demands put on them all the time. The shop, Littleman, was just the excuse they needed and the treatment of Aunt Vie and Azora, especially Aunt Vie, sending them on that wild mongoose chase, even more. We haven't got the power or the right to stop them.'

She got up and went into the kitchen to begin the supper, he joined her minutes later, and she insisted that he express no more of his doubts. 'We have to be confident. We have to be determined to win, even if it takes months, even years. We can't go back now to how it has been. It would be shameful.'

The public meeting had left her with a tremendous sense of optimism. Not since that time when she was about fourteen or fifteen at the onset of her entry into woman, her aunt had called it, had she been so sensitive to and aware of everything, so excited.

At that time it had been as if she had woken from a long restful sleep, or finished one of Azora's cleansing fasts. Every part of her had come alive. She felt the softness of the air she inhaled, her whole body had been thrilled by the lightest touch. The tips of her own fingers touching her lips had sent ripples through her body as had the touch of her hands on her face, her breasts, her thighs. She had seen her world afresh, as if new, noticed what had previously passed unobserved, like a tiny community of black ants labouring together, birds soaring, wild flowers.

Then it had been a wondrous world full of mystery and delightful opportunities and her appetite had been whetted for it. But until she had got her shop, developed her business, renewed her friendship with Littleman, grown closer to Rose-marie, become one with her District again, that period had been suspended, even forgotten. Now there was no way she would be driven away from it or do without any of them again.

In the weeks that followed there was a frenzy of anti-Cleary activity. Hundreds of names were added to petitions demanding the Clearys return Miss Dee's shop. Simultaneously other petitions were drawn up to put the District's Case for land purchase. They were delivered to the Clearys' offices, homes, grocer shops and businesses in town, in Eggsbury and pinned to the barred windows of the big white house on the hill in Top Mountain. All were ignored by the Clearys and there was no sign of capitulation from them. The District became more and more incensed by their silence and stepped up their action to include the rent strike. This brought down, on those who dared, bailiffs from town and fines from the Parish court but they were not to be deterred, gaining confidence as they did from each other's resolve and determination.

After weeks of daily correspondence to the national newspaper from Miss Dee, a journalist from the national newspaper visited Top Mountain, more out of curiosity to meet the supposed mad woman who had nothing better to do than bombard their office with daily handwritten and delivered letters.

He was taken aback by the woman he met, not at all mad, and she immediately challenged his stereotype of country women, she was presentable, confident and articulate. A week after he met Miss Dee he wrote a long article for his newspaper, supporting the District. It appeared with a picture of Miss Dee, Azora and Vie. Top Mountain, the District gloated, had been put on the map at last.

After the highlighting of Miss Dee's letter writing campaign in the newspaper article, the media got on the band wagon. For a brief period, across the Island the District was the subject of phone-in radio programmes, studio discussions, articles and counter articles. Letters from strangers were written to the prime minister, the Governor General, most echoing the points Miss Dee continued to reiterate in her own letters, including the view that the British had been ousted only to be replaced by a set of homegrown exploiters.

The interest of the media and the escalating frustration of the District at their failure so far to get a response from the Clearys, meant that the march to town attracted even more support than the District had expected. It took place some weeks after the initial frenzy of activity. Placards were made, leaflets printed and distributed as the District and its supporters stopped traffic on their journey to and from town. Amused town-folk wagged their head at their antics, most wondering if they could possibly be serious in believing that the mighty Clearys would listen to them.

After the march to town, Ragu even composed a tune entitled 'Slavery no done yet'. Among its lyrics, 'Independence still no come for Top Mountain'. Lines that were to be quoted again and again in speeches, articles and competing reggae and folk songs across the Island.

Yet, the Clearys would not budge and supported by others, more powerful than mere country people, folk singers and transient newspaper reporters and radio talk show presenters, did not seem to have any intention of ever giving in. They simply avoided the District, seeming to await the inevitable and imminent failure of the uproar.

One morning, months after the beginning of the campaign, with mounting frustration and anger palpable in the District at no sign of victory, they awoke to smoke towering from the big white house on the hill and found its remains charred and blacked in daylight.

Many gathered in Vie's yard, fearful of the consequences of such an act, wondering whether their original aims had been lost. 'Who could have done that?' Littleman asked. 'That is bad. Bad. Bad. Bad. We don't need this kind of thing.'

'I think everything gone too far,' Mr Maxton said. Vie played with her fingers and shook her head. But if she or anyone else suspected who might be responsible, no one named names.

The Clearys, who had not appeared in the District for the months that the uproar had continued, came now escorted by armed police and some of their enraged supporters and a band of predatory journalists, to examine the vandalism that had occurred to their house. If he had even considered complying to their request before, John Cleary Junior was quoted later in the papers as saying, he vowed now not to part with a single furlong.

Hours later when the family were well away from the District, the armed police returned. They headed straight for Vie's yard. Ruthlyn, who had been collecting water from the stand-pipe in front of the grocery shop, threw away her pan with the precious water and ran after the police cars, screaming at the top of her voice that they had come for someone, she could not say who. Children playing cricket and marbles in front of the shop dispersed to their homes all over the District, taking the news with them.

Vie and Littleman stood at the foot of the verandah as the policemen left the cars and headed for Vie's house. Miss Dee sat motionless on the verandah stricken with fright. But contrary to what Ruthlyn who kept up the rear felt, they had not come to arrest anyone but to begin questioning those they had been told by the Clearys were the likely perpetrators of the crime against their property.

They did not get very far and left hours later surrounded by the silence of almost everyone from the District who had swarmed on Vie's yard.

They were to come again and again, on one occasion even

arresting Miss Dee and taking her to town for questioning, causing uproar in the District coupled with threats of what would happen to the Clearys if a hair on Miss Dee's head was harmed, but Miss Dee was released that same day with no charges brought for lack of evidence. None was ever to be found.

Chapter 45

Jane was furious at the uproar Miss Dee had caused in the District, parading with banners to town with Azora and Vie, putting her name to ludicrous letters, shouting through loud-speakers at crowds, as if she was a common market woman. But Jane had resolved even before the uproar to wash her hands completely and permanently of her. More than anything she could not tolerate ingratitude and coarse behaviour, especially from women. Yet, their agitation amused her. How could everyone, especially the previously intelligent Miss Dee, be led to believe by the scheming Azora and Vie that they stood any chance to win against the Clearys? Perhaps a hint if the Senior was still in charge but never now that his son was the boss.

Jane had already planned ahead of them and whatever they did would not stop her. She was sure that even though Azora and Vie pretended to the District that it was Cleary they had conflict with, it was to her that they wanted to make a point, it was her that they wanted ostracised from the District, in a feeble attempt to get even with her for their own different reasons.

Jane planned to go to see Bellinda on the first leg of her own plans. She was sure of success, would be killing two birds with one stone; taking Bellinda Jerr out of her poverty and off the conscience of Jacob Cleary, although he showed no sign of having any. And showing Miss Dee that there were plenty who would be grateful for the home and comforts she had spurned, and additionally making it impossible for Miss Dee to have a convenient change of heart when she tired of the cramped conditions and restrictions of Vie's home, especially with the endless days that she would face with nothing to do. Jane felt satisfied. That would be sweeter and more likely to produce the desired effect than going to an obeahman as she had done to such satisfying success before with Amos. Believing so fully in Azora's power, Jane was not at all convinced that any ordinary obeahman could challenge her. If she risked doing her harm and failed, she shuddered to think what Azora would do to her. And Vie, regardless of how everything had turned out, she thought in quiet moments, she could not forget how good a friend Vie had been to her. Yet even in those solitary times, Jane could not fathom why Vie had come to change so much, to hate her so, to choose Azora above her. As far as Cleary was concerned, only occasionally now Jane laid his underpants wistfully on the floor trying to find the strength to seek out an obeahman as she had done for Amos and since nothing else came to mind she would tuck them away again in the shoe box under the bed.

Jane was just about to set out for the Jerr's house when she heard the sound of hooves turning into her lane. She stepped off the verandah and tried to look around the various bends, made impossible by the line of trees and brambles. She did not have to strain long because in a moment, Azora came riding towards her. Jane froze, her mouth dropped open, her eyes fixed on her.

Azora came into the yard, a tentative, hesitant look on her face. 'Good afternoon Jane,' she said finally.

Jane did not or could not answer her. They faced each other without speaking for moments, Azora on her mule, serious; Jane looking up at her speechless. It was as she dismounted and tied the mule away from the yard that Jane found herself, lifted her feet up the steps off the verandah and slumped in one of the chairs.

Azora joined her on the verandah and since Jane had not yet found her tongue, she invited herself to sit down. 'It's been a long time Jane.' Jane did not answer. Eight years silence and her dead baby was too much silence to break. In the turmoil of the District why had she come? What words could she find to tell her anything? The thoughts that flooded Jane's head, drowning rational thoughts and her entrenched fear of Azora, were immediately, to find some way of doing to her what she had done to her poor innocent unborn child. But she could not find her strength or her tongue. Azora's eyes were on her, so intense were they that she could not avoid meeting them. When she did, the hate and anger that filled her, fully grown now after years of germinating and pampering, welled up, choked her.

'I want you to get out of my yard. Now.' She found her strength and stood up shouting at the top of her voice.

'Jane. I know how you must feel.'

Jane scowled. 'Know? Know? Know how *I* feel? You can know nothing about me! So don't tell me what you know.' She was trembling uncontrollably. Azora noticed and seemed to totter between reaching out to her and staying where she was. Jane did not trust herself to speak again immediately or to remain on her feet. She slumped in the seat. In all her life she had never broken down and showed weak tears in front of anyone, man or woman. She bit her lips.

'Jane I did not . . .'

'Yes you did. You killed my baby. You killed my one and only baby. My babyyy.' She screeched holding her stomach and jumping up. 'You are a murderer, a killer of babies, a heartless wicked woman.' Her face contorted. 'But you can't be a woman. You can't be a normal woman. You're not a normal woman. Normal woman don't kill babies. Don't kill babies . . .' Her voice petered out. Tears sprang to her eyes but did not fall.

'Jane, if . .'

'Get ou of my yard. Leave now . . . Leave . . .'

'Jane . . .'

Jane looked at her and somehow Azora read how completely she wanted her away from her. Azora stood up.

'Now,' she said. 'And don't ever come back here. Ever. Or as God liveth, obeahwoman or not, I will chop you up.'

As she passed Jane, Azora paused, seeming again in the valley of indecision. Jane moved away, pushed open the door she had shut to go out, went into her house leaving Azora on the verandah. She heard Azora go down the lane, focused on the mule's hooves as it turned left towards Old Road. Eventually Jane went back out of her room and stared down the lane Azora had left. It seemed more empty than she had ever known it. Suddenly she spun round as if she had lost something in the spaces around her. As if in an incredible dream. Eventually she set off for Mrs Jerr's house, her mind and body numb.

Jane walked slowly as if only just resurrected to a life she abhorred, her head high, trying to shrug the tension and activity of the District. In the last few months, she had avoided coming into the heart of the District. Now she returned what she considered the hypocritical greetings and sarcastic smiles of those she passed, fully convinced that as soon as her back was turned she would be the subject of their vitriolic words. She didn't care, there had not been a time in her life when she had not felt despised, alone, it would not kill her now. She hoped to, but did not bump into those she considered the main conspirators against her and planned to stop at the grocery shop on the way back to see Dora, the only one whom she now had time for and who had time for her. She could endure Ezekiel's sour stare, even enjoy reminding him of what had so soured their relationship. But for poor Dora and the risk that they would only laugh at her in disbelief, she would expose him and Vie to the District even now.

Dorothy Jerr was in the yard washing when Jane called out for someone to hold the dogs. She waited until she was summoned before continuing up the short lane. The house, on Mr Cleary's land, was a raised wooden structure, the two rooms and verandah clearly in need of paint and seemingly important structural repairs. It flashed across Jane's mind that if there was a slight breeze, the family would need to be seeking shelter somewhere else. Jane wondered whether the Jerrs, too, were now refusing to pay rent or had gone on marches with banners and petitions. Perhaps for some other reason if not for land, Jane thought. She mounted the steps to the verandah as requested, Mrs Jerr taking care to dry her hands on the bodice of her dress as she followed her. She seemed to be alone. Jane was disappointed, she had hoped that Bellinda would be there.

'And what brings you up to these parts Miss Aunt Jane?' Mrs Jerr said after she had sat down on the low wall of the verandah, Jane having been shown the only seat there. Jane looked sceptically round the yard, it was if nothing else, neatly swept and tidy. A brood of chickens pecked lazily at worms beside the fragile wattled kitchen. A goat was tethered next to that and from what Jane could tell was with kid. It seems to be catching in this yard, she thought.

'I have come to see Bellinda,' Jane said finally.

'She gone to the clinic at Kitson Town.' She lowered her eyes. 'To get the baby his vaccination.' Jane nodded, remembering their bitter exchange at the Day's Work months before. These people don't take telling, she thought, careful to keep disdain from her face.

'Can I get you a drink, Miss Jane? I made some sour sop juice just now.'

'No. Thank you. A little water would be fine.'

Jane heard her lifting what sounded like the usual sheet of corrugated iron used to cover water drums. She imagined the mosquito lavae lining the bottom of it but she was in need of

312

something to cool her, what with the shock of Azora and the walk from one end of the District to another, she set her mind against her revulsion.

'So can I give Bellinda a message for you?' She paused. 'She has not been troubling you again has she?'

'No. Not at all,' Jane said, thinking, you have due cause to ask me after all the trouble I've had with her over the years with her rudeness and name-calling, her provocation of Miss Dee.

'So I can't be of help then . . . ? As I said, she's out and she was going to town to pick up a few things for the baby now that Miss Dee's shop close . . .' She realised what she was saying and to whom half way into the sentence and petered out almost inaudibly by the time she said the last word. Jane chose to ignore it. She sighed, seeming to turn over in her mind whether she should or should not leave a message. 'Mrs Jerr, I have come to make a proposition to your daughter.' She cleared her throat. 'One that I do not think she will be able to wisely refuse.' Mrs Jerr rubbed her hand down the front of her thighs. Jane imagined that in the poor woman's heart of heart she would wish for a job for at least one of the children who had found little do to since leaving school, in the District or out, short of the season work that came to the District like cleaning the grass verges by the road side and occasionally selling what little surplus her husband could get from the quarter acre they leased from Mr Cleary. Jane wondered whether she too held out hope like the rest of the demented District to buy land for workshops, so that at least one of her five could learn a trade.

'As you know Miss Dee is no longer with me,' Jane said so clinically, as if Miss Dee had died and was not missed, so without ceremony, that the other woman had to stop herself from mourning for both of them with some appropriate interjection. Luckily, she could find none. 'The house I live in was too big for the both of us at the best of times and so you can imagine what it

313

must be like for just me . . .'

'Sorry Miss Aunt Jane but Bellinda won't want to work as a maid now.' It was on the tip of Jane's tongue to ask the woman if she still thought her daughter having a Cleary's child made any difference. But since employing a maid was not her intention she ignored the refusal. She could not afford not to succeed with Bellinda. She was one of the only people in the District who Miss Dee did not just consider herself above, but who she genuinely despised, the only one she had not mellowed towards. So even more than the joy that the eventual and inevitable failure of their campaign with Mr Cleary would give her, Jane treasured the thought of Miss Dee's outrage when she would hear that Bellinda had taken her place. More than that, Bellinda would give her a grandchild and would without further encouragement or incentive, she imagined, give her even more. So long as the girl was her companion, did her share of duties around the house and learnt the dressmaking and tailoring that she intended to teach her, it would not matter to her how loose she was. In fact a certain amount of looseness would be desirable, Jane thought. She would tolerate her long enough to get adoption papers through for the child or children, so when she got tired of her, they could part company amicably and she would be left with the children. Bellinda, she was sure, would be compliant when it was put to her. She would realise that alone or even with her poor parents, she could never have anything to offer her children, Clearys' blood or not, that Jane could not surpass. In fact sooner or later the girl might even get married and her husband would not want her to be lumbered with her pre-marital mistakes.

'Perhaps I had better talk to Bellinda herself. What I have to say may be too complicated to relate secondhand to her. Perhaps you can ask her to come and see me?' Jane stood up. 'If I don't hear from her in a few days I'll come again,' Jane said, careful to use her best town accent.

Mrs Jerr tried to persuade her to leave a message but Jane had made up her mind, she had to talk to the girl herself. It had to be resolved within the week, if not she would go on to the next on her list, Bellinda's friend Sibble.

Chapter 46

Exhausted and dispirited, Top Mountain was quiet again. Outsiders and journalists, having lost interest in their cause, had disappeared as promptly as they had appeared. The big white house remained charred and blackened.

Not that the District had given up, only that there was little now to try that had not already been attempted. Just to continue, now alone, what they had done in the six months since they had become inflamed. But they were tired of it all. Yet only one or two families, tired of odd nights here or there in jail, of fines for failing to pay their rents and leases, went back to paying. The few others who were made examples of, got almost used to jail food, notoriety and mockery from the law.

Ragu made music still but he seemed unable or uninspired to find tunes that were not doleful. Only when Vie got tired of them and strutted over to reprimand him did he find within him more rousing ones. But only until Vie's word had cooled in his ears.

The year 1969 rolled into 1970, and 1971 was fast approaching. The District planned for Christmas, no victory against the Clearys in sight. No change to usher in yet another year. Things would continue as before only now with a greater sense of failure and powerlessness.

Only the news that Babydear was finally coming, her return, her parents informed Aunt Vie, could not be deferred any longer, such was their concern for her health and well-being. After nearly three years in England, hardly a day had passed, they confessed to Vie, when she did not cry for her grandmother and for the District. And although she was coping in school, she failed to thrive physically. Perhaps a little time in Top Mountain, they said privately, would let her appreciate London more.

Most all the District were gathered in Vie's yard to await the return of the taxi from the airport. Miss Dee and Rose-marie had gone to meet her. Vie, overcome with excitement and disbelief that she was actually to see her granddaughter again, could not go with them. She sat on the verandah, her ears cocked, waiting for the droning of the taxi's return.

Ragu too was alert beside her on the verandah, his own ears sharper than the throng around the yard. He was poised with banjo and mouth-organ, 'Ready to pick a celebration tune,' he had said when he took up his position.

When at last Babydear stepped onto the path from Aunt Vie's lane where the taxi had deposited her and started to make her way up the path, there was a hush in the yard. Vie had heard the taxi, Ragu true to his words was playing but Vie could not move. She waited. Waited. Her head fixed on the middle lane, not the one from which her granddaughter came but the one leading to Ezekiel Samuel's pigsty, until Babydear was standing in front of her. She too had not said a word as she came up the lane, half-running, half-hesitant steps, a fixed smile on her fourteen, nearly fifteen-year-old face.

She stood for moments, looking at her grandmother, a smile broadening on her face, water misting her eyes. Vie got up slowly and took a few steps to her, hardly now a drag to her feet, her arms almost totally strong, the sides of her mouth reflecting now only the sign of age not ailment. After the pause, Babydear rushed up the steps and hugged her, saying over and over and over in her grandmother's ears, 'I'm home. I'm back. I'd never given up hope of seeing you again. Never.'

317

Vie kissed her repeatedly. 'But you're skin and bones my baby. There is nothing to you. What has England done to you?' Only then did everyone speak at once echoing Vie's words, shaking their heads in dismay. This was not the Babydear they knew. Where was her waist, her hips, her cheeks? Independently and silently they planned sustaining dinners for her and special tonics and baths made specially by Azora.

As the evening of eating and drinking and celebration wore on, the District realised with some relief, that though physically ravaged by her three years abroad, Babydear had lost none of her spirit. Miss Dee and Rose-marie, in the journey from town to Top Mountain, had filled her in on the activities of the past months. Now washed and fed, basking in the welcome home hugs and kisses, Babydear enthused about the prospect of joining in the fight against the Clearys. Most looked at her with wary smiles, not able to tell her then how totally exhausted they were of it all. How much their energies were sapped. How near they were to giving up.

But a fresh, young and optimistic presence in the District was just the injection that was needed.

After days of her unrelenting encouragement, Miss Dee started working again. With Rose-marie, she designed and sewed, selling their goods out of boxes from Vie's verandah and took up in addition learning from Azora about herbal medicines. But despite Babydear's presence, it was not the Miss Dee of old. She had undergone many changes; from a superficial girl to a mature woman who had strutted through the District and town campaigning and speech making, a prolific letter writer and a newspaper journalist, to becoming introverted and cast down. Though she was still making a living, she did not like the circumstances in which she worked. As Jane had known she was fast becoming intolerant to sharing a room not only with Vie but now with Babydear too. Rose-marie suggested that she

318

moved in with them but that house was crowded too. She had offers too from Azora and various others around the District, even Littleman wanted to move out of the yard and give her his room but she could not throw him out or take another change elsewhere. She wanted her shop, her own space back.

Babydear, now begging her grandma to register her at a high school in town, was determined that she was not going back to England. In the meantime she threw herself behind her grandmother's and Azora's determination that the District should not give up. With fresh eye and mind, slowly she helped to raise Miss Dee's spirits and with hers those of Rose-marie and the still besotted Littleman.

Azora and Vie *had* not wavered in their resolve. They had seen a lot more of life and understood the sentiments of the almighty, that a day was like a thousand years and a thousand years like a day. So as far as they were concerned, a six or eight months, even a year, time lag was just an irritant, like a mosquito, an irrelevance in the greater scheme of life.

So tireless and with iron determination, Vie and Azora were sitting late on yet another night, trying to find another way. Christmas had come and gone, 1971 was no longer new, Easter was only two months away.

'You know something Azora, I feel the mistake we making is keeping the fight too far from the Clearys.'

'How you mean?'

'We should carry the fight right outside their front door, to town. Force them to see us face to face. Tell us to our faces that they will not sell.'

'They'll never agree to it. You know they've been hiding in town, not even the brazen Jacob show his face, they just biding their time. They're counting that we'll get tired soon, cool down, then they'll strut back and take up where they left off, even come with a truck load of free food.'

Vie was affronted by the mere thought of it. 'We'll order a

taxi and just turn up. I do think it would be better to see the Senior. Age may have mellowed him. The Junior and Jacob, with his vendetta against Miss Dee, won't budge.' She shook her head. 'No those two are prepared to fight us to the death,' Vie said.

Azora smiled. 'Yes let's go. But why order a taxi. Why not saddle up two of my mules?' Vie roared with laughter at the thought until she realised Azora was serious.

They arranged the date and after a week of riding lessons for Vie, who had only ever ridden donkeys and was more than intimidated by the size of the mules, they set out for Kingston.

Riding through the town they attracted a great deal of attention, two old women on over-sized mules was not an every day sight but eccentric country-folks were not unheard of, even in town and only a few took more than a second glance. It was when they turned up in the lavish surrounds of the hills of St Andrew overlooking Kingston that police cars descended on them and they were redirected back to the District. But they did the journey again the next day and the next. Memories were eventually jogged about the conflict with the Clearys that many had thought over and done with and the Clearys back in charge.

Amused by them, with only a tinge of admiration, the police eventually let them be. The superintendent, whom Vie and Azora had spent hours reasoning with, helped no doubt by a few bottles of Azora's special tonics, concluded that they were doing no harm. He would leave them alone, he warned good naturedly, so long as they did not disturb the peace and cleaned up thoroughly after their mules.

The residents of Gainers Town on the hills, overlooking it seemed the whole of the Island, were outraged that the police had taken the side of the country women and tried to take the law into their own hands, threatening and ridiculing the two women, hoping that would drive them away. But Vie and Azora were not to be intimidated. Each day they rode up the hill, dismounted, tethered their mules, unfolded the stools Ragu and Littleman had specially made for them and sat under a tree which sheltered them from the sun. As residents slowed their lavish over-sized American limousines to gawk, they encouraged a few to stop and to those, they outlined their case, even befriending those who were befriendable. At lunch times, they unpacked their wholesome country lunches and ate with ceremony and relish, feeding the mules afterwards and watering them. The afternoons would be spent in the same way as their mornings. As dusk came, they cleaned up after themselves and left to resume their vigil the following day. They did not miss a day, not even Sunday to the consternation of the church-going residents of Gainers Town.

As the days passed, they exercised great restraint in ignoring the snide insults and ridicules of the Clearys' helpers and servants whom they thought should automatically be on their sides. The school children who would forego their usual chauffeured ride to and from school at least for part of the way, to see what the two old women were up to, were humoured sometimes, counselled and reprimanded at other times about good manners and respect for elders.

Eventually, Vie, still at her most optimistic and charismatic, won to their side slowly but decisively, an odd helper here, an odd servant there and a good share of police officers and residents, charmed as much by her simple presentation of their cause as they were by Azora's eloquence and sharpness. Eventually too they drew the attention of radio and newspaper journalists. This time the Clearys were pilloried without mercy.

The action of Vie and Azora and the attention it got, though most was patronising of their age and gender, revitalised the District and three weeks after their vigil began, John Cleary Senior agreed to see them.

Vie and Azora were shown to a lavish sitting room in the

house outside which they had sat and ate and campaigned for three weeks.

Azora, ready to take an olive branch if handed one, was well aware of Vie's unconciliatory mood and was not about to quieten her.

When John Cleary Senior finally appeared, Vie's expression and her mood had hardened beyond the sympathy that she would normally feel for one so bent with age and affliction, so near to a final exit from life.

As he was lowered into his chair by his helper, Vie was overcome with the bitterest disappointment that senility would most likely have erased from his mind all memory of the tussles he had had with her when she was younger – over rent and leases, over his presumption about all country women – all memory of the wrong he had done the District and its scores of women and, worse still, blurred her together with one of the countless women he had passed through.

'Vieline,' he said. Perhaps no senility after all, she thought, yet his use of her full name without a title as if she was a girl, exacerbated her anger. She refused to allow him to direct their meeting. She took control, stating with quiet emphasis the demands of the District. In the middle of it his son, John Cleary Junior, wandered in and was immediately dismissed by his father. Vie caught Azora's eyes and they shared a wry smile.

Azora did not breathe a word as Vie spoke, but her body language bore the support for Vie's every word as if they were speaking together and with one voice.

When she stopped, Cleary Senior met Vie's eyes and she was certain, although he *had* passed through many women, that he had not confused her with them. That he was able to separate those he had cowed into using and those like herself he had not dared.

'What you are asking, what your District is asking, Miss Vieline . . .'

322

That's better, she thought.

'What you are asking Miss Vieline is a hard thing . . .'

'What I see is that you don't have much choice John,' she said, dwelling on the use of his first name. His eyes shifted restlessly and she imagined that he was glad he would soon be dead.

'After all, we haven't been asking you to *give* us land, although some might say it is the least that you owe us. And I would not like to begin to name who and who in the District your son owe too.' His thin bottom lip folded in. She straightened her back and neck, massaged the back of her hands.

'I have already signed everything over to Junior . . .'

'You are his father and you are not dead, yet,' she added, feeling not a hint of remorse for her hardness of heart. His brows creased in indecision as he returned her gaze. She did not look away. His restless eyes shifted to wander the room. She did not let up, 'Don't force us to start the whole fight again. You can see that the whole Island losing patience with you and your kind. Everybody is tired of you. We have had our fill of you.' She allowed the silence, gave her words time to sink in. 'Anyway,' she took up again with renewed confidence, 'The sum total of what we want to buy hardly come to three hundred acres . . . You have more acres than you can count. You won't miss it.' Azora took up then, taking out the diagrams of where the land they wanted was located, when they would need the papers drawn up, what the going rate per acre was and in whose names they were to be purchased.

John Cleary Senior listened, refusing even to meet Azora's eyes as he had done Vie's. Eventually he asked to be given time to think it through and discuss with his son but Vie would not have that. You might be dead tomorrow, just out of malice, she thought. 'We are happy to wait here until you talk to him in another room,' she insisted. He seemed to reflect on that and she wondered whether he was so humbled by his need for assistance to move that he preferred to give in rather than call out for help.

'What you are asking is hard. All the land has been passed down through generations of my family,' he repeated.

'And our families have worked it for you and kept these big houses over your head,' Vie said coldly.

'My family have lost a lot in the months Top Mountain have been holding us to ransom,' he said, ignoring what Vie had said.

'And we can assure you that you will lose more if we continue,' Vie's tone was sharp and impatient.

John Cleary Senior sighed, 'I don't understand why the change, the older people in Top Mountain, in other Districts even, are happy with the way things are. They don't want the responsibility of land ownership. They prefer to lease.'

'How long you going to continue to tell us what is good for us? We can speak for ourselves. I advise you to listen. For once John Cleary.'

John Cleary looked to Azora now whom he seemed to want to intervene. She held his eyes coldly and said not a word, the same way she had dismissed his servants in the past months, during the conflict, when they had come to her for her usual prescription. She understood he had weakened noticeably since he had been without his medicines from her. She showed no sign now as then that it affected her.

He sighed repeatedly, as if he expected that to make a difference.

'I'm getting too old, tired and weak for all this. I lost the strength long ago to deal with stubborn . . .'

'Country people,' Vie said. 'We don't get any pleasure being cooped up in stuffy wasteful town houses either.'

'You are a very hard woman Vie. I'll not get used to dealing with women like you,' he grunted. 'Nor with believing women like you are normal women. You're too hard.' He shook his head as if that in itself emphasised his abhorrence for her kind.

A long silence followed before he said he would accede to some though not all of their demands. He would sell the shop and ten of the acres on which it stood, the church and its surrounding two acres, and a few other parcels of land around the District, nothing like the hundreds of acres they had demanded.

For a moment Vie especially was deflated but soon recognised that achieving some of their aims was better than total failure. But they pressed him for more before they took their leave but he had done more than he intended, he said, and would not do more. 'My son and grandson won't thank me for giving away their inheritance,' were his final words.

'Selling,' Vie corrected.

Back at the District the news was greeted with a mixture of celebration and determination that it was not the last the Clearys had heard from them. 'They think we done with them. They should think again,' Ragu said. 'The Clearys' time is up now. Land from now on will be ours to buy when we want, our lives will be ours to organise as we want.'

Miss Dee, who with Littleman, Babydear and Rose-marie were spreading the news through the District, was convinced that though the gains were relatively few, it was still a victory for the District, an important step forward.

'We've won the hardest battle,' she said to the others, 'the rest would be inevitable. Before they know it the Clearys will be completely out of our District. Mark my word,' she said using a common district phrase as they went to yet another house to give the news. Azora and Vie's praises rang through the District that night. If they had been elevated before, they were now hoisted higher still, even likened favourably to divine beings. Only greater, some said, provoking the Deacon's and Sister Netta's wrath.

Impulsively, when all but Jane's house had been visited that night and the next morning the group had discussed plans for the lands they would acquire, Miss Dee in her excitement decided to go to her aunt's house. She had not set eyes on her aunt or heard anything about her in months and having nothing to be angry with her for now, Miss Dee was resolved to be on good terms with her. Besides she wanted her to be the first, outside their group, to know what plans they had for extending the shop, building a house apart from it for herself and Rose-marie, for starting a dress-making school for young girls out of all-age school. She planned to solicit her aunt's expertise too, get her involved, to show that all was forgiven. She wanted to boast too about Littleman and Ragu's planned ventures, for building a workshop to teach cabinet-making and carpentry. Jane would see that even her despised Littleman was doing for himself, combining his farming with other projects. She could see that the District had grown and there was still a place for her.

Despite the words which lined up on her tongue, Miss Dee was half prepared to be driven out of her aunt's yard without having had the chance to breathe one of them.

As Miss Dee approached the yard, she thought she heard a baby crying but dismissed it as the sound of some errant cat. When she saw Bellinda appear from behind the house, wiping soap suds on her apron, Miss Dee's mind sifted and found the plausible explanation of maid on duty, her baby awoken from sleep to test the good will of the employing mistress. There was a wry smile on the young mother's face as she mounted the step to her baby, only acknowledging Miss Dee's presence just before entering the house, by throwing her a glance over her shoulder and calling out to tell Jane that she had a visitor. It was strange to see Bellinda, one whom both she and her aunt had always despised and ridiculed, so comfortable and at home. The scene brought confusion to Miss Dee's mind.

Alone for those few minutes, between the call and the appearance of Jane, Miss Dee waivered on the first step of the verandah before finally mounting, hesitating again before taking a seat. The baby's shrill voice was cooed into silence by the melodious purring of its mother's until eventually that too was quiet. But Bellinda did not reappear and Miss Dee was tempted, only for a moment, to go into her old room from which the sound had come, to gaze at mother and baby. But before she became too comfortable, she was confronted with her aunt who received her as she would an out-of-town stranger, aloof, and distant, entertaining her in the same manner with drinks and biscuits, seemingly intent on avoiding any planned manoeuver into topics which hinted at reconciliation.

'I came to say I've got the shop back,' Miss Dee said anyway when Jane sat on the opposite side of the verandah.

Jane looked at her blankly, as if she did not know how that could have significance for her. Finally Jane said, 'I see.'

'I . . . I would like to know if you would sew still . . .'

'I have no interest in doing anything for you again. You of all people should know that I finished with you. I told you that before.'

'But aunt . . .'

'You should know that I don't go back on my word especially since you have worked with others in this District to destroy my life, what more do you want to do to me?' Miss Dee shook her head, deflated and sad.

In the pause, Miss Dee's mind went back to the mother and child, now silent in her old room. What were they doing in her room? While she searched for an answer, Jane called Bellinda from her hiding place. She appeared, a moon-like smile plastered on her face. Without ado, Jane filled Miss Dee in on Bellinda's status in the home. 'Bellinda moved in a few days ago and I can tell you for nothing that she shows more sign of gratitude in that time then you ever did. I knew from day one that I made a mistake in picking you up from the street. So now that I throw you back out you can just leave my yard and I don't think there will be any need for you to come back here again,' she said dryly. The glass almost slipped from Miss Dee's hand. She stared at the two women, one fresh faced and grateful, eyes overflowing with the possibilities of her new life, the other gloriously triumphant.

It would have been useless for Miss Dee to ask why? So many whys? Those of the double standards? The destruction of the past, just to create an even more patchy and uncertain future. She was too weary and did not know where to begin so she scurried away hating the knowing silence that followed her down the lane. Bellinda! Of all the needy girls in the District. Why her? And with Jacob's child? The confusion made her retch. But once she was away from the yard and the long path leading from it, Miss Dee told herself that it was Jane's bitterness that was to be blamed. She had isolated herself from the District, built her own barriers, created enemies of people who would gladly succour her if she was only half-willing.

A month later, the shop, the home Miss Dee and Rose-marie were to share, was back in their hands; the District congregated in their yard to celebrate. Celebrate everything, they said. Baby-dear was to remain in Jamaica though under orders of her parents that if she did not behave herself, tried to take advantage of her sick and frail grandmother, or did not work hard and excel at school, she would have to return to England and the firm hands of her parents. And, the District had forced the hands of the Clearys.

The sense of achievement and victory that had pervaded the District on the day Vie and Azora had returned from town with the news, and their belief that the concession that had been made was not the end, had solidified in the District. As each day had passed and it had sunk in what they had achieved, the more their confidence and joy, under the prompting of Vie and Azora and the young people, grew. 'We *will* own our land, work for ourselves and the benefit of the District. And there should be no more bowing down and scraping the ground to them, no more accepting their free food,' Vie said to the crowd gathered for the